"COME IN WITH ME,"

he whispered.

Her heart raced. She tried to pretend she didn't understand the full meaning of the request, yet deep inside she hoped he meant exactly what she thought he meant. How wrong and improper that would be, how frightening and mysterious, yet how right it was for this moment.

He closed the door and gently led her to a chair. His eyes filled with a mixture of pain and passion. "Shannon, I . . ." He came closer, kneeling in front of her. He placed strong, gentle hands on her knees and ran them up her thighs to her hips. "I can't bear the thought of leaving . . . without making love to you."

"Bryce, I'm scared," she whispered. Then his lips met hers hungrily, urgently, and his hand moved under her dress, sending fire through her blood and breaking down all her resistance. He was removing her clothes and she didn't care. His lips and hands were touching secret places that made her whimper his name. Her cheeks were hot, her whole body flushed. The thrill of his lips made her cry out in desire, made her breathe hard and arch up toward him.

She had only been aware up to this moment of the mystery of man, of things girlfriends had told her about mating. Now it was truly going to happen, and there was no turning back. . . .

ARIZONA BRIDE

BY
F. ROSANNE
BITTNER

ZEBRA BOOKS
KENSINGTON PUBLISHING CORP.

ZEBRA BOOKS

are published by

Kensington Publishing Corp.
850 Third Avenue
New York, NY 10022

Fourth Printing: August 1996

Printed in the United States of America

Author's Note

All episodes in this novel that involve the Apache leaders Cochise and Mangas Coloradas are true. The deceitful capture of Cochise and his family by Lieutenant George Bascom and the ensuing hanging of part of Cochise's family, the battle at Apache Pass with General Carleton, the wounding of Mangas Coloradas and his flight to Mexico with Cochise, and the cruel death of Mangas Coloradas at the hands of United States soldiers, are all actual events. Primary characters in this novel, including the Apache leader Saguaro, are ficticious, and their involvement in the true episodes mentioned above and conversations involved in same, are added from the author's imagination and designed to fit reasonably the actual event that took place. None of the words spoken by characters who actually existed are direct quotations, but are merely supposed, according to records of what actually occurred when these events happened. The events themselves are based on factual printed matter that is available to the public.

Author's Note

All episodes in this novel that involve the Apache
leaders Cochise and Mangas Colorado are true. The
deceitful capture of Cochise and his family by
Lieutenant George Bascom and the ensuing hanging of
part of Cochise's family, the battle at Apache Pass with
General Carleton, the wounding of Mangas Colorado
and his flight to Mexico with Cochise, and the actual
death of Mangas Colorado at the hands of United
States soldiers, are all actual events. Primary characters in this novel, including the Apache leader Bargello,
are fictitious, and their involvement in the true
episodes mentioned above and conversations involved
in some, are culled from the Author's imagination and
designed to fit reasonably the actual event that took
place. None of the words spoken by characters who
actually existed are direct quotations, but are merely
suppositions, according to records of what actually
occurred, when these events happened. The events
themselves are based on factual printed matter that is
available to the public.

up the West. And the drivery rich man who joined at Tedd's birth. And last night he came over and brought with him the most wonderful taste and dashing sound. I don't meet this last night, but I peeked from behind the parlor curtains. Oh, Marney, he's like a prince! And he's leaving for Virginia tomorrow. Today is the only time I'll get a chance to—

"Shannon Fitzgerald, I tol' is only fourteen years old—just this month! I bring them pretty men comin' tonight to dine, and then they's goin' to must be twasel-five. If he's a congressman, what you girl? You should be lookin' at them boys you own age. Shame on you!

Chapter One

The year was 1855, and the month was June. It was a time when life was still soft and sweet in Charleston, Virginia; when life was slow and easy and refined. Virginia was only that then, not divided into Virginia and West Virginia. That break would not come until the bitterness of a civil war.

Shannon Fitzgerald studied her budding bosom in the mirror, frowning at the very small cups of her undergarment. She had stuffed cotton under her breasts to push them up so that they would look fuller beneath the ruffled yellow dress she wore.

"Oh, Marney! Do you think I'll ever grow up to be a woman?" she pouted. The black servant slipped a dress over her head.

"My goodness, child, what is you big hurry? Enjoy you childhood, honey! Bein' growed up ain't all you got a mind it is!"

"But, Marney, did you see that ever so handsome soldier Congressman Rather is going to bring? Mr. Rather is pushing bills through Congress to help open

9

up the West. And he's a very rich man who banks at Daddy's bank. And last night he came over and brought with him the most wonderful, brave, and dashing soldier! I didn't meet him last night, but I peeked from behind the parlor curtains. Oh, Marney, he's like a prince! And he's leaving for Arizona tomorrow. Today is the only time I'll get to meet him."

"Shannon Fitzgerald! You is only fourteen years old—just this month! I brung them gentlemen somethin' to drink, and that there soldier must be twenty-five, if'n he's a day. What's wrong with you, girl? You should be lookin' at them boys you own age. Shame on you!"

Shannon blinked back tears as Marney tied a bow in her hair. No matter what she wore or how she fixed her hair, she still looked like just a little girl. Marney smiled and patted her shoulder.

"I understands it ain't easy for you, honey—what with you mama gone and all. I expect if'n I thought on it real hard, I'd remember how some older gentlemen used to strike my eye when I was younger. My own man is a full ten years older than me, but I was seventeen when I met up with my Parker." She laughed, showing large white teeth and a broad smile. "But then Parker is just a stable master. He ain't no knight in shinin' armor like the man you is talkin' about! I expect a knight can't be nothin' but a white man with a fancy uniform like that one!"

"Then you agree, don't you!" Shannon said excitedly. "He's ever so handsome, isn't he, Marney?"

Marney sobered and turned the girl to face her.

"Now you listen up. Yes, he's about as handsome as a man can be. But you is lookin' to git you heart broke,

10

you hear? Ain't no man looks like him and his age and all gonna' be makin' eyes at a child like you. So don't go inventin' things in you head. The first thing you gotta' learn if you wanna' be growed up is to face reality. And the reality is that you is only fourteen, and that there man is all growed up and more than likely he's had his share of women, and maybe there's a bunch of 'em waitin' in line to walk to the altar with that one! Matter of fact, I expect he's already got a woman he's thinkin' serious about. Seems to me I remember hearin' that Mr. Rather sayin' somethin' about how he ought to get himself a wife afore' he goes back out West. They was jokin' about how lonesome a man gits out there, what with nothin' but dust and them terrible Injuns and all!"

"But . . . but he didn't actually mention any woman in particular, did he, Marney?"

Marney sighed and pursed her lips. "You is impossible!" she remarked in disgust. But she gave the girl a hug. "No. I didn't hear them mention nobody in particular."

Shannon began trying on different necklaces. "He's been a soldier since he was fifteen, Marney, stationed out West since sixteen, and he's a captain already, and might be a lieutenant colonel very soon!"

"Now how does you know all this?" Marney asked, shaking her head in wonder.

"Why, I just asked Daddy this morning at breakfast. You know Daddy tells me anything I want to know. And Daddy said he's very brave. He's fought hand-to-hand with those horrible and wild Apache Indians! He's even been wounded, Marney! And he's not twenty-five. He's twenty-three. He's going back to Arizona tomorrow. Congressman Rather brought him

11

here from Washington to meet Daddy and to see if he couldn't come to the party today to talk politics. Mr. Edwards—I mean, Captain Edwards—that's his name—Bryce Edwards—well, anyway, Captain Edwards knows ever so much about the West and the Indians and all. And Congressman Rather is doing his best to get all Easterners to understand what it's like out there. There are treasures beyond belief out there, Marney! And all the land a man could want! Captain Edwards has been here on leave—in Washington most of the time—and Congressman Rather brought him today to explain to people what it's like out West. And guess what, Marney!"

Marney rolled her eyes and shook her head at Shannon's babbling and the skillful way the child had of finding out anything she wanted to know through her father.

"What, child? It seems like everything you say about this Mister—I mean, Captain Edwards—is 'ever so this' and 'ever so that.' What other 'ever sos' does you have to tell me?"

"He was an orphan at seven years old, Marney! He's got no family at all, so he must be ever so lonely, don't you think? I can understand that. I'm practically an orphan myself, I mean, with Mama gone and all, I can understand his loneliness. Daddy said he was treated ever so badly for a long time. He lived in alleys and all—and he worked in those horrible factories in New York where children are practically slaves and get beat and work until they nearly die!"

Marney raised her eyebrows. "My, my, girl, how you do go on!"

"He joined the army when he was only fifteen, and at

12

sixteen he was out West, and—"

"You done told me all that, child."

"Well, he's a very fine soldier, Marney—very brave and all—and very wise in his decisions. That's why he's a captain already."

Marney chuckled.

"Is this necklace all right?" Shannon asked the black woman who was like a mother to her now. Marney studied it in the mirror, standing behind Shannon.

"It's too much—too big for you," she replied. "Why don't you wear that there tiny diamond you daddy give you?"

"Marney, that's a little girl's necklace. This one is more grown-up." She studied the rather large emerald that had belonged to her mother.

"Well, if'n you want my opinion, I'd say that soldier man would laugh inside hisself if'n he saw that there great big necklace 'round you pretty little neck. Don't wear it, honey."

Shannon pouted and put the necklace down, looking at her lap. "I've never had these funny feelings before about anyone, Marney. He's so . . . wonderful. Oh, Marney, I wish I were older so he would look at me."

Marney sighed and patted the girl's shoulder. "Life can be kind of mean sometimes, honey. I expect in a couple of years you'll get over him and be all a flutter over some other young man. You'll see."

Marney turned away and began folding some of Shannon's other clothes while Shannon toyed with her thick auburn hair a little longer. She did not like what she saw in the mirror. Her bosom was much too small and her frame too bony. She pursed her lips and put on just the tiniest bit of lip coloring and was pleased with

13

only one thing—her only asset, as far as she was concerned—her eyes. They were quite large and catlike—provocatively green, with long, dark lashes. Shannon was old enough to know that men liked lovely eyes on a woman, and that a woman's eyes could be used in very effective ways, if the woman was clever enough. Her only problem was she was not quite sure just how to use them, since she knew next to nothing about grown men. What they expected of a woman was a dark and exciting mystery. All she was sure of was her mother's warning that to deal in such matters before marriage would insure that a young lady would burn in hell for the rest of her life. She wondered about all the women of the street who lived north of town and who did lurid and unspeakable things with men. Surely after death they would all scream with the pain of fire. But then she shrugged off her concern and studied her eyes once more. They made her look older, but her bony body gave away her youth. She wondered if making eyes at a man was considered an unforgivable sin.

"Do you think he's here yet, Marney? I intend to make friends with him," she said, rising and going to the door. "After all, he's got no one in Virginia, and Charleston is such a big and busy town. A man could feel very lonely and lost in a place like this, especially after being out in the desolate West."

"Hmmm. I expect so," Marney said curtly. "You jist go on down there and see if'n he's here. I can see nothin' I say is gonna' change you foolish mind."

Shannon flashed a lovely smile, and Marney could see that this child would some day be a beautiful woman.

14

Heaven help me cope with her growin' up! she thought. Shannon left, and Marney grumbled to herself. "I don't expect no man that looks like that is lonely noplace! Wouldn't surprise me if'n he spent the night with one of them high-class whores north of town."

Shannon glided down the steps in as ladylike a manner as she could, looking around the small ballroom below to see if she could see Bryce Edwards. Most of her father's guests had arrived and refreshments were being served at a large buffet table. The four-piece orchestra was setting up, consisting of three violins and a cello, and the musicians prepared to play some waltzes for the guests. This was the spring party Shannon's mother used to hold annually, and her father, bless his soul, had carried on the tradition in his wife's memory.

Shannon stopped midway down the steps and spotted her father. Jonathan Fitzgerald was a rotund man, with graying hair and reddish cheeks and dancing blue eyes. Her mother had been much younger than he, with reddish hair and beautiful green eyes, and everyone told Shannon she was a replica of her mother. She hoped so. She thought her mother the most beautiful woman she had ever known. Her father had been devastated at her death, and had not been the same man since.

Jonathan Fitzgerald was the only child of an Irish immigrant, and both his parents had died shortly after coming to America from Ireland. Shannon's father had worked hard in his growing-up years, building pennies into dollars, and into hundreds then thousands of dollars through thrift and clever investments. Now he was a prominent banker in Charleston, and his children, fourteen-year-old Shannon and eleven-year-old Bobby, were well provided for. But Shannon now carried with her a secret fear of being orphaned. Her mother was dead and her father was old, and, other than her younger brother, she had no relatives in America.

Since her mother's death, Jonathan's health had failed him miserably, and he saw a doctor regularly. Shannon was sure he must have some dreadful disease, or perhaps his heart was going to fail him. If he died, she and Bobby would surely be sent to an orphanage. She shuddered at the thought of the gruesome stories about what happened to little girls in orphanages—and even to little boys. She swallowed and shook off the thought. Nothing would happen to her father. She prayed too hard. Surely God would not wish such a terrible thing on her. But after all, she was almost grown. If something happened, she would simply carry on by herself and take care of Bobby. Perhaps by then she would be the wife of Captain Bryce Edwards!

She scanned the room and could not see Edwards anywhere, but she heard two men talking just below the banister—something about slavery and freedom.

"Come now, Bartley, it isn't as though we were like the Egyptian rulers who chained and whipped their slaves into submission and starved them to death!" Shannon recognized the voice of a wealthy plantation owner and friend of her father's, Loren McGuire. McGuire was a huge man with a gruff voice, and Shannon had never liked him.

16

"Well, maybe not, Loren—at least not in many cases," the other voice replied. "But it is almost that bad in some cases. I've heard even you have ordered whippings."

McGuire laughed casually. "I treat my slaves quite well on the whole, Bartley," he said jovially. "Once in a while one gets out of hand, that's all. They're ignorant, and they have to be dealt with firmly. It's the only thing they understand—like dogs, you know? But I certainly don't order whippings every day, mind you."

Shannon shuddered at the thought of being a slave. She had never liked slavery. Her father's black servants were free and were paid for their work. They were well treated and happy. She put the thought out of her mind and proceeded down the steps; but before she reached bottom her foot caught on the hem of her dress, and she quickly descended the rest of the way with skirts and petticoats flying, landing headfirst, her skirt covering her head and her legs sprawled out behind her on the steps, revealing mounds of ruffles on pantaloons and petticoats.

Her devastation knew no bounds. She wished there were a way she could melt into the stairway and disappear. She could hear her brother giggling mercilessly, and people gathered around her, some tittering and some seeming to be truly concerned that she was not hurt. She quickly prayed ardently that Bryce Edwards was nowhere around. Someone grasped her arm and helped her up.

"There now. I do hope the charming and beautiful young lady hasn't been injured!" a gentle voice said. She looked up, directly into the face of Bryce Edwards. Shannon reddened to the color of a beet and tears

17

welled in her eyes.

"I . . . I'm . . . not hurt!" she squeaked. She burst into tears and raced back up the stairs, charging into her room with the sound of people's laughter ringing in her ears. Was Bryce Edwards laughing, too? Her father was standing next to Edwards now.

"That lovely little girl who just made her grand entrance is my daughter, Captain Edwards," Jonathan explained with a light laugh. "And at the moment, I'm certain she's embarrassed beyond words. I'm afraid she's rather infatuated with you," the man went on, chuckling again. "She was asking me all kinds of questions about you this morning. I'm sure falling right in front of you has not done much for her plans to impress you today."

Bryce Edwards frowned slightly and took a sip of his drink.

"My goodness, Mr. Fitzgerald, she's awfully young."

"She's fourteen, captain, and . . . uh . . . well, fourteen-year-old girls begin to get the idea they're already all grown-up, you know. It's just a phase she's going through. I hope I haven't insulted you by telling you my little girl has eyes for you."

Bryce flashed a handsome grin. "On the contrary. She's very lovely, Mr. Fitzgerald."

"Well, I'm sure there are several young and very available ladies here today with whom you'd rather occupy your time, right?" Jonathan replied with wink.

Bryce grinned and glanced at two young women who stood nearby eyeing him and whispering behind their fans. Bryce Edwards struck a commanding figure in full uniform. He stood a full six feet two inches tall and had thick sandy hair and alluring gray eyes. His

18

features were near perfection, and the fact that he was unattached was food for much gossip among the young ladies present, who were all but clawing at each other to get his attention.

"Actually," Jonathan Fitzgerald went on, "little Shannon, oh—that's my daughter's name—little Shannon has had some problems adjusting since her mama died two years ago." Fitzgerald sobered. "I guess we all have. Now she seems to think she has to be the woman of the house, you know."

"She's lost her mother, then? I'm sorry to hear that," Bryce told the man, losing his smile. "I didn't know, Mr. Fitzgerald."

"Yes, she died two years ago of pneumonia. How a woman can get pneumonia in Virginia is beyond me. It was quite a shock to all of us. She was a beautiful and gentle woman, and still young."

Bryce remembered how he had felt when he lost his parents in a fire. Shannon had lost only one, but still, it must have left a lonely and frightened feeling in the young girl. He glanced up the stairs, strangely stirred by the embarrassment of Miss Shannon Fitzgerald, who wanted so much to be a grown up young lady this day, and who had no mother to guide her in her tender years.

Shannon came late to the breakfast table, her stomach still aching from the tears and humiliation of the disaster at her father's party. She had barely slept all night for the constant replay of her clumsy entrance to the affair, and, worst of all, the fact that Bryce Edwards himself had helped her up. His handsome face, tanned by the western sun and framed with thick blond hair, was emblazoned forever now in her mind. So close it had been to hers, the face of this fascinating soldier who for some unknown reason made her chest ache and stirred feelings in her young body that she had never before experienced.

She knew it was hopeless infatuation on her part. Many of her friends had had crushes on older men, secret feelings about which they whispered and giggled, sharing their curiosity and always knowing that to be observed as anything but children by those men was impossible.

Yet at this moment Shannon was certain her feelings for Bryce Edwards were much deeper and truer than what any of her friends had ever felt. She had no feelings of true womanly desire for him, for she knew nothing of such matters. Yet her feelings were sincere and painful, and she wondered if she would die if she never saw him again, knowing at the same time that she didn't want to see him again, for she could never face him after her horrible embarrassment.

She hung her head and sat down at the large dining table, glad that Bobby had already left the room, for the boy would probably have started giggling and teasing her and send Shannon into a new fit of tears. Her father watched her quietly.

"Good morning, daughter," Fitgerald said, sipping on a cup of coffee.

"Good morning," she replied quietly, staring at a lace flower on the tablecloth.

"Are you going to eat something, child?"

She shrugged. "I suppose. But only toast. My stomach hurts."

20

Fitzgerald rang a tiny bell, his heart aching for his lovely but devastated daughter. A cook came from the kitchen and he ordered toast and tea for Shannon. He sighed and leaned back in his chair, frowning.

"It isn't the end of the world, Shannon. You're a Fitzgerald, and being a Fitzgerald, I expected you to buff up yesterday and return to the party and show everyone there who the most beautiful young belle of Charleston is. I was very disappointed that you were not present. After all, I hold that party in your mother's memory, and you are a picture of your mother."

Shannon's lips puckered and she blinked back tears. "Mother never would have disgraced herself as I did," she mumbled. "And to have . . . Captain Edwards, of all people . . . standing right there . . ." She swallowed.

Fitzgerald grinned slightly. "I see. So it wasn't that you were that embarrassed in front of the others. It's Edwards you're upset about."

She reddened slightly, as the cook brought her food. "I'm sorry, Father. I humiliated you."

Fitzgerald chuckled. "Don't be silly. You're everything a man could want in a daughter. I couldn't be prouder. You're beautiful and well-mannered and a good girl. And you're the image of your mother. Forget about yesterday." He dabbed at his mouth with a napkin, his eyes twinkling. "Besides, as far as Bryce Edwards is concerned, perhaps it was to your advantage to fall. It drew his attention to you and I believe it also drew on his sympathy. He kept asking about you all evening."

She finally raised her eyes to meet her father's. "He did?"

Fitzgerald smiled. "That he did, Shannon, my girl.

21

All afternoon and evening he kept glancing up those stairs and asking if you would return. When he left, he asked if he might come and say good-bye to you this morning, and if he might write you after he's gone. I told him it was perfectly fine."

Some life came back into Shannon's eyes. "You did?" Her heart pounded furiously. Bryce Edwards had asked about her! Her! Shannon Fitzgerald! He wanted to tell her good-bye!

Fitzgerald rose and walked to her chair, patting her shoulder. "I see no harm in a friendly exchange of letters. I think Edwards wants to make sure you don't feel badly about yesterday. He's a very nice young man, with a genuine concern for people, especially young ones who have lost a parent. He's an orphan himself, you know, has been since he was only seven. At any rate, he leaves for Arizona later today and will be gone two years, so I see little harm in allowing him to write you. I hardly think a man his age has any ulterior motives. He's very well respected." He lit a pipe and puffed it a moment.

"Thank you, Father." Shannon looked up at him, then grasped her excited stomach and rose. "I must change if he's coming this morning!"

"Not until you eat that toast, my dear. And you remember your place and your age, daughter, as well as Bryce Edwards' age. Don't make something out of nothing. The young man is simply being kind, and I don't want you pining away for the impossible when you should be enjoying your youth and your young friends."

She reddened again and sat back down. "Yes, sir."

She picked up a piece of toast and her father left the room. As soon as he was gone, Shannon leaped from her chair again and twirled around the room, embracing herself with her own arms and wanting to cry with joy. Bryce Edwards was coming to see her! Bryce Edwards wanted to write to her! Earlier she had thought she might die of humiliation and despair; now she wondered if she would die from sheer ecstasy.

An hour later Shannon waited in the parlor, her hair neatly coiffed, wearing a lavender cotton dress that accentuated her tiny waist. Again she wished she were not so slender and girlish, but there was nothing to be done about that. Her heart pounded so hard it hurt when she heard Bryce Edwards announce himself at the door, and a moment later he was being ushered in to her by a maid, who announced him, then left.

Edwards walked up to her, putting out his hand and flashing a handsome grin that made her feel weak. She gave him her hand and he kissed the back of it. His own hand was warm, and the kiss made her legs feel like rubber.

"I'm so glad to have this moment to speak with you, Miss Fitzgerald," he was saying to her in his soft, low voice. "I was very disappointed that you didn't return yesterday, and very distraught that you let a simple accident spoil what should have been a wonderful day for you."

She reddened deeply, wishing she were older and knew the right things to say. "I . . . I wasn't certain if I . . . should return. I've never done anything so foolish in my life, Captain Edwards, and I . . ."

He squeezed her hand. "Please don't feel badly about it. I felt so sorry for you, I just wanted to meet you once more under better circumstances." She raised her eyes to his, and he was struck by their beauty, just as he had been the day before when he helped her up. They were large and oval, an amazing green color and much too provocative for a fourteen-year-old child. Her beautiful face gave her the look of someone older, and it disturbed him that one so young could be so fetching.

"I . . . I appreciate your taking the time to come and say good-bye, Captain Edwards," she told him, her voice soft and musical. "I wrote down our address for you. Father said you wanted to write. I . . . I would be very happy to reply to your letters, sir. It must get very lonely out there in that awful place where all those Indians are."

The man smiled and released her hand. "That it does. And I haven't any family to my name. I would enjoy calling you a friend and writing to you. I've never had anyone with whom to correspond before."

She thought about how her girlfriends talked of lonely men like Bryce Edwards visiting the whores. Surely this grown man did such things. But then those were not the kind of women a gentleman would want to write to. He would want to write to a proper lady, like herself.

"I would be honored to write you, captain. I can let you know what is happening here in the East, and you can tell me of your adventures out West. That would be so exciting. None of my friends knows anyone who has fought wild Indians."

24

He smiled warmly. "Well, it's not all some people make it out to be. I even consider some of the Apaches as friends. You just have to know how to treat them. If they were treated fairly by all the whites, there wouldn't be so much trouble. Misunderstanding and suspicion cause most of the problem."

She studied the soft gray eyes. "That's too bad. I do hope you'll be all right, Captain Edwards."

He winked. "I'll be fine. I wish I had more time to visit, but I really must be going. I just wanted to stop by on my way to the train to meet you the right way and tell you to please not be upset about yesterday. You're a very beautiful young girl." He took a piece of paper from his coat pocket. "Here is my address. But wait until you get a letter from me first. Sometimes I have to ride out on duty when I first arrive and I may not be there for a while. Or I might even get transferred to a different post."

She swallowed and smiled, reaching down to a table and picking up a piece of paper of her own. "This is our address. I'll wait for your first letter."

He nodded and took the paper. "Now you can tell all your friends you are corresponding with an Indian fighter. That should make them properly envious, right? Perhaps that will make up for yesterday. If they want to laugh at you, you can just tell them about our letters."

She wanted to cry. How much had her father told him? Was he laughing at her? Surely not. His eyes were too kind.

"Thank you," she found herself saying. "I will pray for your safety, Captain Edwards."

His eyes softened more. "I appreciate that, Miss Fitzgerald. I truly do. I will look forward to your letters."

Jonathan Fitzgerald walked in then, and there was a general exchange of words and good-byes, handshakes and well-wishing. All too quickly Bryce Edwards was walking out the door. Shannon watched from a window as he boarded a carriage, and her chest ached with a feeling she did not understand.

Chapter Two

The letters came, at first very formal. But Shannon's warm, youthful replies made Bryce Edwards begin looking forward to each letter with more pleasure. A sweet innocence shone through them, and even though she was to him a mere child, her letters brightened the long, lonely, hot days of service in the arid West. He felt refreshed at her descriptions of the Virginia weather, entertained by her tales of events surrounding her young life. Sweet anticipation followed every letter he wrote her, for he knew she would always reply, each letter full of her innocent excitement and very obvious concern and friendship, bringing a smile to Bryce's lips and a deep appreciation in his heart that he had a new friend in faraway Virginia.

For her part, Shannon's heart pounded with the receipt of every one of his letters. Two years was a long time, and she was sure Captain Edwards would eventually grow tired of corresponding with the little girl in Virginia he had met only once. But the kind captain always replied, his letters full of news about the

27

West and his duties there, as well as exciting tales about the Apache Indians. To Shannon, Bryce Edwards became a brave hero, and she began praying for his safety among the horrible savages she pictured the Apaches to be. Never in her own letters did she hint of her feelings of tenderness and worship for him, for she feared he might only laugh at her. Surely there were mature women in his life, and Shannon was sure that anything more than a kind friendship was hopeless.

Then came the summer of 1857. Bryce Edwards was returning on leave. He could not now take leave without coming to see Shannon Fitzgerald, and sixteen-year-old Shannon was a flutter of nerves over the wait and excitement, unsure just when he would show up, fearful he would decide not to come at all. On the morning of his arrival, Marney could barely keep up with Shannon's frantic last-minute primping. The girl had matured beautifully, and she was now more composed, with a graceful womanliness that had not been present in the child who had made the disgraceful entrance to her father's party two years earlier.

She breathed deeply for self control before descending the stairway to the parlor where the kind captain waited. When she entered the room to greet him, the woman/child Bryce beheld had developed far beyond his expectations. He had pictured her as the child he had briefly met two years earlier, and the surprise in his eyes could not be hidden.

He rose to greet her, their eyes locking in joy and pleasure, saying everything that needed to be said. Shannon approached him gracefully, her full, firm bosom temptingly revealed at the bodice of her pale pink dress. Her catlike, disturbingly beautiful eyes seemed even greener to him than he remembered. Her auburn hair was piled high on her head, with curls hanging from the back, and she reddened slightly as his eyes roved her body in obvious pleasure.

Shannon stepped closer. "I really never thought I'd see you again, Captain Edwards." She put out her hand and Bryce took it, bending down to kiss it. She felt a pleasant tingle at the touch of his lips to her skin. *You are more handsome than ever!* she wanted to blurt out. Bryce straightened and kept hold of her hand.

"After all those letters, you're going to continue to call me Captain Edwards?" he said softly. "I'd say we should be very good friends by now, Shannon. May I call you that? I'd like you to call me Bryce."

"All right. Would you like to sit down, Bryce? I can have Marney bring some refreshments."

Bryce still had hold of her hand and was squeezing it. He wanted very much to embrace her in his joy at how she had matured and the fact that she was more beautiful than he had expected.

"I . . . uh . . . I prefer to stand a moment longer and . . . just look at you," he told her, his eyes roving over her body again. "Shannon, you are the most beautiful young woman I've ever seen."

She blushed and smiled nervously. "My goodness! Why, thank you, Bryce. That's quite a compliment, coming from a worldly gentleman like yourself." Her voice was still small and slightly childish, and there was a hint of a little girl still trying to act like a woman.

Bryce led her to a loveseat and they sat down together. At first neither one could think of anything to say. All the words they had planned fled their minds. It seemed so odd that they were here together again, after two years of being apart and speaking only through written words.

Then they both started to say something at the same time. Shannon reddened and Bryce grinned, and both relaxed more then. She studied the hard lines of his face, the skin tanned dark from the Arizona sun, the neck firm and muscular, the sandy hair bleached blonder from his outdoor work. He now had a thin mustache that seemed only to add to his manliness, and his soft gray eyes were strangely disturbing. Shannon suddenly felt young and foolish. He was so much man for someone like herself. She wondered if he had paid her the visit just to be nice because of all her letters.

"Shannon, let's not be so formal with each other," he announced. "I'm going to say it right out. I enjoyed your letters very much. I looked forward to every one of them."

"You did?"

He took her hand again. "Yes, I did. And I must admit, I was very curious about you, how you had grown and all, wondering what you looked like now. When I got this leave, I couldn't wait to come here and see you again. And I did not expect to find the beautiful young woman who is sitting here beside me now. I must say, you've certainly grown!" There was the boyish grin again. "I already heard in town that there's some kind of charity ball being held this coming Saturday night. I'd like to take you, Shannon. I'd be very proud to have a young lady as lovely as you to escort."

She swallowed. She wanted to tell him she was already in love with him. She wanted to hug and kiss him. She wanted to cry and have him hold her in his wonderfully strong arms.

30

"I'd be honored to go with you," she replied. She had already promised another boy, but she intended to do what no proper lady ever did—break her commitment. How could she pass up an evening with Bryce Edwards? This was too good to be true!

"I'll be sure to ask your father's permission, of course. Do you think he'll mind?"

He'd better not! she thought to herself. "I'm sure it will be all right with him," she said aloud, already planning to throw a crying fit if her father said no. She could manipulate her father however she chose. That would be no problem. "How—how long will you be here this time?" she asked Bryce, studying the lovely gray eyes.

"About a year," he replied.

"A whole year?" she exclaimed. She forgot her manners and position. This was simply too good to be true! Everything was working out so beautifully! She flung her arms around his neck. "Oh, Bryce, that's wonderful! Now we'll have so much time to talk, and—" She stopped midsentence, just then realizing what she had done. She had acted like a silly little girl again, just what she did not want to do. She started to pull away, but before she could, his arms were encircling her and he held her close for a moment, enjoying every second of it.

Shannon's heart beat so hard her chest hurt, and then, like magic, he was kissing her cheek. She knew she was red all the way to the tips of her fingers.

"Well, he said softly. "That's a far better greeting than just getting to kiss the back of your hand."

"Oh, my!" she said, wishing the redness would go away. "I'm sorry! What a terribly blatant thing to do! I didn't mean . . . I mean, after all, I shouldn't take it for granted that I'm the one you'd be spending your time with . . . I mean, there must be someone—"

"No one," he told her gently. "No one special. And don't be sorry for doing something that gives me great pleasure."

She toyed with some lace on her skirt, looking at her lap. "No one?"

"No one."

"But . . . I mean, a man your age . . . and with your looks and position . . . surely, there's someone."

"Women are hard to come by out West. It's even more difficult when you're stationed at a fort out in the middle of nowhere. Besides, when I met you two years ago, I saw the beginnings of a very beautiful woman— and your sweetness impressed me. And when I started getting those letters, I told myself I'd be cheating myself if I went and married some woman before seeing you again. And now that I've seen you, I'm very glad I waited."

"Are you truly?" she asked, finally looking up at him.

"Truly," he replied. "We've not spoken for two years, Shannon, and we had only minutes to meet before I first left. Yet I feel I know you very well. Through your letters you've told me all about yourself—your dreams, your fears, your hobbies. I know all about you. So, it's not as though we're strangers, now is it?"

Her eyes teared against her will, and one slipped down her cheek. She wanted so desperately to hide her feelings, but it was next to impossible.

"I . . . like you . . . very much, Captain Ed—I mean, Bryce. I have . . . prayed for your safety." She looked down at her lap and sniffed. Bryce put a big, strong hand to the side of her face and forced her to look up at him. He brushed at her tears with his other hand.

"I'm pleased and flattered that you're this emotional over my return. You're very special, Shannon. Very lovely and sweet." He smiled, and she felt on fire when his hand touched her face. "And as far as being embarrassed, I believe that's how we first met. Remember?"

She felt herself relax more, and she smiled. Bryce chuckled. She took out a hanky from a pocket in her skirt and turned away to blow her nose and wipe her eyes.

"I'll tell you something else, Shannon," he told her gently. "You don't know how much it meant to me to actually have someone somewhere who cared about me. For the first time in my career, I actually had someone to come home to. I don't have any family, and no particular place I can call home. And after being out West for so long, I have few friends in the East anymore. It was very nice to think about seeing you again when I came back. Very nice, indeed. For the first time, I had someone waiting for me. I've not had anyone who cared since I was seven years old, Shannon."

"Well, I care very much," she replied, dabbing at her eyes again. "And I worried about you so, Bryce! All those newspaper stories we get here about that horrible Apache leader called Cochise!"

"He's not so bad. He's a very honest and proud man, Shannon."

"You know him?"

He smiled. "Of course I know him. He's a Chiricahua Apache." He took a thin cigar from a breast pocket.

33

"Do you mind if I smoke?"

She smiled softly. "It's quite all right."

His eyes roved over her soft curves again as he lit the cigar. Then he rose. "Let's see," he continued. "I'll name a couple more of their chiefs for you. There's Mangas Coloradas. He's getting old, but he's still quite a specimen of man, Shannon—tall and quite overwhelming to look at. He's a Mimbrenno Apache—and pretty peaceful at that. He is also Cochise' father-in-law. And then there's one called Saguaro. He's a Mescalero Apache. Saguaro is quite temperamental. You step on his toe, and he'll take your whole leg off!" Bryce grinned and shook his head. "The Apaches can be your best friend or your worst enemy, Shannon. It depends on how honest a man is with them. They don't put up with lying and cheating. But that is about all they get from the whites. The whites don't understand how simple and peaceful things could be if they just treated the Indians with a little dignity and fairness. Things are pretty peaceful right now—until some agent or settler or miner decides to cheat an Apache, or rape some squaw or murder some buck for no particular reason. The Apaches are firm believers in an eye for an eye. And when it comes to vengeance—" He shook his head again. "They certainly know how to deal it out. The Apaches are the unquestioned experts at vengeance and torture."

Shannon shuddered at the thought of it. The things she had heard about the dreaded Indians were too terrible for her to even mention.

"The Apaches believe in a supreme being," Bryce went on, pacing in front of the fireplace. "They have a very close relationship with their god, Shannon, and with the earth and the animals—a strong reverence for the land and all the things God has given them for free. They can't understand why the whites insist on claiming everything and owning everything. They believe the land was put there by God for all of us to share equally. Our way of thinking totally confuses them. And we're turning what was once a very loving and generous people into vicious animals—hunted and tortured and chased out of their homes because of our own lust for land and gold."

He smoked quietly and seemed to be lost in his own little world now, speaking aloud his inner thoughts.

"You sound like you like them, Bryce."

"I *do* like them." He turned to face her. "Does that surprise you?"

"I guess it does, a little. But I . . . I'm glad . . . that you care about people like that."

He grinned a little. "Mind you, if I'm caught in combat with them, I'll kill one without hesitation. I just think it's a pity we've come to that point. I feel my work out there is very important, Shannon. I try my best to keep the peace and see that the Indians get fair dealing in the process. It's not an easy job. But it's important, and that's why I keep going back. I understand them. There aren't many of us who do. I'm sorry my work takes me so far away, but I will go back again. I've been offered choices of being stationed at more comfortable and civilized places, but I feel compelled to go back."

"I want to understand that," she told him. "And I think I do . . . a little, anyway." She thought a moment. "Is it true there's a great rivalry between the Apaches and the Mexicans?"

He laughed lightly. "Very great isn't descriptive

35

enough. Heated, violent, extremely hate-filled are better descriptions. So far there are many more raids into Mexico by Apaches than raids by them against the whites. It's a long and bitter rivalry, and no one is quite sure when or why it began. But there is no love lost between Mexicans and Apaches. The crazy part is that they steal each other's women and end up having half-breed babies, in spite of their hatred for each other."

He smiled, but she blushed and looked away. "How awful!" she said in her small voice. "To be stolen away like that!"

Bryce frowned and took her hand again. "I'm sorry, Shannon. I shouldn't be telling you all these frightening tales. Let's get back to you and me."

She smiled and looked up at him again. "Where are you staying?" she asked.

"Uh—at the Carney House, several blocks from here." He had not actually registered there yet, but he did not want to tell her he had spent his first night rollicking in bed with a voluptuous blond prostitute north of town. Bryce Edwards had returned with needs that were very great. He was a virile man who enjoyed women as much or more than most. Back in Arizona, there was one special whorehouse he visited as often as possible, but not nearly as often as he would have liked. And upon arriving in Virginia, it was very pleasant to spend the night with a fashionable, high-class prostitute. He studied Shannon and felt an urgency to know what she would be like in bed.

Very good, no doubt, he thought. A beautiful young virgin who has never been touched by man. The thought both fascinated and stirred him deeply. He liked Shannon Fitzgerald very much. He could not say that he loved her. Not now. But he knew that he could love her. Her sweetness and innocence impressed him. She was charming and slightly submissive—sophisticated, but not conceited. He was suddenly startled that he was already entertaining thoughts of love, when he had been sitting here with her a mere twenty minutes.

"Isn't it expensive there?" she was asking.

"The army pays for part of it," he replied. "I must tell you that I'll be spending part of my time in Washington, Shannon, but not all of it. And the time that I'm here in Charleston, I'd like to spend a lot of that time with you—if you'll oblige me."

She smiled and rose. "You know I will," she said softly. "I'm going to ask Marney to bring us something. You must be hungry, unless you already had lunch."

"Well, actually, I thought maybe we could go for a ride. I rented a carriage. I'd like to take you to some nice little restaurant to eat. Would you like that?"

"Oh, yes!" she said, too eagerly again. Bryce grinned at her almost constant blushing. "I'll . . . I'll get my cape."

He studied the slim waistline as she walked through the doors to get the garment. Yes. It was very pleasant to be back in Virginia.

They attended the ball, and Shannon felt like Cinderella herself. For three weeks they were together at least every other day, going for rides, walking in her father's gardens, and talking, endlessly, learning everything there was to know about each other. But to Shannon there was so much more to learn about Bryce Edwards. After all, he had been so many places and

37

done so many things. She concentrated on everything he said, wanting to understand him, becoming his confidante.

Both knew they were in love, yet it seemed so fast and so ridiculous, considering the short time and their age difference, that neither one could quite admit to his or her feelings openly. They touched often, held hands more often; but as yet, Bryce Edwards had not kissed Shannon Fitzgerald the way he wanted to kiss her. Would it frighten her? Maybe not. What he feared most was that she would respond wholeheartedly; and if she did, and they were alone, he wasn't sure he trusted himself not to take advantage of the situation. He wanted very much to plant himself inside this charming young virgin and feel her naked body next to his and hear her crying out his name in the first pain of intercourse. He loved her. Yes! He must be crazy, but he loved her, nonetheless. For all his twenty-five years, and a string of women too long to remember, he had surprised himself by falling in love so quickly with this young girl who wasn't even quite a woman yet. But he wanted to consume her—to be one with her—to taste her and feel her slim legs wrapped around his waist. He wanted to explore every inch of her and hear her whimpering beneath him. He wanted to subdue her—to claim her—to teach her all the mysteries of love that he was sure she knew nothing about.

Yet she was so very special. He did not want to touch this one unless she was his wife. It just didn't seem proper to have it happen any other way with someone like Shannon. But she was still much too young to marry. He could tell by the way her father talked about her that he, too, did not consider his daughter of marrying age. But perhaps the man was just being selfish, wanting to keep his daughter under his wing as long as possible.

Bryce found himself sleeping more often with the whores than in his own hotel room. His desire for Shannon was too great for him to allow it to build up. He did not intend to spoil the precious child whom he had already decided he was going to marry. At the end of the third week, Bryce was to leave for Washington for three months; and, although he would miss Shannon, he was almost glad he was going to get away. Being with her was almost too much of a strain.

But how quickly the three weeks had flown! He kissed her tears at the train station, and he wanted so much to kiss her sweet, innocent lips. But her father and brother were standing there, and he decided that the kiss he still had not given her would have to wait. Shannon's disappointment shone in her eyes, and it hurt him to see it. He realized that since she knew little about men, she must not understand why, during these past three weeks, he had not kissed her or approached her physically as a lover. He could tell by her eyes that she was thinking that possibly she was nothing more to him than a child and a friend, after all. Perhaps she was afraid he would not come back from Washington. He decided it was time to admit to his feelings. He bent down and whispered in her ear.

"I love you, Shannon." It was the first time he had mentioned love. He straightened and watched the disappointment in her eyes vanish, replaced by such shining love that he would have liked to grab her up then and there and whisk her off to his bed.

"I . . . didn't think—" she squeaked. He put his

39

fingers to her lips and winked.

"You needn't say anything," he told her. "I can see it in your eyes. I'll write—and I will be back. After all, I came back after two years once, didn't I?" He smiled and squeezed her hand, then jumped onto the now moving train.

"Good-bye!" He waved, and she waved back. But he was only a blur through her tears.

Shannon hummed as she repotted some plants in the greenhouse behind her father's mansion. They had a fine gardener, but Shannon liked working with the flowers herself sometimes, and it gave her something to do to pass the time while waiting for Bryce to return. Two months had gone by already. She thought of him lovingly and sniffed at the mum she was transplanting when she heard the door to the greenhouse open and close. She looked over to see Loren McGuire standing there watching her.

"Why, Mr. McGuire! What brings you clear out here?" she asked. The man looked her up and down like she was a piece of pie, and Shannon felt a sudden chill. Forty-eight-year-old Loren McGuire was a huge and graying man, at least six feet four inches tall, and he looked as big as a locomotive to little Shannon.

"I—uh—was looking for your father, Shannon. The maid told me he had come out to the gardens, but I can't find him. I have some business to talk to him about."

"Oh. Well, Father's not here at all. He *was* here, but he left for the bank. You'll find him there," she replied, turning around and digging up another flower.

"I see," the man said. He stood there, staring at her and not moving. Shannon looked over at him again.

"I said he's at the bank," she repeated.

"You—uh—you've really grown up, haven't you, Shannon?" he said in a mockingly friendly tone. She reddened and turned away again. "Are you pretty serious about that soldier fellow you've been seeing?" he asked.

Shannon swallowed and kept her eyes averted. "I would say that is my daddy's business—and mine, Mr. McGuire."

"Hmmm. Well, a soldier just back from the West— he must be pretty hungry for a woman. You must have looked real good to him. 'Course we all know he's been sleeping with the whores most of the time. Did he tell you that?" McGuire delighted in seeing her pale slightly. "'Course, maybe he had enough time left over to teach you a few things. Now you wouldn't be dishonoring your daddy's name, would you?"

Shannon whirled and threw a clod of dirt at McGuire. "What an ungodly filthy thing to say!" she snapped, not even sure what it was he was referring to, but knowing by his voice it was something sinful and lurid. "You get out of here right now, Mr. McGuire, before I scream for the gardener!"

"You wouldn't really do that now, would you?" he threatened, coming closer. "Why, I'm a good friend of your daddy—and a very good customer. You give me trouble, and he'll lose a damned big account. Besides, I can always say you provoked me. Maybe your soldier boy has waked you up to men, and you all of a sudden found out you like men. Him being away and all— maybe you got lonesome." He grinned and came closer, and she held up a gardening fork.

"You touch me and I'll make a mark on you that will disgrace you!" she told him, trying to sound firm. McGuire grinned more.

"I saw you that day you fell down the stairs and your skirts went flying," he told her in a voice gruff with desire. "When I saw those lacy pantaloons, I never forgot it, little Shannon. Too bad we weren't alone that day. I've thought about you and watched you grow ever since!"

He leaped at her and grasped her wrist before she could wield the fork. Shannon screamed at the top of her lungs as he squeezed her wrist and forced her to let go of the fork. Then he bent her arms behind her back, and before she knew it his lips were pressing against hers. She grimaced and squirmed as his saliva ran down her chin and his tongue licked at her mouth. She could smell liquor on his breath and struggled helplessly against his overwhelming strength. When his lips finally left hers, she screamed as loudly as she could again as he pushed her to the dirt floor, still holding her wrists with one hand and tearing at the front of her dress with the other. She started to scream again when he finally managed to expose one breast, but he slapped her hard.

"I just want to see them, honey. You can't tell me your soldier boy hasn't taken you already. Why are you so afraid of it? He's a big man. I expect if he's been inside you, there's nothing I can do to hurt you any worse." He moaned with the want of her, and she gave out one more scream for help. McGuire's desire grew to animal grunts as his free hand moved up her leg while his mouth covered a virgin nipple. He suddenly

42

realized that she actually was still untouched, and it made him want her all the more.

"Git up! Git up now, mistuh!"

McGuire froze at the new voice. He turned his head to see Marney's husband, Parker, standing over them with a shotgun.

"You git yo' white ass off'n that little girl, else ah'll blow a hole in it bigger than the one you already got!"

Shannon whimpered and pulled her dress closed as McGuire stood up. She scooted away from him as the big man turned to face Parker.

"Now you listen here, nigger!" McGuire growled. "You pull that trigger, and you'll die! You know that, don't you? Whether you're defending someone else or yourself, no nigger shoots a white man and gets away with it!"

"It don' matter. If'n ah die fo' keepin' yo' hands off'n that nice little girl, then ah expects ah'd jist have to die. Now you git!" Parker shoved the double-barrel shotgun into McGuire's gut. McGuire looked down at the gun, then looked over at Shannon, who sat whimpering in a corner.

"All right," he said slowly. "I'll leave. But let me warn both of you! Either of you says a word about this to Fitzgerald, or to my own family, and I'll see to it that the name Shannon Fitzgerald carries nothing but disgrace with it! I'll tell everyone in Charleston how I found her in the greenhouse, with her black stableman humping on her. I'll tell all the details of how I saw her lying naked, her little white legs wrapped around her big black stud's body!"

Shannon cried harder, and McGuire smiled.

"How would you like your soldier boy to hear that

43

one!" he sneered. "And you just remember that if I pull my money out of your father's bank, he'd have a hell of a time covering the rest of his accounts! And I'd make sure his other customers would think he was going under, so they'd all come in asking for their money!" He turned back to face Parker. "And you, nigger, would be quickly strung up to the nearest tree for touching a white girl!"

"Ah jist might call yo' bluff!" Parker replied, looking squarely into McGuire's eyes. "Ah's been workin' fo' Mastuh Fitzgerald fo' a long time. Ain't no way he'd believe yo' story."

"Maybe he wouldn't. But considering the way he pampers his blacks, by the time I got through spreading the story around town, people would sure wonder, you black mother! They'd wonder enough so's Shannon Fitzgerald wouldn't be able to hold her head up in public! You remember that, and keep your nigger mouth shut!" He looked back at Shannon, then turned and stormed out of the greenhouse. Parker hurried over to Shannon to help her up.

"Ya'll come on in the house, honey, and let ma' Marney he'p yo'," he said to her in a kind voice. She was trembling and covered with black dirt, and Parker kept a tight arm around her.

"Oh, Parker, thank you!" she whimpered. "If you . . . hadn't come—" She could not finish for her sobbing, and Parker led her to the house, still holding the shotgun in case McGuire returned.

"It's goin' be all right now," he assured her. "Don' you be worryin' 'bout what that there man said. Ain't nobody gonna' believe sech a thing."

"Oh, Parker, you know . . . how people are!" she

said frantically. "I've heard them whisper . . . about Daddy paying you . . . and all. Don't tell *anyone* . . . about this, Parker! Especially Daddy!"

"Yo' should tell yo' daddy, Missy Shannon," he advised.

"No, not yet! Please, Parker! Let me think! With Daddy's weak heart and all . . . and Mr. McGuire might really take his money out of Daddy's bank! I have to think, Parker!"

"Well, ah thinks it's wrong, Missy, but ah'll do whatever yo' wants. But it jist ain't right that man should git away with puttin' his hands on the likes of yo'. I ain't never knowed nicer ladies than yo' and yo' mama, bless her soul." He helped her inside and up the back stairway to her room, where Marney was changing the bed.

"Lordy sakes, what's happened!" Marney exclaimed. Shannon ran to her and cried as Marney held her.

"That there Mr. McGuire—he done tried to molest that girl," Parker told his wife. "If'n ah hadn't heard her screamin' an' come along when ah did, he would o' done more 'n that. Ah come runnin' with a shotgun and ah shooed him off."

Marney's eyes widened. "Parker! You is lookin' to get youself hung!"

"Mebby so. But ah couldn't let the man do what he was fixin' to do."

Marney patted Shannon's back. "No, I expect you is right," she told him. She released Shannon and put an arm around her. "You come into the bathroom now and Marney will fix you a nice hot tub, honey. It's too bad that Captain Edwards weren't here. He'd knock

45

that man from here clean out of town, he would!"

"Oh, Marney, I don't ... want him ... to know!" Shannon sobbed. Parker went out, a little worried about his confrontation with McGuire.

"Now, child, he should know—and so should you daddy!" Marney told Shannon, filling the tub.

"Marney, he ... he did an ... ugly thing! Bryce might not want me anymore ... if he knew! He did something ... oh, Marney, I wanted to save myself ... for Bryce!"

"Honey, if'n he jest touched you, that nice captain would understand that. Goodness knows he'd probably fix that man so's he'd never think about touchin' you agin!"

"Marney, we can't say anything! We can't!" Shannon shook as she removed her clothes. There was a black and blue mark around her left nipple. She felt nauseous at the memory of the animal viciousness of McGuire's attack. Surely it wouldn't be that way with Bryce. Was all sex this ugly and repulsive? Did Bryce grovel over the whores that way?

"Marney, he said .. he'd tell everyone ... that he found me and Parker ... together ... naked in the greenhouse ... if we told anyone!" Shannon whimpered.

Marney frowned and shook her head.

"I expect there's plenty of people who'd like to believe a story like that. People enjoy juicy gossip," she said, swishing her hand in the water and making more suds. "I don' expect my Parker would get no kind of trial and I don' expect nobody would believe you side of the story nor you daddy's. People is funny. They like to believe the worst. Makes themselves feel better 'bout

46

they own sins, I reckon'."

"Marney, I don't want Parker to get in trouble just for helping me! He could get hung for McGuire's lie! And I would never be able to hold my head up again! And . . . and McGuire said he'd pull all of his money out of Daddy's bank! Oh, Marney, what else can I do but keep quiet?"

Marney sighed. "Well, it jest don' seem right, that man gettin' away with what he did. I think you should at least tell Captain Edwards. He's a wise sort—and a man who does things his own way. I say he'd know what to do about it. I thinks you is wrong if'n you don' at least tell him, child."

"Oh, Marney, he'd hate me!"

"Hate you? I expect you got you guilty people a little twisted, honey. You didn't do nothin' wrong at all. Now git in this here tub."

"Marney, tell Parker how much I love him for what he did!" Shannon sniffled as the woman helped her climb into the porcelain tub. "He risked a hanging sticking up for me like that!"

Marney grinned. "Well, now, maybe sometimes a knight in shinin' armor can have black skin, hmmm?" Shannon smiled through her tears and slid down under the suds.

"There now," Marney told her gently. "You jest git youself calmed down. We'll do like you say for now and not say nothin'. But sayin' nothin' can eat away at you, honey. And I expect sooner or later you is gonna' have to tell you soldier man what happened. And in the meantime, you be sure you ain't caught alone agin', understand? And if that man makes a move fo' you agin', you don' worry about me or Parker, or you

47

daddy, or nobody. You worry about you—'cause that's all we usually got in the end, honey. You jest scream and you tell the whole world what that man is doin'. What all did he do, anyway? Parker says he don't think the man raped you."

"I . . . don't even know for sure . . . what rape is," Shannon whimpered. "He . . . tore my dress and . . . he . . . he put his mouth on me!" She started crying harder again, pressing a hot wet cloth to her sore breast. "Oh, God, Marney, he spit on me . . . and made awful sounds . . . like an animal!" She choked in a sob and Marney made her lean forward and gently massaged the girl's back.

"Honey, rape is when a man—well, when he gits inside you—like what a man and wife do to get her a baby. Don' you know about them things?"

"Not . . . very much, Marney."

"Well, maybe I ought to explain to you a little bit, so's if'n you marry that there soldier man, you is gonna' know what a man and woman is supposed to do. Only I don' want you gittin' all scared about it, 'cause it's real nice and pretty when it's with the man you love, honey."

She took the pins from Shannon's hair and poured water over it to soap it up.

"Now the first time a man takes a woman," Marney went on, "it always hurts some, honey. Sometimes it hurts a whole lot—sometimes jest a little. Depends on who's doin' it and how careful he's bein'. If'n it's the man you love, and he's growed up enough and been around enough women so's to know how to treat 'em, then it ain't gonna' hurt so awful much. Besides, after that, it gets better, see? And anyway, you don' mind the

48

hurt 'cause you love him and you is pleasin' him, and that makes you happy—and he might give you a baby, and that makes you even happier. It's only if'n it's with some ugly man you don' wanna have touchin' you that it can be powerful bad and painful."

Marney lathered up the girl's hair and proceeded to explain, to Shannon's shock and curiosity, about men and women and sex and how men were made and how babies were made. Shannon was not at all sure she could do such things—even with Bryce Edwards. But she was fairly sure he would be gentle about it. Yet how could she be certain? Maybe it was best never to have anything to do with men. She suddenly no longer had the desire to be kissed by Bryce Edwards, or by any man—ever.

Chapter Three

"Oh, Master Edwards, it's so good to see you're back!" the maid told Bryce as she ushered him into the parlor. "Miss Shannon hasn't been herself at all for a month now. We all expect it's from pining over you—only don't tell her I said so."

Bryce frowned slightly. "She isn't sick, is she?"

"Well, sir, I don't believe so. But she has become awfully quiet the last month or so. And she won't even leave the house. She just hasn't been herself at all!"

Bryce lit a cigar. "Well, for the last month she hasn't even written me," he told the woman. "Go tell her I'm here, will you? I'm anxious to see her."

"Of course," the maid replied. She quickly left, and Bryce gazed absently around the ornate parlor where guests were received, his mind on Shannon. Chinese vases stood in the corners, with large ferns in them. The rugs were oriental in this room, and covered a gleaming, polished oak floor. The entire Fitzgerald house was gleaming and full of treasures, and Bryce could see that Shannon's mother had had good taste.

51

But the luxury of the Fitzgerald home made him wonder how Shannon would adapt to living out West. Moving from one fort to another would mean that he could not provide her with such a fine home—a three- or four-room cabin would be more like it.

He puffed the cigar and paced, wondering why it was taking Shannon so long to come down. He had expected her to practically run into his arms. At least the girl he had left behind would have. He had already decided he would marry her, when she was old enough. He just hoped she could accept the different life style. But then a girl as sweet as Shannon surely wouldn't mind.

He nervously put out the cigar. He had been gone three months. He had corresponded often with Shannon the first two months, expressing his love. And she had replied with glowing letters, telling him how much she loved him also. But for the last month he had received nothing. Something was terribly wrong, and he intended to get to the bottom of it. Shannon finally appeared at the doorway. She looked pale and thinner and did not make a move toward him. Bryce could not quite read the look in her eyes as he approached her.

"Well!" he said, putting on a smile. "This is not the greeting I expected from the girl I love," he went on teasingly. He bent down and kissed her cheek, but she seemed cold as stone.

Bryce stepped back and crossed his arms. "Not a very warm greeting, Shannon. Would you mind telling me why the sudden change?"

She swallowed and looked him up and down as though he were a dragon come to consume her.

"I . . . I've decided that I don't think . . . it will

work," she said in her small voice. "You and I, I mean." She looked down at the floor. "I don't love you, Bryce. It would be better if . . . if you found someone else."

At first he stood there silently, studying her. She was obviously lying. He frowned and grasped her arms.

"Shannon, what's the matter with you? When I left you were bubbling over with what I thought was love. Your letters were full of love. And for three months I've been telling you I love you. Now I realize that some girls your age are flighty, but I didn't expect that of you, and I still don't! Now I want to know what is really wrong?"

She was breathing in short, frightened gasps now, refusing to look at him. She squirmed to get free of his grasp, and he finally let go of her.

"Just go to your whores north of town!" she whimpered. "They can do all those horrible things men like to do! I can't!" She burst into tears and ran back up the steps. Bryce stood there in bewilderment as the maid returned with some lemonade.

"Why, where did she go, Master Edwards?"

Bryce's face was dark with anger and confusion.

"I want to see that personal servant of hers—Marney, I believe her name is. Get her for me, please."

"Yes, sir." The maid set down the drinks and Bryce lit still another cigar and waited. Marney soon appeared, looking scared to death. Bryce glared at her.

"Get in here and shut those doors!" he commanded. She looked at him wide-eyed for a moment, then obeyed.

"What the hell is wrong with Shannon?" he asked point blank. "And don't you lie to me, Marney, or I'll drag Mr. Fitzgerald in on this!"

53

Marney wrung her hands nervously. "She made me promise not to say nothin', sir. I can't break no promise to Miss Shannon."

Bryce came closer. "The hell you can't!" he fumed. "If you really care about her, then you tell me what's happened! I happen to love that girl, Marney. Now I want to know what's going on! Believe me, it's for her own good if you tell me."

Marney put a shaky hand on his arm. "You got to promise to use you head," she said with begging eyes. "Use you head, or you could git that little girl, and her daddy, and my Parker in trouble."

Bryce calmed down a little. "All right," he said, patting her hand. "I'll use my head." He puffed the cigar and walked over to the fireplace. Marney watched him, feeling confident in his strength and wisdom. She had advised Shannon to tell this man right away. Shannon should have written him, and he would have come back lickety-split, Marney was sure of that.

"She . . . she was . . . molested, Captain Edwards . . . while you was gone."

Bryce stood frozen with his back to her, and she could feel his hurt and rage.

"She weren't raped, sir. No, sir. He just . . . he caught her in the greenhouse . . . about a month ago. From what she says, sir, he . . . he kissed her . . . and he pushed her around . . . held her arms and bruised them up. And he . . . he tore open her dress, Captain Edwards . . . and . . . put his mouth on her." Marney looked down at the floor, her black skin hiding her embarrassment. Bryce threw his cigar into the fireplace and turned around. Marney looked up at eyes so cold

54

they startled her.

"Who was it?" he asked grimly.

"Please don't make me say, sir!" she begged. "It . . . it was a white man . . . a good customer of her daddy's. Shannon made me promise not to tell her daddy, on account of the man said he'd pull all his money out of her daddy's bank and make him go broke. And he said he'd say some bad things about Miss Shannon and my Parker."

Bryce came closer, the look in his eyes frightening her.

"Oh, Captain Edwards, my Parker—he's the one that saved her! He done heard her screamin' and he run in there with a shotgun and scrammed that man out of there 'fore he could violate Miss Shannon. But that man, he threatened my Parker and Shannon both. Said he'd say he found 'em naked together and my Parker havin' . . . havin' a time with Miss Shannon."

Bryce grabbed her arms tightly, and she gasped.

"I'm asking you again—who was it?" he growled.

"Please, Captain Edwards! I beg of you to consider everything about this before actin' on it! You know what happens to black men that gits accused of touchin' a white girl! My Parker—he's good! He saved Miss Shannon! And Miss Shannon would be ruined in society! And her daddy's bank could be ruined!"

"I want a name, Marney, or so help me I'll beat it out of you!" She trembled and began to cry.

"What will you do?" she squeaked.

"Marney, I want you to trust me. I've been around conflict all my life. There's only one way to deal with a man like that—and that's head on. Now believe me, Marney, I *can* deal with this man, and neither Parker, nor Mr. Fitzgerald nor Shannon will get in any trouble, I assure you. Trust me, Marney!"

Their eyes held for a moment, and Marney relaxed.

"I done tole' that girl to tell you right off, Captain Edwards. But she's so young, and everything scares her. I tole' her you'd know what to do, and I believe you do. It . . . it was Loren McGuire, sir."

Bryce let go of her and sighed. "Well, well," he said absently. "That big son-of-a-bitch has crossed the wrong man, Marney." He ran a hand through his hair. "Did he hurt her—physically?" he asked.

"Well, sir, like I said, he bruised up her arms, and he slapped her . . . and . . . well . . . the breast where he put his mouth, it was all bruised from him bein' so violent about it."

Bryce gritted his teeth and paced again.

"Sir, little Shannon . . . well, sir, I think maybe she's thinkin' bein' with a man . . . that they is all animals like that one. It liked to scare her to death. She done started askin' me questions about . . . about men and women and all . . . you know. So I expect she's thinkin' you could be jest like him if'n you had a mind to and if'n you had a little too much whiskey."

"That's ridiculous!" he snapped.

"Sir, I know that! But you got to remember her upbringin' and her age! She don't know nothin' much 'bout men at all, sir. I done tole' her some things, 'cause I felt sorry for her askin' all them questions . . . and her havin' no mama to ask."

"That son-of-a-bitch must have scared the hell out of her."

"Do you . . . do you want me to go and get her to come back down here?" Marney ventured.

"No. Not yet. I'm going to pay Loren McGuire a visit first," he replied, putting on his hat. He was in full uniform, including a revolver.

"What will you do, sir?"

"That's my business. Don't worry, Marney, I'll work it out."

"Don' go gettin' youself in trouble, Captain Edwards. You look out for youself."

He looked at Marney and grinned, and the woman couldn't imagine Shannon Fitzgerald turning away from this man for long.

"Marney, after living around Apache Indians all these years, I'm very accustomed to looking out for myself, believe me. You tell Shannon I'll be back, and she's going to talk to me if I have to break her door down!"

"Yes, sir. I'll make sure, sir." Bryce reached out and patted Marney's cheek.

"Thanks for filling me in, Marney. Don't worry about Parker." He quickly left, and Marney ascended the stairs shaking her head.

"I tole' that silly girl she ought to have tole that there captain 'bout Loren McGuire. My, my! What a man she's got! If'n she don' come around and let him talk to her and hold her, I swear, I'll tan her behind myself!"

Loren McGuire walked toward his house from one of his outbuildings. He had just whipped a black picker for being too slow. He rolled down his shirtsleeves and pondered over whether or not he should drag out the man's lovely, dark-skinned daughter to the shed and rape her as further punishment to the family. The girl

57

was only twelve, but he had been eyeing her for a long time, and the young ones were always the greatest thrill. Few decent-looking black girls who were unlucky enough to belong to the McGuire plantation were left untouched by Loren McGuire.

"Wonderful rhythm," he commented to himself, chuckling. He rounded a bush near his house, and was suddenly confronted by Bryce Edwards. McGuire froze, totally startled and shocked to see Bryce standing there. In one glance he realized that Bryce knew everything.

"Listen, Edwards, I was drunk! And that little slut of yours gave me the eye!"

Before McGuire could prepare for combat, Bryce Edwards's foot came up and landed squarely in McGuire's privates with a vicious thud. McGuire screamed out and doubled over in black pain, and Bryce's large fist came up into the man's face and sent him flying backward. McGuire landed hard and curled up in pain. Bryce leaped on him and rolled him onto his stomach, wrenching one arm up behind McGuire's back and pushing his face into the dirt with his other hand.

"You scream again and I'll break your arm!" he growled to McGuire. McGuire squirmed and grunted, swimming in pain and surprised at Bryce's strength. Although Bryce was a big man himself, McGuire was even bigger, and had always considered himself stronger than anyone he knew. But Bryce Edwards had been in combat with Apache Indians, and there was no better training to be had. Bryce's voice sounded distant as McGuire listened with a head fuzzy from the terrible pain in his privates.

"You messed with my woman, McGuire!" Bryce said

in a low and gruff voice. "My property! I'm very possessive of my belongings! And I consider Shannon Fitzgerald mine. She's a lovely, innocent girl. And I intend to see that she remains that way until I make her my wife!"

Bryce bent the arm more and McGuire groaned and spit dirt from his mouth.

"Now I'm the only one who knows, understand? We'll keep this between you and me, McGuire! And if I hear of you going near Shannon again, or threatening Parker, or withdrawing from Fitzgerald's bank, you'll be signing your death warrant, McGuire! You remember that! I can easily arrange to kill you with no problems at all. And don't think I wouldn't do it!" He wrenched the arm again. "I've been around Apaches a long time, McGuire! I know all about how to torture a man!"

He bent the arm until he heard a snap, and McGuire could not help but scream out from the terrible pain.

"My God, you broke it! You broke it!" he yelled, now sobbing. Bryce only grinned, getting up and shoving the man over onto his back with his foot.

"You remember my warning, McGuire!" he hissed. He kicked the man again—first in the midsection, then in the privates. "And you remember the pain! It's nothing compared to what you'll get if you make trouble for Shannon again!"

Bryce picked up his hat and dusted himself off. He walked to his horse, mounted up and rode away, leaving behind a vomiting and crying Loren McGuire. He rode hard, in a hurry to see Shannon.

Shannon jumped as Bryce came charging through

59

the door to her bedroom, upset that she had still refused to see him after he got back. His anger at Loren McGuire still surged in his blood and burned in his eyes. Shannon sat on the edge of her bed in a robe, and as soon as her eyes met Bryce's she turned away, reddening deeply and wiping at tears.

"Go away!" she said in a near whisper.

"No, ma'am," Bryce said in a determined voice, closing the door and stepping closer. "I love you, Shannon. How in hell could you think I'd ever do anything to hurt you! How can you think I'd attack you like some goddamned animal!"

"Don't cuss—"

"I will cuss if that's what it takes to make you understand a few things!" he replied, raising his voice slightly. "Sure, I go see the ladies north of town once in a while. And do you know why? It helps keep me from talking you into doing things I know you aren't ready for yet! It's because I don't intend to hurt you or take advantage of you. I've never loved and respected a woman like I do you. And if we ever . . . if we . . . got married . . . I'd be kind to you, Shannon. Surely you know that. I wouldn't grovel over you like McGuire did. How could you think I'd be that way!"

She sniffled and kept a hand to her face, still turned around. Her hair was completely undone, and it hung in a cascade of reddish waves past her waist. Bryce wanted very much to touch it—to run his hands through it. He wanted to hold and comfort her. And yes—he wanted to do the very things he was promising her he would not do. But wanting and doing were two different things with such a young and innocent girl.

"Don't turn away from me, Shannon," he told her,

now softening and coming closer. "If we can't talk about something as important as this, then there's no use in going on with our relationship."

"Did you . . . did you just ask me . . . to marry you?" she said in a tiny voice. Bryce grinned a little and scratched his head.

"I guess in a way I did, didn't I? I didn't exactly intend to ask you this way, though. I was going to ask you under much different circumstances."

He saw her shoulders shake, and she flung herself down on her pillow.

"Oh, Bryce!" she sobbed. "It was so . . . terrible! I didn't think . . . you'd want me . . . after what he did!" She choked in a sob. "I didn't want . . . anyone to . . . touch me but you! And now I . . . I don't know if I even want *you* touching me!"

She cried hard now, and he frowned and came over to sit down beside her on the bed, putting a hand on her shoulder.

"Damn it, Shannon, don't cry. I can't stand it." He bent down and grabbed her up in his arms and pulled her onto his lap, and for several minutes he rocked her in his arms, neither of them speaking.

"Shannon, you trust me, don't you?" he finally asked gently.

"Yes," she whimpered, her head on his shoulder.

"Honey, when sex is between the right two people, it's very nice. You must believe that." He held her tightly, and in the next moment his lips were lightly caressing her neck, and she felt a warm tingle in her blood.

"Honey, this is Bryce. If I was anything like Loren McGuire, you'd have known it before this, because I've

61

wanted to bed you since the moment I laid eyes on you when I got back from Arizona."

His lips moved to her cheek, and then they found her lips, and he put a hand to the side of her face and kissed her hungrily. But his lips were ever so sweet and gentle and soft—not pushing and slobbery like Loren McGuire's. He groaned lightly and his lips lingered sweetly on hers as he gently laid her back on the bed. He moved on top of her, fully embracing her, and she felt lost beneath his magnificent frame. One of his hands moved down to lightly press against her hips as he gently forced her lips apart, and she suddenly felt like she was on fire. This was so different from what she had expected! He made her hunger for more. He made her want to give herself to him. It suddenly didn't matter that it might hurt when she became his wife. With Bryce doing this, she knew she wouldn't mind the pain. How lovely and sweet were his lips and the touch of his hand!

He left her lips and moved down to caress her neck with gentle kisses.

"You'd never have to be afraid with me, Shannon," he whispered. Again, his lips found her mouth, and she felt herself returning the kiss and whimpering as he moved off her slightly, and his hand ran over her thighs and belly and on up to her breast. He gently squeezed and caressed the breast through her robe, and she felt her entire body was exploding with a newly awakened ecstasy.

She did not even mind now that he was carefully opening her robe, and the large, strong hand was reaching inside to softly fondle her breast. She drew up her knees and whimpered, smothered by his kisses and feeling like a rag doll beneath this beautiful, golden man who made her want to submit to his desires. She whispered his name as his lips moved down, now lightly tasting the tender young nipple of her breast with lips as soft as velvet and with the gentleness of a kitten. How could she have thought she would not want to do this with this man? How could two men be so different?

"I'd never hurt you, Shannon," he whispered again as he pressed his cheek against the softness of her breast. "Never in God's name could I hurt you."

She felt a painful stirring deep inside her as his eyes rested lovingly for a moment on the exposed breast. He kissed it once more, and then his lips were at her neck again. She embraced him tightly around the neck.

"Oh, Bryce, I'm so sorry about the way I greeted you! But I've been so mixed up! It was so . . . awful . . . and ugly!"

"Hush," he told her softly, showering her with more kisses. "I don't want you to think about it anymore. I've taken care of it."

She clung to him tightly, grateful for his strength and sureness, stirred by his immediate action and his courage, relaxed in the knowledge that he was here now and would take care of her.

"You belong to me now, Shannon," he told her, softly stroking the hair back from her face. "And it will never be anything but beautiful between us."

She felt hot and flushed as he casually pulled the robe back over her breast. He placed a hand to the side of her face.

"I'd love to stay right here on this bed and make you mine," he told her. "But I haven't the right, and you aren't ready."

She closed her eyes and put her hand over his.

"I like when you touch me," she whispered.

"And I love to touch you," he told her. "But I'll not make you mine until you're really ready, and you aren't. You're still very young, and life in Arizona is not easy. I wouldn't be playing fair if I tried to take advantage of this very pleasant situation."

She blushed and he squeezed her hand. Bryce grinned and kissed her forehead.

"But I want you to remember that I've already staked my claim on you, Shannon Fitzgerald. And I'll not let go of you easily, nor will I allow another man to lay a hand on you—unless in the next year or two you change your mind about me."

"I'll never stop loving you," she said softly.

"Well, if we don't get married before I leave, I'm going to see to it that someone is assigned to keep an eye on you at all times. I'll not leave you here as bait for the wolves, Shannon."

"I've got Daddy."

"That's not enough. Besides, your father isn't well. As long as I'm around, I don't want you wandering around without me, understand? And I'll talk to Parker. When you go out to the gardens, you always tell him first so he knows where you are. There is a lot of unrest in Virginia now, Shannon. Sometimes people kind of change. When I leave, I'll provide a reputable man to watch over you and escort you places. I don't want you to be afraid of anything from now on."

"I don't know what I would have done without you to help me in this," she said, her eyes tearing.

"Well, I want your promise that from now on you'll

64

tell me everything, young lady, or I will be very angry with you."

"I promise"

He kissed her again, and she suddenly felt a hot and fierce jealousy at the thought of him lying naked next to the whores and giving them what he should be giving to Shannon Fitzgerald. She decided that once they were married she would make sure Bryce Edwards never again lay in a whore's bed. She would keep him too busy and too tired to think of other women. Yet she wondered if she could bear the terrible, hurting jealousy in the meantime. A little voice inside of her told her he would continue to see women who could please his manly needs. She wished she understood men better. And she wished so very much that she was older.

I'll just pretend he doesn't go there, she told herself as she closed her eyes and returned his kiss in the best fashion her virgin lips knew how. I won't ask him about it. We just won't talk about it, and it will be like he doesn't go at all.

Oh, how warm and safe she felt in these arms! He was her wonderful, strong, courageous and beautiful Bryce! He was a leader of men—and fought the terrible Apache Indians in the West. He had even taken an arrow in his side, and had once offered to show her the scar; but she had been too bashful to look at him without a shirt on. It wasn't ladylike. Now she found herself very curious to see the broad shoulders and muscular arms in the flesh. A man's body was a mystery to her. Surely he looked marvelous—like the statues she had seen of Greek Gods! Someday they would lie together, skin against skin, and the thought

65

of it made her love him all the more. Let him go to the whores to fulfill his needs for now. None of them would ever own this man! He belonged to her and no one else.

"You feeling better about all this now?" he was asking her.

"Oh, yes, Bryce! I feel so relieved that you know everything."

"And you trust me?" He kissed her again.

"Yes."

"You believe me when I say I'd never hurt you or rush you?" Again the kiss.

"Yes," she replied, feeling the crimson blush return.

"Good," he said softly, kissing her again. She looked into the beautiful gray eyes so full of love. This beautiful specimen of a man had just put his lips to her breast, and it had seemed so wonderful and natural. Why on earth had she been afraid he would be cruel to her?

Bryce studied her a moment, her green eyes wide with newfound pleasures and total trust and love. He kissed her again, this time harder—possessively—outraged that the huge and ugly Loren McGuire had slobbered over this lovely creature and frightened her so badly. If not for Parker, this precious child might have been raped. Bryce pressed his lips harder at the thought of it, moving on top of her. This girl belonged to Bryce Edwards, and may any other man who touched her be damned!

Chapter Four

A full year of courtship had passed when Bryce Edwards entered the office of Jonathan Fitzgerald one day and the two men shook hands. "So, what brings you to my place of business, Bryce?" Fitzgerald asked with a smile. "You thinking of investing some funds in the bank?"

"I wish I did have some funds to invest, sir. I'm not a rich man, but I have managed to build a tidy savings from my army pay over the years. It's held in a bank in St. Louis." Both men sat down. "Still, my savings might not put me in the upper class according to some of your friends' standards."

"Well, you're upper class in my book, Bryce," Fitzgerald replied. He leaned back in his chair. "I'm told you're a damned good officer, and since I've known you, I've grown to like you quite well. You're an honest and trustworthy young man."

Bryce smiled almost bashfully. "Thank you."

"When do you go back to Arizona?"

"One month." Their eyes held and Fitzgerald could

67

tell Bryce was nervous. The older man chuckled.

"Something tells me you're here about Shannon."

Bryce shifted in his chair. "Well, actually, yes, I am. I wanted to talk to you without her around."

"To tell me you want to marry her?"

Bryce smiled and nodded. "Yes, sir. I figured you knew I'd ask you soon. I honestly think I loved her clear back when she was only fourteen and I helped her up from that fall. I've been here nearly a year now, and we've seen a lot of each other. I love her very much, sir, and Shannon loves me. I already told you I have quite a bit of money saved, and I have a good career with the army. I can take good care of her."

"You realize, of course, that she's too young to be galavanting off to the kind of life she'd live out West, don't you?"

Bryce sighed. "Yes, sir. I'd just like your permission. I intend to wait for marriage until next year when she turns eighteen. I just thought we could announce the engagement tomorrow at your annual party. And next year, if I can't get a leave to come here and marry her, I'd see that she had proper escort to get her safely out to me. All I want from you is your permission, and your promise that you'll send her out to me next year, no matter what."

"She's all I have, Bryce—besides Bobby, of course. But being around Shannon—well, it's like being around her mother."

"I understand that, sir. But she's young and her whole life is ahead of her. You have to let her do what's important to her future. I love her very much. I can promise I'd take damned good care of her. She won't live in luxury, but she won't want for things, either.

68

And she would be safe and protected inside the fort. I don't want to wait more than another year, sir. I'm twenty-six years old and I want to have children. I never had any family of my own. I'd like one very much."

Fitzgerald studied the younger man intently. "All right," he finally replied, to Bryce's relief. "I can't let the loss of her mother chain her to my side forever, I know that. And I truly cannot think of a better man to marry her. You may not be a rich man, but wealth isn't everything. I don't doubt you could make her as happy or happier than any man with money. I see how she looks at you. I'll make some kind of arrangements so that after she leaves, if something happens to me, little Bobby will be looked after."

"You can send him out West, too, if you like. I'd be glad to raise him for you, Mr. Fitzgerald."

"My goodness, if you're going to be my son-in-law, please call me Jonathan. And I'm sure Bobby would love to go out West. He thinks the world of you, you know. Wants to be a big army man, like you."

They both chuckled, and Fitzgerald leaned back in his chair.

"I'm just glad you agree she should wait one more year. I think eighteen is a much better age for her to—uh—become a woman, if you know what I mean. I'm trusting you haven't already overstepped your bounds in that area. Shannon is very desirable, and I don't doubt you're skilled enough with women to woo her into anything you like."

Bryce lit a thin cigar and took a deep drag, wondering if he should tell Fitzgerald about Loren McGuire. But he decided against it. Fitzgerald's health was not good, and there was always the risk of his exploding at McGuire and losing the man's account. Bryce wanted to be sure that while he was gone there would be no danger to Shannon's financial welfare.

"She's a lady," he replied soberly. "I respect her."

"I'm sure you'll be good to her, Bryce. But what about other women? You're unusually handsome. And that uniform you wear only adds to your charisma. Women come to you like bees to flowers."

"I'm not interested in any woman but Shannon. She's charming and full of love, and I know she'll make a lovely wife and mother."

"Well, I just want you to be sure. As for Shannon being sure, another year should tell her that, also. I'm sorry for the personal questions, but you can understand. All in all, I think you're a man of fine character, and I'd be proud to have you as a son-in-law. I admire how fast you've moved up in rank over the last ten years. You're a man of courage and accomplishment—and you put duty above all. You know you're needed out West, and godforsaken as the place is, you're going back again. I admire that."

"I considered asking to be stationed closer to Virginia next year for Shannon's sake, but the way things are going over this slavery business, it would be next to impossible now. With the few men they're leaving out West, good leaders are essential. The Indians take very special treatment, Jonathan. You make one wrong move, and you've got slaughter on your hands."

"I understand, Bryce. I'm disturbed over this slavery issue myself. You know where I stand. No man should be the property of another. It just isn't right. I pay my

70

blacks and I treat them well. But there are many who do neither. It's becoming such a heated debate that I'm beginning to lose some of my friends and customers over it. More and more people are taking deliberate sides in the matter now. I don't like the looks of it at all."

"Nor do I. And I don't want Shannon or little Bobby getting caught in the middle if things flare up. I'd like your promise you'll send them West if guns start going off in Virginia. Just wire me and I'll be sure she has safe escort once she leaves Missouri and heads for the wild country."

"I'll do that. I don't want her mixed up in it either."

"I also want to arrange for a man to kind of keep an eye on her for me—escort her when she goes shopping—things like that. You're a busy man, and Bobby is too young to be of any use."

Fitzgerald frowned.

"You seem more concerned than necessary, Bryce. Charleston is quite a civilized town."

Bryce avoided the issue of McGuire.

"Let's just say Shannon is very beautiful—and very gullible. She trusts too many people. And when people start dividing themselves up like they are over slavery now, sometimes their personalities begin to change. They begin to feel desperate and afraid. You already admitted you're beginning to make a few enemies. People can find strange ways of taking their vengeance, if you know what I mean."

Fitzgerald pursed his lips. "Yes, I do. I hadn't thought about it that much, but you're right. You're around violence more than I, Bryce. You understand it better. And I'm very glad that you're so concerned. I

71

can certainly see I needn't worry about Shannon's welfare with you around!" He smiled, but Bryce remained sober.

"I'd die to keep her from being harmed," he told Fitzgerald, his eyes hardening slightly at the thought of Loren McGuire. Fitzgerald lost his smile.

"And pity the man who harms her," he replied with raised eyebrows. He stood up and put out his hand to Bryce. "Thank you for loving her so much. In my delicate health, it is very comforting to know she has someone like you if something happens to me."

Bryce stood up and they shook hands firmly.

"I ... uh ... I already bought a ring ... in the hopes you'd have no objection. I'd like to go and see her right now, if it's all right," Bryce said, now smiling again.

"Certainly. And won't she be walking around with her nose in the air and you on her arm tomorrow at the party?"

Both men laughed. "She's exciting to be around," Bryce told the older man. "She's so much like a little girl in some ways yet—including trying so hard to act older. But that's partly what I love about her—that innocence and that sweet personality."

Fitzgerald smiled sadly. "That's what I loved about her mother. If she's at all the kind of wife her mother was, you'll be a very happy man, Bryce Edwards." The old man's eyes teared, and Bryce knew he had made the right choice. The next year of waiting would be difficult indeed.

Bryce watched with delight as Shannon moved

among the guests, showing off the ring he had presented to her that afternoon. It had taken a good chunk of his savings to buy it, but the pleasure in her eyes was worth it. He studied her grace and beauty as she glided from person to person to flash the large stone and accept congratulations.

How he wanted her! He could hardly believe something this wonderful could happen to him, after the lonely, neglected life he had suffered in his younger years. One more year. One more long, lonely year, and she would belong to him.

She was coming toward him then, her auburn hair sweeping upward to the crown of her head and hanging in long curls at one shouder; her emerald-green eyes dancing with the youth of a seventeen-year-old; her fetching young breasts teasingly revealed in her low-cut mint-green gown. Her white skin looked like velvet. He wanted so much to touch all of her before he left—to have her just once before he returned to Arizona.

"Bryce, we're going to dance alone!" she said, coming up and giving him her hand. "Everyone wants us to dance, and I want to show you off."

He smiled and shook his head. "You make me sound like a trophy," he told her, putting a hand to her waist and whisking her out to the center of the crowd.

"You are!" she replied. "When I was fourteen I was so devastated because you wouldn't look at me like a woman. And now you do! I was so afraid when you left that first time that you'd never come back again—that you'd find some woman and marry her."

"With all your letters reminding me of you?" he replied. Their eyes held and hers teared.

"Oh, Bryce, I love you so much! The ring is so

73

beautiful! Thank you for thinking of giving it to me in time for the party. But how on earth am I going to stand the next year without you! I'll miss you so, Bryce!"

"It will probably be good for you. I want you to be sure, Shannon. And it will give your father one more year with you. Once you come West, you may not see him for a long time, honey. And in his condition, you may never see him again, for that matter." Her eyes teared more and he patted her at the waist.

"I don't mean to make you unhappy, honey," he went on. "Not tonight, of all nights. I just want you to be aware of all the angles. Over the next year, without me around, you'll have a lot of time to think things out. The way it looks now, I'll probably be stationed out West for quite some time. You'll be leaving luxury and your family for something very different, and it won't be easy. I'll love and protect you, and I'll give you all of the comforts possible, darling. But it will be nothing like floating around in this mansion of a house, with maids and such."

"I don't care. I'll be with you, and that's all that matters."

"Well, I'm just trying to be fair about it. I'm not going to paint you some glorious picture of what it will be like. The army is my life and my future. As I move up even more, I'll have more choice as to where I want to be stationed, and I'll make more money. But even that won't happen until we see how this slavery situation works out. It puts a slight dent in our list of choices. Things may not be easy at first, but they will get better—and some day I'll be able to support you in the manner to which you are accustomed."

"Bryce, Daddy would give you all the money you needed if you wanted to quit—"

"Shannon Fitzgerald!" he said firmly but quietly. The dance ended, and he led her out onto the veranda, smiling to others and shaking hands as they walked. He got her through the double french doors and they took a deep breath of the night air. "If you think for one minute that I intend to move in on your father's money, you think again, Shannon," he told her, turning her to face him. "That's the first time I've heard you suggest such a thing."

"I just—I want to help however I can—"

"Shannon, if I am going to make it in life, it will be on my own. I'll not live off someone else's money."

"Oh, Bryce, I didn't mean it that way at all. I wouldn't love you as much if you were that type of man. I just . . . I want to do something, too . . . to help us . . . to help you, because I love you." She sniffed and he pulled her close.

"I'm sorry, Shannon. I'm just . . . I guess I'm upset over having so little time left with you, and I worry just a little that you'll change your mind and not come out to me at all."

"How can you think such a thing!" she whispered, putting her arms around his middle and resting her head against his chest. "Oh, Bryce, I don't even want to think about you going away. I want to enjoy this last month together." She looked up into the soft gray eyes and he caressed her cheek with the back of his hand. "Bryce, will you be in danger? Those horrible Indians and all!"

He smiled. "Don't worry about that. I'll worry more about you than you should about me. By the way, I got a reply from Washington this morning, and they're sending a man to be your escort while I'm gone. Your father will help pay his fee. I managed to convince him that you should be watched—what with all the enemies he's made. The man's name is Carl Danner. He's about thirty-five and a widower, so he has no other responsibilities but to watch after you. I understand he's very dependable. He'd better be, for what he costs."

"Oh, Bryce, it all seems so silly and unnecessary."

"Silly or not, I'll rest easier knowing you're protected. These are bad times, Shannon. You've already seen how your father's friends can turn on you." She paled at the memory and he held her close again. "Promise me that you'll not go out without Mr. Danner. He's being paid well to keep you safe. He should be here in a couple more weeks."

"I promise," she said with a sigh.

He kissed her forehead. "And spend a lot of time with your father and brother this next year," he added. "Your father promised to send Bobby out to us if anything happens to him. His lawyers know what to do. He'll have everything all worked out so by the time you come out to me, there will be nothing for you to worry your pretty little head about."

"Well, I do worry about Bobby, Bryce. He's only fourteen, almost fifteen, but he's already saying that if we have a war over slavery, he wants to be in it. He thinks he can put on a uniform and suddenly become an experienced soldier like you. Bryce, if anything happened to Bobby, I don't know what Daddy would do."

"I'll have a little talk with the boy and make him

76

realize he's the man of the family now and should stay home," Bryce told her, giving her a squeeze.

"Would you? He worships you, Bryce. He'd listen to you."

"Then it's done. Now, my lovely princess, shall we rejoin the party?"

She met his eyes. "I like being alone with you."

He bent down and kissed her hungrily, fully embracing her, wanting her.

"Oh, Bryce, hold me! Hold me tight!" she whispered when he released the kiss. He could feel her trembling and she choked in a sob.

"Hey, what's this? Tears at your own engagement party?"

"Bryce, I'm so scared! What if there's a war soon? What will happen to Daddy—and Virginia—and Bobby? What will happen to all of us!"

He embraced her reassuringly.

"That will be enough of that talk. Now I told you your father has everything worked out with his attorneys. And I'll talk to Bobby. And you'll be well guarded. And I highly doubt there will be any kind of war in just one year, darling. You'll hear a lot of talk, and there may even be some small skirmishes between small groups of people. But an all-out war won't come that soon." He kissed her hair. "I'm afraid it will lead to that, though, Shannon. But by the time it does, you'll be safe and sound with me in Arizona. Now I don't want you to be afraid of anything, not anything, understand?

They kissed again, and nearly forgot all about the party until they heard loud voices coming from inside. Bryce lifted his head and looked toward the folding doors to see a young private standing there, looking embarrassed at having seen them kissing.

"What the hell do you want?" Bryce asked, a little irritated. Shannon gasped slightly at the words and turned to see the young man.

"Oh, my!" she said, reddening.

"Ex . . . excuse me, sir, but . . . I was sent here with new orders for you."

Shannon's chest tightened at the words. Bryce kept a firm arm around her as they walked toward the private. Shannon put the back of her hand to her hot cheeks, embarrassed at being flushed from Bryce's kiss.

"What's everybody yelling about inside?" Bryce asked as he took the telegram.

"Well, sir, I just got here. But I think they're arguing about Kansas, sir. The Lincoln-Douglas debates were being discussed as far as I could tell. I . . . uh . . . I'll be leaving now, sir. I was to bring you that note. Good evening, Captain Edwards."

The young man saluted, and Bryce saluted in return. The private quickly left and Bryce opened the note. Shannon watched his face cloud as he read it. "Damn!" he finally swore, crumpling the note and turning away.

"Bryce? What is it?" Shannon asked in alarm.

He sighed deeply. "I have to leave tomorrow evening," he answered. "They've . . . changed my orders." His voice was choked. "Tomorrow!" he groaned. "I leave on a train . . . around six o'clock."

"Oh, Bryce!"

He turned and she could see the tears in his own eyes. "I don't want to leave you so quickly," he whispered. They embraced, Shannon breaking down into tears.

"Oh, Bryce, why so soon? Why?"

"It's partly the trouble in Kansas. People are forming mobs there . . . some arguing whether it should be a free state, and others saying it should be a slave state," he answered in a strained voice. "Washington wants me to get the hell back to Arizona. They're removing even more troops from the West, including officers. Damn! I don't like any of this, Shannon."

"Oh, where will it end! Even our engagement party has been ruined because of this stupid slavery argument!"

He held her tightly as she wept, but their intimate moment was interrupted by a loud crash from inside the house. Bryce pulled away and kept hold of her hand as both ran back into the ballroom to see Jonathan Fitzgerald lying flat out on the floor and people standing around staring.

"Daddy!" Shannon gasped, running to kneel beside him. Two large men stood nearby, fists clenched, as Shannon bent over and helped her father sit up.

"What the hell has happened here!" Bryce roared.

"Those two men—they crashed the party and started an argument about Kansas and slavery!" one of Fitzgerald's friends spoke up. "The next thing we knew, one of them punched Fitzgerald."

Bryce stepped up to the men, both of whom were as big as he.

"Who the hell are you?"

"We're representin' some people that don't like Fitzgerald's way of thinkin!" one of them sneered. "We was hired to come over here today and make sure Fitzgerald and all his friends know they're in for trouble if they keep up this talk about freein' slaves! It's against everything the South stands for."

79

People screamed as Bryce suddenly landed a fist into the speaking man's middle, then came up with a hard uppercut to the man's jaw, sending him flying backward. The second man charged into Bryce and Shannon held her father's head in her lap and watched wide-eyed as Bryce's foot came up at the last minute and landed in the man's throat. The would-be assailant made a strange grunting and gagging noise and bent over. Bryce backhanded the man while he was gasping for breath and knocked him sideways to the floor. People gasped, and the young women stared in awe at Bryce Edwards's skillful fighting.

"Somebody throw these men out into the street!" Bryce said angrily. Four men hurriedly picked up the two half-conscious men and carried them out the door. Bryce was panting. He smoothed back his hair and turned to Shannon, who was crying as her father struggled to get up. Bryce grasped Fitzgerald under the arms and helped him to his feet.

"Are you all right, Jonathan?" he asked in concern.

"Oh, yes! Yes!" Fitzgerald grinned and looked around at the crowd. "Quite a future son-in-law I've got here, isn't he?" he said, trying to revive the party spirit.

Shannon stood between Bryce and her father, fighting tears of concern for her father and for Bryce's bleeding knuckles. Several people came up and expressed their verbal support of Fitzgerald's cause, and the whole room was suddenly a rumble of voices, nearly all conversation centered on freedom and slavery, the Lincoln-Douglas debates, and Kansas.

"Jonathan, you do have friends who agree with you," one man spoke up. "We should have stepped forward sooner. Forgive us for standing back."

"Times are coming when we are going to have to stick together, David," Fitzgerald replied.

"I don't want to hear all this political talk at my engagement party!" Shannon sniffled. "Everything has been ruined!"

"We must discuss it," Fitzgerald told his daughter, patting her arm. "I'm sorry, darling, but after what's happened here, it's time to organize and time to find out just who is behind me and who isn't." Shannon sniffled again and Bryce embraced her as several more men came up to Fitzgerald.

"The only way to stop the horror of slavery is to end slavery!" one man spoke up. "We all know how some of them are treated—and by men who call themselves Southern gentlemen! Loren McGuire is a good example! I noticed he isn't here today! That tells us where he stands!"

Shannon looked up at Bryce.

"Everyone knows how McGuire treats his slaves," another put in. "I don't care how wealthy the man is, I can't call him a friend any longer. He's ordered brutal whippings, and there's a rumor he does . . . things . . . to the young black women and girls."

Shannon moaned and Bryce held her close and scowled at the man. "That remark wasn't necessary!" he barked.

"Some things are necessary to say!" the man replied. He then looked around at the rest of the crowd. "I say we divide the state of Virginia! It's West Virginia that's antislavery! I want to be a part of Virginia, but I don't want to be a part of a slave state! I'm for the State of Virginia and the State of West Virginia!"

Several guests cheered and put up their fists. But one man scowled and stepped up to Fitzgerald. He was Noel Jackson, a good friend of Loren McGuire.

"Nigger lover!" he sneered under his breath quietly to Fitzgerald. "So, you use your own daughter's engagement party to take your stand on slavery! How dare you and your friends suggest dividing Virginia!"

"They're your friends also, Noel," Fitzgerald replied. "And I'm not a nigger lover. I'm a man who loves freedom, and who believes no human should be owned and treated like an animal—sometimes lower than animals!"

"They—and you—are not my friends!" Jackson snapped, now speaking loudly. "And before this is over, it won't be just friend against friend, Fitzgerald! It will be father against son—and brother against brother!"

People gasped and quieted at the remark. "You'll destroy the South!" Jackson added. He grabbed his wife's arm and left in a storm. Most of the guests began leaving then, but not without first giving Jonathan their thanks and support and apologizing for the turn the party had taken. They all gave their best to Bryce and Shannon.

"Don't worry, Jonathan," another man said as he left. "You have a lot of people on your side. As for Kansas, I think we need to do something. I don't know what. But it will only make it more difficult to eliminate slavery and make this a truly free country if another state is allowed to enter the Union as a slave state."

"Thank you for your support, Robert. I'll—uh—see you at the meeting tomorrow."

The man nodded and left. When the last guest was

out the door, Shannon, still sniffling, began helping the maid remove dishes from the buffet table, just to have something to do to try and forget about the terrible ending to her party.

"What meeting was that last man talking about?" Bryce asked his future father-in-law. Fitzgerald cleared his throat and walked over to the table to pour both of them a drink. He turned to face Bryce, handing him the glass.

"Some of us are meeting tomorrow to decide just where we stand in case of an all-out civil war, Bryce," the older man finally replied. Shannon felt her heart quicken, and she hurriedly carried a bowl out of the room, not wanting to hear any more of this talk that frightened her. Fitzgerald lit a cigar. "I expect we'll be a separate state before this is over, Bryce—West Virginia."

"Jonathan, I admire your courage in taking a stand on this," Bryce said, lighting a cigarette. "But like I said before, I don't want Shannon or even Bobby getting caught in the middle."

"I think it's exciting!" Bobby spoke up. The boy walked up to the two of them, putting his hands on his hips. Unlike Shannon, he was big-boned and tall for his age, and very dark. There was little resemblance between Shannon and Bobby. The boy's blue eyes glittered with pride. "If we go to war, I'm gonna go out there and fight for what Daddy believes in!" the boy said proudly. "And I'll be a good soldier, just like you, Bryce!"

"Son, I'm proud of your desire and determination," Fitzgerald told him. "But you'll not be out there fighting at your age. There are many other ways to be of service. I've lost your mother, I don't intend to lose my precious son."

"I'm old enough right now to go and fight!" the boy balked. "It wouldn't be any fun sitting around here hearing about all the battles. I want to be a part of them! You'll see. Some day I'll be an officer, just like Bryce. He was only fifteen when he joined the army, weren't you, Bryce?"

Bryce sighed and ran a hand through his hair. "Listen, Bobby, when I was fifteen . . . well, I'd already been living a pretty damned rugged life. I was accustomed to hard knocks. I didn't have a nice home like this, and people who loved me. For me it was just . . . something to do with my life, I guess. It gave me some direction. Now you, on the other hand, have advantages I never had. You have the opportunity to further your education, maybe help out some day as a doctor or a lawyer who's worked his way into Congress where you can help change the laws. Your father's right. There are other ways to help, and your father and sister both need you here at home."

Bobby's face fell.

"I'd rather go to war," he pouted. Bryce looked over at Shannon and detected the fear in her eyes at her brother's words.

"Bobby, war isn't anything like you think it is," Bryce said to the young man. "It isn't glorious and exciting. It's ugly, Bobby. It's bloody and ugly and painful. You see things that make you want to vomit, and sometimes you do vomit. And you may do what people term brave acts of heroism—but inside you're scared to death and you want to cry, and sometimes you want to die."

84

"I'll bet you've never been scared of anything!" the boy declared. Bryce grinned a little and shook his head.

"Bobby, I want you to picture a huge, dark Indian straddled over your body while you're lying on the ground injured. And that Indian is raising a tomahawk, screaming in ungodly war cries, his face painted monstrously, his arm poised to bring down the hatchet and split your skull, and you tell me you wouldn't be afraid," Bryce replied. Shannon stood over at the table quietly listening. She grasped her stomach at the thought of something happening to Bryce.

"Did that happen to you?" Bobby asked, wide-eyed.

"You bet it did. And if not for a good soldier friend of mine being quick and a good aim with his rifle, I sure as hell wouldn't be here today."

"Stop it! Stop all of this horrible, bloody talk!" Shannon spoke up. Her eyes met Bryce's, and he immediately regretted having mentioned the incident in front of her. Shannon turned and hurried up the stairs to her room. Bryce looked at Fitzgerald and frowned.

"You remember that promise, Jonathan," he said. "If things get worse, she comes out to me, even if the year isn't up yet. That man I've hired to watch over her will be here in a couple of weeks. I'll feel very good knowing he's around."

"Well, whatever you wish, Bryce. I do think it's a little unnecessary in a civilized place like Charleston, but then, after today, I can see where some people might get a little rough. I deeply appreciate your giving me one more year with my daughter and letting her grow a little more before making a pioneer wife out of her. And with that man here to protect her, you can

85

concentrate on fighting Indians without worrying about Shannon back here. The important thing is that nothing happens to you now. You're her future, Bryce. And I have no doubts she'll be a very happy young woman."

Bryce finished his drink and walked over to Bobby, who was shoving several more cookies into his mouth before the maid carried them away.

"You remember what I said, Bobby," Bryce told the boy quietly, speaking low enough that Fitzgerald could not hear. "Cool your heels and stay here where there are people who love you and need you. It could be you'll be the only man of the family sooner than you think."

Bobby frowned and shoved his hands into the pockets of his well-tailored, expensive suit.

"I want to get out and see things . . . do things," he grumbled. "I don't like being stuck here, and I hate school and stuffy parties and such. I want to do something exciting."

"Well, Shannon may need you right here. At least wait until she's safely out West with me. That's only a year, Bobby. But that isn't as important as the fact that your father has already lost your mother. Don't destroy him by causing him to lose his only son."

Bobby's eyes met Bryce's, and Bryce could see he was not completely getting through to the boy.

"There's more to being a good soldier than fighting in hand-to-hand combat, Bobby. And bullets hurt, son. They hurt like hell. You remember that." Bryce looked steadily at the boy, trying to get through the young man's thirst for excitement.

Bobby sighed. "Yes, sir," he said dejectedly. He

turned and went up to his room. Fitzgerald had poured himself another drink and approached Bryce.

"Listen, Bryce, if you'd like to go up and talk to Shannon, it's all right with me. I do believe the little princess is rather upset right now, what with all this talk of war and her party being spoiled."

"Well, it isn't just that, sir. I got new orders tonight. I go back tomorrow instead of in a month."

Fitzgerald scowled. "Oh, I'm damned sorry to hear that, Bryce. Too bad for both of you. We'll all miss you very much." He puffed on his cigar. "But at least we have matters all straightened out. Next spring, if Shannon is still determined to go running out into the hot desert sun to marry her prince, I'll send her on her way with my best wishes; unless, of course, you can get a leave to come here to marry her."

"I'd love to be able to do that. But I have a feeling that this time there'll be no coming back for quite a while, Jonathan. Not with war pending here and skeleton troops out West. The Apaches aren't going to care much about whether or not we're at civil war in the East. They'll go on about their raiding and looting just like always—not that I always blame them, mind you. If you think some slaves are treated badly, you should see how Indians get treated!"

"Mmmm. That's too bad. Too bad. Our arrogance gets us into some sorry messes, doesn't it? I'll say one thing, though. After watching you fight tonight, I'd say the Apache Indians hadn't better cross you too often. That was quite a show you put on, Bryce. And I appreciate it. You really gave those two mugs what for."

Bryce grinned. "What about you? Are you sure

you're all right?"

"Oh, I'll be fine. I have a very sore jaw right now, and I pretty much ache all over, but I don't think any real damage was done."

"Well, I think I'll go upstairs and see Shannon then," Bryce told him. "Good night, Jonathan." The two men shook hands and Bryce went upstairs with a heavy heart, depressed at having to leave so much sooner than he had planned.

He tapped on the door to Shannon's room, and after several seconds she finally opened it. He looked down at her pouted lips and red, puffy eyes.

"I'm sorry I mentioned that bit about the Indians," he said softly. She broke down into renewed tears, and Bryce stepped inside and pulled her into his arms.

"Oh, Bryce!" she cried. "It seems like there's war everywhere! Why can't people . . . just get along! Even if . . . you stayed here . . . you'd end up getting caught in the fighting between the states! There's no getting away from it. Bryce, I'm scared!"

He kissed her hair and held her tightly. "Now you just stop that talk," he said gently. "Everything will be all right. I'll keep in constant touch. And before you know it, you'll be coming out to me and we will forget all of this mess and just enjoy being in each other's arms and being in love and having babies."

He ran his hand through her now-undone hair, relishing its softness and thick beauty, and in the next moment they were kissing with the passion of lovers about to part, as he pressed the back of her head while his lips searched her own, and with his other hand he grasped her hips gently and pressed her against his hardness. She felt the strange yet exciting fear of the unknown, still not even sure how a man looked unclothed, yet filled with an intense desire to know—to experience making love with her handsome lieutenant colonel, who would be so gentle and kind with her.

Bryce's lips left hers and he embraced her so tightly she could barely breathe.

"God, I love you, Shannon!" he whispered. "I'll not rest well at night until I have you beside me and we can be one."

"Oh, Bryce!" she whispered. He kissed her again, then bent down to caress the white of her breasts with his lips. He could feel her trembling. His lips moved back up her neck and found her mouth again. Yes, she was still half child. And he would thoroughly enjoy bringing out the hidden woman. Bryce Edwards and only Bryce Edwards would experience the joy of hearing her cry out at that first intercourse. But he would be ever so gentle with her. He would not allow her for one moment to be afraid or to experience great pain. No harm would ever come to Shannon Fitzgerald.

The thought of taking her and getting it over with passed through his mind, but he tried to ignore it. The sudden change in orders brought on an unexpected urgency, and former rules of respect suddenly seemed unimportant.

"I love you, Bryce!" she was saying. "I'll be dreaming about you constantly—praying for you constantly."

"It won't be so long, Shannon," he said, in a voice gruff with desire. "In one more year you will be mine, and damn everything and everyone else. We'll never be apart again, and your age or the war or the hardships in Arizona or your ties here—none of it will matter. You will be Mrs. Bryce Edwards, and we'll not let anything stop us."

They kissed again, hungrily, and then his lips moved to her neck, as his mind raced with apprehension. Could he truly leave this beautiful girl he loved without branding her first as his own? It would be difficult to sleep this night.

"I'll pick you up early tomorrow, Shannon," he whispered. "We'll spend the day together."

Chapter Five

The carriage splashed through puddles left from a light rain. Shannon thought how fitting the gloomy, gray day was, for this would be the last day she saw Bryce before the long year of waiting to become his wife. The events of the night before, combined with Bryce's having to leave this evening, left a cloud of depression over both of them, a feeling of urgency that obliterated any thoughts of what was proper. All that mattered was that he was going away, and they paid the driver to wander aimlessly while they sat embraced beneath the carriage hood, often kissing, wanting time to stop.

They had only this day, this one, short day, and not even all of that. Shannon was overwhelmed by a new fear, brought on by the argument at their engagement party the night before. Maybe she would never see him again. Maybe he would be killed by Apaches, or she would be killed by her father's enemies. Everything seemed to close in on them now, so that she could not truly enjoy the elegant luncheon Bryce had offered her at the elite French restaurant where he had taken her after first picking her up. Both of them left half their food, wanting only to be alone.

Now they clung to the moment, savoring it, she nestled in his shoulder, flushed from the heat of love, not caring when his hand sometimes moved over her breasts. She wanted him to touch her, wanted to remember his gentleness. They rode that way for an hour, embracing, kissing, touching, whispering words of love. He was so lonely. She was so afraid. And both were so very much in love.

Bryce thought his body would burst with desire for her, a sudden need to have her now that there was little time left. So what if she was not his wife? She soon would be. He had a right to touch her, taste her sweet mouth, share his passion with her. She was his betrothed. To take liberties meant no dishonor. He knew she would do these things with no other man, respected her sweet innocence and devoted love for him. He had been alone for so long, having no one in the world who cared about him. Now there was sweet, beautiful Shannon Fitzgerald, who put her total trust in him, gave her total love to him, was even willing to leave the comforts of home one day and follow him West. He ordered the driver to the address of the small apartment where he had been staying.

"I have to get my things packed," he told Shannon. "I'll get my bag and then we can spend the rest of the afternoon together riding before I catch the train."

"Oh, Bryce, don't talk about it." Her tears came again and he held her tightly, his body screaming with desire to have her and get it over with. It seemed only moments before the carriage stopped. Bryce pulled back and drank in her beauty, as she sat there in a bright pink dress and bonnet, her red hair even redder where the sun hit it, her green eyes greener from crying. Their eyes held, and the words came out in uncontrolled passion.

"Come in with me," he whispered.

Her heart raced. Her subconscious told her what he really meant by the words, yet she pushed the thought away. She would pretend she didn't understand the full meaning of the request, yet deep inside she hoped he meant exactly what she thought he meant. How wrong and improper that would be, how frightening and mysterious, yet how right it was for this moment.

"I . . . I shouldn't be seen. . . ."

"There is no one around here who knows you, not in this neighborhood. Come inside with me, Shannon, just for a little while. I don't want to spend the whole day in this carriage. We can talk better inside."

She reddened and looked down. "All right," she answered.

Bryce exited the carriage and helped her down. Her legs felt weak and he seemed to sense it, keeping a firm arm around her as he paid the driver to be on his way. He quickly whisked her up the steps and through the double-door entranceway, with its lace curtains on the glass. He led her down a hall to another door, slipping a key into it and going inside. He closed the door and removed his hat, then gently led her to a chair.

"Would you like some tea or something?"

Their eyes held again, and she shook her head. He suddenly looked nervous as he began opening the drawers of a bureau. Shannon glanced around the small, one-room apartment, kitchen cabinets, sink, fireplace, two chairs and a bed, all in the same room. She glanced at a door in the corner, which she suspected was the water closet.

"It's not much, but a single man on the move doesn't need much," he told her.

She met his eyes again. "It's cozy," she replied.

His eyes filled with a mixture of pain and passion. "Shannon, I . . ." He came closer, kneeling in front of her. He placed big, gentle hands on her knees and ran them up her thighs to her hips. "I can't bear the thought of leaving . . . without making love to you," he told her, his voice gruff with passion. He closed his eyes and rested his head in her lap. "I'm sorry. I deliberately brought you in here, hoping . . ." He pulled away and rose. "I'm sorry. I'll pack as quickly as I can and get you out of here." He pulled out a duffel bag and began stuffing clothes into it. When she did not reply, he finally turned to face her. His heart raced when he saw that she had removed her hat and had taken the pins from her hair.

"I want to stay," she told him in a shaking voice. "I . . . feel the same as you. What if . . . what if we never see each other again? I wouldn't want . . . any other man to . . . to . . . be the one."

Her face reddened, and in the next moment he was sweeping her out of the chair, pressing her close, his lips searching her own hungrily, urgently, both of them crying.

"Shannon, my Shannon!" he whispered, moving his lips to her neck, her shoulders. He picked her up and carried her to the bed, gently laying her down and moving onto the bed beside her.

"Bryce, I'm scared," she whimpered. "I . . . I want

94

to, but . . . please don't hurt me, Bryce."

He raised up and stroked her hair. "I would never hurt you. We have time to make love more than once. After the first time it will be better. He kissed her eyes. "Trust me, sweet Shannon. I love you so. You're going to be my wife some day, and we'll never be apart again."

His lips met hers again, and his hand moved under her dress, touching new places and sending fire through her blood that broke down all her resistance. The only important thing was to make this beautiful man happy, to please him, give him something to remember and cherish, something that would ensure he never forgot her, no matter what.

Everything became unreal, as her movements seemed more like a dream. He was removing her clothes and she didn't care. His lips and hands were touching secret places that made her whimper his name. Her cheeks were hot, her whole body flushed, and the thrill of his lips tasting the fruits of her breasts removed all fear; the magic he worked with his hands removed all modesty. Her youthful passion could not be controlled, no more than his own manly needs could be.

She curled up bashfully when he stopped momentarily to remove his own clothing, and for the first time in her life she looked upon a naked man. He was like the statues of Greek Gods she had seen, broad and strong and muscular. He lay down beside her again, taking her hand and gently pressing it against that part of him that made him most manly, and she found herself lightly exploring with her fingers and kissing his chest.

95

"Don't be afraid of it, darling," he told her. He kissed her neck and moved his own hand to that magic place that made her cry out in desire, and in the next moment she felt an explosion inside that she had never before experienced. It made her breathe hard and arch up toward him, saying his name over and over as he moved on top of her. It made her want to open her legs, want to take this man inside of herself. She had only been aware up to this moment of the mystery of men, of things girlfriends had told her about mating. Now it was truly going to happen, and there was no turning back.

She cried out when he entered her, the pain worse than she had expected. He embraced her and she dug her nails into his shoulders, screaming his name.

"It's all right," he consoled her. "In a moment it will be done." In his great passion and the excitement of stealing her virginity, he could not control himself as he would have liked to, but perhaps it was better for this first time that it was done quickly. His life poured into her small belly, amid groaning kisses and the thrill of skin against skin. In a moment it was done, and they lay limp and kissing, both crying again, expressing words of love. It was done. Their love was sealed for all time. He was her man and she was his woman, and no matter what happened from then on, nothing could change it. This was their moment. No one could take it from them, not a civil war, not the Apaches, not a year of waiting to make the marriage legal on a piece of paper. In heart and body, and as far as Shannon was concerned, before the eyes of God, they were married, for they had been as one.

"Now we have something no one can take from us,"

Bryce whispered. "My God, Shannon, I love you so." He raised up and kissed her tears. "Are you all right, darling?"

"I'm not sure. It hurt . . . more than I thought it would."

"I'll draw a hot bath for you. You sit in it a while and you'll feel better. Maybe then . . . maybe we could . . ."

She put delicate fingers to his lips, studying the beautiful, finely etched lines of his face, the square jaw and gentle gray eyes. "I want to do it again, even if it hurts," she told him. "I'll be all right. I don't want to waste this beautiful day, Bryce. It's all we have."

He smiled softly and kissed her fingers. "Then you aren't angry for what I've done?"

"I told you I wanted to stay. What about you? Please tell me you don't think less of me."

He caressed her hair. "You are my sweet Shannon. What you've done was out of love, and I've wanted to be loved for so long. How could I think less of you? I brought you here, hoping it would come to this. I am the only one to blame, the only one who could have stopped this. But I can't resist you, Shannon Fitzgerald, and if it damns me to hell to take your virginity this way, then I'll gladly go to hell. But I'll not go back to Arizona without making you mine—totally mine."

She reached up and traced his lips. "God would never send my sweet Bryce to hell. I will love you forever. Forever and ever."

The next three hours passed all too quickly. Twice more they gloried in their newfound ecstasy, he

97

claiming the woman-child he so passionately desired; she learning about man and how to satisfy a man and in return realize her own deep joy and satisfaction. Never had she dreamed it could be so wonderful. Never had she truly believed a man the size of Bryce Edwards could be so gentle and sweet and understanding. If only there had been more time to think and plan. If only her father would give his permission for her to be married now. Perhaps they would have done everything differently. But being rushed made it impossible to reason out anything. The army was Bryce Edwards's life and income. If he was going to marry someone like Shannon, he must not risk his career. He was ordered to report, and report he must.

A year. Only a year. It seemed like forever, but perhaps it would go faster than they expected. They floated on the bed in the tiny room, blocking out all thoughts that brought them pain and sorrow, relishing in each other's touch and body, whispering promises, exploring secret places, discovering to their great joy that this would most certainly be a satisfying part of their marriage. Yes. It would be good, so good! She didn't care what he did with her. She wanted him to remember her, to claim her totally. She wanted to be Bryce Edwards's woman and to show him how she could please him. Such wonder and joy she had never known. Bryce! It was Bryce who had broken her into womanhood, Bryce who took privileges, who claimed her, devoured her, invaded her.

And then it was over and they were dressing. Her heart pounded with sorrow as he called a carriage and they stood silently on the street as it came to a halt in front of them. They looked at each other before getting into the carriage. Shannon burst into tears as the vehicle headed for the train station. Bryce's throat hurt too much to talk. He only held her.

All the way to the station their minds raced. What lay ahead for Virginia, for Shannon's family? What was in store for Bryce in Arizona? They felt their hearts being torn in many directions, grieving over a broken nation, and over their own separation. Both knew the next year would be the longest and loneliest of their lives. They could already hear the drums of war beating—beating. Or was it only their own hearts they heard?

It was all happening too quickly now! They left the carriage and Bryce paid the driver to wait for Shannon to take her home as soon as Bryce boarded the train. They sat on a bench to wait, her head on his shoulder.

"Are you okay, Shannon?" he finally asked in a strained voice. "Are you sure I didn't hurt you?"

"No more than any girl would be hurt the first time. I'm all right. Anyway, it was worth it."

The train arrived and she looked into his eyes. "I love you, Bryce Edwards. I will always love you."

His own eyes teared. "You come out no matter what next year, understand? And if anything bad happens before that, you come out right away. Promise me."

"You know I will."

"The man I hired will take good care of you. You'll be safe as long as you stay with him. You go straight home, and I don't want you running around town until he arrives, understand?"

"I understand."

Their eyes held. "God, I love you, Shannon." A tear slipped down his cheek. "I love you so goddamned much. I'll never forget this day. Never. He kissed her lips lightly. "Thank you. Thank you for giving yourself to me. I'll cherish the memory the rest of my life."

"And so will I," she answered. She burst into tears and hugged him tightly around the neck. "Oh, Bryce, Bryce, how will I live without you?"

"We'll be all right. Write me, Shannon. Write me every day, darling."

"I will. Oh, Bryce, I love you so! I love you, I love you, I love you!"

He pulled her arms from around his neck and kissed her hard, an almost brutal kiss of possessiveness, then quickly stood up. "Remember you're mine now, Shannon. Only mine. I love you. As soon as I'm aboard, you get to the carriage and go straight home."

She nodded, tears streaming down her face. "I'll pray for you. I'll light a candle at church for you."

He smiled, a sad but utterly handsome grin. "Then I'll surely be safe." He stood there looking at her like a lost little boy, then turned and ran to the train, jumping onto the steps of a passenger coach as the train started moving. Their eyes held as he went by. "I love you," he called out, tears on his own cheeks. "I love you, Shannon."

"I love you," she called back. She watched him as the train moved faster, taking him away. He waved, leaning from the steps of the coach, until he became a small dot and then disappeared. She felt a wrenching pain in her chest that actually made her bend over for a moment. A terrible emptiness engulfed her. Bryce. One moment she had been lying naked in his arms, feeling him, touching him, giving herself to him, abandoning her virginity to him willingly and with great passion.

Now the warmth of his arms was gone. It was almost a shock to be suddenly alone.

She made her legs move to the carriage. She must get home! She must get to Marney. Marney would understand. Marney would hold her and comfort her. Thank God for Marney. The carriage pulled away. It was done. He was gone.

Chapter Six

Bryce awoke in a sweat, and he knew the day would be dreadfully hot. Summer seemed to come early and stay forever in Arizona, if, indeed, it ever left at all; and this June day of 1859 would be hotter than usual. The sounds of the morning maneuvers could be heard outside as his skeleton supply of troops greeted a new day at Fort Buchanan. Problems with the Apaches were mounting again, and the leaders of Arizona Territory were screaming for better protection. But there simply were not enough soldiers to cover the entire area adequately.

"If people would keep a few promises, there wouldn't be a problem in the first place!" Bryce grumbled, more upset by his long, lonely year without Shannon than over Indian problems.

How many restless, frustrated nights had he spent aching to hold her soft flesh against his own? He longed to again cup her full breasts in his hands, to taste their sweet fruit and push himself inside her eager, welcoming body, glorying in a mixture of sorrow over the pain

103

he caused her and joy at the realization that the pain meant she was his and his alone.

Thank God, it wouldn't be long now. Soon her sweet letters would be replaced by her own sweet lips, the light touch of her delicate fingers on his body, her soft, whispered words of love instead of mere ink on paper.

He shook off his thoughts of her. It was time for matters at hand, and he rose to dress and to face another day of the difficult task of keeping the peace.

In his eleven years of dealing with the Indians, he had come to consider many of them his friends. He had a deep appreciation for their way of life and their spiritual closeness with the earth and nature, their simple openness and honesty. The proud and mighty Apache race, as well as other Indians, were being swept away by land-hungry settlers and gold-hungry miners who spit at treaties and boundary lines and sacred grounds. Many of the whites thought the Indians of no more worth than the snakes who crawled in the desert, and they shot them just as easily. And so the skirmishes went on, and Bryce knew it would get worse before it got better. The Indians were merely fighting for what they felt was rightfully theirs; and the whites retaliated in their lust for land and gold and water rights.

Bryce walked out to his office, where a young private had coffee ready for him. "Good morning, sir," the private greeted him with a salute. "It's going to be a hot one."

"Morning, Reynolds. At ease. You're right about the heat." Bryce, now a colonel, stretched.

The young man turned and poured some coffee and handed it to Bryce. "You got a letter, sir. Came in by stage real early this morning."

104

Bryce's heart leaped. He had written Shannon nearly two months earlier, wanting to know when she would be coming out and telling her to wire him immediately when things were set and he would make sure she had escort. According to wired responses to his telegrams, Shannon was fine and had not had any major problems from her father's involvement in the slavery issue. And she was very pleased with Carl Danner, who watched her like a hawk. Bryce knew there would be a letter coming soon. The wired messages were simply to inquire about her well-being. But their personal feelings and expressions of love could only be conveyed through their letters, which took considerable time to deliver. He was a little worried now that something had gone wrong. If she were ready to come out, he would have received a wire instead.

Reynolds grinned as he handed his commander the envelope. "It's from her, sir. Postmarked Virginia."

Bryce grinned in response and took the letter. "Open the rest of the mail, Reynolds, while I read this."

"Yes, sir."

Bryce sat down behind his desk and held the letter under his nose, smelling the light lilac scent and feeling a dull ache at the thought of Shannon. He sipped some coffee and opened the letter.

My dearest Bryce,

The most dreadful thing has happened! I asked Mr. Danner not to tell you by wire, but rather let me write you instead. Bobby has run off to Kansas! Daddy's heart is crushed. You are probably aware of the terrible fighting that is going on in Kansas right now between the pro-slavery groups and the abolitionists. They even call the territory 'bleeding Kansas.' We're both so afraid for Bobby. Bryce, he is only sixteen. But he thinks he's so grown up. He left a note saying he was going to fight with someone named John Brown. We've heard he is an abolitionist, but more like a crazy man—a murderer. Daddy has sent men to search for Bobby, but until he is found, I simply cannot come out to you. How can I leave now, with Bobby missing? If Daddy loses him, it will destroy him! I can't leave him alone when it's possible he'll discover his son has been killed.

Private Reynolds glanced over at Bryce to see the man's face paling and his eyes actually tearing.

"Sir? Has something happened to Miss Fitzgerald?"

Bryce laid the letter down. There were several pages yet to go. He didn't reply right away, but rather closed his eyes and swallowed.

"She—uh—can't come yet," he said in a near whisper. He raised his eyes to meet Reynolds's. "Her brother's run off to Kansas. He's only sixteen, and her father needs her there until they get word of what happened to the boy." He sighed. "Damn! I have a terrible premonition that I'll always regret not bringing her with me last year when I returned. I don't like this."

Reynolds frowned. "I'm sorry, sir. I'm sure it will work out somehow."

"Yeah," Bryce replied. "Listen, Reynolds, I want you to get on the telegraph and I want you to find out all you can about an abolitionist named John Brown. I also want to know just how bad things are getting in Kansas. And I want to send a telegram to Miss Fitzgerald." Bryce stood up now and began pacing, running a hand through his hair. "She has to be pretty upset," he continued, lighting a thin cigar and puffing on it for a moment. "I don't want her to have to wait for my reply. I want her to rest easy and know that I understand."

"Yes, sir."

"Go find out what you can about this John Brown and I'll get a message ready."

Reynolds left and Bryce turned and slammed a fist against his desktop.

"Goddamn *all* of them!" he growled to himself. "Damn! Damn! Damn! Damn the slaves and the slaveowners and the abolitionists! Goddamn John Brown—and the whole damned world!"

He had looked forward to Shannon's arrival with near painful excitement, envisioning her soft green eyes, her auburn hair tumbling down long and thick over her bare shoulders and hiding the nipples of her young breasts. How sweet it was going to be! How he loved her! And he was so lonely. He wanted a wife, a home, children. Now it would all have to wait even longer. The memory of their one afternoon together would be even more painful now.

He picked up his coffee cup and threw it against a wall, splattering coffee on the wall and floor. He breathed deeply to gain control of himself and went back to pick up the letter and read the rest of it. It did not help his loneliness. She wrote only of how much she loved him, how much she regretted not being able to come, how lonely she herself was, how her heart ached for him and how she longed to be in his arms again.

She also voiced her fear over the increasing

107

bitterness between free and slave states, and the fact that many of her father's friends had all but deserted him for his beliefs. The entire situation made Bryce uneasy. Was it possible men were pulling their money out of Fitzgerald's bank? The man could be in financial trouble and not tell Shannon about it, not wanting to worry her. Bryce decided that if Bobby wasn't found within six months or less, he would wire her and insist she come West at once, no matter what. Things were getting too dangerous.

He contemplated telling her if she didn't come out right away he would not marry her at all, but he knew he could not pose such a decision to her. And he couldn't live without her now. It would be impossible. Not only did he love her desperately, but he had claimed her as his own personal property. Guilty as he felt about what he had done, he could not truly regret it. He was glad he had taken advantage of her youthful passion. He would always treasure the memory of their afternoon of ecstasy and sweet parting. He had that much to keep him going, the comfort of knowing she was unquestioningly Bryce Edwards's woman, the memory of that glorious afternoon of heated passion, the most beautiful sexual encounter he had ever experienced. The thought of her slender thighs and her whimpers from the pain of first intercourse made him feel hot with a mixture of guilt and savage desire. He sat thinking for several minutes, alone and lonely. Then he turned and took out a sheet of paper.

"Shannon, I understand," he wrote. "Don't worry and don't be frightened. I'll use whatever influence I have to help find Bobby. Will wire all the top brass I know. Anxiously waiting for the day you can come to me. Will write longer letter right away. Love, Bryce."

It was short, but necessarily so. He would write her a letter later that evening and tell her his more personal thoughts. Private Reynolds entered and handed Bryce a note.

"I got a quick answer from St. Joseph, Missouri, sir. I asked them to relay the messages on to Washington, but this is what I got from them for now."

Bryce quickly grabbed the telegram, which read: "John Brown violent abolitionist. Kansas in civil war. Brown and followers suspected of several murders."

Bryce sighed and looked up at Reynolds, who was eyeing the coffee cup and the splattered liquid on the floor.

"I'm a little upset this morning, Reynolds," Bryce mumbled. "Clean that up, will you?"

"Yes, sir."

"And—uh—take this message over and get it sent right away to Charleston for Shannon. In fact, do that first." He handed the young man his note.

"I really am sorry, sir—about Miss Fitzgerald. I know how anxious you've been for her to come here. Sounds to me like there's gonna be a civil war, Colonel Edwards."

Bryce folded Shannon's letter. "I'm terribly afraid you're right, Reynolds," he replied.

"Yo! Indians! A lot of them ridin' up to the fort!" a guard shouted from his post outside. Men began running to their posts, and Bryce grabbed his holster and hat and hurried out, scowling with impatience.— He was not in any mood for an argument with the Indians. A soldier came running up to Bryce and saluted.

"What's going on, Captain Marx?" Bryce asked

the man.

"Not sure, sir. They look peaceful, but most of them are painted up. There's about fifty of them, sir— waving a truce flag. They want to talk to the man in charge. Cochise is one of them."

Bryce scowled. "Well, I'm the one in charge. So I guess I'd better go out."

"You want some men behind you, sir?"

"No," Bryce replied curtly. He removed his hat and wiped sweat from his head, then put his hat back on. "Open the gates!" he barked.

Two men pulled open the large wooden stockade doors and Bryce walked out to face a rather threatening band of Indians, led by none other than the tall and handsome Cochise, chief of the Chiricahuas. Beside him, perched on a sturdy stallion, was a young buck of equal stature, his eyes blazing with an unnerving hatred. He was the Mescalero leader called Saguaro. Bryce nodded to Cochise and Saguaro, and pushed his hat back.

"What's the problem, Cochise?" he asked.

"Maybe you have problem, my friend."

Bryce folded his arms in front of him. "Well, at least you're still calling me friend. What's wrong?"

"Your people, my friend, think of Apache as equal only to lizard!"

Bryce glanced at the handsome Saguaro. Both Cochise and Saguaro were clean and neat, their hair hanging straight and shiny, their muscular bronze arms glowing in the morning sun, copper bands around their wrists and biceps. Saguaro was painted as though for war, and his eyes told Bryce he would like nothing better than to drive a lance through the soldier. "Get to the point, Cochise. You know I'm a fair man. What's happened now?"

"Saguaro. He married to woman of my tribe—the Chiracahuas."

"And?"

"She is dead. Saguaro's two small sons also dead. All killed by white men. They beat and shot them with no cause!"

"Where? When?" Bryce asked anxiously.

"East of Apache Pass, near Pelongillo Mountains. Saguaro go there to visit his Mescalero family. When they return to our village, they were attacked by six white men. Saguaro had only his knife and lance. White men shot him in leg. Tie him and make him watch while they rape his wife. All take turns with her, then torture her and kill little boys before Saguaro's eyes!"

"Jesus!" Bryce whispered, his anger building at hearing of the atrocity. "When did this happen? Which way did they go?"

"They ride East. Saguaro hear one say El Paso. But it has been long time. Saguaro was injured and full of grief and hatred. He not think clearly to come—tell the People right away. He think only of wife and babies, who lie dead! He gather them and take them into mountains. There he bury them and mourn for them and cry out to our Father to accept their spirits. After many days he come down from mountains and tell us this terrible thing. I tell Saguaro you can help find white men who do this, but it is long time. To find them not be easy. Saguaro is full of rage and hatred that will not soon die, my friend. If these men are found, there should be justice for Saguaro."

111

"I'll do what I can, but Saguaro must understand that those men are probably hundreds of miles from here by now."

"Soldiers only here to protect the whites!" Saguaro spoke up bitterly. He spit at the ground. "They not care what happen to Indian! Nothing will be done! White man make promises, then break them! He lie and cheat! Kill and rape! Only Indian is punished for doing bad, not white man!"

"Saguaro, it isn't always that way."

"I believe no white man! They are like sands of desert. They steal our land until we are squashed against one another! What I have seen burns in Saguaro's belly and screams in Saguaro's mind! Soldiers will hear more from Saguaro!" The Indian threw his lance and it landed between Bryce's feet. Bryce did not move.

"Don't do this, Saguaro. Give me some time."

"Saguaro does what he chooses to do!" the man sneered. "Just like the white man does! Saguaro great warrior! He has suffered tortures of bravest Apache men. Yet he was made to lie helpless while his woman was killed. A day does not go by that Saguaro does not hear her screams, and the crying of his sons. Saguaro feels shame that he could not help them! Saguaro never forget! Never!"

Bryce sighed and grasped the lance, pulling it out of the ground. He handed it to Saguaro, the pointed end toward himself. Saguaro grasped it.

"I could push on this now and kill you!" he said with a smirk. Bryce studied the fiery, dark eyes and the magnificent build on the young warrior.

"I wouldn't do that, Saguaro," Bryce said calmly.

112

"But if I were in your position, I'd feel the same way. I'm a man. And there is a woman I love. If something happened to her, I'd be out for blood, just as you are. I'm asking you to give me a little time. I'll try to help—try to find those men. I'm here to help everyone, Saguaro—not just the whites."

"This man is good, Saguaro," Cochise told the man. "He speak truth. I know him. If he say he will search out the white men, he will do so."

"You become too soft, Cochise!" Saguaro snarled. "You allow white man's stage to travel through Apache Pass. You even cut wood for station! But stage only bring more whites! You will see. Some day they not listen to your demands to stay off our land! They will swarm over you like honey bees, and they will sting you!" He looked back at Bryce and let go of the lance. "I give you from full moon to full moon to find these men," he warned in a cold voice. "If nothing is done, you will hear my name groaned from the lips of dying whites! Saguaro! Remember the name!"

The tall, vicious-looking Indian whirled his horse and galloped off with some of his own men behind him. Cochise and the rest of the band remained.

"I'll do what I can, Cochise," Bryce told the man. "But after this long, I don't even know where to start."

"Go to the place called El Paso. Their leader was big man. He wear cloth over one eye."

"Well, it's not a lot to go on, Cochise. But I'll try my best." He stuck the lance into the ground angrily. "I'm sorry, Cochise. What did Saguaro do about his leg injury?"

"He cut it open—remove bullet himself. It is healing." Bryce raised his eyebrows in surprise.

113

"Saguaro full of sorrow. Not feel pain," Cochise explained. "He is brave man. He can bear pain when it is necessary. He is very proud. What he see burns in his memory. Proud men need revenge like baby needs its mother's milk."

"He'll only get himself killed, Cochise."

The striking Indian leader smiled. "Death is not new to the Apache. Better to die proud than to live in shame! A man must do what he must do!" The Indian turned his horse and shouted a command to his followers. They all let out piercing war whoops, wanting to impress Bryce Edwards and the others inside the fort.

"Reynolds!" Bryce shouted angrily, wanting to hit out at everything and everyone.

"Yes, sir!" The private came running.

"Get me about eight men and pack up my horse. I'm leaving Captain Marx in charge and riding to El Paso. It's the least I can do."

"Yes, sir!" Reynolds ran off to do the man's bidding.

Bryce went inside his office and plunked down at his desk, taking out some paper to write a hasty letter to Shannon, worried that he would get a telegram while he was away and be unaware of further trouble the girl might get into. The black fear of possibly having made a grave mistake in leaving her behind a year earlier engulfed him. He put his head down on the desk.

"God in heaven, protect her!" he whispered.

"My darling Shannon," Bryce wrote from a brothel in El Paso. "Not only is there unrest in Virginia and Kansas, but also out here. I have just arrested several men who committed a vile and unspeakable crime against an Apache woman and her children. They were all killed at these men's hands, yet out here, you only make enemies when you try to do anything that means justice to the Indians. I got into quite a scrap over the arrest, not only with the men who committed the crimes, but with the townspeople themselves! The men are in jail here in El Paso. I must wait here now for the traveling judge."

He paused, reflecting on the incident. It had been easier to find the men than he had thought it would be. They had indeed gone to El Paso, and had remained there, actually admitting to their actions and bragging about it to the local citizens. No one cared much, since it was an Indian woman who had suffered the rape. He decided not to tell Shannon about how he had nearly been shot when he confronted the rapists. The bearded, one-eyed outlaw leader had pulled a gun on Bryce, but Bryce had managed to kick the weapon out of the man's hand before the shot went off. It was then that the leader had charged into Bryce, quickly joined by his companions. The soldiers who had accompanied Bryce inside to make the arrest then joined in on the battle of fists, and the other patrons in the tavern jumped on the soldiers. The arrest was made only after an all-out brawl, with tables and drinks flying and women screaming.

The brawl ended when the local sheriff entered the tavern with two of his deputies and fired his guns into the air. A group of very bloody men finally came to order; and Bryce, his uniform torn and his mouth bleeding, made the Federal arrest. He had not been overly surprised when the others in the tavern had defended the outlaws. Killing a squaw and her children merely meant more Apaches had been eliminated, which was good for the settlers.

"The worst part is that I doubt there will be a conviction," he wrote on. "This is all a waste of time. My arrest will end up being just a token act, to show the Indians that we do our best to see that justice is done. But the Apaches will not be allowed to testify in court, and who else is there to accuse these men? White men can speak out in court against the Indians, but Indians have no say. These criminals will simply say they were attacked and fought back in self-defense. They will not mention the rape. They will not mention the fact that there was only one Indian involved, against six men. The Indian involved was the woman's husband, none other than the Mescalero Apache I told you about once—Saguaro. The little boys were his sons. Saguaro is quite a handsome Apache, but full of hatred and vengeance. I try and try to keep the peace, but it's next to impossible when the whites commit these crimes against the Indians without cause. Already I have heard of a ranch Saguaro raided, killing the whole family. I suppose I will have to return to Fort Buchanan and search him out to arrest him. Yet I honestly cannot blame the man for the way he feels."

He put the pen down and glanced over at the prostitute who lay in the bed nearby, her eyes closed and a smile on her face. Her name was Mona Jackson, and in her understanding of his loneliness and his heartache over his betrothed's being unable to come out to him, the woman had become more than just a body to him. She was a good friend. She understood what he was going through. If not for Mona, he sometimes wondered if he would keep his sanity. He knew the woman had feelings for him, feelings he could never return. But he was grateful for her willingness to see him whenever he was in town, though she knew he was only using her.

"I love you, Shannon," he continued. "I ache for you. Bobby had better turn up soon, or I'll go AWOL and come to get you myself, before I go mad with desire for you."

"Bryce, honey, come back to bed," Mona said in a sultry voice.

"In a minute, baby."

"Do you know you called me Shannon when you were making love to me?"

"Did I? I'm sorry." He kept writing another few minutes, then put down the pen and walked over to the bed. Mona studied his magnificent build as he stood there naked, then she opened the covers and he climbed in beside her. He stretched out on his back and she slithered on top of him, kissing him hungrily. Bryce closed his eyes and imagined that it was Shannon's lips he tasted. Between his natural needs and his longing for Shannon, he had decided he would take every opportunity while in El Paso to get his desires out of his system.

"There's a woman I need," he whispered.

"I understand," she replied. He rolled her over and she welcomed him inside. If letting him pretend she was someone else was the only way she could enjoy this magnificent man with the golden hair and gray eyes, then she didn't mind.

Chapter Seven

(November, 1859)

"Bryce," the letter read. "By now you have heard about Harper's Ferry in eastern Virginia. John Brown seized the U.S. arsenal there in October, vowing to give weapons to the Negroes and free all of them. He was arrested by Colonel Lee, tried for murder, and hung. Some Northerners consider him a martyr, and most Southerners are frightened to death now of a Negro uprising. But that is not the worst. Oh, Bryce, how can I tell you? Bobby is dead! He was at Harper's Ferry!"

"My God!" Bryce whispered as he read. "Damn! Damn!" He sat up straighter in his bed and leaned toward the lantern to see better.

"I would have told you by wire, but how could I tell you such a thing in such a cold and sudden way? Bryce, I'm so afraid! And Daddy is desolate! He has taken ill. He had a stroke, and he is almost completely helpless. Bryce, I'm so alone. But I'm doing my best to be grown-up about all this. I'm handling things I never thought I would have to handle. I wish I was stronger. I cry constantly. First Mama—then Bobby. And now the doctor thinks Daddy won't live much longer. I wish so much that you could be here to hold me! I would be fine if I were in your arms. But how can I come to you now, with Daddy on his deathbed? I'm handling things as best I can, and Daddy's lawyer says not to worry about anything. He's taking care of all financial matters. I'm going to sell the house and take a loss, I might add, what with all this civil unrest. But with Daddy so ill, I must be ready to come out to you immediately when he dies. Dear God, I can't bear to think of it! My whole family, Bryce! But I have to think about it, because it's real, horrible as it is.

"I know you will be thinking you should not have left me behind, Bryce, but you are not to blame yourself. How could we have known such terrible things would happen? And I still have Mr. Danner, who is ever so kind and watchful, so you needn't worry. When I leave, I'll wire you, and you can arrange the escort you told me about. All will be well in the end when I can at last be in your arms, Bryce."

Bryce's jaw flexed in anger at himself for Shannon's lonely predicament. He decided he would write back right away—no, a wire. He would urge her to leave just as soon as possible when and if her father died. She was to waste no time. The midst of a cruel civil war was not a good place for an innocent young woman alone.

"I know now we made the right decision," he read on. "What if this had happened—Bobby's death and Daddy's stroke—and I had not been here to help poor Daddy? I help nurse him day and night, and I can tell by his eyes how much he needs me with him. I am his very last living relative. I'm so glad I can be with him,

120

Bryce. But it breaks my heart to have to again put off my coming West. I can hardly believe it's been almost a year and a half since you left. I'll make it all up to you when I get there. I'll be a good wife, Bryce, and a good mother. You will be all I have, and I will be all you have, as neither of us has any family now. We must cling to each other, at all costs, and never let anything come between us. I never want to lose another loved one. It hurts so very much!"

He could see the blotches where she had apparently cried while writing and her tears had dripped onto the stationery. "My poor, sweet Shannon," he groaned. How lonely and afraid she had to be. Yet there was a tone of maturity in her letter. He longed to see how she had grown and changed.

"Please don't worry. Mr. Danner is a constant companion, and I am in no danger. My financial matters are taken care of. But how I long for your comforting arms, Bryce. How I long to come to you and let you be the strong one. I love you so."

Bryce put down the letter and sat quietly in his quarters. A coyote howled outside, and he wondered if it was really an animal or an Indian. At the end of July, Saguaro had returned to the fort with several warriors, demanding to see Bryce. Bryce had been forced to tell him the awful news that the men who had raped and killed Saguaro's wife and sons had gone free. Since learning that news, Saguaro was making quite a name for himself—raiding and looting and killing—always fleeing across the Mexican border into the Sierra Madre mountains, there to rest and rearm for another attack, either on a small town, or a ranch, sometimes a fort, settlers and miners. Always there were deaths and looting. Children and women were sometimes kidnapped and held for ransom—for guns, food, or horses.

The attacks were scattered, but Bryce could already see the future. The men who had raped and killed Saguaro's family had been released by a circuit judge. The reason?

"We cannot punish whites for mistreating the Indians," the judge had stated. "If we do that, all whites will be afraid to defend themselves when necessary, for fear of being arrested."

Bryce felt ill at the memory of the verdict. In essence, the whites were being given free license to do whatever they wished to the Indians whether the Indian deserved it or not. But the Indians would continue to be arrested and beaten and hung for any acts against the whites. And against these odds, soldiers were expected to keep the peace. It was ludicrous to think about. To top off Bryce's rage, the outlaws' only punishment was to be banishment from Arizona—they had been told to move on to other parts, so as not to "instigate Indian uprisings" by their continued presence in the area. The judge decided that if the outlaws were nowhere around, the entire incident would be forgotten and the one called Saguaro would cool down.

But Bryce knew Saguaro. There was no way the man would forget this outrage. He stood up and lit a cigar and paced. Now his problems with the Indians were compounded by this new development with Shannon and her family. How could he concentrate on his job knowing the poor girl was back in Virginia watching her father die?

"And poor little Bobby," he thought. "He considered

122

himself such a man . . . wanted so much to be grown up. And now my little Shannon has to be a woman in the truest sense."

His heart ached for her. He wanted desperately to go to her, comfort her, help her. Now it was not just his need to have her in his arms and be one with her again, but his manly instinct to protect and defend the woman he loved. But there were so very many miles between them, and now each of them had a duty to attend to.

"I just don' feel right leavin' you, child," Marney fussed again as she packed her carpet bag, new tears coming. "You is like my own."

Shannon sat sniffling on the bed, her heart torn. "I know, Marney, but I have Mr. Danner. Father hasn't much longer . . . to live," she sobbed, "and I'll be going out to Bryce just as soon as . . . as—" She could not finish, but burst into a new fit of tears. Marney sat down beside her, putting her arm around the girl.

"This is all that no-good Barrett Carter's fault!" she said angrily. "He done called hisself your pa's best friend, and then he done went and cheated him out of everything. And cheated you, too, leavin' you with practically nothin'."

She patted Shannon's shoulder as the girl wept. Barrett Carter, her father's attorney and trusted friend, had cleverly maneuvered her father's financial empire into ruin while Jonathan Fitzgerald lay sick and helpless. He had called Shannon into his office only two days earlier to inform her there was no Fitzgerald money left, only enough to bury her father and a small amount of spending money for Shannon—"to get you to your soldier in Arizona," he had told her with a sneer.

The house would be auctioned off, to be occupied as soon as Fitzgerald was dead and Shannon was on her way to Arizona. The news had been a shock to the already distraught Shannon, who still mourned the loss of her brother, and whose time was spent mostly nursing her ailing father. Never had she dreamed Barrett Carter would scheme to leave them penniless; but these were bad times, when friend turned against friend, brother against brother. Barrett Carter was pro-slavery. Shannon was helpless to fight what she knew was blatant robbery and embezzlement. But she could not prove it and did not have the money to hire anyone who could. Besides that, there were enemies all around her. She could trust no one. Only Bryce could be trusted. Only Bryce would love and help her now. He was her only goal, her only refuge. Bryce! She could still see him standing on the steps of the passenger car. How wonderful it would be to feel his arms around her again! How safe and loved she would be once more! He was all that was left.

"I'll be all right, Marney," she whispered. "All I need is Bryce. And I'll be safe with Mr. Danner until I can get out there."

"I surely hope so. You promise me, child, that you will git youself out there to your man jist as fast as you little feet will take you, you hear? That there soldier man is a good man, and he done took you and made you his, and I expect he's gonna be the happiest man in the world to see you. You git out there to him and you won' never have to be afraid or alone agin. I thanks God you done found that man."

"Oh, so do I, Marney." Shannon pulled away and wiped at her eyes. "I wish you could stay till I leave, but we don't know how long that will be, and the hatred is getting so bad here in Charleston. I love you and Parker both so much. I couldn't stand losing anyone else that I love. I want you to get yourselves out of here. Go up North, Marney, where it will be safe for you. Terrible things are going to happen here. I just know it. Even Mr. Carter warned me that you two had better leave, as though he knew someone had plans for you. It might be that awful Loren McGuire. He always hated Daddy for paying you for your help and making you free. God only knows." She blew her nose. "I only know you should get away quickly. Mr. Danner also feels you should leave. And I can't pay you any more now, anyway."

Marney grunted and shook her head, rising to pack again. "Do you think I care that you can't pay me and Parker? That don' matter to me. But I love my Parker, and I feels like you. With you father so sick, that there McGuire might come along and make good on his threat to say bad things about you and my Parker and get my Parker hanged. He'd like nothin' better than to smear your reputation and get back at Parker fo' that day he done held a gun on him. I ain't leavin' jist because I's afraid fo' myself. It's because I's afraid fo' Parker . . . and fo' you, child. And even at that, I'll only go because you have that there Mr. Danner to look after you, and he's a good man; and because I know he'll see you git to your soldier man fast as lightnin' soon as your pa is—" She swallowed back new tears. The tragedies in the once lively, happy Fitzgerald household were overwhelming. First Mrs. Fitzgerald,

125

then little Bobby, and now Jonathan Fitzgerald was near death. The family had gone from wealth to poverty. All the servants were gone now, and soon she and Parker would have to leave. "It ain't fair," she mumbled. "It jist ain't fair."

The packing was finished all too soon, for Marney and Parker Washington had little in the way of personal possessions. A carriage was called, and there was a last farewell to Jonathan Fitzgerald, although the man just lay and stared, unaware of his own financial misfortune and the departure of his trusted servants.

The carriage arrived, and Shannon found herself standing at the doorway saying good-bye to the woman who had become like a mother to her, and the man who had saved her from Loren McGuire's cruel attack three years earlier. It all seemed so unreal. Everything in her life seemed unreal now, like a nightmare. How she wished she could wake up and find everything the way it once was! But it was all true, so horribly true. She was penniless, her family was gone, and Marney and Parker must get themselves North for their own safety.

"Do you have your papers saying you're free?" she asked Parker,

"Yes, ma'am," he replied, tears in his eyes. He shook his head. "I's awful sorry, Miss Shannon. Awful sorry for all of it."

"So am I, Parker." She hugged the man tightly, then turned to Marney. The two women wept in each other's arms for several long seconds before Shannon finally pulled herself away. She turned to Carl Danner, who had become not only a faithful "watchdog" but a trusted friend. The man put an arm around her shoulders and Shannon faced Marney and Parker once more. "God be with you both," Shannon told them. Their eyes held and Marney just put a hanky over her mouth.

"And . . . with you, child," she wept. She turned and quickly hurried down the steps. Parker nodded to Shannon, a tear slipping down his cheek, then followed his wife. The door closed. It seemed to Shannon that many doors were closing on her. How many doors would be shut?

She left Danner and sank into a chair, weeping. Danner walked over and patted her on the head. "I wish you'd let me send a wire to Bryce," he told her.

She shook her head. "Not yet, Mr. Danner. Please. I want him to think everything is fine. Poor Bryce has enough to worry about. If he has something like this on his mind, he might get caught off guard in some Indian skirmish and get himself killed." She blew her nose. "Besides, there is nothing he can do about it. As long as I have you, I'm safe. When father passes away and I'm ready to go out to Bryce, that's soon enough to wire him."

"Well, I think you're wrong. But I'll bend to your wishes. I can see your point to a certain extent, and I must say you've become very strong and mature since I first came here to keep an eye on you. Bryce Edwards will be proud of you."

She wiped at her eyes. "I'm not that strong, Mr. Danner. I'm just doing what must be done. I'm not sure how much more I can bear."

The man knelt down and took her hands. "I'm sorry about all this. But it will be over soon. I'll see you safely out to Bryce and return to Washington and find out

127

what my next duty is." He patted her hands. "I must say I've enjoyed taking care of you, Shannon. You are like a daughter to me. I want you and Bryce to keep in touch once in a while. I'll want to know how you're doing."

She sniffed and managed a smile. "Thank you, Mr. Danner. I'm so glad Bryce thought to hire you. I . . . I haven't any money left, but Bryce will see that you get paid."

"I'm not worried about it. I'll just be glad when all of this is over for you."

She closed her eyes. "So will I, Mr. Danner. I never dreamed a person's life could take such a sudden change. My whole world is falling apart. Bryce is all I have left."

Within two months after Marney and Parker's departure, Jonathan Fitzgerald was dead. Shannon had made sure her father never knew of his financial ruin, refusing to bring him any worry or unhappiness in his last days. But it was quite possible he never would have understood anyway.

All too quickly she found herself standing at his graveside, weeping not just over his death, but over the whole trauma of losing her mother, brother, father, everything. Everything was gone. Everything. All her loved ones, her precious Marney and Parker, and even her money. All security was gone, for most of her family's friends had deserted. Only Carl Danner remained, reliable Carl Danner. Bryce became more and more her only hope now for happiness. But even he could not be here now. The year they were to have been apart had turned into two years. Now there was nothing more important than to get to Arizona—to Bryce's arms—to the strength and love only Bryce Edwards could bring her.

The Fitzgerald mansion sat empty now, waiting for its new owner. Everything had been sold. Practically the only pieces of furniture left were the beds Shannon and her father had slept in, and a small cot Carl Danner slept on downstairs. The new owner was anxious to move in. When the funeral was over, Shannon would go home, pack necessary belongings, and go to Bryce. Carl Danner was this very moment taking two of Shannon's trunks to the train station, where he would send a wire to Bryce, then come back and pick Shannon up after the funeral. It hurt just to leave everything she had ever known, all her former security, her own father's fresh grave beside those of her mother and brother. But there was nothing left now for her but her beloved Bryce.

She stared at her father's casket without really seeing it. She wondered how things could have turned out so miserably. How quickly time could change things! Eight years ago, when her mother was alive, everything had been so bright and wonderful. She had been a child, without a care in the world. And at fourteen, in spite of her mother's death, she had at least had her father and brother—a fourteen-year-old belle of Virginia, in love with the twenty-three-year-old hero, Bryce Edwards. And even at sixteen, only three years ago, she had been happy and secure, with a home and wealth, a father and brother, her precious Marney— and Bryce. And then there had been that glorious moment when she gave her virginity to her beloved

129

Bryce. It seemed like only a dream now, a warm, beautiful, precious dream that came alive in the deep of the night. Clinging to that burning memory kept her alive and gave her hope, constantly reminding her there was something beautiful in life after all; that there was someone gentle but strong who loved her and would protect and keep her forever more. She had belonged to Bryce Edwards since that moment, body and soul, and in her mind and heart they were already married. She knew it was the same for Bryce. It was only a matter of a few weeks now, and she would finally be in his strong, supportive arms, never to be afraid and alone again.

"Ashes to ashes," the priest was saying. Shannon sniffed and fought a complete breakdown. She had to be strong. Strong—until she could fall into Bryce's arms. She dared not break down until then. It was all too much to handle alone. She still had not even wired Bryce that her father was dead, and he still was not aware of her poor financial condition.

"I'll tell him everything when I get there," she determined. The telegram she had given Danner to send simply said that her father had died and that she was leaving, and when and where the troops should meet her. She felt very mature now, having handled everything alone without worrying poor Bryce. He would be very proud when he discovered how well she had done, considering all the odds she had been up against—a dying father and no money. She had decided she could not always be pouting on Bryce's shoulder like a baby once they were married. So, she must start now. She was nineteen—a woman. And she

130

would go out to Bryce as a woman—and become his woman.

Only a handful of friends and neighbors stood at the graveside. Shannon's father's beliefs about freedom for the slaves had won him many enemies.

The ceremony was soon over, and Shannon was shocked to realize she had been aware of hardly two words that had been said. People came up to give her their condolences and wish her well on her trip to Arizona, telling her they were happy she would at least be able to go to Bryce now and get out of the South before war broke out in full force. She found herself hugging some of them, telling them she would pray for their safety in whatever was to come. She felt removed from herself, and knew that when the day came that she faced up to the horror of the past two years, she would collapse into a fit of crying that would last for days. But there was no time for that now. No time.

"Mama!" she screamed inside herself. "Bobby! Daddy! God help me! Help me get to Bryce and to keep my sanity!"

She stood at the graveside long after everyone had left, looking at the three graves of her only family. She knew it was quite possible she would never even see the graves again. When she died, it would probably be somewhere out West. Her life would become very different now. Her whole world would change. But it didn't matter. She would have Bryce.

She forced herself to leave the graves and climb into her rented carriage, sitting back and closing her eyes as it splashed through the streets, carrying her back to the big empty house.

"Danner should be there by now," she thought. He was to accompany her to the station and stay with her until she reached St. Louis, Missouri, where the troops Bryce would request would be waiting for her.

She fought her terrible depression as she climbed out of the carriage and told the man to go on. Danner would be inside waiting for her, but they could flag down another carriage a little while later. She wanted to take some time to say good-bye to the only home she had ever known. Danner would understand. He would wait. Thank God for Danner! How could she have made it through all of this without his generous help?

She went inside, closing the door and gazing around at the empty house, remembering better times and the lovely annual party her mother had so loved. It would have been held this very month if— She covered her face and wept. Then the uglier memories came. She thought about the horrible two-day auction— watching people put greedy hands on precious family treasures and practically steal them with their low bids. But at least it had given her a little more money to take West with her. She remembered the terrible parting with Marney and Parker. She remembered her father's collapse at the sight of his dead son. She remembered— "No! Not now!" she told herself. "Wait until you get to Bryce! Stay strong, Shannon! Hang on!"

She removed her cape. "Mr. Danner," she called out. The house was deathly quiet. She wondered why Danner was not back yet. She didn't like being in the big house alone. Everyone was gone now, all the servants, everyone. She felt desolate and suddenly frightened. She felt a presence—an evil presence. Her

132

body chilled. "Mr. Danner," she called out again. It was then she heard the footsteps. She gasped and whirled, and there by the stairway stood Loren McGuire! Her heart and feet froze! She looked at him, wide-eyed and speechless.

"Hello, my sweet virgin child," he sneered.

Chapter Eight

Shannon swallowed, repulsed by Loren McGuire's cold stare and wicked grin. "Mr. Danner!" she screamed at the top of her lungs. McGuire laughed, a deep, ugly laugh from the depths of his hellish soul.

"Don't bother, my lovely Shannon. Your Mr. Danner is dead. I . . . arranged . . . to have him robbed and killed at the train station."

Shannon's breath came in short gasps as her mind reeled with a rapid succession of defensive thoughts. Her confrontation with this man three years earlier still haunted her with its horror, and now there was no Parker and apparently no Carl Danner to come to her defense. She was alone, and there was no doubt what Loren McGuire had in mind. He would finish what he had started in the greenhouse three years earlier.

McGuire grinned. "Yes, my dear. I can read your thoughts. There is no one to come to your rescue this time. No nigger Parker, no snoopy watchdog Danner, and no brave, heroic Bryce Edwards. There is just you and me, my lovely."

135

Shannon found her faculties and charged for the front door, but McGuire caught her dress and violently ripped part of it off. She screamed in horror as he caught her, and in the next instant a large hand slammed across her face and she felt herself passing out. Someone grasped her, and now she was struggling violently. Everything seemed to happen in a daze as she scratched and kicked. Something hit her hard on her ear and she felt as though she were falling into a black pit. Bryce! She belonged to Bryce Edwards! No other man must ever touch her! She fought to keep her senses. She was defenseless. To fight this huge, ruthless man could only bring more blows and perhaps total unconsciousness or death, and an inability to stop him from taking what belonged to Bryce. She could not let this evil monster spoil the beautiful moment she had shared with Bryce, yet how could she stop him?

Her ears rang painfully and there was another blow, this time to her rib. She thought she heard screaming, but was not certain the sound came from her own lips. She felt herself being carried up a stairway as she swallowed blood from a cut inside her mouth.

"Please, Mr. McGuire, don't . . . do this!" she found herself begging, wondering how she had found her voice.

His reply was only an ugly laugh and a tighter grip as he kicked open a door. She sensed they were in her own bedroom, where her bed remained, having been sold with the rest of the house. She grunted when the man dropped her onto the bare mattress.

She felt her clothes being removed as she lay on the bed. Now there was hot breath against her face, her shoulders, a warm wetness on her breasts, ugly, animal

136

sounds. She weighed a mere hundred pounds, packed into a five-foot-two-inch frame. Loren McGuire stood well over six feet tall and weighed at least two hundred pounds, if not more. How could she prevent the inevitable?

She broke into resigned weeping, feeling vomit in her throat. Bryce! She belonged to Bryce! But now this ugly, brutal man was leaning over her, touching her, putting his fat lips on places that Bryce had already claimed in their beautiful act of love. Now Loren McGuire was desecrating that special moment, stealing another man's property, preparing to ruin the wonderful memory and rob her of her most sacred possession, that which she had given to one man alone in a moment of blessed love; that which she had vowed to give to no other man.

She watched in stunned shock and through blurred vision as McGuire stood up for a moment to remove his own clothes. She wanted to try to run then, but her body would not react and she knew she could not possibly move fast enough to get away from this cruel, demented rapist. She suddenly realized that throughout her beating and her clothes being viciously torn from her, she had somehow clung to the strings of her handbag. She could almost have laughed at the humor of it, clinging to her handbag as though to keep it from being stolen, when this hideous animal was preparing to steal something much more precious.

"*God, help me!*" she prayed inwardly. "*Help me!*"

Now McGuire was moving over her again, uttering ugly suggestions, laughing his grotesque laugh. She felt ill at his odor and could feel his sweat.

It was then she thought again about the handbag.

The handbag! Carl Danner had purchased a small handgun for her, insisting she carry it for her own protection. She had argued and protested. She didn't like guns and had never used it, but she carried it to appease Danner. Now it was right beside her—in the handbag! God had brought her a miracle after all! But could she truly use the weapon on another human being?

There was no time to wonder and question. This hideous man was grasping her legs, painfully gripping them as he forced them apart and moved between them so there was no way for her to avoid the sickening inevitable. There was no one to hear her screams of terror. McGuire's cruel words and foul breath made her groan with nausea, and she turned her head sideways, grasping at the handbag with one hand as McGuire slobbered at her neck.

She groped for the gun, not even sure how to use it. She prayed it was properly loaded and ready to shoot, and her heart leaped when she found the handle. Thank goodness McGuire was taking his time, planning to enjoy himself thoroughly. He had not yet taken her, and he was so lost in his act of violence and lust that he did not even notice what she was doing with her free hand.

There was no time to falter or question. She grasped the gun and found the trigger. All was a daze now, her movements seemingly disconnected from her own body. The gun was in his ribs, and she pulled the trigger.

She heard a strange grunt and a moment later she felt McGuire's enormous weight crushing her. "You . . . bitch!" he groaned.

Shannon squeezed her eyes shut and pushed at the man's body, then felt a huge hand squeezing around her throat. "Bitch!" he repeated. "You . . . shot me!"

He squeezed harder and she had no choice as he began cutting off her air in a last effort to kill her for shooting him. She struggled to get the gun closer to his chest and she fired again. Seconds later his grip at her throat lightened.

Shannon groaned in revulsion as she struggled with her last ounce of strength to get out from under the man. His dead, sweaty body scraped over hers as she finally managed to slide away and roll off the bed to the floor. She went to her knees, shaking violently and still gripping the gun. She bent over and vomited, then sat there rocking and moaning for several minutes before managing to grip the side of the bed and push herself to her feet.

At first she just stared wide-eyed at McGuire's huge naked body sprawled on the bed. There was no sign of life, and a gaping hole was open in his back, another in his ribs, where bullets had exited his body from the two gunshots. She looked down at the gun, then saw blood on her own naked chest and belly. She gasped and dropped the gun, overwhelmed now with the realization of what she had done. She put her hands to the sides of her head, and screams of horror rose from her throat, over and over until she had hardly any voice left.

Finally she tore her eyes from McGuire's grotesque body and stumbled to the bathroom, wanting only to bathe and wash away the man's filthy touch. She thanked God that at least she had not been raped, yet the fact remained that she had committed an atrocious crime.

What would Bryce think? Surely he would understand, for she had had to defend herself and her honor. Bryce was the most understanding man she had ever known. Surely he would understand this. And he already knew Loren McGuire had tried to harm her once before.

She began hurriedly bathing herself, suddenly realizing speed was now all important. She blocked out her terror and guilt and allowed her mind to overrule her emotions. Bryce! She must think only of Bryce! At least she still belonged only to her sweet Bryce. She had been brave and resourceful and had saved herself for the only man who had a right to touch her. She must go to Bryce right away! She must hurry! Time was of the essence now. She had killed a man. She had not one friend or family member to help her out of this. Her father's enemies would accuse her of seducing Loren McGuire. She could not depend on anyone to help her—not now in this time of fear and hatred. She would have to leave. It was the only answer. And quickly! If Loren McGuire was found before she could get out of town, she would be imprisoned, perhaps hung!

How she made herself move she was not sure. She finished bathing and walked back to the bedroom to dress, forcing herself not to look at McGuire's ugly, dead body. She decided she would be able to cover most of her bruises with her clothing. If anyone asked about her bruised face, which she would try to hide as much as possible under the hood of her cape, she would simply say that she fell.

She hurriedly finished dressing, then packed a few

140

belongings. Every movement was painful torture as her body began feeling the results of McGuire's beating. She knew she needed rest and a doctor, but there was no time now. And she did not want to be identified by anyone. She must get away!

She moved cautiously back to where she had dropped the gun. She might need it. She swallowed, moving around the bed and keeping her back to it, not wanting to look at McGuire, and having the irrational feeling he might somehow come back alive and grab her. She shook in a cold sweat as she cautiously bent down and picked up the gun and her handbag, then quickly ran back to the other side of the room.

She stuffed the gun into her carpet bag, along with most of the money she had saved for the trip. The rest of the money she stuffed into the bodice of her dress, except for a few dollars she carried in her handbag. She removed her engagement ring and put it on a chain around her neck beside a Crucifix she wore, then tucked both into her dress. She didn't want to wear any expensive jewelry in obvious places, fearful someone might harm her to rob her. She put a little powder over the bruises on her face, straightened her hair and threw on her spare cape. Then, before she got out of the room, she was engulfed in a new wave of sorrow over Carl Danner. No! She must not think of him now! She must not think of anything but running! She swallowed back the tears of sorrow, humiliation, rage, and utter despair and drew on a strength deep inside herself that she never realized she possessed. She had only herself to depend on now. She must get to Bryce before she collapsed.

She breathed deeply and ran out of the room,

hurrying down the stairway. Some of her torn clothes still lay on the hardwood floor below, where McGuire had first grabbed her. She would leave them. It was best that everything remain untouched and that Loren McGuire be found naked on the bed. At least the police would know what had likely occurred, that he had attacked her viciously. So what if his family was shamed and embarrassed? It would serve them right. Still, her innocence in the attack could be turned around by her father's enemies to make her look like the guilty one, and she could not take that risk. She dared not wait for hearings and trials. She could not bear any more pressure. She was almost crazy already. She could not take the strain of inquests and personal, probing, intimate questions shouted cruelly by an eager prosecutor. She could not bear the humiliation alone. She wanted only Bryce! She must get out to his warm, strong arms. She had to get away from all this horror and never come back! Bryce would know what to do, if only she could get to him!

She walked through the front door, closing and locking it. She descended the steps. Everything hurt. She wondered if she might actually be badly injured and die without a doctor's help. But she dared not draw any attention to herself now. There was no way she could go to any doctor. But the pain! The awful pain!

She pulled her hood over her head and began walking, already deciding she would not take the route she had mapped out for Bryce—the route that was to have been included in Danner's telegram to Bryce. She suddenly wondered if Bryce would ever even get the message. Probably not. All the better. She would leave on a different train and use a fake name. No one would know who she was, and no one would be looking for her. If she were caught, she might be arrested—maybe even go to prison for murder! No! She could not be caught! She would hide and make her way as best she could. It would be best if Bryce never got the telegram. That way, no one would be aware of her plans or her route of travel. She would leave her trunks at the station. It was too risky to try to pick them up now. Besides, she must travel light, as she might spend part of her trip walking.

"God, help me!" she whispered, making a sign of the cross. "Bryce! Bryce!" Bryce had no idea now that she was financially ruined and that Jonathan Fitzgerald was dead. She was alone in this awful nightmare. She must get to him. She flagged down a passing carriage for hire and asked to be taken to the train station, where she would try to board a different train from the one she had originally intended to take.

As she struggled to climb into the carriage, Danner's body was being discovered. The police rummaged through the man's clothes for identification and came across the written note:

Leaving on afternoon train to St. Louis. Will take riverboat from there to Memphis. Butterfield Stage west. Have troops waiting at Memphis by June 20. Father is dead. I am fine. Danner will accompany me to St. Louis and on to Memphis. Do not worry. We will be together soon, darling. How I long for the comfort and safety of your arms.

"I wonder who the hell wrote this," a policeman muttered. "And who it was going to." He folded the note and put it into his pocket.

Bryce looked up from his desk at Private Reynolds, who saluted the officer almost hesitantly. "Well?" Bryce asked, quickly saluting in return.

"I . . . uh . . . I sent your telegram, sir."

Bryce's heart quickened. "And? What was Danner's reply? Is something wrong with Miss Fitzgerald?"

Reynolds swallowed. "She . . . uh . . . she seems to be missing, sir."

The look in Bryce's eyes was enough to put great fear in anyone's heart. Reynolds had not wanted to give Bryce the news, aware as he was of how anxiously Bryce had been waiting for Miss Fitzgerald to come West and marry him.

"What do you mean—missing?" Bryce asked, slowly rising. His jaw flexed in building, seething anger.

Reynolds shifted nervously. "Well, sir, I sent the message like you said. And you know it always takes a few hours for the answer. Sergeant Harris sent a messenger for me, saying the answer was coming in, so I went over there . . . after telling you . . . and—"

"Goddamn it, Reynolds, get to the point!" Bryce snapped, his eyes blazing. Reynolds twisted his gloves in nervous hands.

"Well, sir, the man that delivered the telegram found the house officially closed . . . by the police, sir. So he told his boss . . . and they . . . they checked with the police. Come to find out Mr. Fitzgerald, he's been dead for over a week, sir. And . . . a dead body was found in the house . . . some man by the name of Loren McGuire."

Bryce's eyes widened and he paled. "McGuire!" he whispered. "My God!"

"Do you know him, sir?" Reynolds was almost shocked to see Bryce actually trembling.

"What else, Reynolds?" he asked in a strained voice.

"Well, sir, the police claim it looked like Miss Fitzgerald . . . like she . . . killed this Mr. McGuire . . . maybe for his money. They've found out she's clean broke. The Fitzgerald fortune is gone, sir. And Miss Fitzgerald has disappeared. The police want her for questioning for the murder of Loren McGuire. No one has seen her since June twentieth, the day of her father's funeral."

Bryce stood there staring at the young man in disbelief. Never had Reynolds pitied a man more than he pitied Bryce Edwards right now.

"It's a lie!" Bryce finally growled, now taking on the look of an officer ready for battle. "What about Danner? Did they find out about him? Where in hell was Danner?"

"He—uh—he's dead, sir. Police say he was killed during a robbery."

"The hell he was! It was a setup! Someone is covering up for Loren McGuire. He attacked her, that's what he did! He got rid of Danner and he attacked her! He probably—" He stopped midsentence and violently shoved everything off his desk. Reynolds stared in confusion and amazement, as Bryce hunched over then and grabbed his stomach as though he were ill. He slumped into his chair.

"Sir?" Reynolds spoke up, concerned. "Is there . . . anything . . . I can do?"

"I should have brought her back with me!" Bryce

145

said in a choked voice.

"I'm awful damned sorry, sir," Reynolds said quietly, feeling awkward being present during this very personal and tragic moment in the senior officer's life. He stood there waiting, afraid to approach the colonel. Bryce finally stood up, throwing his head back and breathing deeply. He quickly wiped at his eyes with his shirtsleeve.

"I've got some wires to send," he said, his voice now as cold as ice. He wiped his eyes again. "I'll get to the bottom of this!" He stormed out and Reynolds followed him. Bryce went directly to the small building where the telegraph was located and dictated a message to the private investigating firm for whom Carl Danner had worked.

"Suspect Carl Danner robbery and murder a cover," the message read. "Suspect a setup by Loren McGuire and possible payoff by McGuire's family to hide truth. Suspect Danner's murder arranged by McGuire, and Danner's client, Shannon Fitzgerald, attacked by same man. Investigate McGuire murder. Also investigate status of Fitzgerald financial situation. Cost no object. Urgent!"

Reynolds and the sergeant taking down the telegram looked at each other, the sergeant only suspecting the woman called Shannon Fitzgerald was someone special to his commanding officer. Private Reynolds was the only man who knew anything about Bryce Edwards's private life, and that only because he was his personal aid. Bryce trusted the young man to keep what little he knew to himself.

Bryce ran a hand through his hair. "I have another message to send," he told the sergeant in a hoarse voice.

146

"Send this same message to Fort Washington in Ohio, Fort Harrison in Indiana, Fort Leavenworth and Fort Osage in Missouri . . . uh . . . Fort Prudhomme in Tennessee, Fort Smith in Arkansas and . . . where's a damned map!"

The sergeant whipped one out and Bryce studied it.

"O.K. We've got to try and figure what route she might take. Also send this to Fort Jesup in Texas—and, also in Texas, Fort Reno, Fort Sill, Fort Richardson and Fort Stockton. Fort Sumner in New Mexico. And send it to the authorities in El Paso, Texas; Independence and St. Louis, Missouri and Memphis, Tennessee. Have the train depots notified, too. Tell all of the forts that I suspect a Miss Shannon Fitzgerald is trying to get out to me. I'd like them to make their scouts aware of the situation and to keep their eyes open. She might even find a way to hide out on a wagon train. Also have the authorities in the cities mentioned and at the railroad stations watch for her. If she's found, she is to be sent directly to me, not back East. Make that clear. She is not to be sent back. If anyone sends her back, they'll have the whole United States Army on their tails!"

"Yes, sir," the sergeant replied, scribbling fast. "I . . . uh . . . I need a description, sir."

The room quieted as Bryce swallowed and turned away, his eyes filled with pain and fury. "Auburn hair," he finally spoke up in a strained voice. "Quite . . . long and thick. In the sun it . . . glows quite red. She's slight of build . . . maybe five feet and a couple inches . . . maybe a hundred pounds. Very fair complected. She's nineteen. She has lovely green eyes . . . oval-shaped—long, dark lashes . . . very beautiful. Her eyes are what

147

make her look older. She's all . . . lady. Speaks well. Well-educated and well-dressed. She may be wearing a diamond engagement ring. She's just a kid. That's all she is. Just a kid." He turned to face the sergeant, his face suddenly haggard. "I'm sorry. I . . . gave you more detail than necessary. Get on all that fast, sergeant. I'll be in my office." He left quickly, walking dejectedly to his quarters. He plunked down behind his desk with a bottle of whiskey and began slugging down the alcohol, not bothering with a glass.

148

Chapter Nine

Bryce Edwards existed in a vacuum for the next three days, waiting for word from someone, anyone. The silence penetrated him like a bullet. He cared little about his own men or the Apaches or the settlers or the miners. They could all go to hell as far as he was concerned. He was not going to do a damned thing until he heard something. The reply finally came on the fourth day, as Bryce sat at his desk staring at Shannon's last letter. It gave no hint of any problems, no suggestion that she might be broke.

"She was trying to spare me until she got here," he thought. He closed his eyes and rested his head in his hands. "My God, I'll never forgive myself!" he whispered. "Why, oh why, didn't I bring her out here two years ago! Shannon! Shannon!"

Private Reynolds entered hesitantly. "We—uh—got a couple of answers, sir."

Bryce looked up with hollow, bloodshot eyes, his heart pounding.

"That investigation firm—they got to the bottom of

it for you. They had already been working on it before they got your telegram because they suspected foul play in Danner's death."

"And?"

"Well, sir—" Reynolds sighed and looked down at the floor. "Come to find out—McGuire was found . . . in the nude, sir."

The young man reddened and his chest hurt at what he had to say. "He was . . . shot at very close range, sir . . . twice. One bullet penetrated the heart. He was . . . lying on a bed upstairs. His family paid off the sheriff not to tell how he was found. There was blood on the bed . . . and a woman's torn clothes on the floor. The man's face and body were . . . were scratched up pretty bad. More torn clothing was found downstairs at the entranceway."

Bryce's color faded to a deathly gray and his jaw flexed. "Miss Fitzgerald?"

Reynolds felt his heart breaking for his senior officer. "Still no sign of her, sir. Not anywhere. The investigator says some lawyer by the name of Barrett Carter claims the Fitzgerald fortune was lost by a run on his bank and bad deals. There was just enough to pay for Fitzgerald's care and burial, and a little left over for Miss Fitzgerald. The house and everything in it were sold, sir. A—uh—a note was found on Danner's body. Apparently it was a telegram he was to send to you. It said Miss Fitzgerald was leaving that day— June twentieth, sir—to come out to you. I guess he never got to send the wire. Two of Miss Fitzgerald's trunks were found at the station. Best they can figure, Danner went to the station to get the tickets and take her trunks and all and was supposed to go back and get

150

her. But he never got there, sir. The investigator has turned everything over to the prosecutor. It will all be straightened out. I'm sure Miss Fitzgerald will be cleared in the shooting, sir."

"But she doesn't know that!" Bryce growled. "Don't you see? She's running, Reynolds! She's trying to get to me! And the poor kid doesn't know a thing about how to get here, or who to trust or—" He leaned forward and put his head in his hands.

"You . . . you know this Loren McGuire, sir?"

There was a moment of silence. "It's a long story, Reynolds. It doesn't matter anymore. All that matters is that Shannon is out there somewhere scared and alone and trying to get to me. God only knows where she is, what she's been through."

"Sir, there are a lot of people looking for her. I'm sure she'll be found."

Bryce shook his head and took some deep breaths. "She'll do her best to hide her identity and duck away from any authorities," he answered. He rose and walked to a window. "She thinks they'll take her back East. I know how she thinks . . . how scared she must be right now. She had no one left back home to help her. Even her father's lawyer turned out to be a crook. She knows there would be ugly questions and accusations. Shannon isn't designed to handle situations like that. She's too vulnerable . . . too delicate. She's running scared, Reynolds. Running scared trying to get to me. She's out there . . . somewhere. And it wouldn't even do any good for me to go and look myself. I have no idea where in hell I would begin. All I can do is hope that out of all the people searching for her, she'll be found."

"Your request to be given a leave has been denied, sir," Reynolds said quietly to Bryce. "You've been ordered to go farther east over to that new fort—Fort Bowie—by Apache Pass. Washington says you're needed very badly right here. They simply can't let you go running all over the South looking for one woman. There's an all-out civil war going on now. It's real bad, Colonel Edwards. There's just no way they can spare you now. They opened that new fort near Apache Pass to help protect the Butterfield Stage station there. So it's just possible, if Miss Fitzgerald manages to get on a stagecoach coming this way, heck, maybe she'll show up at Apache Pass, sir. You never know."

Bryce turned to look at him, the gray eyes cold and desperate. "When do we go to Fort Bowie?" he asked curtly.

"In six weeks, sir. It's not quite finished."

Their eyes held. "So, that's it, that's all," Bryce said with a sneer. "Saddle my horse, Reynolds." He walked over and picked up his hat.

"For what, sir?"

"I'm going for a ride—alone."

"Sir, you shouldn't go out there alone. Saguaro is still raiding and—"

"Do as I say, Reynolds!" Bryce snapped. "I've got to get away from here and think!"

Reynolds sighed. "Yes, sir." The young man went out, and Bryce went to his desk and took out a bottle of whiskey. After a few minutes he put on his gun and walked out, mounting his horse and ordering the gates opened. He rode out and did not return until late into the night, slouching on his mount and ordering the gates opened with a slurred command. Reynolds, who had been watching for him, was first out the gate, taking the horse's bridle and quickly leading it to Bryce's quarters, not wanting too many men to see their leader drunk. He was glad it was late at night and only two men were standing guard.

The private caught Bryce as he half fell from his horse. "Salute your colonel!" Bryce said sarcastically. "Salute your brave hero of the West!" He held up an empty bottle as Reynolds whisked him inside. "That's what she called me, Reynolds," Bryce was mumbling. "Her brave hero!" Bryce laughed as he fell back onto his cot and Reynolds pulled off his boots. "Some hero!" He laughed and rolled over. "Some damned hero."

Reynolds covered Bryce and sighed, not sure of all the details about Bryce Edwards and Shannon Fitzgerald, but sure enough that Edwards had loved the girl and intended to marry her. The young man's soft heart ached for Edwards, who he knew to be himself a compassionate, honest man, and a man who was also very lonely.

"What a mess!" the boy muttered.

Mid-August of 1860 found a desolate Bryce Edwards leading a squad of twelve men east toward Fort Bowie. Their transfer there had been delayed because the fort had not been completed on time. But now the new stone garrison was ready for Colonel Bryce Edwards and its new battalion already stationed there—all very young men fresh from the East.

Bryce did not relish the task before him—to train eight hundred to a thousand men who knew nothing about fighting Indians. The Union was keeping its best and most experienced men in the East now because of the war there. Bryce was being left with not only too few men, but men who were green. Nearly a third of his men at Fort Bowie would go on to other forts in the West after their training.

Bryce was thinner now, hollow-eyed and rather spiritless. There had not been one word about Shannon. The massive search he had instigated came up with nothing. And since Shannon was so young and inexperienced, he could hardly believe she was clever enough to have hidden herself for two full months. She should have arrived by now, if she was going to get to him at all. The only dreadful conclusion he could come to now was that she was very likely dead, either in some swamp at the hands of riverboat men; or perhaps strangled and robbed of her money and diamond ring by some gambler who had promised to help her; or maybe raped and tortured to death by the Apaches or Comanches. Who could tell? His torture at not knowing for sure was worse than having positive proof that she was truly dead. Maybe she was being held prisoner by someone.

The entire incident was a nightmare that he would probably have to live with forever. Things had finally been straightened out in Charleston, and Shannon had been cleared. But she had no way of knowing that. The vision of his beautiful, frightened woman-child crying and ducking through alleys and begging men for secret rides burned at his guts so that he had not been able to eat or sleep. The strain showed vividly. But he would stay on now in the Arizona heat and do his duty. What was left now? It was all he knew. He would have to

154

hang on and just hope and pray that somewhere, sometime, Shannon would turn up in one piece. But that hope seemed very thin at the moment.

The worst part was that she had suffered so much alone. The shock of her brother's and then her father's death, then finding out she was penniless, and then the attack and possible rape, a horrible, and, Bryce didn't doubt, brutal struggle. Sometimes he felt he would go insane at the thought of it. God only knew what all McGuire had done to her. Probably no one would ever know. Her mental torture over the attack, as well as over having killed another human being, must be excruciating. And what was she going through now— A beautiful young woman traveling alone, inexperienced, afraid, no money and no friends?

He sighed, wondering how he would ever be able to stop his thoughts from whirling over and over the same tortures. Would he go on like this forever?

"She'll turn up somewhere, sir. I feel it in my bones," Reynolds spoke up. Bryce looked over at the young man. He managed a slight grin.

"You always know what I'm thinking, don't you, Reynolds?"

"I've been with you quite a while, sir."

Bryce turned and looked forward again.

"Smoke to our left, sir!" someone from behind shouted. "Just over that hill!"

Bryce halted the squad of men and studied the black omen of trouble.

"Should we go and investigate, sir?" Reynolds asked.

Bryce studied the smoke silently. "I wish I had more men. We could be riding into trouble."

"We could go to Fort Bowie first and get more

155

men, sir."

"There could also be women and children over there who are still alive and need our help. We'd better go take a look. Keep your eyes open."

"Yes, sir."

Bryce waved the men forward, veering to the left now and heading for the smoke at a fast gallop. They made their way through a maze of large boulders and precarious crevices, climbing the hill and cresting it to see several Indians, perhaps twenty or so, rounding up four horses they planned to steal. A squatter's wagon lay in smoldering ruin and four bodies, including a woman's, were on the ground beside it. A half-built shack was torn down and burning.

Bryce did not like riding into battle against twice as many men, but he had a duty now. The Arizona authorities were hopping mad about all of Saguaro's raids, although Bryce had no idea if these were Saguaro's men. Arizona citizens were demanding better protection from the hated Apaches, and they expected more action out of the United States Army, which was supposed to be there to protect them.

But guarding hundreds of square miles of twisting, puzzling, rocky, mountainous terrain was not easy, especially when the Apaches had ways of hiding that defied the best white scout's ability to find them.

Bryce had been careful to be as fair as possible with the Indians, but when he caught them in the act as he had now, he had no choice but to move in and try to capture some of them, to have them imprisoned or sent to the reservations they hated vehemently. He ordered a full charge, and the soldiers galloped down the hill toward the marauding Indians.

The Apaches began firing and heading for cover, but many fell under the soldiers' surprise bullets. The raiders let go of the stolen horses and began running. Bryce was sure the very short battle was over and turned to call a halt to the shooting, only to see at least thirty more Apaches behind them on the crest of the hill.

"Take cover!" he shouted. "Every man for himself!"

The Apaches were soon on them from both sides now. Bryce was furious at allowing himself to be trapped. He wondered where in hell the additional Indians had come from. They seemed to have a way of appearing right out of the sands of the desert. No one could hide better than an Apache. The ratio was now at least three Indians to one soldier, and Bryce and his men found themselves in hand-to-hand combat.

Bryce was soon ducking tomahawks and knives. He fought well, his vast experience now standing him in good stead. But there were so many. He swung his rifle butt and managed to slam three Indians off their horses. A fourth Indian leaped from his mount onto Bryce, and they both tumbled farther down the hill. Bryce managed to pull his large knife, and the Indian held a tomahawk. They pushed at each other's arms. This would be a life and death battle. The Indian was young and very strong—and out to prove his manhood in battle. He pinned Bryce down and raised his tomahawk, swinging it violently downward and barely missing Bryce's skull as Bryce rolled out of the way. They tumbled more, then got to their feet and circled around, facing each other, each lashing out at opportune moments.

Bryce could hear his men's cries of death, but he had

to concentrate on the battle at hand and not allow himself to think about the fact that probably all of his men would die—along with himself.

The young buck who was bent on killing Bryce charged again, screaming a bloodcurdling war cry and slashing out with his tomahawk. Bryce felt the razor-sharp edge of the blade split the skin of his chest. The Indian laughed with joy at the sight of Bryce's blood and swung again. Bryce ducked and landed into the man's legs, grabbing them and causing the Indian to fall over Bryce's back, as he was already in forward motion. Bryce swung around as the Indian hit the ground and quickly kicked the Indian's wrist. The redskin released his hold on the tomahawk and dropped it. Bryce kicked it out of the way quickly and then kicked the Indian in the head as hard as he could. The stunned buck lay there for one or two seconds, just long enough for Bryce to leap onto him and quickly ram his knife into the Indian's heart. Blood spurted from the bare-chested brave, spraying Bryce in the face. The Indian let out a grotesque grunt, then went limp.

Bryce, filthy, sweaty, and bleeding heavily now from his own chest wound, struggled to get up, only to turn and see himself surrounded by at least thirty Apaches. He just then realized that all was quiet and the rest of the battle was over. He wondered how long these Indians had been standing there amusing themselves by watching the battle between Bryce and his opponent.

A tall, commanding Apache stepped forward and held a rifle on Bryce.

"You fight very good, my white soldier friend."

Bryce grasped at his chest. "Well," he said, panting, "I've been looking for you for a long time, Saguaro."

"You remember me, then."

Bryce looked around at the burned wagon and dead bodies of the squatters.

"You don't let people forget you, Saguaro. Why did you do this?"

"They make their home on our sacred burial grounds. We ask them to leave. They do not go. Always the white man thinks he has right to plant himself wherever he chooses on our land! Always he takes what is not his! Always he ignores the treaties!"

"These people were at Fort Buchanan a month ago. I warned them not to settle here." The pain in his chest worsened, and his words were becoming more difficult. "They . . . talked like they were . . . going to heed my warning."

"They were fools. They not listen to you. When we send someone to warn them to leave, they shoot three of our men! One was Saguaro's cousin! They take our lives. We take theirs!"

Bryce sighed and looked up into the hills, his heart aching for the bloody, dead bodies of his men that lay sprawled among the rocks.

"And what . . . are your plans for me . . . Saguaro?" he asked, growing weaker. "Torture?"

Saguaro grinned. "It is a thought."

"Go ahead then . . . and get it over with," Bryce said in a strained voice. "I'm . . . bleeding to death anyway." Their eyes held and Saguaro frowned.

"I see no spirit in your eyes, white soldier. I see you fight for life, and now you tell Saguaro to take your life." He ripped open Bryce's uniform, and Bryce grunted with pain, expecting the Indian to string him up then and cut him more. "Once you try help Saguaro by searching out those who kill Saguaro's family. Saguaro does not kill those who help him," the big Indian declared. "Apache also have honor, white soldier. White man not understand our ways. If Saguaro help white man, do you think white man would not kill Saguaro later if he could?"

"Some would . . . some wouldn't," Bryce choked out. Saguaro studied Bryce's muscular build. The two men were not much different in stature. Saguaro grunted a command in his own tongue to one of his men, and the Apache buck walked up to Bryce. He reached into a pouch and smeared something smelly on Bryce's wound.

"It is a healing herb," Saguaro told Bryce. "Soon bleeding will slow. You very brave and strong, my white soldier friend. I find myself liking you. Now we are even. You try help me—I help you." The magnificent Indian turned and stretched out his arms while the buck who had dressed Bryce's wound shoved a stick into Bryce's hand to be used as a cane. Bryce leaned on it, not sure how long he could stay on his feet. "Once . . . plains—mountains, prairies, forests—all covered with the Indian, and with great buffalo that fed and sheltered Indian," Saguaro was saying. "Now, both soon be gone." He whirled. "But that not happen here! This Apache country! Your white friends steal our gold—our women—our land." His dark eyes flashed with anger. "What gives white man this right? Tell me, white soldier. What gives him this right?"

"I can't answer that, Saguaro. I can give you no reasons but greed and lust. I am only here to try my best

160

to keep things peaceful and to work out . . . reasonable solutions and to . . . punish those who harm innocent people." His breathing was becoming more labored.

Saguaro sneered. "You try that with men who kill my family. But your own people let them go! Your ways not work, white soldier. Your people not be happy until they have it all! Cochise not agree with Saguaro yet, but soon he will also see. Now we barely speak, but soon we will fight white man together! You will see. You not know how bad it is. No one knows! Great Father in place called Washington not come out—see for himself how bad it is! He tell us we must live on tiny pieces of land, where Apaches are pushed together to live like dogs! Saguaro not sit on backside and stick out tongue so someone put food on it! Saguaro survives his own way! He is proud! He is man, not dog!"

The Indian noticed a strange sadness in Bryce Edwards's eyes. "I understand everything you're saying, Saguaro," Bryce replied. "I even understand about your woman. Believe me, I understand. A man needs his revenge. And when he can't get it, it eats at him inside. He takes it out . . . on everything and everyone around him. But . . . it doesn't really help."

Saguaro studied Bryce silently a moment. He seemed to soften slightly, but just as suddenly, his eyes were cold again.

"Saguaro finds it hard to feel pity or friendship," he stated. "My feelings have left me, except for hate! I do not remember your name, white soldier. Nor do I want to know it. If I meet you in battle again, I will kill you if I can. Yet I will not like it, because you are different from others. Saguaro sees honesty in your white eyes. I let you go—this time." He smiled rather sarcastically. "But you will be busy protecting your white brothers. Saguaro will continue to raid and kill until the whites leave this land forever!"

"You'll die trying, Saguaro."

"Perhaps. But to live without my woman and without my pride is worse than death, so it not matter! She and my sons were my life . . . my very blood! You not understand this."

"I do understand, Saguaro." Their eyes held again and each felt strangely warmed to the other. "I understand more than you think I do."

"We will meet again," Saguaro said calmly. It was almost more of a prediction than a speculation.

"We will," Bryce replied, studying the tall and powerful Indian. He thought about what a waste it was for such a handsome and intelligent man to have to live a life of fighting and hiding.

"I leave you now, white soldier. You not be bothered on your journey to your new home. See? I know all of your movements. You are journeying to new fort built of stone near Apache Pass. I will be watching you, my friend. Look into the hills, and you will see me! When you look again, I will be gone."

"To the Sierra Madres?"

Saguaro smiled. "White soldier can never find us, can he? No one knows this land better than Apache!" His smile was bright and almost mischievous, and Bryce found himself liking the man.

"Saguaro, if circumstances were different, you and I might be good friends."

"Your people not allow that. Indian and white man can never be good friends!" The Indian lost his smile.

162

He let out a war whoop and was quickly joined in the eerie cries by the rest of the Apaches. Bryce stood still while they rounded up the horses again and picked up their dead to take back to camp for a proper burial—wherever camp was. It seemed only moments before they had all disappeared just as quickly as they had appeared, and Bryce was left standing alone amid the ruins and dead bodies. He struggled painfully up the hill, but the Apaches had melted into the hills and all was now eerily quiet. He stood there alone, still bleeding, listening to the desolate sound of the hot Arizona wind whining and moaning through the rocks and hills. He felt a heavy sorrow. Shannon was probably dead. Some day the proud Indians would all be dead. His men were more than likely all dead. And he felt dead inside. It was as though everything that mattered to him was dying. And, having been orphaned at seven, he wondered if that was the way life was to be for him—always losing those he loved.

He stumbled back down the hill and searched for Private Reynolds. He found the young man lying facedown beside a large rock. Bryce knelt down and grunted with pain as he rolled Reynolds's body over. The man's pantleg and one sleeve were covered with blood.

"Reynolds?" Bryce asked, after finding a pulse. "Can you hear me, son?"

"Colonel Edwards?" the man said weakly. His bright red hair was caked with dirt and sweat and his hat was missing. He opened his pale blue eyes, and, in spite of his nineteen years, he looked like a five-year-old boy who was frightened. "It . . . hurts bad . . . sir!" he said, blinking back tears.

"I know it does," Bryce replied. "I'll see if I can't get the bleeding to slow." He patted the young man's cheek and gave him a smile. He ignored his own pain and ripped open Reynolds's uniform and undershirt, tearing apart the undershirt and tying it around the bleeding shoulder as best he could. Then he tied his own neckscarf tightly around Reynolds's upper thigh to help stop the bleeding in his leg.

"I'm not . . . gonna' die . . . am I?" Reynolds asked weekly

Bryce took his hand and squeezed it. "Hell no, Reynolds!" he assured the young man. But he was already wondering about himself. If help didn't come soon, the last two remaining men of this siege would be dead—Bryce Edwards and Private John Reynolds. "I'm going to see if there's anyone else alive," Bryce added, squeezing the young man's hand again.

Bryce managed to crawl around to examine the others, every movement making him weaker. But he had a responsibility to these men, many whom he knew well. Not one other man was left alive. Bryce fought a desire to break down and weep. He contemplated trying to get himself and Reynolds to Fort Bowie, but everything was becoming more and more gray and blurry. He made his way back to Reynolds.

"I'll . . . stay right with you, Reynolds," he told the boy. "Don't worry . . . about a thing. Someone will . . . come along . . . as soon as we're missed at Fort Bowie. I'll—"

Bryce's bleeding had slowed from the treatment Saguaro had given him, but he had already lost too much blood. Everything went black, and he slumped over beside Reynolds.

"Colonel Edwards!" Reynolds yelled. "Colonel Edwards, don't die and leave me here! Colonel Edwards!" The boy reached down and touched Bryce's head with his good arm. "Colonel Edwards?" The boy broke into sobbing and the hot sun burned unmercifully into his face. He tried to move, but it was fruitless. "God, don't let me die here like this!" he sobbed. He tried to rouse Bryce again, but the man appeared to be dead.

"You three!" the young, green lieutenant from Fort Bowie shouted to three men from his platoon. "Ride back to Fort Bowie—on the double! Come back with more men as fast as you can to help us bury these men, and for protection in case of another attack!"

"Yes, sir!"

"And send word East to General Hathaway about what has happened here! Tell him Bryce Edwards and all of his men have been massacred! Tell him the Apaches are at it again and we simply must have more men out here if we are to protect the citizens of Arizona properly!"

"Yes, sir! Right away!" The three excited men turned their horses and galloped off.

"Damn!" the lieutenant fumed to a companion. "That settler was right about Saguaro being at it again!"

Everything was commotion, and fear gripped the remaining men as they looked at the dead and bloody bodies of the Edwards platoon—bodies sprawled grotesquely on the side of the hill. The ruins of the squatters' wagon and half-built house still smoldered.

"It's almost dark, sir," the companion told the lieutenant.

"That's good. The Indians seldom do anything after dark. It's their stupid religion—something about spirits being active after dark. Damn! Edwards was one of the best! We needed him at Fort Bowie! Look where all his knowledge and experience got him! This shows you those animals can't be trusted!"

"Do you think they're all dead, sir?"

"Hell yes! How could any man live through this! If one did, the Apaches would make sure he was dead before they left! Damn! Let's get on with the burial!"

Chapter Ten

Shannon sat nervously fingering her gloves, avoiding the stare of the stage station attendant. Outside, the driver was in the process of unhitching his worn team, to be replaced by fresh horses kept at the station. Shannon was not positive where she was, but she was sure she could not be far from Bryce now. The driver had said they were in the White Mountains of Arizona—someplace called Doubtful Canyon.

"Unless the Apaches get to us first, we'll hit Apache Pass next, lady. That's near Fort Bowie," the driver had informed her. "That's a brand new fort they just put up. The Indians have been raidin' more, I hear. I feel sorry for them soldiers havin' to try and keep up with it all. Them goddamned Apaches—oh, excuse me for my language, miss—but I can't think of nothin' better to call them redskins. Anyway, they've been raidin' and killin' somethin' awful lately. We'd best get you to Apache Pass and Fort Bowie. Some of the troops there can see that you get safely to Fort Buchanan from there. Who are you fixin' to meet at

167

Fort Buchanan, anyway?"

"My—uh—brother," she had told him. "Our parents both died, and he's all I have left."

"That's too bad, ma'am. Well, all I have to do is change this team and we'll be ready to roll. You go on inside the station and wait. It's safer and cooler inside."

Shannon had obeyed, gripping her carpetbag and the few possessions she had in it. She still wore the diamond ring around her neck. But when she entered the station, she had chilled at the look in the old attendant's eyes when he caught sight of her. His look reminded her of Loren McGuire. While she waited, she sat in a corner, and, other than asking for a drink of water, she avoided conversation with the old man.

The fear and horror she had experienced over the last two months of her desperate journey floated through her mind. How wonderful it was to be this close to Bryce now! How she had made it this far was nothing less than a miracle. She had very little money left, having had to pay dearly to get people to help her.

She was learning a lot about her own strength and determination, as well as learning about people and the real world. But her struggle and her rude awakening to the harsh side of life were causing her to lose her own identity. Where was the real Shannon Fitzgerald? Surely, when she reached Bryce, she would not be anything like the girl he had left behind. Would he still want her at all? Perhaps she could find herself again in his arms. Perhaps then her sweet and loving side would return. But now she felt cold and hard, her nature suspicious and almost cunning.

How she longed for someone she could talk to, someone like Marney. But soon she would have Bryce.

He would help. She would have a friend, someone who loved her. She could pour out her horror, tell him the truth about what had happened. She had forced herself not to think about the murder itself, hardly able to believe she had actually killed another human being. Would she go to hell for it? To think about it made her more miserable, and she could not help but wonder if even Bryce would want her once he knew. Perhaps he already knew.

There had been nights when she wept until there were no more tears, nights when hopelessness, fear and despair had even caused her to contemplate suicide. All she would have to do was take out her handgun, put it to her temple and pull the trigger. It was that simple. But her hope of finding Bryce and seeing love in his eyes had kept her from doing so, as well as her religious belief that suicide was the ultimate sin.

The last few weeks had been filled with only one goal for her—survival. She must survive and get to Bryce. Then she would know whether she wanted to live or die. It would all depend on how he felt about her. She had scratched and crawled her way this far, and in spite of her ignorance and inexperience, she had made it! Bryce was close now!

Would he be proud of her strength and courage? Or would he hate her? She was no longer the sweet, innocent child he had left behind. But there had been that one beautiful afternoon of passion and sweet love they had shared. Surely he would cling to that just as she had done. Surely his love had been real and would remain loyal.

She wondered if the authorities were still searching for her. She would do anything but go back East and

169

face the horrible questioning and possible imprison-
ment. She would never go back, no matter what. If
Bryce didn't want her, she would kill herself, after all.
But would she have the courage even to do that?

"What's a pretty thing like you doin' travelin' alone,
missy?" the old station attendant asked. Shannon
jumped, startled, at the words, for she had been lost in
her thoughts. She was at once defensive. What did this
man know?

"I . . . I'm on my way . . . to meet my fiance," she
spoke aloud with a confident air. Why not tell him the
truth? She was almost at Bryce's doorstep. "He's a
colonel in the United States Army, and he's stationed
not many miles from here." She tried to appear calm
and sure of herself.

"That so? What's his name? Maybe I know him."

"It's—" Should she tell him? Of course. Out here
everyone must know the name. This old lecher would
know he'd better beware once he knew who she
belonged to. "It's Colonel Bryce Edwards," she said
matter-of-factly. "He was promoted to colonel not
long ago. He's expecting me by tomorrow," she lied.
"In fact, he's riding this way with troops to meet me at
Apache Pass." She glared at the old man. "And I'd
better show up in one piece, or Colonel Edwards will be
after whoever dares to lay a hand on me."

The old man chuckled with delight.

"What are you laughing at!" Shannon demanded,
rising.

"Colonel Edwards ain't gonna' be ridin' to nobody's
rescue, pretty lady," the man said, laughing harder.

Shannon's heart pounded. Had she spoken too
soon? Was Bryce stationed someplace else now—

perhaps hundreds of miles away?

"What are you talking about?" she demanded, trying to appear confident.

"Bryce Edwards is dead, little miss. Killed yesterday in an Apache raid. Him and twelve other men."

Shannon paled and nearly fainted, grasping onto the back of a chair. "You're—lying!" she gasped.

"No, ma'am. Came across the telegraph just yesterday. I done took the message myself to relay it on East. Edwards was on his way from Fort Buchanan to Fort Bowie with a platoon of men. They was all attacked by Apaches. Every last one of them was killed, lady. And believe me, that telegram couldn't have been wrong. 'Cause Indians don't never leave no white man alive. Ain't no such thing as one man survivin' a battle with Apaches. Nope. Your big, brave colonel done got his throat slit, and more than likely he got his scalp lifted. Must have really been outnumbered and took by surprise. That's the Apaches for ya."

The old man watched with pleasure as Shannon stood there trembling. She blinked rapidly, struggling to think straight, while at the same time wanting to scream out her torment. This couldn't be true! It just couldn't be! Not Bryce! What would she do now? She couldn't go back! Never! They would persecute her— say vile things, throw her in prison. Maybe even hang her! No one would believe her side of the story. There was too much money behind the McGuire name, and she was penniless! Even her father's attorney would not help her now!

"Please—don't lie to me!" she found herself gasping out, clinging to the chair so firmly that her knuckles were white.

"It's the truth, little miss. I wouldn't lie about somethin' like that and risk facin' no colonel for it. Sorry to have to break it to you so cold and hard, but them's the facts, lady." He stepped closer. "What will you do now?" he asked. "Maybe I can help."

"I . . . I . . . " She chilled at his look. Now she was totally vulnerable. She had no defenses left! No money, and no Bryce to back her up. No one and nothing! "I'll . . . go on to California," she said in a near whisper, moving away from the man and walking on rubbery legs to a chair to sit down. Yes. That was what she would do. She must get as far away from Virginia as possible. If she could make it to California, maybe— maybe what? What was in California? Maybe she should just kill herself right now and get it over with. Her mind whirled with indecision and the horrible news. "Bryce! Bryce!" she wanted to scream. She looked up at the old man. "Does the Butterfield—go to California?" she asked in a shaky voice.

It seemed her voice was coming from some other world. Her breath was short as she pulled out a hanky to wipe at the tears that were now spilling down her cheeks. Everything seemed to be swirling, the walls closing in on her. All she could see was Bryce's face— the wonderful smile and the gentle gray eyes. Never would the strong, comforting arms hold her now! Never would she taste his lips again, be one with him again. No! It could not be! She could not take this final loss! All her struggles had brought her to nothing and nowhere.

"Yes, ma'am," the old man was saying. "If you got the money I can get you anyplace."

"I . . . I—" She swallowed. "I have . . . about forty dollars."

The old man chuckled. "Honey, that won't get you to California." He leaned closer and pushed a piece of her hair behind her ear, then looked down at her bosom.

"Now—uh—I know a way to give you free passage to California. Know what I mean, honey?"

Shannon felt nauseous and couldn't even move. She couldn't go back! And Bryce was gone! Gone! Dead! Everyone in the whole world she had ever loved and who loved her was dead! The old man touched her breast with the back of his hand and bent forward to kiss her neck.

"My ring!" she said in desperation. "It's worth a lot of money. Take my ring!" She couldn't believe what she was saying. What had the last weeks of hardships and loss done to her?

The man rose and fingered the ring, letting his hand touch her bosom. "Lady, as long as a man has to go out here without a woman, ain't no ring worth near as much as a pretty piece like you."

"Please!" She quickly got up and backed away, her soul filled with desperation at the thought of Bryce's being dead, and with horrible indecision over what to do next. Bryce! Her beloved Bryce! She couldn't think! Never had such black sorrow engulfed her as now. Words stuck in her throat as the old man came closer, but suddenly there was the sound of horses and war whoops, mingled with piercing rifle shots. The attendant ran to a window.

"Apaches!" he growled. "What a time for Indians to come!" He ran for his rifle, and Shannon, confused and totally terrified, bolted for a back room, where she knelt in a corner, covering her ears against the sounds of vicious savages. What more horror must she suffer? She heard a bloodcurdling war cry just outside the window, and a flaming arrow came crashing through it, landing on a small cot. The bed was immediately in flames, and Shannon ran out to the main room, screaming in terror, leaving her handbag behind.

"The building's on fire!" she screamed at the old man, who was at a front window, shooting his rifle. Another flaming arrow came through that window and immediately the desk behind them was in flames. "We've got to get out!" Shannon screamed at the old man, grasping his shoulders and shaking him. "We'll burn to death!"

"What's out there is worse than burnin' to death!" he growled, shoving her away. Shannon screamed over and over and covered her ears as the firing continued and screeching Indians circled the stage station. Shannon wanted to get to her bag and quickly shoot herself before the horrible savages could get hold of her, but her bag now sat behind flames and she could not get to it. Suddenly the old man was grabbing her, tearing her dress from her shoulders, ripping at it savagely.

"No! What are you doing?" she screamed.

"I have only one chance of savin' myself, lady! You're my insurance! Them redskins will go wild when they see you!"

"No! No! Stop it!" she screamed, struggling violently. He punched her hard in the face and she fell backward, stunned and dizzy. There were the hands again, ripping and tearing as Loren McGuire had done.

174

She felt herself being dragged, and suddenly she was out in the sunlight. She opened her eyes and saw the stage driver, pinioned to a post by a lance driven through his middle. His body was twitching grotesquely, and some of the Indians were circling him, stabbing at him with their lances. Shannon screamed and began struggling more violently than she had thought herself capable of. Surely now these horrible Apache warriors would all violently rape her and then torture her to death. The old man held her tightly and held up his rifle.

The marauding Indians suddenly quieted, and the band of about twenty bucks circled Shannon and the old man, halting their horses and surrounding the two captives. Never had Shannon been more terrified.

"Here!" the old man was saying to the Indians. "I give you this white woman as a gift! Spare me and take her! Look! Look how pretty she is! All white! Yes, sir! She's fresh! You can have her!"

Shannon stood in only her pantaloons and a torn petticoat, sobbing and trying to cover her breasts.

"Let go of her!" a voice spoke up. The old man let go of her, and Shannon fell to the ground. She lay there and wept, then saw the feet of a horse beside her. "Get up!" a voice commanded. Shannon struggled first to her knees, then to her feet. Someone grabbed her hair and jerked her head back. She squinted and waited for some kind of horrible blow from a lance or a knife.

"Who are you?" a voice demanded to know. Shannon could not find her voice.

"Answer the man, you dumb bitch!" the old man told her.

"You! Keep your mouth shut!" the voice demanded

175

of the old man. Shannon felt a hand on her face—a strangely gentle hand. "You have beat this woman?" the voice asked.

"I never touched her, you hear? She's still fresh! I'll let you have her," the old man yelled.

The Indian still had hold of Shannon by the hair of her head.

"You were going to rape her," the Indian sneered. "Indians say white man's manpart is always big!"

Shannon did not hear a reply. She suddenly heard the old man grunt strangely, and then two bucks were dragging his bloody body past her. They picked the old man up and threw him into the flames of the burning station. She heard a short scream—then nothing. Her eyes widened and she began squirming to get away from whoever was holding her. The hand tightened on her hair.

"Who are you?" the Apache asked again. "Are you important? White men pay money for you? Give rifles?"

Shannon covered her mouth and sobbed. "No," she squeaked. "I'm . . . worthless! Go ahead . . . and kill me. I'm worthless to you! I . . . have nothing! No one! No one!" Her sobbing heightened to near hysteria now. "Do . . . whatever . . . you're going to do!" she screamed. "Do it . . . and kill me . . . and have it over with! I don't want to live anyway! Do . . . me a favor . . . and kill me!" Her body jerked in resigned sobs.

"Her hair make prize scalp, Saguaro!" one of the other Apaches shouted. "Look at its color!"

Saguaro! In spite of the heat, Shannon felt a chill at the name. *This was the hated Saguaro Bryce had mentioned in his letters*! What would this vicious Apache warrior do to her?

Saguaro slid from his horse and stood in front of her. "Apache not take scalps!" he boomed out to the others. "No scalps!" The big Indian grasped her arms and she looked up at him, but she could not see him well because of the tears in her eyes. He began running his hands over her body, feeling her breasts and belly, her hips and thighs, as though she were a horse for trade. Then he circled her, looking her over.

"We not kill or scalp this one!" he shouted to the others. "I like how she look—her youth—her strange green eyes—hair the color of red earth. She has colors of land—green grass, red earth, pink skin like flowers in spring. I keep this one! She belong to Saguaro! Others not touch her!"

Shannon sank to the ground at the thought of being carried off by this savage. But then she felt a soft blanket being put around her. Strong hands were pulling her back up with gentleness. She felt a large and powerful presence standing before her, and she pulled the blanket close around her to cover her nakedness as two hands were placed at either side of her face. She looked up, startled at the gentleness of the touch, and looked squarely into the face of her captor. His dark face was painted grotesquely, yet his handsomeness could not be hidden. She was almost shocked at how clean and neat he appeared to be, his hair shining straight and long over his shoulders, jet black and soft-looking. He was nothing like she had always imagined that an Indian would look. And there was a concern in his eyes that startled her.

"I am Saguaro," he told her. "I am leader of this

band of Mescaleros. I speak your tongue. I learn from white missionaries. That was many moons ago, when I trusted white man. Those days are gone. Saguaro spares you, because your tears remind Saguaro of another. White man cruel to you, even though you are also white. I have seen what white men do to women . . . squaws and white women. Saguaro not hurt you. You come with Saguaro now."

"Where?" she whispered.

"To Mexico . . . Sierra Madre Mountains, where we find safety. Do not be afraid."

She glanced at the burning station and the stage driver pinned to the post. Did she have any choice? And could going with this Apache warrior be any worse than what the old man had intended for her—or worse than Loren McGuire? Her fate was horrible no matter how she looked at it. And she had absolutely no place where she could go now.

"Do not make me force you," Saguaro was saying. "I not want hurt you."

So, she thought. I am to end up an Apache slave somewhere in Mexico, no one even knowing I exist any longer. She thought of Bryce and her heart felt shattered. Her hope was gone.

"You won't . . . hurt me?" she whimpered.

"No. But Apache warrior cannot show gentleness in front of other Apache bucks. Until we reach my home, you not speak or make trouble, or Saguaro will hit you. Be obedient, like good Apache squaw. Do not shame Saguaro by speaking out or trying to escape or by crying too much."

Even while you rape me? she thought.

"I say we scalp her!" the other buck spoke up again.

"Why you want that skinny white squaw?"

Saguaro turned from Shannon, and she watched in amazement as he walked over to the protesting warrior and suddenly grasped the man's arm, jerking him off his horse. Saguaro kicked the other buck in the stomach and then in the jaw. He pulled his knife and was immediately on top of the man, the knife at his throat.

"Saguaro has spoken!" the leader growled. "You touch her—you answer to Saguaro!"

The other Indian looked terrified. "Do what you wish with her!" he told Saguaro in a frightened voice. Saguaro got up and the other Indian rose slowly, holding his stomach. He looked darkly at Saguaro and remounted his horse.

"Go look for food!" Saguaro ordered. "Find guns in coach—round up horses! We must leave quickly now! Soldiers will come!"

The warriors began scurrying around to Saguaro's commands, and Saguaro turned to face Shannon again.

"Saguaro not really think soldiers will come," he said rather haughtily. "Saguaro is smarter than soldiers. This morning Saguaro cut talking line so thay cannot send messages."

Because of the cut lines, the old man at the station had never heard the second message—that Bryce Edwards and a Private Reynolds had lived through the massacre near Fort Bowie the day before. Saguaro lifted Shannon to his horse with little effort, as though she were no more than a feather. Then he deftly leaped up onto the animal behind her. There was no saddle on the horse—only a blanket. Saguaro reached around

179

her with bronze, muscular arms that shone smooth and reddish-brown in the hot Arizona sun. Shannon wondered what horrible fate awaited her at the hands of this powerful savage once he got her into his own private dwelling. He would more than likely have his way with her until he tired of her, then turn her over to the other bucks, or perhaps sell her to some bandit, or kill her. The choice would be his. She would have no say in it.

She forced back tears. He had told her not to cry too much. It was a next to impossible demand, as she sat there thinking of Bryce, dying a lonely, savage death, having never seen her again. Now they would never fulfill their love. Her former years and life, and her moments with her dashing, handsome soldier, all seemed a dream, as though it had all happened to another person and not to Shannon Fitzgerald. She wondered if the Indian who now held her was one of those who had killed Bryce. She should hate him. But there were no feelings left. No love, and, strangely, no hate. And what seemed even more strange was that she felt she could trust the savage perched behind her on the horse. If not for the horror of the last several minutes, she could almost have laughed over the irony of the entire situation. Since McGuire's attack, there had not been one white man she had felt she could trust, except for Bryce. Yet now, as she trembled with fright and jerked with silent tears, the dark-skinned savage behind her reached around her and gripped her tightly for a moment. She felt strangely comforted.

"Saguaro tell you not to be afraid, yet you tremble like a newborn pup exposed to cold," he said quietly. "Saguaro not lie. Apache never lies. Tell me. Do you have a man? Children?"

"My man . . . is dead," she said flatly. "I . . . have no family. No one." She choked in a sob and he did not reply. He glanced over her shoulder, down at the whiteness of her skin, intrigued by its velvety look. Then he pulled the blanket closer around her throat.

"You belong to Saguaro now," he said softly. "The others will not look upon you again. Men like that old white one will not touch you that way again."

The other Indians finished with the looting. Saguaro gave out a yipping war cry that made Shannon jump. He turned his horse and they were off. Shannon wondered just how much more she could bear without losing her mind completely. She would never see Bryce again—or her family—or Virginia. And now she would never reach California.

Her life would be dictated now—by fate. Shannon Fitzgerald had completely lost control over her destiny. Her future would totally depend on the unpredictable Apache warrior named Saguaro. She felt that they were disappearing into the horizon, heading south to Mexico and the Sierra Madre mountains.

Chapter Eleven

For three days after her abduction, Shannon Fitzgerald rode with Saguaro. She did not speak. She did not cry. She only sat or moved in a frightened daze. She helped gather firewood in the evenings, as dictated by Saguaro, who watched her like a hawk. He never left her side. She was not sure if it was because he feared she would try to escape, or if he did not trust his men not to harm her. At night he slept sitting up, with Shannon lying at his feet. He did not harm her or touch her rudely. When she needed to go to the bathroom, he stayed beside her, but he always turned around. He allowed her to eat, but it was difficult for her to choke down the roots and dried meat the others ate.

The day before they were to arrive at their destination, Saguaro left her for the first time, not telling her where he was going. The other Indians did not come near her, and it was obvious they all feared Saguaro's reprisal if they touched her. The one who had argued about keeping her watched her sullenly, but did not speak, which was fine with Shannon.

Saguaro soon returned with a leather bag full of peaches, dropping the fruit in front of her. "Eat!" he commanded. "It is white man's food. Apache like sweet fruit also, but not so much as white man. It is very pleasing to the tongue. Eat."

Shannon looked wide-eyed at the beautiful peaches.

"Saguaro steal them for you," he said proudly. "Eat."

Shannon reached out and picked up a large, ripe one, gently running her hand over the soft fuzz. For some reason the lovely fruit stirred something inside of her. It was soft and sweet. It reminded her of Virginia. She looked up at Saguaro, and his eyes told her that he had wanted to give her the fruit with a smile and a touch, but he dared not show his softness before his men.

"Thank you," she said in a small voice.

"Do not thank me!" he said tersely. "You not eat our food. Saguaro not like his women too skinny."

His back was turned to his men and she studied his eyes. He suddenly grinned a little, but not wickedly as Loren McGuire had grinned at her, or the old man at the station. Shannon dropped her eyes and bit into the fruit. She could not help the silent tears that came when she tasted its sweetness, and she thought of the days when she had sat down to a grand table in her father's mansion and food such as this had been peeled and chilled for her, and she had eaten without a thought that some day she might lose all that she had.

Their fourth day was spent winding through a maze of rocks and canyons in the Sierra Madres. It was

184

obvious now to Shannon why Bryce had often written that it was next to impossible to find the Apaches. She was certain she never could have found this place, and she knew she would never be able to find her way back out again once they got where they were going. Her doom was sealed. She would be buried alive forever in these mountains with these savages to live out her life as a white Apache slave woman.

When they reached Saguaro's village, women quickly gathered, chattering and giggling and pointing at Shannon. They clamored around Saguaro's horse and he grunted a command to them in his own tongue. They quickly stepped back. Dogs jumped around and barked. Shannon looked around at tipis and wickiups, guessing there were at least two hundred dwellings in this village. Campfires were burning and she could smell meat cooking. She wondered what kind. There seemed to be little in the way of game in these barren, rocky mountains. But that was not of much concern to her now. She was hot and tired and afraid of these strange people who ran around excitedly, babbling in their own clipped tongue.

Many of the women were running to the other braves now, grinning and giggling and welcoming the men back home. Saguaro slid off his horse.

"Get down," he grunted to her. Shannon slid off the horse and stood on shaky legs as the women gathered around her again, smiling and touching her. She watched them—some of them beautiful, some old and wrinkled, some with kind eyes, others glaring with hatred. She could not understand anything they were saying. Some touched her hair, intrigued with its red glint in the sun. They studied her strange, green eyes.

185

Saguaro shooed them away and grabbed Shannon's arm and led her to a large brush wickiup, pushing her inside.

"Stay," he commanded. "Rest. I will council with my people. Then I will return. Fix a fire. I bring you water to wash." He immediately left the confused girl. Shannon looked around the wickiup. It was composed mostly of brush and branches. She was fascinated that people could actually build a house out of sticks that would stand—like a bird making its nest. She walked over and took hold of a small branch and wiggled it, half expecting the entire dwelling to tumble down on her head. But she was amazed that it barely budged. She pushed at it harder, and it was as firm as any stucco wall. She had noticed that the outside of the very large wickiup was covered with hides. She could see parts of the covering through the brush. There was a hole in the top at the very center.

She walked around, surprised that people could stand inside these primitive homes. She had never dreamed that tipis and wickiups could be so large. There was a strange, sweet odor inside, but far from unpleasant. She decided it must be a mixture of the earth, smoke, and the Indians' body odor, which she had discovered was not offensive at all. Over the past few days of riding with Saguaro and being with him constantly, she had noticed his odor was different from that of whites, but pleasant and manly. He kept himself clean. Most of the people she had seen in the village at first glance also seemed reasonably clean—much cleaner than she had imagined wild Indians would keep themselves.

Her eyes rested on three tunics that hung from little

186

twigs that stuck out from the sides of the walls. Next to them hung a cradleboard. She walked up to touch them.

The cradleboard was covered with fine, soft deerskin, brightly beaded. The tunics were also of soft deerskin, one bleached white. They were fringed and brightly beaded and small. She tried to picture the woman who had worn them, and it was then that she began to connect Saguaro with Bryce's letters. Of course! What handsome buck like Saguaro would be without a woman. This man had been married. These were his wife's clothes.

"Saguaro!" she whispered to no one. Saguaro was the one whom Bryce had written about—the one whose wife and little boys had been killed by white men. Did he intend to savagely rape her in his revenge? The last she knew from Bryce's letters, Saguaro was the only Apache making trouble at the time—because of what had happened to his family. Panick rose in her chest.

The thought of Bryce's letters brought back the awful realization that Bryce Edwards was dead and she was entirely at the mercy of this wild savage.

"Oh, Bryce! Bryce!" she whimpered. "My God, my poor Bryce! He died all alone! All alone out here in this desolate land!" She wondered how much he had suffered. Had he called for her? How could things have turned out so horribly? Why was God so angry with her that He had done all of these terrible things to her? What more could happen? Bryce's death finally engulfed her, and she was swamped with great waves of sorrow and hopelessness. She sat down on a pile of straw and gave in to her great agony and fear. The tears came now—a waterfall of uncontrolled sobs, so violent

187

she thought she might choke.

She did not know how long she cried. She was aware of nothing, not even of the fact that Saguaro had returned to find her crying. He had left again and returned with an old copper bucket filled with heated water. He set the water down and went to her side. Shannon jumped and gasped when he touched her shoulder. Then she moved back like a frightened deer. Saguaro watched her quietly for a moment. Then he stood up and walked over, taking down one of the tunics that hung on the wall.

"You small like my woman was. You can wear this. Take off blanket—wash—put this on."

She sat there frozen. Saguaro sighed and came over to her side, reaching out to remove the blanket. She pushed his hand out of the way and he grabbed her wrist and jerked her forward.

"Why you not believe Saguaro when he tell you not to be afraid?" he asked. "Is it because you are used to white men's lies? Saguaro not lie! Saguaro only want to help you wash—make you comfortable so you can sleep. You must sleep. You not strong like Apache women. You must learn. I not make you work too hard."

She pulled back and he jerked her forward again.

"You are my woman now!" he told her. "Now I can look upon you. I not wish to harm you. My only wish is to help you!"

"I know what you wish to do!" she spit out. "You wish to rape me!"

"No," he replied in a softer voice. "Saguaro not rape. Saguaro want only to wash you—make you sleep. Saguaro wishes to look upon soft skin of white woman,

188

but only to look. Let Saguaro bathe you. If you fight Saguaro, Saguaro will hurt you when he does not want to."

He touched her face gently and then pulled the blanket off of her. Shannon sat there and let him, knowing that a struggle was hopeless. Soon this man would be using her like an object. She reddened under his gaze, and he gently touched the whites of her breasts with the back of his hand.

"You are . . . beautiful," he said softly. He ran a hand over her belly. "You are soft—pink, like peach fruit. Your eyes make Saguaro weak like puppy."

The remark surprised her, coming from a man of Saguaro's savage reputation. He brought the bucket of water closer and showed her a bar of soap.

"Look!" he said with a grin. "Saguaro know what white women like for washing. Saguaro has stolen this white wax for you that smells like flowers! You will like it!"

He dipped the soap into the water and lathered his hands, then gently rubbed the soap over her neck and arms, under her arms and over her breasts. In spite of her humiliation, the fresh soap smelled wonderful, and his gentle, massaging hands were wonderfully relaxing as they moved gently over her tired body. He wiped her off with a soft cloth.

"Get up," he commanded. She had no choice but to obey. She rose, then gasped in frozen dread as he jerked off her pantaloons and unbuttoned her shoes, ordering her out of them. He pulled off her stockings and ordered her to stand in the bucket. He dipped the soap again and lathered up her legs and bottom. Her heart pounded with dread, yet strangely, he did nothing insulting. He rinsed her off and dried her, even laying out a cloth for her to step on when she got out of the bucket so she would not get dirt on her still-wet feet.

"There now. Does that not feel better?" he asked her, slipping the tunic over her head and gently helping her sit down on the straw.

"Yes," she answered in an almost inaudible voice, pulling the tunic as far over her knees as possible and wondering just when he intended to have his way with her. Saguaro turned to build a small fire, and she watched him curiously. She could not quite determine just what this man had in mind. Surely it was something dreadful. Yet so far he had only been kind to her. She removed a barrette from the side of her hair and pulled all of her hair back, fastening it at the neck with the barrette. She pulled out her chain and cross, grasping the cross and the ring in her hand and praying that by some miracle she was not going to be harmed. Saguaro turned to look at her.

"What is that around your neck?" he asked her.

"You should know," she replied. "You said you knew some missionaries once."

"Their crosses did not have a man on them."

"I . . . I'm Catholic. Our crosses mean the same thing—faith in the Christ. Only our crosses show the body of Christ on them. That's how he died . . . on a cross. He was killed, and through his death our . . . sins . . . are forgiven." She grasped the cross tighter and blinked back tears. Would God forgive her for killing a man?

"I know of this Christ," Saguaro spoke up. "He is no different from our God. He die for cause, just as Apaches die for cause. Your missionaries say your God

190

make heavens and all land. Apaches believe same—that one God make sky and earth. Apache God is Usen. Usen make earth for all men, not to own in little pieces, but to share. Your people not follow their faith. They are filled with greed for land—gold—power. Want to own all Apache land and all Apaches, too. But they will never own Saguaro!"

Shannon gripped the cross tightly, fingering the ring next to it and wishing Bryce Edwards would come with his men and rescue her. But there would be no knight in shining armor now. There was only this very handsome but very frightening Indian chief on whom she could rely.

"Greedy white men—they kill my woman—my two sons! My woman was young, kind, beautiful. They rape her! Six of them! Many times over!" He was growling the words, pacing and clenching his fists. Shannon waited for him to come over and beat her and rape her for his revenge. "They cut up my baby sons, then torture and kill my wife. My whole family—killed before Saguaro's eyes while Saguaro was tied and forced to watch! This is how whites are! Saguaro will never forget. Never!"

"And . . . that's why you do . . . all this killing and looting now?" she asked, surprised that she had even been able to open her mouth and speak. Saguaro whirled and looked at her with fiery brown eyes.

"For that and for many other reasons! White man come to steal our land. Our women. Our horses. They take everything. Apache proud. He cannot sit and watch this happen. And he cannot live on filthy reservations, begging for food like dog! Apache must be free—strong—like wild animals!"

191

The way he ranted and raved reminded her of just such a wild animal, caged and frightened. She glanced down and pulled at a piece of straw.

"There is much pain and death on both sides, Saguaro, Your woman was killed by white men. And my man . . . the man I came out here to marry . . . was killed by Apaches. So, it goes on and on."

He softened slightly. "So," he said in a quieter voice. "You feel about your man as Saguaro feels about his woman. Death is cruel for those who are left behind. But those who die, they go to better life in great beyond. Sometimes I envy them."

Shannon's tears spilled down her cheeks and she wiped at them with shaking hands. Saguaro came closer and knelt in front of her, and she quickly pulled her tunic down even farther over her knees, praying she would not have to pull it back up so that this man could put her through the horror of rape.

"What are you called?" he asked her gently.

"Just . . . Shannon," she said, sniffing and wiping at more tears.

"Shannon," he repeated. "My woman, she was small like you. She was called Yellow Flower. Saguaro call you White Flower, because you are small like her, but you are fair like lilly." He wiped at her tears with wide, strong fingers. "Saguaro wishes to know about you. I have told you about my woman and my sons. Now, you tell Saguaro why you at station alone. Tell Saguaro about it. It is good to talk of such things."

She broke into sobbing and he pulled her onto his lap and gently rocked her. She knew she had done this before. Bryce! Bryce had held her this way after the awful attack by McGuire in the greenhouse.

192

"Stop crying and tell Saguaro what has happened," he told her calmly, still rocking her.

This is insane! she thought. Had she lost her mind, after all? She actually wanted to tell him. She actually wanted him to hold her, simply because she needed so much to be held. She needed someone else to be the strong one. And who else on God's earth did she have now but this man? Was he really telling the truth when he said he would not hurt her? Had she found a friend in this half-crazy savage Apache warrior? Who ever would have thought two years ago that Shannon Fitzgerald would end up sobbing in a primitive wickiup, dressed in a common tunic and spilling out her troubles on the shoulder of an Apache warrior?

Her story came pouring forth, and she wondered if it was truly she speaking to this Apache savage as though he were a friend. Yes. Surely she had lost her mind completely now. She no longer knew who she was, where she was. She ended by shouting that the soldier she was to marry had been killed by Apaches.

"Apaches!" she repeated, hate in her eyes. "Everything is so . . . so ugly and black and horrible! I wish . . . I was dead! Please kill me, Saguaro! Have your way with me and get it over with!" She covered her face and her shoulders shook with sorrow and shame and fear. "Why do you taunt me like this," she wept. "Making me wonder when you're going to put me through the awful pain and humiliation and torture!"

Saguaro scowled. "I already tell you. Apache not rape. But white man good at raping women. He has strange hunger for women—no control. From time he is born, Apache brave is taught strength, courage, patience and control. He is taught pride—"

"You're no different from the others!" she interrupted in a near hiss. "Go ahead and have your way, Apache savage! But you'll not have me willingly!"

Saguaro actually grinned and shook his head. "Still you not believe Saguaro. Why do you think Saguaro kill that man who hurt you? After seeing what happen to my Yellow Flower, no white man live who hurt woman. I save you from that man. If I wanted to take you, I would have done so by now. I tell you again, Apache not rape. Sometimes we sell our captives, but mostly we kill them or hold them for ransom."

"Then you will have to kill me or sell me!" she replied. "There is not a person alive now who would pay a cent for me! I'm worthless to you, Saguaro!"

Saguaro sighed and removed his quiver of arrows. The muscles of his powerful arms and shoulders rippled as he did so. He looked her over.

"Still you do not understand."

The softness in his voice and the gentleness in his eyes surprised her. She was trying very hard to hate this man—to bring out whatever horrible thing he intended for her. But nothing was working. Was he actually telling the truth?"

"You are most beautiful creature Saguaro ever see," he told her. "All over you are soft—white. Your nipples are color of flowers instead of brown. Your eyes are color of leaves and grass. Your hair shine like red clay. You are like part of earth. Saguaro keep you for himself and you not be harmed."

"If keeping me means taking me to your bed, then you do rape!" she sobbed. "Because that is all it would be!"

194

He shook his head and knelt in front of her. She stiffened as he reached out and touched her cheek.

"I tell you now, White Flower. Day will come when you will want Saguaro as a woman wants her own man. That is when Saguaro will make you his squaw. Saguaro not touch you until you smile at him and embrace him willingly."

"I'll never want another man! Let alone a savage killer! Your kind killed my man!"

"And your kind killed my woman! But it not matter now. None of us is really so different. I am man, you are woman. Saguaro treasures you like gold."

He unlaced her tunic and pulled it down over her shoulders to her waist, gazing lovingly at her breasts and gently touching them for a brief moment.

"All women need man—and all men need woman. It is what God wants. It is beautiful and right. It is not for mating that you need man. It is for his strength—his protection—and for man to plant life in your belly."

She felt sick at the thought that now he would push her down and she would be forced to give him what belonged to only one man. Now that man was dead, she would give herself to no one. But to her surprise he pulled the tunic back up and laced it as he continued to speak.

"Man need woman in many ways also," he told her. "He need her softness—her gentle touch. Man and woman draw on each other. Feed on each other. This is how it was with Saguaro and Yellow Flower. All was beautiful. Losing her was like losing my own life blood. Saguaro has wept alone many times over loss of family. At night Saguaro still hears their cries and screams. Saguaro need someone to take away blackness—

195

terrible sadness. Just as you need someone to do same for you after your attack and loss of your man. So . . . we will help each other."

Much as she wanted to argue the point, his words made sense. "I . . . I can't stay here, Saguaro," she told him, confused now. "I don't belong here."

"And where do you belong now? You say you cannot go back to place called Virginia. You say you have no one now. Your family is dead. Your man is dead. White man is cruel to you. You are alone and weak. If Saguaro take you back to your world, you will be abused, perhaps put in prison. You are better off with ten Apache bucks than even one white man! Would you rather Saguaro had not come, so that old man at station could hurt you?"

Her eyes teared anew. She could not answer his logic. Never had she felt so lost and alone. There was no other choice for her. Saguaro leaned forward and rubbed her cheek with his own.

"Saguaro not hurt you," he reassured her again. He suddenly left without another word, and minutes later he returned with a fistful of flowers. He handed them to her. Shannon took the flowers in near shock. This man was trying his best to please her. He was acting like a lovesick suitor.

"See?" he said with a dashing and unexpected grin. "Saguaro know what women like! I pick those earlier, when I saw you crying. But I want talk to you before I give them to you."

She studied the brilliant bouquet of mountain flowers. She thought of Bryce again and the night he had given her the beautiful ring. That had been over two years ago now. All of her plans and dreams were shattered. She would never see Bryce again. She would be wise now to accept this man's kindness as a godsend and not run from it. Where would she run?

"You won't . . . force yourself on me?" she asked, staring at the flowers.

"Saguaro is patient man," he told her. "It get dark now. We will sleep. Tomorrow you will meet all our women. Our women are kind—helpful. They teach you what is expected of squaw. They teach you to cook and gather wood and weave blankets. They teach you to make deerskin soft so that it is pleasant against skin when it is worn. They teach you how build house of sticks, and tipi, and how make food from things you would think cannot be eaten. You will have friends here—protection." He handed her another peach. "Here. Eat."

She took the peach quietly and bit into it.

"Saguaro himself will protect you," he continued. "He will be strong for you so you not cry alone. Saguaro no longer have to sleep alone and bear pain of his dreams about his wife and babies." He took the flowers she still held in one hand and plunked them into a can. "You like?"

"Yes, Saguaro. Thank you," she replied, relaxing a little more. The man flashed the handsome grin again.

"Saguaro keep himself clean," he said proudly. The way he was talking and trying to please her sounded strange, coming from such a big and powerful man. He removed his knee-high cowhide boots, which were brightly beaded. He removed his vest and jewelry. She was nearly finished with the peach, but could not finish it when she began to panic as he stood up and, to her complete shock, removed his pants and loincloth. He

197

stood before her completely naked. He was an amazingly handsome specimen of man, but that was her least concern at the moment. She moved back, wide-eyed, pulling her tunic as far over her legs as she could make it go. So, he had meant to have his way with her all along!

Saguaro grinned. "Saguaro never wear clothes when he sleep," he told her, throwing a blanket over the straw. "Come—lie down," he commanded rather sternly. "My woman must rest now."

She sat frozen in place. Saguaro sighed and shook his head.

"It is sad thing—the terrible fear men have planted in your heart, my White Flower. Now you think all men ugly and mean. Some day Saguaro show you this is not so. When will you learn to trust Saguaro?"

He grasped her arm, gently but firmly, and forced her over to the straw. "You must always obey your man," he told her sternly. "It is first rule of Apache buck. Disobedient woman shames her man. I am leader of this village. Do not shame me." He lay down beside her and pulled two blankets over them. "You not good squaw tonight. You not build fire like Saguaro tell you to do. But Saguaro not scold you this time. You are learning. You are tired and afraid."

Scold me! she thought. Saguaro pulled her close so that her back was to him. He bent his knees and fit them into the back of her legs, pulling the blankets over them and hugging her tightly, her head just beneath his chin.

"Now Saguaro not be alone at night. This has been good decision. You not have to be alone now—or afraid. See? Saguaro's arms protect you. Saguaro is strong and brave. He fears nothing."

It was all said matter-of-factly, without an ounce of conceit. Just simple fact. The bed was soft and very welcome after the hard ground she had slept on for three nights. And, much as she hated to admit it, his arms were welcome, after all. She began to believe he told the truth about not raping her. She closed her eyes and pushed herself even closer to him, and Saguaro smiled. She suddenly felt like a little girl in her father's arms, and she decided that for the moment, considering her predicament, this place was far better than what awaited her back East, or anyplace else, for that matter.

She thought of Bryce, wishing the arms around her were his. Yes, once she had known kindness in a man's arms, one glorious, beautiful afternoon, the last time she would ever see Bryce Edwards alive. She was glad now, glad she had been one with him, glad she had given him joy and pleasure, love and beauty in what was to become their last time together.

She wondered if she would wake up in the morning to find that the kindness Saguaro now offered her was going to change to cruelty and unbearable slavery. She drifted into a badly needed sleep, deciding that all she could do now was live each day and give no thought to the future. She had no future.

Chapter Twelve

Bryce Edwards sat alone behind his desk, smoking and drinking. Outside the coyotes howled, mingled with other strange sounds of the cool November night. He had come close to death after the grave wound he suffered at the hands of the Apache warrior, and very likely would have died if not for the strange ointment Saguaro had ordered smeared on his wound to slow the bleeding. Bryce knew that he literally owed his life to Saguaro, who could easily have taken it that day, and he had often thought about Saguaro since then, wishing he could know the man under different circumstances.

Because of his wound, Bryce was granted a month's leave as soon as he was well, to allow him to search for Shannon. He spent all of October searching, going as far east as El Paso. From there he had pursued his last hope—the Apaches. Cochise of the Chiricahuas and his father-in-law, Mangas Coloradas, were both at relative peace with the whites at that time. Bryce rode alone into Apache country to search out the men. He felt no particular fear. It was rumored the only chief causing trouble was Saguaro, who was hiding out in Mexico.

Bryce's hopes were dashed even more when, after long talks with both Apache chiefs, he was informed they knew nothing of any white woman captive. If Cochise or Coloradas knew of one, Bryce was certain they would have said so, and haughtily, demanding rifles for her return. Both men claimed Saguaro was in Mexico, but they did not know of any white woman captive with the marauding warrior. Bryce knew how rapidly the Indians could communicate their news to each other, through smoke signals and runners. No such messages had been sent to either Cochise or Coloradas.

The last remaining possibility, the one Bryce dreaded most, was that Shannon might be a slave of some Mexican bandit. Mexicans, not just the bandits but often the wealthier ranchers, bought and sold white women. The thought of it was torture to him. He had seen the results of such slavery. He had dispatched soldiers and spies into Mexico to search and ask questions, but they had come up with nothing, and, for the first time, Bryce was glad. He would rather find Shannon dead than to find her, or what would be left of her, at the hands of a Mexican.

Yet the only alternative was that she surely must be dead. He smoked quietly, staring vacantly at the wall. Death was the only conclusion he could reach. He would have to try to go from here and somehow manage without her. He would have to stop hoping and planning. There would be no life with Shannon Fitzgerald. He must try to forget her now—forget the

202

past and Virginia. He would never return there. It would be too painful. He had been full circle—rage, hatred, frustration, fits of temper, drinking, weeping, bedding Mona Jackson, sometimes almost violently, trying to wipe out all desire for Shannon.

Now he sat alone, with no feeings at all. He had decided his career and his life would be here in Arizona for good. Maybe someday, somehow, he would find a woman he could love enough to marry. It didn't much matter. He had wanted only Shannon that way. She would have been a sweet and good wife, a loving mother. But he would not feel her softness again, or hear her sweet voice. The poor girl had left a life of wealth and beauty in Virginia, driven out hurriedly by a torturous attack and probably rape, forced to kill a man and then flee to her own death. And Bryce Edwards would never forgive himself for not having married her before he left and forcing her to come West with him right then and there. If he had done that, his beloved Shannon would still be alive. She would be in his arms every night. She would—

The door opened and Private Reynolds entered. The young man's right arm hung limp at his side. It had been useless since he had been wounded by Saguaro's men three months earlier. There was now an even closer bond between Reynolds and Bryce, since they had been the only survivors of the massacre. Reynolds felt a deep allegiance to Bryce, certain that Bryce's quick action in bandaging up his wounds, in spite of his own pain and bleeding, had saved his life. Now Reynolds's arm was useless, but at least he was alive. He saluted Bryce with his left hand. Their eyes held in an unspoken bond.

"There's a man by the name of John Ward outside to see you, sir," Reynolds told Bryce. The young man felt deeply sorry for Bryce, knowing the inner torture he had suffered over the last several months. Bryce was a changed man. He seldom smiled now. He did not make ready conversation. He was harder. Yet he had retained his ability to be reasonable about the Indians.

"What does he want?" Bryce asked quietly.

"Says Apaches attacked his ranch, sir. Stole cattle and his little boy."

Bryce stood up, excited that possibly the Apaches had been Saguaro's Mescaleros. Saguaro was the only Indian he had not been able to question regarding Shannon. Even though Cochise and Mangas Coloradas knew of no white woman, that was not conclusive evidence that Saguaro did not know something. They had not seen or spoken to Saguaro in many months, because of their disagreement over Saguaro's raiding.

"Send him in!" Bryce commanded. Reynolds went out and returned moments later with a middle-aged man who stormed in, his eyes blazing.

"I'm Colonel Edwards, Mr. Ward. Have a seat," Bryce told the man.

"No, thank you!" the man snapped. "My stepson has been stolen! What are you going to do about it?"

"We'll do all we can, Mr. Ward. But you have to understand that we are very short of men out here. Tell me what happened."

"I've already reported it to Fort Buchanan. But they gave me the same answer you've just given me!" The man removed his hat and slapped it down on Bryce's desk. "I've got me a ranch east of here. My wife, Jesusa,

204

is a Mexican woman. She was captured a few years back by the Apaches and one of the bucks made her his woman. She had a son by the man. His name is Felix. She finally escaped to her own people. She's married to me now! She kept the boy because she was his ma and she loved him. But the Apaches came back last week and attacked us. Stole most of my cattle and stole the boy back! It was Cochise and his men!"

"Cochise?" Bryce was almost disappointed it was not Saguaro. And he also found the story hard to believe. "How do you know it was Cochise?"

"It was Cochise's bunch that captured her in the first place a few years back. So they're the likely ones who would want Felix. The Indians take great pride in their sons. I tell you it was Cochise!"

"I can't believe that, Ward." Bryce said tersely. "I know Cochise. He wouldn't just raid some ranch without a reason. He's been quite peaceful lately, and he even cuts wood for the Butterfield Overland. Besides, nearly all Apache raids are against Mexicans below the border. If Cochise had a beef with you, he would have come and told me about it first. He's a man of his word, and his last word was that he would cause no more trouble with the settlers, unless the settlers cause trouble for him."

"I said it was Cochise! My wife is a Mexican! She don't count as one of us in an Apache's eyes!"

"Then I'll go and talk to Cochise myself."

"Talk! If that's all you're gonna do, I'm gonna send word for more help out here—men who'll wipe out the Indians like they ought to be doin'! What the hell kind of lily-livered soldiers are they sendin' us, anyway! You ought to be out there cleanin' the Apaches out of the hills and the mountains and puttin' them on the reservation where they belong—or puttin' them in their graves! My woman's beside herself with grief, and all you're gonna do is talk?"

"Jumping to conclusions as you're doing will only lead to more bloodshed!" Bryce told the man. "This is how the wars get started, Ward! You have no proof whatsoever it was Cochise! Did you actually see Cochise himself?"

"Well, no, but—"

"Would you know him if you saw him?"

The man sighed. "No."

"Do you know how to tell one tribe from another? Can you tell a Chiricahua from a Mimbreno? A Mescalero from a Pinal Apache? Do you even know the difference between a Ute Indian and an Apache Indian? The Utes have been known to take women and children captives, Ward! Can you recognize a Navaho, or a Paiute?"

"Well, I—I know how to identify some of them—"

"But not all of them, right?"

"No!"

"Then let someone handle this who knows Indians and how to deal with them, Ward! Now I said I'd look into it, and I will!"

"I want Felix back! If you don't do it, I'll find someone who will!"

"And start a new wave of Indian wars?"

Ward stepped up closer to Bryce. "All I know is I've got me a cryin' woman who wants her son back! If every Apache in the territory, and every Ute and every Navaho has to be wiped out to find him, then so be it!"

*   *   *

206

Shannon lay in a fever in Saguaro's tipi. The combination of the delayed shock of her attack by Loren McGuire, the ordeal of her trip West and learning of Bryce's death, along with the terror of being taken captive and adjusting to an entirely different style of living, had taken their toll. She had been treated kindly by Saguaro, just as he had promised, but that had not been enough to ward off the inevitable collapse.

The past five months had simply handed Shannon Fitzgerald more than she was capable of enduring. She had lost too much too fast, and all of Saguaro's kindness and gentle caring could not make up for it. Now she had taken ill. No one was quite sure what her ailment was. But she had a dangerously high fever and frequent vomiting. Saguaro, who had very strong feelings for her now, sat by her side, while a painted and feathered medicine man voiced strange incantations over her, dusting her with strange herbs and waving magic instruments over her body and praying to their God.

Shannon clung to Saguaro's hand, aware now only of his presence. He had become her only refuge, this wickiup her only home, his people her only friends. In three months of living with this man and sleeping with him every night, Saguaro had never once offended her. He was her strength and her constant companion. She had even held him often in the night when he would wake up weeping for his dead wife and tiny sons, remembering the horror of their murders. She had lost all fear of this Apache chief who could be vicious and unforgiving outside of their little world.

Now Saguaro sat close to tears for fear of also losing his White Flower to death. He faithfully bathed her face in cool water and held her hair back from her face when she vomited. He kept her covered with a blanket she had helped to weave herself, remembering the day she had shown him her finished product and had presented it to him as a gift. He remembered the pride and the pleasure in her eyes.

"Saguaro, look what I've made!" she told him excitedly. "I've never made anything this beautiful before!"

Saguaro had taken the colorful blanket from her and studied it carefully.

"This is well done, White Flower," he told her. "It is woven so tightly it would hold water. I can tell. You learn quickly, my white squaw."

"It's . . . for you," she had told him bashfully. "For helping me . . . for giving me shelter and food and protection. You . . . you won't give me back, will you, Saguaro? You could probably get money for me from the white authorities." The old fear returned to her eyes.

"No," he had told her, touching her face. "You belong Saguaro now. Saguaro never take you back. And you are more Apache than you think," he added with a grin. "You killed the man who hurt you. That is good! You are good warrior."

Shannon smiled for him. "I don't want to talk about my past, Saguaro," she told him. "I would rather forget all of it . . . everything."

"It cannot be forgotten until you allow hurt to flow out of you, White Flower. You have not yet done this. You pretend you have forgotten. But Saguaro knows different. Day will come when pain will flow from you in crying and sickness. Only then will you be free from

208

it. You not talk about it. You not tell Saguaro truth when you say you forget. Saguaro see how you look upon the shining ring that your white man give you. Inside you still weep for him; and inside you still scream with fear at thought of that other man touching you."

He pulled her close and she rested her head on his broad, firm chest. "Day will come when you are ready, and you will be Saguaro's woman. Saguaro will know," he had told her then.

It had not been long after that when a small band of Mexicans had come across Shannon and three other Apache squaws bathing. The bandits had attacked the women, excited at seeing a white one among them. The women's screams had brought the Apache bucks running to their rescue. In minutes the bandits were captured and dragged back to camp to be properly punished for their attack. Saguaro had been especially cruel with them because of his fury at Shannon's having come close to being harmed. The men had suffered torture and mutilation.

But the attack on Shannon had taken its toll. She had sat in a stupor for a full day, Saguaro talking to her, trying to comfort her. And then the sickness had come, after several hours of uncontrolled sobbing and screaming. The medicine doctor told Saguaro it was her mind and her soul ridding itself of bad memories and deep fear.

"If she does not die, she will be stronger when she is well," he told Saguaro. "It will be better then. She will smile from the inside then, instead of just on the outside. She has not smiled from the inside for many moons."

And so, Saguaro sat and waited, studying the calluses on her delicate white hands, put there by work she was not accustomed to. But she had not complained, and had actually seemed to enjoy working and seeing the fruits of her labor.

Several times in her fever she had called out for the one named Bryce. Saguaro knew it was the name of the white man she had loved. She had never spoken the full name, and in consciousness had never voiced the name over the past three months—afraid that it would bring back all her sorrow. The name was familiar to Saguaro, but he could not remember why. It did not matter now. The man was dead. Saguaro would be her man now. He would love her as much as any man had loved her. She would not cry so much anymore.

To Saguaro's great relief, Shannon finally improved, after three days of tossing in a fever. She opened her eyes to see Saguaro still beside her, watching her with deep concern. He smiled.

"You are better?"

"I . . . what happened? The last thing I remember is those . . . those bandits!" Her breathing quickened, and he squeezed her hand.

"Do not move too much, White Flower. You are weak. You have been very sick. Do not think about the bandits. Dancing Bear, our medicine chief, has been praying to our God for you and has annointed you with healing herbs. He say your sorrows and your fears were crawling out of your skin to leave you forever, so that you can smile from the inside. Was he right?"

Shannon studied the handsome Apache who had been her whole world for three months now. "Do you . . . love me, Saguaro?"

He did not reply right away. He smoothed back her hair and thought for a moment. "You do not know this?" he finally replied. "All these days I have stayed by your side. I not leave you. I pray for you—even hold cross you wear and pray to your God. I hold your hand for many hours. I bathe you in cool water. And you do not know if I love you?"

"Why?" she asked, a tear slipping down the side of her face.

He smiled softly. "First day Saguaro see you, your weeping make him think of Yellow Flower. He see same look in your eyes—the fear. He see goodness in you, too. And he remember terrible screams of Yellow Flower. Saguaro want show you that Apache not always bad like whites think. He does not always torture, or attack without reason. He can be kind. Saguaro want help you. Saguaro has very . . . very strong . . . feelings for you." Their eyes held. "Saguaro want very much to make you his woman in body, but he has kept his word to you, has he not?"

"Yes, you have. You've been wonderful to me, Saguaro. If not for you—"

"And what are your feelings for Saguaro? Do you love Saguaro?"

She studied his perfect physique and the dark, handsome face.

"I . . . I'm not sure yet, Saguaro. I think I must love you. Yet I'm not ready to fulfill that love. And my heart is still so full of someone else."

211

"It is enough to hear you say that much," he replied with a smile. He tucked the blankets around her. "You rest now."

Shannon rested for three more days, Saguaro not allowing her to get up. On the fourth day he came inside painted fiercely and bedecked with ornaments around his neck and around his muscular biceps, beads and feathers woven into his lustrous hair. He looked grand, by Indian standards, and just as grand by white standards, yet his painted, dark body almost frightened Shannon. He whisked her up in his arms, keeping a blanket wrapped around her.

"Come! Today we celebrate your recovery! Saguaro declare day of feasting—dancing—games. You will watch Saguaro win all the games!"

He made the statement matter-of-factly, and Shannon had to laugh. Indians had a strange way of boasting without really being conceited. An Indian buck was apparently expected to brag about anything he was good at. Saguaro had told her many times over about some of his exploits and great battles.

Outside everything was commotion. Drums beat rhythmically, while men and women alike danced in circles, dressed in costumes so magnificent that Shannon couldn't think of words to describe them. Every color there ever was seemed to be included in the beads and jewelry and feathers—and every color was brilliant and deep. Bells jingled on ankles and wrists, in timing with the stomping feet and jerking movements of the dancers' bodies.

Women walked up to Shannon and laughed and

showered her with flowers, and Saguaro carried her around, proudly displaying her as though she were a prized treasure. He placed her on a rock to watch the dancing and the games.

For the rest of the day, women brought her food of every variety. Vegetables and venison. Peaches and beans. And Shannon could see that this was going to be Saguaro's day to show off for her. This was his day to show Shannon Fitzgerald that she had the strongest, fastest, bravest Apache man in the whole tribe.

The first thing Saguaro did was join the dancing, letting out a chilling scream and jumping into the center of the circle of dancers. He began a one-man war dance, gyrating and bending, circling and screaming terrifying war whoops that would put fear in any man's heart. He was a commanding and hypnotic figure as he swung hatchets and lances.

"Saguaro very brave chief," one of the older women told Shannon. There were no more than one or two women in the entire village who could speak Shannon's language. "He has even gone through torture of proving his courage and manhood. Have you not seen scars on his chest and the insides of his arms?"

"Yes, but I thought perhaps an animal—"

"They are scars of one who has endured pain beyond consciousness. Pain to test his strength. Have you not heard of this test for the bravest of Apache bucks?"

"I . . . I know little about your people," Shannon replied, watching Saguaro jump and scream.

"The flesh is pierced, and pieces of bone are inserted through it . . . at the breasts, arms, legs. Leather strings are hooked to bone, and warrior is hung by skin for many hours."

213

Shannon's eyes widened and she turned to look at the woman.

"Ai," the woman said with a smile, enjoying the shock in Shannon's eyes. "Saguaro go through this test. For days before that, he not allowed to eat, so that he was weakened even more. I remember how Yellow Flower wept for him, but she was not allowed to go to him. The test was his choice, something he learn from Cheyenne and Comanche. But his faith was strong. Our God helped him survive. And he is a stronger man for it. Saguaro is great leader."

Shannon swallowed and began to perspire.

"You are liked by our people," the old woman went on. "But Saguaro's love for you will be his ruin. Nothing and no one has ever defeated Saguaro. But you are different. You come from the white man's world, and one day you will want to go back to it. And when you do, Saguaro will never be same. He will be broken man."

The woman quickly left, and Shannon watched after her for a moment. The words left her with a strange, uneasy feeling. How could she go back to her own world now? There was nothing there for her. No. She would always stay with Saguaro. She was learning the Apache ways, and she was beginning to feel safe and settled and secure for the first time in a very long time. It was comforting.

Saguaro concluded his dance, then took a long drink from a leather pouch. He brought the pouch over to Shannon.

"You like my dancing?"

She glanced at his scars. Was she actually falling in love with this wild, primitive man who allowed himself

214

to be hung by the flesh just to prove his manhood?

"Yes, I did, Saguaro," she told him with a smile. He held up the pouch to her.

"It is called *tizwin*. It is good drink made from corn. The Indian buck drinks it when he wants to feel happy—like the firewater the white man drinks. You have some. It good for casting out the sickness."

Shannon took the pouch and smelled the home-made liquor. She wrinkled her nose.

"Oh! No thank you, Saguaro! I'll get well my own way!"

Saguaro laughed and took a long swallow. As he drank, he saw the old fear coming back into her eyes. He finished drinking and handed the pouch to another buck.

"You think Saguaro get drunk and not be kind to his woman, ai?"

"Something like that," she said, losing her smile.

"Then I will drink no more *tizwin*. There. See? Saguaro want only to please you."

He walked off to begin the games. For the rest of the afternoon Shannon watched him win at wrestling, hatchet throwing, arrow shooting and racing. He came close to being defeated in the race, but he drew on his inner determination to show White Flower that he was the best, and in one last spurt he defeated his opponent.

Everyone cheered, and Shannon found herself yelling and laughing and clapping along with the others. It suddenly hit her that she was enjoying herself for the first time in over two years. She was safe here. She was cared for. And she was loved. It felt so good to be loved. Saguaro was coming toward her now, raising his arms in victory. When he reached her their eyes held, and his heart leaped at the new look in her eyes. She was looking at him as a man instead of just a friend or a brother. He grabbed her up in his arms.

"Saguaro hot from race. And you need to bathe after your long sickness. We will go now together to bathing pool."

He snapped an order to one of the squaws, who giggled and ran to Saguaro's tipi, returning with clean clothes for both of them, and a blanket. Shannon reddened as the others laughed and made remarks that she could not understand, but which she knew were teasing remarks about their great leader taking his white squaw to bathe. Saguaro walked off with an unprotesting Shannon.

"No one will bother us," he assured her. She put her arms around his neck and her head on his shoulder as they walked. They reached the splashing waterfall and sparkling clear stream, deep in a very small canyon of the Sierra Madres, and Saguaro set Shannon on her feet.

"How you feel?" he asked her. "Can you stand?"

"I'm fine, Saguaro," she replied. He watched her blush as she always did when he removed her clothes. He then removed his own and carried her into the water, taking along the bar of white woman's soap. Then he lathered her up, even washing her hair. She stayed in the water and swam around while Saguaro washed. He watched her nude body beneath the water. He wanted her as he had never wanted her before, but he did not want to frighten her. He dove back into the water, then came up beside her. Shannon screamed as he grabbed her. Then they both fell back into the water laughing.

"I must get you out before you get too cold," he told her. He stood up and lifted her out of the water, carrying her to the blanket. He set her on it and wrapped it around her.

"You feel better now?" he asked her.

"Oh, yes, Saguaro!" she replied excitedly.

"Our medicine man was right," Saguaro told her, standing up and wringing out his hair. "You smile from inside now." He sat down naked in the grass beside her. Shannon threw her head back so that the warm sun could soak into it.

"Saguaro," she spoke up, her head back and her eyes closed. "Tell me how you got your name. What does it mean?"

"Saguaro is name of tallest cactus plant of the whole Apache country! It stand for courage and strength. The saguaro cactus grows taller than all others," he said, waving his hand. "It can bear all things—heat, cold, water, drought. It only grows taller and stronger each year, its arms reaching up to heavens. It is also a provider. Its fruit can be eaten and can be made into many things."

He stood up and faced her, holding out his arms. "Is not Saguaro like the tall cactus that can withstand all things?"

Shannon studied the magnificent physique, and for the first time since her beautiful afternoon with Bryce she allowed her eyes to rest for a moment on that part of a man that she had learned through Bryce could be beautiful, but that had become ugly to her after the attack by Loren McGuire. She felt a desire she had not experienced since Bryce Edwards had spent that one lovely afternoon teaching her about man and love and

217

being one, sharing bodies in glorious giving and taking. She had been so curious then, so afraid. How long ago had that been? Two and a half years already! She had wanted Bryce so much then. She remembered the mysterious thrill she had felt when he grasped her hips and pressed her against himself, the first beautiful pain of intercourse, and then the ecstasy of sharing him again without the pain.

She looked down at the ground then. "Yes, Saguaro. You are like the tall and strong cactus."

Saguaro had seen the new and strange look in her eyes. His heart leaped with joy. He sat down beside her.

"I must tell you I am leaving you soon, White Flower," he said. "My people are getting hungry. This feast we had today—we used our best foods to celebrate. But there is not much left, and hunting here is not so good right now. I go to hunt for a place farther north where we be safe and where hunting is better. And I will do more raiding and get us more supplies."

Shannon felt her heart breaking at the thought of his leaving her. "Saguaro, don't leave me alone!" she told him, her breathing quickening.

"It not be for long. Perhaps one moon—maybe two."

"Two months! What will I do without you for two months! Saguaro, I need you! You're my protection—my friend!"

Saguaro turned to face her, putting a hand to the side of her face. "Many braves will stay to protect you. You can stay with some of the other women whose husbands will go with me. You will not be alone or unprotected. Saguaro must do this."

"But what if you don't come back!" she suggested,

her eyes tearing.

"My people would care for you, because you were Saguaro's squaw. You would always have home here. This is their promise to Saguaro. You not be traded or sold or forced to take another man against your will."

"But I wouldn't want to be here without . . . without you!" she whispered. She turned away from him and Saguaro moved closer. He pulled the blanket off her shoulders and gently massaged her neck and shoulders as he spoke.

"When an Apache buck rides off into danger, it is custom for his squaw to let him mate with her first. It give his mind something to dwell on if he is wounded, it help him want to stay alive. He must return to his woman."

He was afraid she would turn away from him completely at the remark. But she reached up and touched his hand, then turned to face him.

"One of the old women of your tribe . . . told me . . . I would ruin you," she said quietly. "Because I come from a different world, I will some day destroy you. I would never want to do that, Saguaro."

Their eyes held as they spoke. Both knew what the other was thinking.

"You should not listen to the old women," he replied.

"I want . . . to give you something to come home to, Saguaro," she whispered, closing her eyes. Tears trickled down her cheeks. Saguaro's heart beat hard with joy and desire. She wanted him! She finally wanted him!

"I have only . . . been with a man once," she continued, reddening. "My . . . soldier. It was . . . a day much like this one. He was also going away. I was so afraid. And I loved him so! We both wanted . . . wanted to make sure that if something happened . . ." She met the dark eyes. "It was the last time I ever saw him alive." More tears slipped down her cheeks and he leaned forward and brushed her cheek with his own.

"It will not be our last time," he whispered. He opened the blanket the rest of the way and laid it out flat behind her. He bent down and lightly tasted one nipple, and she whimpered with a mixture of fear and intense desire. She touched his hair, and he moved up to her neck and her cheek, lightly touching her skin with his tongue.

"I . . . it was . . . so long ago," she whispered. "It might hurt."

"Saguaro not hurt you, Saguaro make you cry out with pleasure."

He encircled her with one arm and pressed against her, his chest pushing on her breasts as he gently forced her down onto the blanket. "My White Flower!" he whispered reverently. "You take away Saguaro's deep pain for the want of his dead wife! I have wanted you for so long!"

"Please don't hurt me!" she begged.

"Saguaro never harm his woman," he told her, gently running one hand over her breasts and belly, ever downward until his fingers gently probed between her thighs. She closed her eyes, waves of acute excitement flowing through her.

For a moment memories of Bryce pierced her heart. His touch had sent the same fire through her veins, making her want to open herself to him as Saguaro was now making her want to do. But this was not Bryce. This was Saguaro, and she must think only of him now, because he was all she had. He was good to her. He loved her.

"Saguaro make you cry out in pleasure, not fear and pain," he was telling her. He rubbed his chest against her breasts and lightly licked them while his fingers continued to stroke her in places she never dreamed she would be able to allow a man to touch again. She found herself running her hands over his rock-hard arms and shoulders.

Shannon opened her eyes and noticed the contrast between her lily-white hands and his very dark skin. He hovered over her, dwarfing her beneath his large frame. Their eyes met, and she saw nothing but glorious love in his deep, dark, Apache eyes that now burned with passion instead of hatred and revenge.

"You be Saguaro's squaw now," he told her. "Do not be afraid, my White Flower. You are like the lily—delicate and fragrant. You are Saguaro's gift from God—just as our God gives us the gift of air and water, food and animals."

She closed her eyes again as he tasted her breasts and his lips moved down to her belly. She wanted very much to rediscover the beauty of this act, to love and be loved, to belong someplace, to someone.

Saguaro gently caressed her belly with his cheek, then moved back to her breasts and neck, cautiously pushing her legs apart with his knees. He felt her stiffen. "Do not be afraid, White Flower," he assured her again.

She closed her eyes and gritted her teeth and he suddenly pushed. She screamed out at first. It had been a long time and it was almost like the first time all over again. But then Saguaro was there, close, reaching

221

under her back, pulling her up tight against himself, whispering to her of love, praising her beauty.

He spoke softly and moved rhythmically, and she found herself beginning to move with him then, wanting him, filled with a great joy and pleasure, excited that she could truly enjoy this act once again. It was not Bryce. If only it could be! But this man loved her and would protect her. He had saved her life and then had sat faithfully by her side when she was violently ill.

His hands moved down to reach under her hips, grasping her and pushing her up as she cried out his name. She felt a sudden pulsating desire, and her fingers dug into his back. Moments later, with one hard thrust deep in her belly, Saguaro's life poured into her.

They both lay limp and sweetly satisfied, not speaking for several seconds.

"You are all right?" he finally asked. Shannon hugged him around the neck.

"I am very happy, Saguaro!" she said, half crying. "Will you look forward to coming back now?"

Saguaro raised up and smiled his broad and fetching grin.

"Ai," he told her. "Saguaro has much to look forward to. And yet today, we will be married Apache way. It will be good ending to my day of celebration. You give me much to celebrate. We will marry, and all will know you belong only to Saguaro—forever."

"I . . . never thought . . . it could be like this for me, Saguaro," she told him. "I know that my white man would have made it like this for me. He wasn't like the others. He was good and kind like you. Strong and brave like you. He knew how to be gentle with his woman, like you. But he is dead now. You will be my man, Saguaro. I want very much to be your squaw. I will be good. Perhaps I will give you sons who will help you bear the loss of the little sons that you lost."

"Perhaps. Saguaro has planted seed in your belly. Saguaro pray that seed takes root."

"And I will pray for the same, Saguaro. I want a child, to help me forget the past and look to the future."

Saguaro pulled her close and spoke in a whispered voice.

"Tonight we will do this again. We will do it many times before Saguaro leaves White Flower in two days. Tonight the drums will beat and the men will dance while Saguaro and White Flower are melted together in their newfound love."

Shannon gripped him tightly around the neck. "Hold me, Saguaro!" she whispered. "It's so wonderful to have someone who loves me! So wonderful to feel safe!"

They lay there for several minutes, then he picked her up and carried her back to the stream.

"Now Saguaro must wash you all over again!" he said with a grin. Shannon laughed as he fell into the water with her.

"Saguaro, I want to show you something!" she told him, hanging on to his neck.

"You have already shown me everything, my white squaw," he teased. Shannon blushed and put her head on his shoulder.

"No. There is one little thing I want to show you. It is something the white man and woman do to show their affection."

223

"And what is that?"

She grasped his face between her hands and parted her lips slightly, then placed them against his. At first Saguaro did not react, and Shannon kept kissing him until he suddenly moaned lightly and parted his lips slightly, moving his head and sitting down in the water with her. He ran a hand over her body and kissed her harder, quickly catching on to the very nice white man's custom. He finally released her and their eyes held.

"That is a kiss," Shannon told him. "And there is usually a lot of it done between a man and a woman who have strong feelings for each other."

Saguaro grinned. "Saguaro likes this kissing," he told her. He planted his lips on hers again and pulled her close, and Shannon knew she had found a new world and a new life—and a new love. She would truly be Saguaro's woman now—completely.

224

Chapter Thirteen

It was late January of 1861 when the very young man appeared at Bryce Edwards's desk and put out his hand confidently, speaking in a haughty voice. "Colonel Edwards, I'm Lieutenant George Bascom."

Bryce met the young man's eyes, seeing already that the young officer, fresh from the East with fifty-four of his own men, was eager to make a name for himself in this new frontier. Bryce sighed, tired of inexperienced men. He had spent the entire day drilling more green troops, and the news he had just received of Bascom's arrival did not set well with him.

He rose from his chair and returned Bascom's salute. "Bascom," he replied coolly. "And what are you and your men doing here?" he asked wearily.

"Well, sir, Washington knows how busy you are, and shorthanded. So they've sent me out with orders to root out this Apache called Cochise and punish him for the kidnapping of one Felix Ward. I'm also to recover the cattle Cochise stole. This Ward fellow has all of Arizona in an uproar, of which I'm sure you are already aware."

225

Bryce almost laughed at the casual way the young man had stated his duty, as though finding Cochise would be like chasing down a child and spanking its bottom.

"Whose orders are you under?" he asked, sitting down on the edge of his desk and lighting a cigar.

"Colonel Hardin—of Washington, sir. I am merely here to meet you and pay a formal visit and inform you of my mission. However, you have no control over my actions, sir, if you'll pardon the tone of that statement. No disrespect intended."

"Mmmm-hmmm." Bryce puffed the cigar. "Well, Lieutenant Bascom, it so happens I know the Apaches like the back of my hand, and I'm telling you Cochise did not take those cattle or the boy. I've already met with the man. He claims it was probably Pinal Apaches that did it."

Bascom grinned and paced. "Come now, Colonel Edwards. We all know how tricky the Indians are—and how they lie."

Bryce bristled and stood up. "Do we? I only know how we lie to the Indians!"

Bascom reddened slightly as Bryce continued. "Do you know how to tell one Apache tribe from another—or even how to tell an Apache from a Navaho, Lieutenant Bascom?"

"That is beside the point," the young man snapped. "I merely came here to pay you a cordial visit, Colonel Edwards, and to ask for your help. But I can see you'll be of no help whatsoever."

"You don't want my help, Bascom. You're enjoying your authority and you want to rub it in. Makes you

226

feel important."

"You have no right—"

"I have every right!" Bryce snapped. "I've been through hell out here trying to keep the peace. You go making trouble for Cochise, and Arizona will have a lot more trouble on its hands than the raiding of a few ranches. He'll join up with Saguaro of the Mescaleros, and Mangas Coloradas of the Mimbrenos, and no settler, no miner, and not even the towns will be safe. Up to this point, most Apache raids and wars have been against the Mexicans, with whom they have had a long and bitter dispute. The whites are relatively safe around here right now. I've worked hard at keeping that peace. Cochise and Mangas Coloradas have both been peaceful lately and have kept their promises of no raiding. Cochise even has an agreement with the stage line to cut wood for the station at Apache Pass. The only troublemaker we've had has been Saguaro, and even he has been quiet lately." He sighed and put out his cigar. "I can't understand why in hell the government sends boys out here who are still wet behind the ears."

Bascom's face turned beet red. His jaw flexed in anger. "I am aware, Colonel Edwards, of your long experience with the Indians. Perhaps you have been out here too long." The man's eyes gleamed. "Perhaps you have become too close with the Apaches to think logically any longer."

Bryce's eyes blazed. "My purpose out here has been and always will be to keep the peace. There have been some terrible wrongdoings on both sides, Bascom. If the army begins to join the rest of the whites out here in

227

their ignorant prejudice against the red man, there will be nothing but more bloodshed to pay. I'm warning you to leave Cochise alone. He is not the man you want. John Ward has been stirring up trouble against Cochise ever since that raid. And he has not one ounce of proof that it was Cochise and his men who took the boy."

The very proud Lieutenant Bascom tried to stand a little taller, but he was unable to talk to Bryce without looking up slightly, which irritated him. He blocked out everything Bryce had said, reminding himself that Washington considered his mission very important, and that if he succeeded, he could get a promotion and no longer be under the thumb of senior officers such as Bryce Edwards.

"I have my orders," he said, glaring at Bryce. "I intend to show Cochise and all the others that the army means business! They cannot get away with these raids!"

Bryce snickered. "You'll find out what they can get away with!"

Bascom sighed and fingered his hat. "My men and I will be staying here at the fort tonight. In the morning we move out to the station at Apache Pass, where I will attempt to make contact with Cochise myself."

"And?"

Bascom cleared his throat. "I'll . . . talk to the man. I simply want to meet him for myself and hear his story from his own lips. I certainly can't go back to Washington without even having a little powwow now, can I?"

"No tricks, Bascom, or there'll be hell to pay."

"No tricks," Bascom replied. He saluted briskly to Bryce and quickly left.

It was easier to contact Cochise than Bascom had thought possible. He merely visited James Wallace, the station attendant at Apache Pass, and discovered Wallace knew Cochise well and could contact the man with messages. Bascom left Ward the message that he was there on a peaceful mission to bring Cochise news from Washington, then moved his troops out of Apache Pass to be sure he could not be trapped by Indians who might lurk among the canyon walls. Then it was only a matter of waiting, for he could see that Cochise trusted James Wallace.

By the second morning of his encampment, Cochise, with his wife Nahlekadeya, his son Nachise, and a brother and two nephews rode into Bascom's encampment, trusting the bluecoat soldier that he was only there to talk. Cochise sat tall and proud on his mount, halting the horse and telling one of the soldiers to go and tell Lieutenant Bascom that he had come to parlay with him, with only friendly intentions.

"Oh, yes sir, Mr. Cochise!" the young and excited sergeant told the Indian. He ran toward a large tent on the far side of the circle of tents, and Cochise studied the young man as he hurried away.

"A boy," he thought. The soldier had not looked like much of a warrior to Cochise. The proud Indian dismounted and the rest of his family followed suit. The sergeant came hurrying back and ordered two other men to take care of the Indians' horses.

"Just follow me," the sergeant told Cochise. Cochise thought the man seemed overly excited and nervous, but he merely attributed it to the fact that the young man from the East had probably never seen an Indian before. Cochise thought it rather humorous. Did the boy expect Cochise to lift his scalp? The Indian almost laughed as he and his family followed the sergeant into a very large tent, where a man in a fancy uniform stood to greet them.

"I'm George Bascom," the bluecoat said with a friendly smile. He put out his hand to Cochise. Cochise shook it. The Indian introduced his family, and Bascom greeted all of them warmly. Outside, soldiers were surrounding the tent, unknown to Cochise. Only the back, which was next to wild shrubbery, was left unguarded.

Bascom visited with Cochise for several minutes, asking how he liked getting paid to bring wood to Apache Pass, what problems he was having with settlers and miners, and other small talk. Cochise complained that his father-in-law, Mangas Coloradas, was having considerable trouble being hassled by the unruly miners from the new mining town, Pinos Altos, which had sprung up like a mushroom after a new gold strike the year before in New Mexico. Bascom swore he would look into those problems. Cochise was about to go into another problem when Bascom looked at the entrance to the tent and suddenly rose from the circle in which they had been sitting on the floor. His face immediately changed to a frightening hardness, his eyes now filled with hate and icy condemnation. Cochise was amazed at the sudden drastic change, and totally confused. What had he said? Bascom pointed an accusing finger at Cochise, standing in front of the man with his feet apart.

"Where are you keeping the boy, Felix!" he demanded. "Tell me, Cochise, or it will not go well for you and your family!"

Cochise looked at his family in surprise. All were alarmed and puzzled. They rose, and Cochise now looked down at Bascom.

"I not know what you mean," the Indian said truthfully to Bascom. "I do not understand—"

"You know exactly what I'm talking about!" Bascom roared, his face reddening with anger. "You are now my prisoner, Cochise! You tell me who raided the Ward ranch and where the boy Felix is at this very moment. You have him, don't you? You took the boy Felix and stole Mr. Ward's cattle. I demand their return, or you will be my prisoner forever. I will allow you to send one of your nephews back to get the boy!"

Cochise's eyes turned to stone. He looked down a proud nose at the young upstart of a lieutenant.

"Cochise has already spoken to Colonel Edwards about the Ward raid," the Indian said, his voice now cold and unfriendly. "Cochise not commit this crime. Cochise not lie! I give word that I will try harder to find who did this thing. I will get boy and cattle back for you, if I can."

"Your word?" Bascom sneered. "The word of a warring, filthy, ignorant Apache renegade? You're a liar, Cochise! You already know exactly where that boy is! You'll soon learn you can't toy with the United States Army, Cochise! And I'm no patsy like Colonel

Edwards! I'll have you imprisoned and beaten until you tell me where that boy can be found. My duty is to find him, and find him I will!"

Cochise could hardly believe the way this bluecoat was behaving. He ranted and raved like a child having a temper tantrum. Cochise actually snickered. "Surely you joke!" he told Bascom. "I already tell you, Cochise knows nothing of boy. It is my belief it was Pinal Apaches who take child. Perhaps Coyoteros. Cochise will ask. It is possible they will accept ransom for boy and cattle."

"How stupid do you think I am, Cochise? I let you out of here to do your dealing, and you never come back. When I'm through with you and your family, someone will tell me the truth!"

It finally hit Cochise that this man truly meant to keep him as a prisoner.

"Cochise not lie!" the Indian snarled. "White soldier lies! And white man at stage station lie!"

Before Bascom realized what was happening, Cochise moved his hand to his side and whipped out a large knife, just as soldierse began entering the tent to arrest all of the Apaches. Cochise slashed out at Bascom, and the soldier jumped back as Cochise moved fast as lightning to slash a large hole in the back of the tent, through which he disappeared.

"Get him, men!" Bascom screamed the order. Those ouside the tent thought Cochise was still inside, and more soldiers poured in so that all was confusion in the small enclosure. Those already inside the tent scrambled to get through the hole Cochise had cut, but they all struggled at once and none could get through.

"You idiots!" Bascom seethed. "He's getting away!"

232

Cochise's wife clung to her son in terror as soldiers surrounded the rest of Cochise's family. "Take them all away and tie them!" Bascom growled, thoroughly irritated at Cochise's wily escape. He was furious at being outwitted by the Indian and totally embarrassed. "Watch that woman and boy—and those men!" he screamed out to his men. "Cochise is bound to come back for them! I'll be damned if I'll go back to Washington without accomplishing my mission here! We'll use his family as ransom for the Ward boy!"

Guns were being fired outside, and Nahlekadeya began to cry for fear of what was happening to her husband. Nachise watched everything in wide-eyed fascination, confused as to why these bluecoats were trying to hurt his father. But Cochise was already far into the hills, paying no heed to a bleeding side where he had been grazed by a soldier's bullet. He only kept running, filled now with rage and humiliation and fear for his family.

In minutes, the soldiers camp was far behind the Indian chief. He made his way on foot through rocks and gulleys, through streams and canyons, running—running back to his village as fast as he could go, vowing to take revenge for the trick that had been played on him. The first one to suffer would be Wallace, who he was sure had conspired with Bascom to get Cochise to go to the soldier's camp to be trapped there. He reached his own village by nightfall.

That night the drums beat loud and long in Cochise's village, as warriors danced around fires, praying for their God to fill them with the courage and fortitude they would need for battle.

"They will all pay for their trick!" Cochise vowed over and over. The painted, screaming dancers joined in his thirst for vengeance. By morning, seventy warriors with grotesquely painted masks and grand apparel and an array of weapons were ready to make war on the white soldiers. Cochise would never again trust the white man. There would be no more peace! From now on the Apache name would fill the white man with a fear he had never before known!

It did not even dawn on the thoroughly upset and angry Lieutenant Bascom until late the next morning that perhaps he should dispatch a few men to Apache Pass to warn James Wallace that Cochise might be after him. He sent four men to carry the message and kept the rest of his enforcements camped on the same spot where they had been the day before when Cochise escaped their trap. Bascom prepared for a fight, as he expected Cochise to descend upon them at any time to rescue his family. He thought of seeking out Bryce Edwards's advice, but he simply could not bring himself to admit to Bryce that he had bungled his mission.

Cochise arrived at Apache Pass ahead of the soldiers who had been sent to warn Wallace. He called Wallace out of the station, and the man walked out to Cochise quite willingly, unaware of what had taken place in Bascom's tent. He was, in fact, accompanied by two other men, Charles Culver, the station agent, and another man, by the name of Walsh. Both men wanted Wallace to introduce them to the famous Cochise. But as soon as they got close to the Indian chief, they were immediately surrounded by Cochise's warriors, who had remained in hiding until that moment.

"What the hell is this?" Wallace demanded to know.

"You call yourself my friend, white man!" Cochise sneered. "Cochise was fool to trust pale-faced liars who smile at him and put out hand to him!"

Wallace swallowed. "Cochise, I don't know what you're talkin' about! What happened?"

"Soldiers hold my woman—my son!" The chief lashed out with a small whip and knocked the man to the ground. The two men who accompanied Wallace started running, and the four soldiers sent by Bascom just then arrived. The man named Culver was shot in the back by an Apache warrior as he reached the door to the stage depot. He screamed out, throwing his arms out and falling forward. In the confusion, as the man named Walsh also ran from Cochise, one of the soldiers shot him by mistake, thinking he was one of Cochise's men because he had long hair.

The soldiers ducked behind rocks as Cochise and his men circled their horses around the stage station, yipping and howling their war cries and dragging a screaming Wallace behind Cochise's horse on a rope.

Then Cochise stopped and dismounted, picking up the bleeding Wallace and throwing him facedown over the neck of his horse. He remounted and shouted out to the hiding soldiers.

"Tell your leader—Bascom—he has not heard last of Cochise!" the Indian shouted. "Tell him come here—to station at Apache Pass—at sunrise. We will talk! Tell him bring Cochise family—or Wallace dies! Cochise has spoken!"

The Indians fired shots into the air and quickly melted into the rocks. A dry wind howled through Apache Pass, where all was now eerily silent.

"I think we've got ourselves an Indian war," one of the soldiers commented to the others. "And I ain't lookin' forward to tomorrow."

Chapter Fourteen

The next morning Cochise and his warriors rode for Apache Pass, attacking a wagon train on the way and leaving eight Mexicans tied to the wheels of the burning wagons. All members of the wagon train were brutally murdered, and two American men were taken prisoner. At Apache Pass, Bascom and his men waited. They buried the two men who had been killed there the day before. Birds sang and it was a beautiful day. It was a chilling thought that such a lovely morning just might turn into a day of death and disaster.

"Do you think we're in for a big one, sir?" a private asked Lieutenant Bascom.

"We'll see," Bascom replied quietly, gazing around nervously at the rocky canyon and feeling an eerie presence. He half wished Bryce Edwards were there with them. He knew nothing about fighting Indians, and Bryce knew everything. But there was no way he was going to go to Bryce for help.

It was only an hour later when war cries could be heard, along with thundering horses, somewhere beyond the canyon. The frightening sounds came closer, and the soldiers took their places as the Indians suddenly appeared out of the hills and rock formations. Bascom walked out to stand before the approaching Apaches, looking brave but starched. Beneath his uniform he was sweating profusely. Cochise's family was kept hidden inside a tent. The Indians stopped at one end of the canyon and Cochise's voice boomed out for all to hear, as it echoed through the high canyon walls of Apache Pass.

"Bascom!" the Indian called. He rode in a little closer, pulling Wallace along on a lariat tether. Wallace was groaning and weeping. Bascom faced Cochise halfway between the troops and the large band of painted Apaches. Cochise looked fierce and hard now, and Bascom was determined not to let the man intimidate him with his grotesque warpaint and commanding size. The fearful-looking Indian chief rode up close to Bascom and looked down his nose at the bluecoat.

"White Father in Washington stupid!" Cochise sneered. "He send child to deal with men!"

"Now wait a minute!" Bascom growled. Cochise placed a lance against the man's chest and Bascom swallowed and stood frozen.

"I want my family—all of them! Now! I have two other prisoners besides Wallace! Give me my people now, or all die!"

Bascom's eyes hardened. "You kill me, and every soldier in the nation will be after you, Cochise!" he snapped. "I'll not give your people back."

"Listen to him!" Wallace begged. He sobbed as he pleaded with Bascom. "They're gonna kill me, you

238

ignorant bastard! They think I tricked them into going to you so you could capture them. Tell them it's a lie!"

Bascom remained silent, affronted at being called names by the worthless civilian who stood there pleading for his life. He refused to meet Wallace's eyes. Instead, Bascom kept his eyes on Cochise.

"You Indians must learn that the army will not be so soft from now on!" he said haughtily.

"There is difference between softness and wisdom!" Cochise snapped. "You not know difference. Bring out my family, or lives of three of your people will be on your head!"

"You underestimate our determination, Cochise!" Bascom replied. "Do you really think you can ride in here and dictate what we should do? You go back and you get the boy Felix. You bring him here, and then I will let your family go."

"I not care about boy now!" Cochise growled. His muscular arms glistened in the sun as he continued to hold the lance to Bascom's chest. "Before I would have helped you find him. But you not listen to truth! Now you will bring my wife and son, brother and nephews out to me!"

"No! I want the boy first, Cochise. I'll not return to Washington until I have found him."

"Bascom, don't do this!" Wallace begged. "You can't argue with Cochise! He means what he says! He'll kill me!"

"The man is bluffing, Wallace!" Bascom replied, his eyes still on Cochise. "You won't be harmed. After all, you're supposed to be his friend."

"Bascom!" Wallace screamed. "Go get Bryce Edwards! He'll tell you what you should do!"

Bascom hardened even more. He glared at the bleeding Wallace.

"This mission is under my control!" he sneered. "I'll handle it as I see fit! I will not back down to this savage!"

"So," Cochise said coldly. "You refuse my request?"

"I most certainly do!" Bascom replied.

"Then the bargaining is over." Cochise whirled his horse and rode off at a fast gallop, dragging a screaming Wallace along behind him. The Indians all yelped and hollered as they rode away into the hills and soon disappeared into the nearby mountains. Bascom turned and walked back to his men.

"He'll be back," he commented tersely to one of them. "I still have his family. Be ready."

"Sir, maybe we should—"

"Should what, soldier!" Bascom snapped at the man who had dared to speak up. "I was told to deal harshly with these wild Indians, and not to give one inch. I intend to stick to that, no matter what Cochise threatens to do!" He went to his tent, and the soldiers all looked at each other, wondering what kind of man their officer was.

Two hours later the Apaches returned full force, descending on the soldiers from all sides of the canyon. For nearly an hour the battle raged, Indians yelping and howling, guns firing, and men shouting. Many soldiers went down under lances and arrows and rifle fire, and many Indians were felled by the army rifles. Horses squealed and fell.

Everywhere the soldiers turned, there were more

240

Apaches. They seemed to flow from the ground like water. When the Indians finally withdrew, many soldiers lay dead beside the Indians, and men could be heard moaning from wounds.

Within the hour Cochise returned, again pulling Wallace with a lariat. He sat some distance away, letting his voice echo through the canyon again to Bascom.

"This is last chance, Bascom! This time when I leave, I not return! You not find me. My prisoners will die, and you will be to blame! Let us end this now, Bascom!"

No one moved, and Wallace's crying could be heard, mixed with the ominous wailing of the canyon winds.

"Maybe we should give them back, sir," a captain suggested in a whisper to Bascom.

"I'll not be ordered around by an ignorant savage!" Bascom hissed. He climbed up on an overturned wagon, in full view of Cochise.

"I'll not turn over your family until I have the boy!" he shouted, the veins sticking out on his neck.

"What shall be, shall be!" Cochise replied. The Indian turned and rode off.

"Bring the boy!" Bascom shouted after him. But the Indian chief soon disappeared, and war whoops and thundering hooves could be heard in the distance. The soldiers all sat rigid with fear, and it was so quiet, the Indians could be heard until they were a great distance away. Finally, men began moving around again.

"Sir, we need more men," a sergeant told Bascom. "If Cochise comes back full force—"

"You don't need to tell me!" Bascom snapped. "Get in the station and send a wire to Fort Buchanan

241

for reinforcements!"

"Sir, I can't. The Apaches cut the wires. And Fort Buchanan is too damned far from here to send men for help. It would take two or three days at least, maybe more. Fort Bowie is a hell of a lot closer. We could be back with men by tomorrow."

"Led by none other than Bryce Edwards, no doubt," Bascom mumbled.

"What, sir?"

"Never mind. Go ahead. Take a couple of men and get down to Fort Bowie. Be back here by morning. I don't think Cochise will come back anymore today."

"Yes, sir." The sergeant rounded up two more men and they were off. Bascom watched them ride off, then turned and glared at Cochise's trembling wife, who sat close to her brother-in-law with her hands tied behind her back.

"Damned Indians!" he mumbled.

Fires burned brightly all night, with several men on watch while others treated wounds and buried the dead. Nahlekadeya sniffled all night, having recognized some of the Indians who were shoved into one common hole for burial. Cochise's brother and nephews felt the anger and revenge building in their hearts. They had originally come with Cochise to visit this lying bluecoat with nothing but friendliness and good will in their hearts.

All night and most of the next morning was spent in anxious waiting for a return of the Apaches. Bascom decided the Indians were not coming and wished he had not sent for Bryce. He ordered his men to break

242

camp. They would leave and scour the mountains for the Indians and their captives.

"We'll take Cochise's people with us," he told the men who guarded Cochise's relatives. "Keep their hands tied. No special favors. They're only Indians."

"Sir, the woman's wrists are getting raw," one soldier protested. "And when she has to go to the bathroom, I have to help her. She cries somethin' awful. Hell, she ain't gonna' hurt anything. Surely we can untie—"

"You do as I say!" Bascom roared. The soldier gritted his teeth and returned to the prisoners, but moments later a furious Bryce Edwards came galloping in with an extra forty men. He had already been told what had transpired. He had barely dismounted before he landed into Bascom, ripping through the man with sharp words and lashing ridicule for the man's bungling, not allowing Bascom to get a word in edgewise. Bascom's men stood and watched with mixed emotions. They felt a loyalty to their officer, but few of them agreed with the way the man had behaved.

Bryce stormed over to check out the prisoners.

"Why in hell are that woman's hands tied!" he roared at Bascom. "And the boy's. Do you think they'll attack you?"

"No Indian can be trusted!" Bascom roared back.

Bryce whipped out his knife and cut the ropes on the woman and child. He said something softly to Nahlekadeya in her own tongue. She dropped her eyes and embraced Nachise, looking fearfully at Bascom. Bryce whirled to face the man again.

"I can't believe what you've done!" Bryce fumed.

"I did as I was ordered!" Bascom replied curtly. "How dare you come here and try to—"

"You've put an Apache's lance into the hearts of every settler and every miner and half the soldiers in Arizona and New Mexico!" Bryce interrupted. "I hope you can sleep with that, Bascom!"

The young lieutenant paled slightly but remained rigid.

"You exaggerate, Colonel Edwards"

"Like hell I do! If anything, I've probably underestimated the magnitude of Cochise's revenge! Why didn't you contact me sooner and get my advice on this? I've been out here for close to thirteen years. What the hell makes you think you can come out here for three weeks and solve all the Indians' problems!"

"I told you—I had my orders."

"There's such a thing as reason and common sense," Bryce seethed. "I'm sure Washington intended for you to use some! Now let's go search for those captives. Not that it will do much good. I can tell you right now how we'll find them. Because if Cochise said he would kill them, then that's what he'll do!"

Bryce ordered everyone to mount up and get in line to move out to search for Cochise and his prisoners. He suggested that they break up into two groups in order to cover more ground. Cochise's family would be split up, the male relatives riding with Bascom's men, and the wife and son riding with Bryce's men. Bryce saw the fear in Nahlekadeya's eyes when she looked at Bascom, and he was not about to let her go with the man.

"Keep an eye on her and treat her with some respect!" he ordered the two men who were to watch the two prisoners.

"Yes, sir," the men answered, not about to cross

244

Bryce Edwards at this moment. All Bryce could see when he looked at Cochise's young and lovely wife was Shannon. Maybe he could make up just a little for whatever happened to her by caring for this woman, hoping that maybe someone, somewhere was affording Shannon the same respect, if she was even alive.

"If we split up the prisoners, it gives both our groups something to bargain with if one of us comes across Cochise," Bryce explained to his men. Bascom, to Bryce's surprise, had agreed, but Bryce knew the man was only trying to save face now. "These prisoners are our protection and our best weapon right now," Bryce went on. "I hope somehow we can keep the bargaining table open." He glanced over at Bascom, who was mounting up in the distance, wishing very much that he could kill the man.

The men moved out, and for the next several days they battled the heat of the foothills as they scoured them for some sign of the Indian Cochise. One of Bryce's men was bitten by a rattler, and in minutes the man died. Bryce's rage at Bascom mounted, as he blamed Bascom for his men having to be out searching in the first place. They climbed higher into the mountains, then back down again, moving from cool, grassy, forested spots to hot, dusty, rocky canyons and reddish, sandy deserts. Men cursed and fumed at the heat and their sweaty uniforms.

The trip began to tell on Cochise's tired wife, who Bryce often caught beginning to slump over on her horse. He finally took her from her own horse and kept her in front of him on his so that he could hang on to her and do his best to reassure her no harm would come to her.

245

He kept his arms around her and spoke frequently to her in her own tongue. Not only did he feel sorry for the innocent woman and her son, but he also knew that killing her would bring on revenge not only from Cochise, but also from her own father, the great war chief of the Mimbreno Apaches, Mangas Coloradas. The combined forces of Cochise and Coloradas would be dreadful indeed. And there was always the possibility of Saguaro's also joining forces with them.

On the sixth day of their searching, the bodies of the American captives were found by Bascom's men.

"Here, sir!" someone shouted. Bascom quickly rode to the spot, where two soldiers stood throwing up. He dismounted and walked over to find the horribly mutilated bodies of Wallace and the two Americans captured from the wagon train.

"My God!" he whispered. "The man's family will pay for this!" He ordered the bodies, or what was left of them after being lanced hundreds of times, to be buried.

"Where's Edwards?" Bascom asked one of his men.

"He's about a mile from here, sir."

"Good. Then I'll act before he returns. Whether he likes it or not, this is still my mission. I don't need his permission for a thing. I cannot let this atrocious act go lightly! Get Cochise's brother and nephews and hang them from the closest tree!"

"But, sir, they didn't really do anything."

"Are you going against my orders, private?" Bascom growled. "I could have you hung right along with them! I'm under command from Washington—not Bryce Edwards, and certainly not you!"

The private swallowed. "Y—yes, sir." He ran to the men who guarded Cochise's male relatives and explained the order. The men looked in shock at Bascom. But an order was an order, and they had seen the mutilated bodies of Cochise's prisoners, which fueled their hatred for the Apaches.

The soldiers threw three ropes over an old tree not far from the sight where the bodies of Cochise's captives had been discovered. Cochise's brother and nephews were quickly dragged, fighting and struggling, to the dreaded hoops. They were hoisted up onto horses, now wide-eyed with fright as the nooses were slipped over their heads. And without a word from Bascom, the horses' rumps were slapped and the three bodies hung grotesquely, jerking and wiggling in a slow, strangling death. Their faces soon turned blue. Their eyes bulged and their mouths moved in hideous sneers. And then they were finally dead.

When Bryce arrived a half hour later, the three men's bodies still hung, while nearby soldiers laughed and ate. Nahlekadeya screamed and went into an eerie wailing at the sight. Bryce clung to her and held back, ordering Reynolds, who rode with Cochise's son, Nachise, to hang on to the boy as best he could with his one good arm, but another of Bryce's men had to go and help the one-armed man with the struggling Nachise, who began crying and fighting as furiously and vengefully as any good Apache warrior would do at such a sight. His uncle and cousins hung dead, their bodies already swelling—killed for no reason. The extra man worked to calm down Nachise as Bascom approached Bryce and Nahlekadeya.

"I will remind you again that my orders come from Washington, Colonel Edwards," Bascom said matter-of-factly. "I have done what our government would want me to do. Now release that woman. She hangs, also. We'll hold the boy until Ward's son is returned. Cochise mutilated and murdered the three American prisoners! If you saw them, you'd have done what I did. Cochise went too far, Colonel Edwards! I know Washington will agree with me."

Bryce whipped out his rifle with one hand, cocking it in midair and then pointing it at Bascom.

"You've done all the damage you're going to do, Bascom!" he snarled, backing his horse up more. All of Bryce's men lined up behind and beside him. "You touch this woman and I'll put a hole right between your eyes! And I'll gladly suffer the consequences!"

Bascom paled. "Don't do something foolish, Edwards—"

"Colonel Edwards, Lieutenant Bascom! You've underestimated my power, lieutenant! I intend to give a full report of how you've bungled this job! You've started something that might take years to settle and cost the lives of hundreds of innocent people! Your name will go down in the history books, Bascom—as a young fool who started the Apache wars!"

"I've done what is proper!" Bascom retorted.

"You take your troops and you get the hell out of my territory, Bascom! I'm taking this woman and child to Cochise, and you'd better be gone when I return, or by God I'll hang you up there with Cochise's nephews and brother! That's an order, Lieutenant Bascom!"

Bascom eyed the rifle. Bryce looked eager to pull the

4 BESTSELLING HISTORICAL ROMANCES BY YOUR FAVORITE AUTHORS CAN BE YOURS, FREE!

Kensington Choice, our newest book club now brings you historical romances by your favorite bestselling authors including Janelle Taylor, Shannon Drake, Rosanne Bittner, Jo Beverley, and Georgina Gentry, just to name a few! Each book is filled with passion, adventure and the excitement of bygone times!

To introduce you to this great new club which is part of Zebra Home Subscription Service, we'd like to send you your first 4 bestselling historical romances, absolutely free! And once you get these 4 free books to savor at home, we'll rush you the next 4 brand-new books at the lowest prices available, as soon as they are published.

The way the club works is that after your initial FREE shipment, you will get our 4 newest bestselling historical romances delivered to your doorstep each month at the preferred subscriber's rate of only $4.20 per book, a savings of up to $7.16 per month (since these titles sell in bookstores for $4.99-$5.99)! All books are sent on a 10-day free examination basis and there is no minimum number of books to buy. (And no charge for shipping.) Plus as a regular subscriber, you'll receive our FREE monthly newsletter, *Zebra/Pinnacle Romance News*, which features author profiles, contests, subscriber benefits, book previews and more!

So start today by returning the FREE BOOK CERTIFICATE provided. We'll send you 4 FREE BOOKS with no further obligation: A FREE gift offering you hours of reading pleasure with no obligation...how can you lose?

We have 4 FREE BOOKS for you
as your introduction to
KENSINGTON CHOICE!
To get your FREE BOOKS, worth
up to $23.96, mail the card below.

FREE BOOK CERTIFICATE

Yes! Please send me 4 Kensington Choice (the best of Zebra and Pinnacle Books) Historical Romances without cost or obligation (worth up to $23.96). As a Kensington Choice subscriber, I will then receive 4 brand-new romances to preview each month for 10 days FREE. I can return any books I decide not to keep and owe nothing. The publisher's prices for Kensington Choice romances range from $4.99-$5.99, but as a preferred subscriber I will get these books for only $4.20 per book or $16.80 for all four titles. There is no minimum number of books to buy and I may cancel my subscription at any time, plus there is no additional charge for postage and handling. No matter what I decide to do, my first 4 books are mine to keep, absolutely FREE!

Name _____

Address _____ Apt. _____

City_____ State_____ Zip_____

Telephone ( )_____

Signature _____

(If under 18, parent or guardian must sign)

Subscription subject to acceptance. Terms and prices subject to change.

KF0896

AFFIX
STAMP
HERE

KENSINGTON CHOICE
Zebra Home Subscription Service, Inc.
120 Brighton Road
P.O.Box 5214
Clifton, NJ 07015-5214

trigger. The man suddenly wondered if he truly had made a wrong move. How would this look in Washington?

"Look, Colonel Edwards, let's both go out and talk to Cochise. We've had an eye for an eye now."

"You'll never learn, will you, Bascom?" Bryce sneered. "The Apache gives a man only one chance! You've had yours. And you'll not get another! And I'll be damned if you're going to use me to make yourself look better in Washington!"

Bryce backed up his horse even more. "Reynolds, you come with me. Hasty—Randall—you come, too. Help Reynolds with the boy!"

"Yes, sir," the two extra men shouted out.

"Captain Jacobs!" Bryce yelled louder to his next-in-command.

"Sir!"

"Camp here and wait for me. I'm taking Nahlekadeya and Nachise to find Cochise so he can have them back!"

"Yes, sir!"

"Sir, they'll kill you," another of Bryce's men protested.

"I don't think so," Bryce replied, still watching the furious Bascom. "You know, Bascom," he went on, "right now I trust Cochise one hell of a lot more than I trust you!"

"You'll end up like the three men we found!" Bascom retorted.

"If I do, my men will see to it that Washington knows it was your fault I had to go out there in the first place, Bascom! The army is already short of men. Losing experienced ones out here won't set too good in Washington. You had no right hanging those Indians without consulting me first! They should have been taken back to the fort and imprisoned, at the very most. They should never even have been held in the first place. My guess is you won't be welcomed too eagerly in Washington—if you can even *get* back without being massacred by the Apaches! My advice to you is to cut down fast to the Rio Grande. Cochise rode north. Get moving! I don't want you around here stirring up any more trouble. I'll have enough problems straightening out the damage you've already done!"

Bryce whirled his horse and galloped off, followed by Reynolds and the other two soldiers.

For three more days Bryce and his men rode aimlessly through Apache territory with Nahlekadeya and Nachise, making themselves easy targets, wanting to be found by Cochise. Bryce knew the man would show himself as soon as he was sure Bryce's presence was not a trick.

On the fourth morning, Bryce and his men awoke to find their camp surrounded by Cochise and about forty warriors, all on horses. Nahlekadeya gasped with joy and ran to her husband's side, followed by Nachise. The woman wept and grasped Cochise's leg, putting her head against it and sobbing out how his nephews and brother had been hung.

"I already know this," Cochise told her. "Cochise has many eyes in these mountains." He reached down for a moment to gently touch Nahlekadeya's hair, overjoyed that she was safe. He glanced at his son and smiled at the boy. Then he turned his eyes back to Bryce and lost his smile.

"You risk much bringing her here, white soldier!"

"I risk nothing," Bryce replied. "I know Cochise. I've brought you your wife and son. You will kill me for this?"

Nahlekadeya spoke rapidly in her Apache tongue, gesturing to Bryce. She looked from Cochise to Bryce.

"Bascom wanted to hang my wife?" Cochise asked.

"I told him I'd put a hole between his eyes first," Bryce replied. Cochise grinned.

"So Nahlekadeya tells me. It is a debt Cochise will not forget. You are free to go, white soldier. If I meet you in battle, I will try to spare you."

"And will there be a battle?" Bryce asked.

"As surely as the sun rises," Cochise replied, almost sadly. "Cochise has been made a fool. He has been humiliated and insulted. His nephews and brother were hung without cause."

"And the men you killed? What were they guilty of?"

"Wallace was guilty of treachery. The others were killed because Cochise keeps his word! I gave white soldier choice. He not listen to me. It was only way to show him Cochise not lie or change mind. If white soldier had been honest and told Cochise he would hang my nephews and brother, I might have bargained more with him. But he not tell me he would do this. He hung them in act of treachery. They were innocent! I tell Bascom exactly what I will do with *my* prisoners. But what does it matter now how it all began? It has been proven to Cochise that white man cannot be

251

trusted. My warriors and Mescalero chief, Saguaro, have often told me I am foolish to put faith in white man. They were right. Cochise will not be fool before his warriors any longer. Soon all white intruders will know that this land—as far as eye can see and beyond—belong to Apache. We have allowed you to sit on it long enough. The visit is over, white soldier! Soon this land will hold only Apaches again. I know I can count on Saguaro's help, and soon I will convince Mangas Coloradas to join me!"

"The white movement can't be stopped, Cochise. They'll keep coming, no matter what. End it now, my red brother, before more of your people are violated and killed."

"Even you do not understand the fierce pride of the Apache. If a man is to live, he must live as a man, and not as a beggar, or as a puppy, whining and licking its master's hand. It is better to die a man, than live like a dog."

Cochise lifted his wife to his steed and another warrior took the man's son.

"Cochise is grateful for return of his wife," the Indian told Bryce. "In all of this, I believe you alone have been honest. I am sorry our friendship must end."

The Indian whirled his horse and he and his warriors rode off. Bryce watched after them, then glanced at Reynolds with grief-filled eyes. He said nothing as he turned and walked over to saddle his horse, ordering his men to do the same. They headed south, back to Fort Bowie.

It seemed to Bryce that more things had gone wrong of late in his life than had ever gone wrong in all of his other twenty-eight years, including his being orphaned.

He wondered what he had done to deserve it. He felt a sudden longing to be able to hear Shannon's delightful voice, to talk to her, lie in bed with her and let her hold him. Her face suddenly appeared very clearly in his mind. It had been so very long since he had seen her! And he would probably never see her again! But he would never forget the childlike face, with the unusual catlike green eyes that seemed too womanly for the rest of her; her thick reddish hair; her soft skin; her lovely young breasts that he had tasted and caressed; the glory of entering her sweet body. He dug his heels into his horse's sides and rode the animal hard, taking out his sorrow on his horse while the others rode hard to keep up with him.

Shannon was dead! Dead! Dead! It had been eight months since she had fled Virginia. Let the Apaches come! He hoped he would be killed.

For two months after the incident at Apache Pass, Cochise and his warriors struck with a mighty vengeance. Even the towns were attacked. By late March of 1861, over two hundred people—settlers, wagon train travelers, miners and townspeople—met their deaths; some quickly, some by torture. Many people fled for their lives from southeastern Arizona and southwestern New Mexico, leaving the territory never to return. Bryce was kept so busy that he had little time to lie around dwelling on the loss of Shannon. His green recruits were fast becoming experienced, as they rode out on mission after mission, chasing the ever-elusive Apaches, helping wounded citizens, often getting caught in the middle of raids and return attacks. Guns fired, horses reared and snorted, and buglers blew their horns in the call to attack or retreat in countless battles.

Washington was in an uproar. They had enough on their hands, they shouted, without having to send more men out west. Men in command argued back and forth about the fateful sending out of Lieutenant Bascom to take care of the incident over Felix Ward.

"I told you to let Edwards handle it!" one general shouted to a colonel. "The man has experience!"

"But nothing was being done!"

"Edwards moves cautiously—and rightfully so!" the general shouted in reply. "Now you can see what moving too fast with the Apaches can do. That damned Bascom had stars in his eyes, colonel. Like the kind I wear on my shoulders. Sure, Edwards takes more time. But he knows the Indians. He would have found a way to settle this without all the bloodshed. Now he's left out there with that skeleton crew of men trying to keep ahead of Cochise. It's a losing battle."

The colonel frowned and began to pace. "We seem to have complete unrest everywhere, don't we, sir?"

"We certainly do," the general replied, plopping down in his chair. "The war here—the Apaches out West." He sighed. "I wonder if Edwards ever heard anything about that Fitzgerald girl."

"I don't think so, sir. She's presumed dead. It's been nine months since she disappeared from Virginia."

The general shook his head. "That's too bad. I did everything I could for Bryce on this end. If she had been found, I'd have made sure there would be no trial or jail for her. Anyone can see from the evidence what happened. The poor girl was just defending herself. She

254

must have been terribly afraid and lonely to have run off by herself like that." The man sighed again. "Too bad," he repeated. "Bryce Edwards has certainly had his problems this past year."

"And they don't look like they'll get better, sir."

"No. They certainly don't, thanks to George Bascom!"

Chapter Fifteen

In the Sierra Madres of northern Mexico, Shannon struggled to adjust to a new life of work harder than she had ever imagined she was capable of doing. Her skin reddened, and it was difficult to keep her long, thick hair from tangling. She kept to herself, except for a few friendships she had managed to form out of the necessity of sharing work, using a crude form of sign language to communicate. But she stayed away from most of the Apaches, not out of fear for her life, but because she was afraid that she might in some way offend their customs and religion and be cast out or sold before Saguaro returned, for there were a few who still eyed her with hatred and suspicion, although she felt fairly confident that, because she was Saguaro's woman, no harm would come to her.

Still, she must remember how different, how passionate and volatile these people could be, and, if she unkowingly committed any major affront to them, especially the priest or the shaman, even Saguaro might be forced to beat her or even kill her. She trusted in his sweet, gentle love, but he was first an Apache, a leader, bound to live by the rules of his people. And Saguaro and these people were all she had now. She wanted to stay here in this peaceful little village, where each day ran into the next, with no worry about time, and where she need never worry about the authorities in the East ever finding her.

Her only worry was what would happen to her if Saguaro should be killed. He had left and returned twice now, only gone about two weeks each time, bringing back blankets and utensils and women's toiletries for Shannon; and food, mostly stolen, she was certain. But she no longer blamed Saguaro. She only feared he could be killed during a raid. The area where he had always lived and where the Mescaleros had always hunted and provided for themselves had been completely overrun by settlers and miners. He and his people were forced to live as outcasts in the barren mountains of northern Mexico, where hunting was not plentiful enough to provide all the needs of the now one thousand or so people of the village.

And now Saguaro was a hunted man—hunted not only by the white soldiers for the crimes he had committed after his wife and sons had been tortured and killed, but also by the hated Mexicans, who often raided Apache camps, killing all the men and taking the women and children to be used as slaves. A Mexican raid was the main thing Shannon feared now, after the attack by the Mexican bandits several months earlier. But at least this was a very large village, and no common band of thieves or bandits would dare to attack such a large Apache settlement. Saguaro had left many men behind for security.

This was the third time Saguaro had left her, gone to find provisions and to do his own hunting. He still talked of moving back north to his own lands. This time he had been gone a month, and Shannon was afraid for him—and for herself. Should she just stay here forever if he did not come back?

She missed him. The tender love she had found in the arms of her Apache warrior had been welcome sweetness to a young woman totally lost and alone. Saguaro had saved her life more than once. He had been loyal and tender. He had given her a home. He was her lover, her friend, her father, protector, and provider. In her confused and tortured mind he had become her whole world.

She looked down at her still flat stomach and touched it. She was almost four months pregnant, as best she could determine, and her waist was getting thicker. She and Saguaro had made love several times before he left after their marriage, and now she was carrying his child. She had not told him yet. She wanted to be sure. She was excited about carrying life in her belly. A child! Now, no matter what happened, she would have something to love. She would have a reason to keep going. She would never be alone again. She would have a child of her own and a reason to be truly happy. She knew that Saguaro would be overjoyed at the news when he returned, and she was aching to tell him, praying daily that he would come back soon. Saguaro needed a child to help fill the terrible vacuum left in his heart by the loss of his two sons.

She put more wood on her fire and threw some of the fruit from the saguaro cactus into a big pot. She had learned to cook the fruit many ways, and watching it begin to bubble now reminded her of her Apache husband, who was named for the great cactus that stood tall and strong. Today she would make jelly from the fruit, letting it cook slowly while she went out to watch the continuing puberty celebration.

She stirred the fruit and left the wickiup, walking out into the bright sunlight to join the dancing and laughing Apaches. A twelve-year-old Apache girl was being joyfully initiated into womanhood. The "Coming-of-Age" celebration was cause for great merriment among these people. This would be the third day that the young girl, dressed in golden buckskin and covered from head to foot with golden pollen, danced until midnight around a tray of ritual objects inside her sacred tipi, watched and prompted by her mother and grandmother to keep going in spite of her tired condition. For three days the dancing and laughter had gone on, in spite of the fact that these peple really had no place to call home any longer. They were slowly starving and dying of white man's diseases. Yet they could smile, and the children ran and played games. Shannon loved watching the bright-eyed, dark-haired Indian children. Apache children were loved and pampered. Family and children were all-important to these people, and Shannon could fully understand now Saguaro's great rage at the deaths of his wife and sons.

Drums beat rhythmically, and Shannon watched as warriors, wearing bizarre headdresses to identify them as mountain spirits, danced and sang around sacred objects near a fire. Their ritual was to ensure a long and full life for the young virgin, who had finally had her time of flowing and was now able to bear children. She was a woman now, and would probably be married soon. Shannon had learned not to be shocked any more by their early marriages or other strange customs. She was a stranger among them. She spent her nights praying to the Virgin Mary, using her own cross, begging for forgiveness for murdering Loren McGuire and praying for the safety of herself and her child. She often wondered what Bryce Edwards would think of her now, if he were alive. She bore little resemblance to the girl he had left behind in Virginia, at least not in spirit and innocence.

Thank God he's dead, she found herself thinking, wanting to weep at the statement. Better dead than for him to find me now—knowing that I have killed a man, and now am pregnant by an Apache warrior.

She loved Saguaro. She did not resent him for what he was, and she was not ashamed. But she knew that no white man, including Bryce, could possibly understand why she loved Saguaro and why she was now carrying the man's child. She would be branded a whore who liked the Apache bucks. No one could possibly understand that she truly loved Saguaro—that he had not taken her by force, but by sweet consent—that she was his wife, not his squaw. It would be even more impossible now for her to return to her own world. Her child would be a half-breed. Better a full-blooded Indian than a half-breed.

She pushed the terrible agony of her past out of her mind. This was a day to be happy and to celebrate. She thought of Saguaro's strong arms and whispered words and she said a short prayer for his quick return. She did not like being alone now. She had had enough of being alone.

*　　　*　　　*

It was early April when Saguaro returned again. Shannon heard war cries and thundering horses. She rushed out of the wickiup to see not only Saguaro coming, but also more Indians than had left with him. At least three hundred additional Indians accompanied Saguaro and his own hundred and fifty men.

Indians poured out of tipis and wickiups to greet the returning men, whose faces were strangely painted. The women wept with joy and cheered, but hung back, as it was forbidden to show affection outwardly between wives and their returning husbands. That would come later. The men sat proud and straight on their horses, mostly pintos, some palominos and a few Appaloosas.

There was an ominous atmosphere around these men, and Shannon's heart sank at the sight of the additional Indians. Something surely had happened! She guessed the added Indians, whom she was sure were not Mescaleros, were coming there to hide. One very tall and handsome one rode next to Saguaro, and she guessed that, whoever he was, he was the leader of the additional men.

Saguaro only glanced at Shannon and nodded to her, but she knew he wanted to leap down from his horse and hold her. She smiled for him, and the other Indian leader looked at her strangely, as though he knew her. She nodded to him and he turned his eyes from her. The men rode on by and all went to sit immediately in council. All the villagers were very excited and curious now as they ran to watch the proceedings and find out what was happening.

Shannon hurried to join the others, standing beside Bright Sun, a very young girl she had befriended more than the others. Between the two of them they were learning each other's language, and Shannon hoped that she could understand the girl well enough to discover what was happening. Saguaro, the other Apache leader, and several of the best warriors from both tribes, including Bright Sun's husband, formed a council circle, and the village quieted as the men began conversing.

"Bright Sun! Who are those other Indians?" Shannon asked the girl in sign language.

Bright Sun replied in a mixture of broken English and sign language. "Chiricahuas!" she said excitedly. "They are our brothers! The one beside Saguaro is Cochise!"

"Cochise!" Shannon almost gasped the name aloud. She had heard many tales about the great Apache leader, and here she was, looking right at him. She decided if she ever lived to old age, and if in some way she found herself living in the white man's world, she would certainly have some tales to tell her grandchildren. "What are they talking about?" she asked Bright Sun.

"War!"

Shannon's heart froze. "Why?" she asked, grabbing the girl's hand. "What has happened?"

"Shhh! I must listen first!" the girl replied, putting her fingers to Shannon's lips. Shannon waited impatiently as the Indian leaders spoke rapidly. Saguaro got up and stormed around, waving his arms and speaking in a thunderous voice, and Bright Sun translated for Shannon.

"Your husband speaks again of the white men who kill his wife and sons. He tells the others of his hatred for the white man." She waited a moment. "Cochise asks him about the white squaw he sees when he rides into Saguaro's village."

Shannon's eyes widened as Saguaro stopped still and turned to Cochise, speaking in a calmer voice.

"She not like others," Bright Sun interpreted to Shannon in a whisper as Saguaro spoke to Cochise. "Saguaro take her for slave. But she is like us—homeless. Saguaro find her pleasing. She touches his heart. She his wife. She not white. She is Apache!"

Cochise looked curiously at Shannon again, and she glanced down, as any good squaw would do. She wondered what he was thinking and why he seemed to know something about her. Cochise himself was remembering a day when the white soldier called Bryce Edwards had come to him to inquire about the possibility of a white woman's being taken captive. Could this be the woman?

Bright Sun continued to interpret for Shannon as the council continued with their meeting. "Soldier called Bascom come to Apache Pass," she told Shannon in a broken mixture of English and Apache, as she waved her hands excitedly. "He welcome Cochise like friend, then take him prisoner, and also take his wife and son—two nephews and one brother prisoner! He say Cochise steal Mexican boy. Cochise not do this thing. Cochise escape—take three white men to trade for freedom of his family. The one called Bascom not trade!" The girl listened as Cochise ranted and raved. "Cochise kill the white men, and Bascom hang Cochise's brother and two nephews!"

"Hung them! But they didn't do anything!" Shannon gasped in a whisper.

Bright Sun hung her head. "Now there will be war," she said quietly. "Cochise not forget tricks and lies of soldier called Bascom. He say all whites must leave our land or die now. He has attacked ranchers and miners—even towns!" She listened another moment, then turned to Shannon. "Saguaro has joined Cochise in the raiding, because of his own hatred of white man. Cochise come here with his warriors to hide and rest. He hope great chief of Membrenos, Mangas Coloradas, who is also his father-in-law, will join him in raiding. As yet, he has not done so."

Shannon found her feelings mixed. The man who was now her husband was killing and looting her own kind. She felt sorry for everyone on both sides. Even her own kind were probably at war with each other by now. She wondered what was happening in Virginia and with the Union in the skirmish she had fled. Were they in a full-scale war? Would she ever know anything about home again? She thought about her little brother, her father, Bryce.

"Bryce!" she whispered, her eyes tearing. She thought she had taught herself to forget him. But how could she forget him as she watched these Apache warriors? Bryce had served faithfully out in this forsaken land—working with *both* sides—only to earn death as his final medal. How ironic it all was! Perhaps the man who had killed him was right here among these warriors. Yet she could not feel hate. Not now. This had become her home.

There was more talk and more shouting, as the warriors worked themselves into a frenzy. Drums began beating and men began dancing, and things became so noisy it was frightening. The looks on the men's faces gave Shannon the chills. She was the only one present out of these twelve hundred or so people who was white—the very kind they intended to wipe out once and for all. She made her way back to her dwelling to wait for Saguaro.

It was not until the wee hours of the morning that Saguaro came to her. Shannon was still awake, and she looked up at her handsome Apache warrior as he entered. He broke into a grin, and she went to him, flinging her arms around his neck. Saguaro hugged her tightly.

"Oh, Saguaro, I was so afraid! You were gone so long!" she told him, beginning to cry.

"And now I am returned, just as I said," he replied, kissing her hair and patting her shoulder.

"Saguaro, what's happening? I'm afraid for you! I don't want you getting into war!"

She looked up at him and they kissed hungrily. Then he held her another moment before releasing her and removing his headdress and most of his clothing, except for his loincloth.

"It must be done," he told her. "You must understand Apache pride. It is clear white man speaks with forked tongue. No treaties will be kept. No promise will be honored. None of our land will be sacred. It will all be taken from us—but not without a fight!"

"Saguaro, you'll be killed!" she whimpered, her eyes filled with fright. He studied her lovingly and walked over to take her face in his hands.

"Good Apache squaw not argue with her man about

such things. It is his decision," he said firmly, but gently. "Squaw should be proud."

"But I'm—" she sniffed and tried to stifle her tears. "I'm pregnant, Saguaro. I'm going to have a baby— around the end of summer, I think. I've lost all track of time."

She stood there sniffling and looking down, and when he did not reply right away, she met his eyes, to see them filled with love—and tears.

"You are sure?"

"I am."

Saguaro smiled. "Then you are good Apache squaw!" he told her. "You take away Saguaro's pain." He grabbed her close and breathed deeply of her sweet scent. "Thank you, White Flower," he whispered. "My heart is filled with love for you!" He released her and held her at arm's length. "You are strong enough?"

"I think so. I feel fine."

Their eyes held a moment. "Saguaro needs you," he told her gently, running a hand over her breasts, his eyes filling now with passion and desire.

"And I need you," she whispered.

He untied her tunic and let it fall. She stood before him naked, reddening as he ran his hands over her body, then pulled her close against him. She kissed the broad, powerful chest. Saguaro picked her up in his arms and carried her to their bed of robes.

"I love you, Saguaro," she said in a small voice, as his lips moved to her breasts. "I'm afraid when you aren't here." She stroked the long, dark hair, and noticed her own skin was a little darker now from the Mexican sun. She felt that soon she would forget she was white altogether. It was not long before Saguaro was pushing himself inside of her, and she knew where she belonged.

Outside, as he slept under the stars with his men, Cochise thought about many things. He prayed to his God to protect his precious wife, who was staying with Mangas Coloradas, her father; and for his children.

Then Cochise's thoughts turned to Saguaro's white squaw. He would meet her in the morning. He must decide if he should say anything about the white soldier, Bryce Edwards. Was it his woman Saguaro had married? Cochise needed Saguaro for his war. If telling Saguaro of Edwards could mean the white woman would want to go to the soldier, Saguaro would be heartbroken.

A man is weak when he loses his woman, Cochise reasoned. Saguaro would be even weaker, because he has already lost one woman and two sons. He is happy with this white woman. He has told me she is obedient and satisfies his bed. I will not tell white soldier what I have seen here. He thinks woman is dead. Woman thinks he is dead. Cochise will tell neither of them the truth. Cochise needs Saguaro to be strong and full of life—not weak and sad. She here many moons—marry Saguaro. She is Apache now. She must forget her own kind and cling to Saguaro. The great leader sighed and turned on his side. The safety of these Sierra Madres was welcome.

Bryce shook his head as he read the telegram from Washington. "Well, Reynolds, it looks like if Miss Fitzgerald hadn't left Virginia, she'd have ended up in as much trouble there as she did out here," he commented. He wiped sweat from his brow. Mid-August had brought a relentless heat.

"More fighting, sir?"

"There's been a second encounter at Bull Run— almost twenty thousand casualties. Damn! Do you realize there have been more than twenty-five thousand men killed or wounded on both sides already? And I'm afraid this is only the beginning, Reynolds. This is going to be bloody, bloody war. God knows when it will end. A lot of young boys are going to grow up fast before this is over, and I have a distinct feeling the South will never be the same. They've regained most of Virginia, but it won't last."

"You don't think they have much of a chance, do you, sir?"

"Not really. They're far outnumbered. But I know the Southerners. They're proud and stubborn, and they won't back down easily. They may have Virginia now, but in the end the Union will charge through the South like a bull, and a lot of innocent people will suffer for it. How do you feel about all of it, Reynolds?" He rolled and lit a cigarette and looked up at the boy.

Reynolds shrugged.

"I'm from Ohio, sir. I guess I'd have to be on the Union's side. But out here, it doesn't seem to matter much."

"I don't really have any place I can call home," Bryce told him. He took a deep drag on his cigarette. "The worst part about this whole civil war is that our problems out here are going to get shoveled right under the rug. And more and more people keep pouring into the Territory, running from their troubles back East.

269

They just keep right on coming, in spite of the warnings about the Apaches. Then the Apaches feel more and more desperate and retaliate with even worse raids. It's a vicious circle, and I'll get little help or understanding from Washington. I guess none of them—the men in Congress or the fresh settlers from the East—believe how bad it is, or how bad the Indians can be. Today it's Cochise and Saguaro, and soon Coloradas will join them. You just watch."

Bryce got up and paced and smoked silently, then went to a window and looked out at the distant mountains.

"You still think about her a lot, don't you, sir?" Reynolds commented, pouring himself some coffee.

Bryce sighed. "I try and try to convince myself she must be dead, Reynolds. But something keeps eating at me. I just can't quite swallow the very obvious conclusion that she has to be dead. Yet I don't know where the hell else to look, and Cochise and Coloradas both have told me they know of no white woman captive. And if Cochise had discovered that Saguaro or one of his men knew something about her, I think he would tell me, even now, with all this fighting. After all, I did save his wife from a hanging. So she can't be with the Apaches." He turned to go and sit at his desk. "I guess I'll just stick to my duty here. It's going to take a long time for me to get her out of my blood. One thing is for sure. I'll never marry. It hurts too much to love someone."

Reynolds sat down on the other side of the desk and began to open some mail. "I sure am sorry, sir, about Miss Fitzgerald."

"Thank you, Reynolds. And what about you? Don't

270

you want to get married?"

"Maybe. Someday. When I finish my hitch in the army, I'll think about it more."

"Why did you join the army, anyway?" Bryce asked.

"Just to get out and go places—do new things, I guess," the boy replied. Bryce watched him fumble to open a letter with his one good arm.

"It didn't exactly turn out the way you planned it, did it, Reynolds?" he said in a sympathetic voice. "I'm damned sorry about your arm."

"Well, sir, it's just like you losing Miss Fitzgerald. Things don't turn out right for a lot of us. There's all kinds of losses, sir. Physical and emotional. Sometimes the emotional can be worse than the physical. I've seen how you have suffered. I just wish there was something I could do, that's all." The young man reddened a little and opened the envelope, keeping his eyes averted.

"I appreciate your concern," Bryce told him. "It helps to know someone cares a little." He started to fill out a written report of a small skirmish with some Apaches the day before.

"As long as we're being open and personal, sir—"

Bryce looked up from his writing. "What is it, Reynolds?"

"Well, sir, what if . . . well, what if you *did* find Miss Fitzgerald. And what if she'd been a Mexican slave . . . maybe forced into . . . into prostitution . . . or . . . or held captive and abused by the Apaches? Would you still want her? I mean, it wouldn't be anything that was her fault, you know. But some men—"

"I am not some men!" Bryce interrupted. He paled and his eyes teared slightly. "Of course I'd want her," he

271

continued in a barely audible voice. "I'll always want her."

He turned away, feeling as though a knife were being twisted in his heart. He wondered if the strange, heavy pain in his chest would ever leave him. How long would it take to get over losing his precious Shannon? Shannon! Shannon!

Chapter Sixteen

Shannon lumbered into the wickiup with some wood, and Saguaro immediately took it from her, angered that she had even carried it.

"What has Saguaro told you?" he said, frowning. "If not for size of that belly, Saguaro would thrash you good. Look at your feet—swollen! You should not be working!" He helped her to sit down. Shannon wondered if she would explode before she had her baby, she was so large.

"Saguaro, I can't just sit around doing nothing. The other squaws work when they're pregnant."

"They not Saguaro's squaws. And they not so small like you. This child is important to Saguaro."

She sighed and put a hand on his arm.

"Will you still want me if I have a daughter?" she asked him. "I know how proud Apache men are of their sons."

"It does not matter. It is up to Usen. Saguaro wants a son, but daughters become mothers and carry on the sons. A daughter is good. And we will have more.

There will be a son."

Shannon raised her eyebrows. "Not right away, I hope!"

Saguaro grinned and patted her stomach. "It is the custom that a man does not touch his wife while she is nursing. You not have another child soon."

"Saguaro, that could be a year or two!"

"Saguaro will wait."

"But—you won't get yourself another wife, will you?"

Saguaro laughed. "You not want me marry one of the other squaws to satisfy me and have more sons while I wait?"

Shannon pouted slightly and looked down at her belly. "No, I don't," she replied quietly. Saguaro sobered and touched her hair.

"Saguaro not want another wife. Saguaro is pleased with White Flower. She is soft as moss on banks of stream—as colorful as flowers in spring. And she needs Saguaro, as Saguaro needs her. Saguaro not fail those who need him."

He pulled her close and she rested her head on his shoulder. It was good to have him here now, with her being due any time. Saguaro had left and returned numerous times since he first arrived with Cochise. Sometimes Cochise was with him, and sometimes he stayed behind, hiding someplace else. After the latest venture, Cochise had again returned with Saguaro to the Sierra Madres.

"Saguaro, I'm scared. Is it forbidden to be afraid to have a baby?"

He rubbed her stomach gently. "No. But there are many squaws here who will help you. They know what

274

to do. Do not be afraid, my White Flower."

"I want *you* with me."

"It is not custom. It is bad medicine for father to watch. It is not our way. The women will help you, and Saguaro will be nearby."

"Then you won't go out again until the baby is born?"

"No. Saguaro will wait. I will not leave you now, White Flower."

Shannon started to say something more when women suddenly began screaming outside and shots could be heard. Saguaro jumped up and grabbed his quiver of arrows and his rifle. He shoved a hatchet and a knife into his leather belt.

"Do not come out of this dwelling!" he ordered on his way out.

"Saguaro, what is it?" she screamed after him. But he did not have time to answer. Shannon's heart pounded as she moved to the entrance of the wickiup to look out. Everywhere she looked she saw Mexicans cutting down Apaches—men, women and even the children. She gasped and ducked back inside.

"Oh, Dear God! Help us!" she whimpered, crouching down.

Saguaro had explained to Shannon how the Apaches and the Mexicans had warred for generations, and how the Mexicans stole women to sell as slaves in Mexico. She groaned with fear. She did not want to be at the hands of one of the men she had seen. She was glad Cochise and his men were there, and that the Mexicans had hit when the Apaches were at full force in camp.

The screaming and shooting and bloodcurdling war

whoops continued as Shannon sat frozen and beside herself with fear. Suddenly someone ripped through the side of the wickiup, and three Mexicans pushed their way inside. They grinned with pleasure at the sight of a white woman. She knew by the look in their eyes exactly what they were thinking. She would not be killed. She would be taken alive. Better to be dead.

"Saguaro! Saguaro!" she screamed, picking up a heavy pan and raising it. In a flash her Indian husband was inside. He fired a rifle into two of the men immediately, and Shannon screamed as the third man managed to grab the barrel of Saguaro's gun before he could fire again. Shannon noticed Saguaro was already bleeding.

"God, help him!" she screamed. One of the other Mexicans moved, and Shannon smashed him over the head with the heavy pan, as Saguaro and the third Mexican wrestled with the gun and went crashing through the side of the wickiup. The entire dwelling collapsed and Shannon found herself struggling to get out of it while Saguaro and the Mexican continued to fight. Saguaro got the gun away from the Mexican and swung it, smashing the man in the side of the face.

Another Mexican came charging up to Saguaro on a horse, and Shannon screamed to Saguaro to watch out. Saguaro turned, and the Mexican curled a large bullwhip around his body. Shannon screamed as blood appeared in a long, red cut around Saguaro's back and ribs; but Saguaro grabbed the whip and held on so that the Mexican could not pull it back and swing it again. The Indian yanked on the whip and pulled the man off his horse, and, almost faster than Shannon's eyes could decipher, Saguaro had plunged a knife into the man's heart and then deftly removed his scalp.

Shannon covered her mouth and felt faint, but someone grabbed her from behind and began dragging her off. Shannon screamed and Saguaro charged into the man, pulling Shannon from the Mexican's arms. She fell to the ground and Saguaro and the Mexican rolled on the ground while Shannon began crawling toward a large rock where she might find shelter. She looked over and saw Bright Sun, lying dead and bloody.

"Oh, no! No!" she whimpered. Not far from Bright Sun lay the body of her husband, Eagle Feather. Would Saguaro die, too? "God, help him!" she screamed again. She crawled to the rock and covered her ears and hid her face, waiting for some horrible Mexican to come and drag her off. Maybe they would slice the baby out of her belly and rape her.

A horse thundered by, and she looked up to see if Saguaro was still near and alive. He was still struggling with the Mexican who had grabbed Shannon, but it looked as though the rest of the Mexicans were now fleeing. Several Apache warriors were chasing after them. Shannon watched in horror as Saguaro grabbed his hatchet and brought it down into his opponent's face, obliterating the man's head. The Mexican lay dead, and Saguaro, filthy and bloody, stumbled to Shannon's side. She sat wide-eyed and trembling, still looking at the Mexican. Saguaro immediately picked her up and carried her a few feet away.

"Bright Sun!" she gasped, the tears now coming.

"Her spirit is happy now," Saguaro told her quietly.

Shannon choked in a sob and put her arms around Saguaro's neck. He laid her down in the grass and had a

277

difficult time pulling her arms off of him. He held her arms at her side and bent down to kiss her forehead.

"They—did not hurt you?" he asked, looking her over.

"I—don't even know!" she whimpered. "It all—happened so fast! What are we going to do! Will they come back?"

Saguaro looked around the village. It looked like a battlefield. Bodies lay everywhere. Some tipis were burning, children cried, and women walked around wailing and searching for loved ones.

"Ai," he replied, breathing deeply and wiping his forehead. "They will come back. They must have seen us and followed us to this place when Cochise and Saguaro return from north. We must leave here for a while, White Flower—go back north."

"But all the soldiers are looking for you across the border, aren't they?"

"Better to answer to soldiers than to Mexicans! We go north and find a place to hide and rest. Then we come back here and take out our vengeance on these Mexicans!" His dark eyes flashed. She saw that he was bleeding from a shoulder wound and from the cut made by the bullwhip.

"Saguaro, are you injured badly?" she asked. She removed the cloth band she wore around her forehead to keep her hair out of her face and pressed it against the shoulder wound. "Oh, look how you're bleeding!" Saguaro watched her quietly for a moment, then put a hand over the one she held to his wound.

"It not good for you here. Saguaro not want to make you travel with child so large in your belly, but it is better if you are taken by soldiers than Mexicans. Far

278

better. You are white. Mexicans would do terrible things to you."

"I don't want . . . to be taken by anyone! The soldiers would send me back home, Saguaro! I . . . don't want to go there! I just want to stay with you!"

Saguaro wiped at her tears with his fingers and kissed her hair. "Saguaro never let anything happen to White Flower," he told her. "Saguaro want you to stop crying now. It not good. You make baby come too soon."

"I . . . can't help it!" she choked. "I was so . . . afraid for you!"

"For Saguaro?" He put on a smile for her. "Saguaro is good fighter! It takes more than a few Mexicans to get Saguaro, ai?"

Shannon tried to smile, but couldn't. "Three times . . . you've saved me . . . from a fate worse than death," she told him, still trying to stop his bleeding. "You saved me . . . from that old man at the stage station . . . and from the Mexicans who attacked me so many months ago . . . and now today. And you've . . . been so good to me, Saguaro. I love you. I don't . . . want to lose you, Saguaro!"

She wept harder again and he pulled her close.

"Saguaro would die for you," he told her flatly. "It is not such a big thing. Saguaro loves you."

Cochise approached them and knelt down beside them.

"Your woman is hurt?"

"No. Just frightened. I fear for the child."

"And you?"

"A Mexican's knife found its way into my shoulder—and a bullwhip tasted my flesh. But Saguaro

279

has been hurt worse."

"We must go north," Cochise stated. He looked at Shannon with the strangely familiar look in his eyes that she always felt when he looked at her—as though he already knew her before he had found her with Saguaro. It made her uneasy. But she was not afraid of Cochise.

"Ai," Saguaro was agreeing. "We will come back later when things have quieted. We will find new hiding place."

"Always we must hide!" Cochise growled, rising. "There was a day when all of this land was ours! Now we are hunted like buffalo and snake. This is no way for a man to live!" He spoke through gritted teeth, as his eyes scanned the bodies of the dead and wounded. "To be Indian today is to be cursed. And what did we do to start this? Nothing! If not for the white settlers, we could go north now and live wherever we choose— safely away from the Mexicans! We will continue to raid their homes and their towns until they leave!"

"Ai. I think we should try Dragoon Mountains, Cochise. They are close to forts and to Apache Pass. They not think to look for us so close to white soldiers. Besides, white soldiers can never find us. They not know mountains like Apache knows them!"

"We will do this. And I will get my wife and children." Cochise met Shannon's eyes. She wished she knew what it was he wanted to tell her. "Tell me, White Flower," he said. "Do you not miss the world you came from?"

Shannon looked at him in surprise at the strange question. It seemed out of place at a time like this. Even Saguaro looked surprised.

"I . . . I have no one in that world," she replied. "I feel at home with Saguaro now . . . wherever that might be. I am carrying his child, and I love him. Do you think I would betray you? Is that why you always look at me so strangely?"

Cochise glanced at Saguaro and back to Shannon. "No," he said quietly. "I only worry that something might take you from Saguaro."

"He is my husband. And my hair may be red and my eyes green, but I am more Apache than white now."

Cochise studied her a moment, feeling rather sad. He remembered that Bryce Edwards had saved his own wife from hanging. But what was past was past, and now he was at war with all white men, even Edwards. And Saguaro had already lost a wife and two sons. Cochise would not be the cause of more sadness for him.

Cochise reached out and touched Shannon's hair. "I believe you are truly one of us now," he told her aloud. His worry stemmed from the fact that they would now be moving into soldier territory. If she was spotted, there could be hell to pay if the soldiers misunderstood. He pushed the thought from his mind and turned to Saguaro. "We have some captives," he said, now changing the subject. "We will teach them what happens to men who raid Apache camps and kill women and children! Ai?"

"Ai!" Saguaro replied excitedly. He stood up and helped Shannon to her feet. "Stake some of them out in the sun with no clothing and fill their mouths with sand!" Saguaro was saying, now getting wrapped up in revenge. "Let the women spit on them! Put some in a pit with snakes! Burn out the eyes of some and tie some

281

to stakes and lance them to death! We will set an example for those who return!"

Shannon felt faint at the words. She could hear a man screaming horribly in the background. How could these men who were so gentle with her be so fierce and bloodthirsty? Torture and murder were as nothing to them, as long as they thought they were right and were doing it for revenge. Cochise actually smiled now.

"A Mescalero not need tell Chiricahua how to torture a man," he sneered. "We will have contest and see who can cause most pain. Already I have cut the eyelids of one and tied him and set the ants on him! He is the one you hear screaming!"

Both men laughed and Shannon paled and turned away. Cochise glanced at her and turned back to Saguaro. "In some ways she will never be Apache," he told him.

"We must leave quickly, before Mexicans return with more men," Saguaro was saying as he packed their travois. "They know we are here now. They steal our women and children. Trip will take five, six days. Saguaro make you rest safely on travois. I am sorry for this, White Flower. Child may come while we travel, but there will be women to help you. Do not be afraid."

She reached up and touched his bandaged shoulder. "Are you all right, Saguaro?"

"Saguaro is sore. It go away soon." He bent down and kissed her cheek. "We must leave now. We buried our dead quickly beneath rocks. There is nothing else we can do here."

"How many were killed, Saguaro?"

282

"Fifty perhaps. Many more wounded."

Shannon closed her eyes. "Oh, Saguaro, Bright Sun! And Eagle Feather! I liked them so very much. I love all of them. And Bright Sun was so sweet, such a happy child."

He touched her cheek. "Do not weep, White Flower. Save your tears, if there are any left. To weep is bad for you."

"I don't want to leave this place," she said sadly. "I liked it here. I was happy here. Now God only knows what will happen to us."

Saguaro grasped her arms firmly. "Nothing will happen," he said gently. "Not to my White Flower." He bent down and pressed his cheek against hers. "Now you know," he said in a near-whisper, petting her hair. "You know, my white squaw, what it has been like for Apache—always chased from their homeland, until there is nothing left we can call our own. It will be like this and worse before it is over. But Saguaro will protect and comfort you, no matter what happens. You have Saguaro's promise."

She suddenly hated the Mexicans and even her own people. She closed her eyes and kissed Saguaro's cheek. "I will go wherever you go," she whispered. "My home is with you."

The morning of August 28, 1861, found Shannon Fitzgerald and Bryce Edwards unknowingly moving closer to each other. Bryce left Fort Bowie that morning with a company of 150 men, having been informed by scouts that a large band of Apaches had been spotted moving north. The soldiers headed southeast, warning settlers along the way to be on the lookout and promising to keep the area well guarded.

That same morning, Shannon lay on a travois, bumping over the rugged terrain. The Indians moved silently over the desert country of the Rio Grande between the Sierra Madres and the Dragoon Mountains. It was an eerie silence. Mothers covered the mouths of their babies and let them nurse more often to keep them quiet. When dogs barked, they were kicked. Horses were muzzled. It was imperative that they travel under as much cover and in as much silence as possible. Women cried silent tears over loved ones left behind.

Shannon felt strangely separated from all of them, again finding it incredible that she was here at all and actually feeling sorry for these lost wanderers whom she had once feared so greatly. They reminded her of the lost people from the Bible stories she had been told when she was a small girl in Virginia.

Virginia! she thought, feeling a pain in her chest at the memory. There was cool shade there, and soft, green grass. She thought about the lovely dresses she used to wear, her elegant hairdos and the beautiful house she had once lived in. She thought about poor Marney and wondered where she and Parker were now. Wouldn't Marney carry on if she knew what had happened to Shannon! How strange it all seemed. It was as though that life belonged to a different girl, not the one who lay on this travois, dressed in a common tunic and about to bear the child of an Apache chief! How strange life was. And then she thought of Bryce.

It had been over three years now since their last day together. She still wore his ring around her neck. She closed her eyes and dared to think of his kiss that beautiful afternoon, the glory of giving her virginity to the handsome, lonely soldier who had loved her so and had gently claimed her in that moment of great need and passion.

But that was another time, another place, another Shannon.

Early the next morning, as they camped in the foothills of the Dragoons, the black pain suddenly ripped through Shannon's insides, and she cried out, forgetting she was supposed to be quiet. Saguaro hurried to her side and clamped a hand over her mouth.

"The baby is coming?" he asked anxiously. Shannon nodded her head with frightened eyes, wanting to scream out again, the pain seeming worse because she could not yell.

"Please try not to cry out with the pain," Saguaro pleaded.

She closed her eyes and felt the tears coming—tears of pain and fright. Was she to give birth out here in this desolate land? They were so close to their destination. If only the baby had waited. Saguaro ordered a wickiup to be erected quickly, so that Shannon could be placed inside, out of the hot sun. He hurried over to Cochise's camp.

"The child comes," he told Cochise. "You must take others and go to safety. I camp here until child comes."

"It will be dangerous, Saguaro!"

"Saguaro knows this. But Saguaro must think of woman and child now. I keep two squaws with me to help with birth."

"You should also keep at least thirty warriors to help

protect you in case some soldiers or miners discover you."

"Ai. Saguaro do this. But no more than thirty. If something should happen, it will only take away too many men from you, Cochise."

The two men clasped hands. "Good luck to you then, Saguaro."

"And good luck to you, Cochise, my friend. Soon you be with your own woman. I will join you soon—at the Valley of Purple Rocks."

"Ai. That is where we will make camp and wait for you. Soldiers not find us there. Soon we will again go to war." He smiled. "I hope it is a son, Saguaro."

Saguaro nodded. Their eyes held in friendship, then Saguaro left to hurry back to Shannon. Thirty warriors and two squaws remained behind as the rest of the massive Apache tribe moved on with Cochise, and the long and painful ordeal began for Shannon Fitzgerald.

She was not designed well for delivering babies, and she needed medical help. But there was none to be had. She squatted the way the Apache squaws instructed her, and clung to a post buried in the ground for support so that she would have something to hold on to as she panted and moaned in agony.

Saguaro paced outside the tipi. It would not be a quick birth. The wind howled mournfully, mingling with Shannon's cries of pain and fear—pain that took her into another world, removed from the one in which she was physically located. She wondered if she was going to die as the long, gnarled fingers of pain reached inside her belly and pulled mercilessly at a child that was not quite ready to make its exit into the harsh life of the Apache world.

The waiting went on for hours, and Saguaro feared for the life of his delicate white squaw and the child she was delivering. He blamed himself for having to take her on this strenuous journey, but they had had no choice. It had been difficult enough even for the healthy ones, let alone a woman about to give birth. He cursed the hot sun. He cursed the Mexicans who had chased them out. And he cursed the white settlers who had taken so much of their land that they were forever moving from place to place. Shannon screamed again, and Saguaro walked away from the area to pray for her and for his child.

The day drifted into dusk, and the sun hung low in the west. Saguaro and his men still waited, talking little. And Bryce Edwards made camp with his men only a half mile away, just over a high and rocky hill, in a small canyon, where he had remained undetected by Saguaro's men.

Bryce squatted by a small fire, kept small so that there would not be too much smoke. He poured himself some coffee, then looked up at the canyon wall when he heard a strange, eerie cry—unlike any animal he had ever heard before. He looked at Reynolds, who also heard the sound.

"Go tell the rest of the men to be completely silent for a minute and to muzzle the horses," he told Reynolds in a near-whisper.

"Yes, sir."

Everyone quieted and listened. Reynolds returned to Bryce, and they strained their ears. There was the sound again!

"That's no animal, Reynolds," Bryce said quietly.

"Sounds more like a woman to me, sir," Reynolds replied. "Maybe somebody's in trouble."

"Let's take a look. Round up a few men—quietly. I think we can get up that canyon wall. Sounds to me like it's coming from the other side."

Reynolds gathered six more men and Bryce signaled silently for them to follow him up the embankment. They moved quickly and quietly, and when they reached the top, they could see the small Indian camp. Bryce signaled for the telescope. He held it up and adjusted it. Then he broke into a grin.

"Well, I'll be goddamned!" he remarked. "We may not have Cochise, Reynolds, but we've got the next best thing. That's Saguaro down there! By God, I don't intend to let him get away! He just might know something about Shannon Fitzgerald!"

"Why do you suppose there's so few of them, sir?"

"From the sound of things, some squaw is having her kid. Let's try to take them peacefully, for the woman's sake. I can't pass this up, Reynolds, baby or no baby. If Saguaro had anything to do with harming Miss Fitzgerald, he's one Indian I won't mind hanging myself!"

"Sir, he spared your life once."

"And he said that evened us up! When it comes to harming a woman like Shannon Fitzgerald, there's no room for mercy or old friendships, Reynolds!"

Bryce moved quickly and quietly back down the canyon wall and alerted the rest of the men, who took up arms. He ordered about half of them back up the canyon, to move in on one side of the Indian camp on foot, while the rest of them would ride around the hill on horseback and approach from the other side. All were given orders not to kill Saguaro, so as to be sure Bryce would be able to question the man about Shannon.

The foot soldiers gave Bryce and the others time to make the long ride around to the other side, and then they swooped down from above, cocking their rifles and shouting orders to the Indians not to resist, as they were outnumbered. Shannon could hear the voices and shouting.

"Saguaro!" she screamed. "Saguaro, what's happening!" Then the horrible pain hit her again, and it didn't matter what was going on outside. The two squaws fled in fright from the wickiup at the sound of the English-speaking voices outside. The startled Indian bucks began firing back before Saguaro could give any orders. Shannon groaned and wept as she heard the firing of guns.

"Oh, God, no! No! Not now!" she wailed, as another pain engulfed her and removed her mind from the present battle. She screamed as the wicked hands of labor again pushed and pulled at her insides, and she grasped the pole tightly and pushed automatically, but nothing came. She felt she would go crazy from pain and the sounds of battle outside the wickiup.

"Saguaro!" she screamed again. "Saguaro! Saguaro!"

Five of Saguaro's men fell under the soldiers' surprise bullets, and the two squaws fled in fright and quickly disappeared into the rocks, sure that the white soldiers would rape them if they made themselves evident. Bryce and his men rode at a gallop into the camp, and Saguaro whirled and aimed a rifle at Bryce, who kicked the gun from the Indian's hands, then pushed Saguaro in the chest with his foot and knocked the man down.

"Tell your men to stop fighting—now!" he ordered Saguaro. "You're outnumbered, Saguaro! This time I'm the one springing the surprise! Give it up, Saguaro! I don't want to kill you!" He held his revolver on Saguaro and remained on his horse as he shouted the orders. Saguaro got up slowly. He growled a command to his men in his own tongue, and the other Apaches stopped fighting. The Indians threw down their weapons and looked around at each other, not sure what to expect. The two squaws kept running, deciding to search out Cochise and tell him Saguaro needed help.

"So, white soldier, we meet again!" Saguaro hissed.

"I've been looking for you for months!" Bryce told the man, now dismounting.

"We owe each other nothing now. So, you may kill me, white soldier!"

"I don't intend to kill you, Saguaro—not unless I find out you've had something to do with harming a woman I've been looking for for over a year. You're my prisoner now, and it will go a lot easier on you if you answer my questions truthfully. After some of the raids and killings you've committed, I could hang you right here and now, and no one would give a damn!"

"What questions? What woman?" Saguaro asked, becoming alarmed.

Bryce poked the man in the chest with his revolver. "Not here," he grumbled. "Whatever vile things might have happened to my woman, I don't want the rest of my men knowing the sordid details! Get over there,

290

away from camp." He motioned to his right, and the two men walked several yards away while the rest of the soldiers rounded up their prisoners. Reynolds watched after Bryce, ready to come to his defense if necessary.

Bryce walked Saguaro behind a huge boulder. "One move and I'll shoot out your knees!" he warned quietly. His eyes glittered with eagerness. Finally he had someone new he could ask about Shannon!

"I've been searching for a white woman," he continued in a low voice. "I asked Cochise and Coloradas about her, but they knew nothing. The only one I could never find to ask was you. She was to come out here and marry me, but she disappeared, and I've been searching for her ever since. I want to know if you know anything about a white woman. Did you kidnap one and sell her to the Mexicans?"

Saguaro stood there speechless at first. Bryce cocked his pistol. "Answer me, Saguaro!" he growled. But he felt himself softening when a strange, desperate look came into Saguaro's dark eyes, which actually appeared to have tears in them.

"You . . . not take her back!" he pleaded. "You not take her! They will put her in their prison. She is mine. Mine!"

The words cut through Bryce like a butcher knife, and his eyes widened with disbelief. "Explain yourself!" he hissed.

"Saguaro!" Shannon screamed from inside the wickiup, almost crazy with fear and confusion. Bryce looked toward the wickiup, sensing something in the voice vaguely familiar. His heart pounded furiously with dread.

"You!" Saguaro hissed, looking at Bryce as though

he were an apparition. "You are the soldier she was to marry! I did not know! You are not dead then!"

"Dead? Who said I was dead?"

"She say you are! She not say name, only that she is told you are dead!" Saguaro breathed hard from excitement and fear for Shannon. "She alone . . . afraid! Saguaro not hurt her! Saguaro loves her! Please promise you will not hurt my White Flower!"

"*Your* White Flower?" Bryce was beet red with rage at the realization that this man had a white woman. "What do you mean?"

Saguaro trembled with fear for Shannon. "Your woman . . . have red hair . . . like clay; eyes . . . color of grass?"

Bryce stood stock still and speechless. His eyes began to tear.

"My God!" he whispered.

"She say she is once called . . . Shannon . . . from far in the East, a place called Virginia."

Bryce's eyes filled with hate and rage. He grasped Saguaro's vest in his fists and gave the man a jerk, the gun barrel under Saguaro's chin. "Where is she!" he demanded. "What have you done with her!"

Saguaro looked him squarely in the eyes, standing straight and proud. "I have only loved her," he replied calmly. "I protected her . . . gave her home. If not for Saguaro, she would be dead now, or lost and alone . . . perhaps a Mexican slave. Saguaro not hurt her. She is Saguaro's wife."

Bryce felt himself exploding inside, his thoughts whirling and confused. He didn't know whether to be happy or outraged or sad, whether to kill this man or thank him. "Your . . . wife!" he hissed.

292

"Ai. Even now she gives birth to Saguaro's child."

Bryce let go of the man and backed away. He could not bear the thought of it. "No!" he groaned. "You're lying! You lying bastard!"

"Saguaro does not lie!" the Indian replied defensively, himself in agony. What would this white man do to him now? What would happen to his precious White Flower? "Go and see for yourself," he said dejectedly. "She is in wickiup, giving birth. It is Saguaro's life she carries—willingly!"

Bryce stepped closer. "Why would she give herself to an Apache buck willingly!" he sneered. "You forced her!"

Saguaro shook his head. "No. I not force or hurt her. But you must not think she has been bad woman. She sweet and good. She told you are dead. She alone and afraid. She think your own people will put her in prison. She abused by her own kind, hunted. She think her people will hang her for killing a man who beat her and try to rape her. You must promise Saguaro you not harm her or send her back! If you do, by the God of the Sun, Saguaro will hunt you down and kill you, slowly and painfully!"

"Saguaro!" the woman screamed again, and went on, in English, "Where are you? Help me!"

Bryce's face drained of all color. The voice! Even screamed in the pains of childbirth he could recognize it. He would never forget the voice. And she had called out in English. Apache women had their own strange wail and chant when giving birth. He only hoped none of the other men would suspect.

He struggled to keep his composure, reminding himself of the kind of sweet, innocent child Shannon had been when he had left her. The way she called for Saguaro was not the way a woman called to a man she hated and feared. But could she truly have given herself to this man willingly? He put the barrel of his pistol against Saguaro's throat. "We're going back to the others, and we'll keep this quiet for the moment," he growled. "Understand?"

Saguaro held Bryce's eyes, jealous that this handsome soldier had been Shannon's first man, yet glad her lover had been a man of strength and bravery, as he knew this one to be. "Saguaro understands," he replied, trying to control his own desolation. "You are ashamed for your men to know your woman has been with an Apache man. But it is not the way you see it. You must never blame her or be ashamed of her. And please . . . do not harm her."

Bryce pulled the revolver away. "Harm Shannon? I love her. I've searched for her for a year!" How he wanted to pull the trigger! But he had to see Shannon first, find out from her what was the truth. Shannon! Not Shannon! He must keep this quiet, if possible. He must guard her honor, keep her from suffering the humiliation of how the other men might look at her. But he must also control his own reaction. He must not let her see shame or rejection in his eyes, at least not yet. He must first hear her side. And yet it didn't seem to matter. The thought that she could even be alive was too wonderful, too miraculous! Shannon! Was it truly she in the wickiup?

He motioned for Saguaro to return to the camp. "If she tells me you forced yourself on her, you're a dead man, Saguaro!" he warned. "I'll hack your balls off and feed them to the dogs and skin you alive!"

Saguaro turned away sadly, afraid now only for Shannon. They returned to the other men.

"I don't want this man harmed!" Bryce ordered. "Save him for me!"

Saguaro met Bryce's eyes, his own pleading. For a moment their eyes held in mutual understanding. Saguaro looked as though someone had stuck him with a lance and Bryce was moved by the look of devastation on his face.

"I have already lost a woman and sons," Saguaro spoke up. "Do not take this woman and child from me!"

Bryce turned away and walked toward the wickiup, his legs feeling weak. Reynolds watched curiously, wondering at the looks of sorrow on each man's face.

Bryce entered the wickiup hesitantly, then stopped still to look upon what could be a white woman. Her arms were tanned dark. She was squatted on a blanket on her knees and clinging to a pole, bent over and crying and moaning, her back to him. Bryce felt his heart shattering, piece by piece. He studied the reddish hair, worn in a thick braid down her back and tied with pretty beads. He was almost afraid to speak. He swallowed.

"Shannon?" he asked gently.

She gasped and turned to look at him. Her eyes widened. She began shaking her head and trembling. She went into a strange wail and scooted away from him.

"You're . . . alive!" she screamed. "My God! You're alive!"

Chapter Seventeen

Bryce stood rigid for a moment, staring at her in disbelief. He could hardly convince himself that the tanned woman in the common tunic and Indian beads who sat trembling in the corner was the young girl he had left behind in Virginia three years earlier. His first reaction was horror and near revulsion. She was the wife of an Apache! His Shannon! She saw the look in his eyes.

"The man at the station told me you were dead!" she screamed in her humiliation. She wanted so much to run to him—to touch him and to have him hold her. Bryce! Bryce! But his eyes!

"My God," she screamed, her breath coming in short, desperate gasps, as she felt another pain coming, "he told me you were dead! Dead. Saguaro . . . helped me. He helped me! He loves me! I . . . had no one. No one!" She began to sob. "What have you done . . . with Saguaro? Where's Saguaro!"

She covered her face with her arms and bent over in another pain, groaning and sobbing, her pain increased by what she was sure Bryce was thinking of her. How must she look! He must think her a white whore who groveled in an Indian's bed and was now having his bastard son. But suddenly he was at her side. There was the familiar hand on her arm.

"Be still, Shannon," he told her softly. "I'm trying to keep your identity from the others, for your own protection and Saguaro's. Saguaro hasn't been harmed." She trembled in his arms and he held her tighter. "It's all right, Shannon. I just . . . my God, Shannon, this is all such a shock! I've searched for you for so long! I had finally come to the conclusion you were dead, and now, here you are!"

She suddenly tried to pull away from him. "You hate me!" she whimpered. "I know what you're thinking!" She struggled to be free of him, but he would not let go. "It's not . . . like that at all! Oh, God, Bryce, I . . . didn't have anybody. I couldn't . . . go back to Virginia. They'd put me in prison . . . for . . . McGuire. God, Bryce, McGuire! He was so . . . ugly . . . and brutal. He beat me and was going to . . . steal what . . . belonged to you! God help me, I killed him! I killed him!"

He grabbed her close against her will and held her tightly against his chest, he himself now in tears, a mixture of joy at finding her alive and terrible inner pain at the thought of all that had happened to her. He held her firmly until she began to calm down. Then she grasped at his sleeve and doubled over with another pain. He held her until it subsided.

"Hang on, love," he whispered, kissing her hair. "This will all work out. Right now let's get this baby born. There'll be time enough later for talking. How

298

long have you been in labor?" He wiped at his eyes with his sleeve.

"I . . . don't know . . . anymore. Since . . . before dawn," she gasped. She breathed in rapid pants. Bryce took her small chin in his large hand and raised her face, forcing her to look at him. He could barely talk when he looked into the beautiful, beloved green eyes. Tears spilled down his cheeks.

"My God, Shannon! Please . . . forgive me!" he choked out. "I should have . . . brought you with me . . . three years ago!"

He grabbed her close and wept like a child. She reached around his neck. Oh, how good it felt to be held by him again! It was really Bryce! And perhaps he didn't hate her, after all!

"Bryce . . . I thought . . . the man . . . at the station . . . he said you were killed . . . when I mentioned your name. And when he knew I was alone . . . he tried to force me to . . ." She began sobbing harder now, wanting to scream out her devastation. "If not for Saguaro . . . he would have raped me . . . and maybe he'd have sold me . . . or . . . I don't know! He—"

"Not now, Shannon," he whispered, now kissing her over and over, her hair, her cheeks, her eyes, her lips, filled with hunger and passion and joy and remorse. "Shannon! Shannon!" he whispered. He sat all the way down and pulled her onto his lap. "What's happened to my beautiful Shannon!" He wept again and rocked her in his arms.

"Oh, Bryce, how did it ever end up like this?" she sobbed. "I loved you . . . so much. I tried so hard to get to you. Oh, Bryce, it was all . . . so horrible! Loren McGuire—"

299

"Shhhh. Not now, honey. Not now. I know all about it, Shannon—everything. You've been cleared of everything. You've nothing to fear. And we'll worry about what we're going to do about all of this later." He pulled back a little and gently touched her stomach. "The damned war has taken its toll on all of us, hasn't it?" he said in a strained voice.

"Oh, Bryce!" She drew her knees up in another pain. He held her until it was over. "They're getting . . . worse!" she panted. "Bryce, help me!"

He gently laid her down on the blanket.

"Get . . . the two squaws," she whimpered.

"They ran off, honey. They aren't here."

"Oh, my God! Bryce! I'm afraid! Who's going to help me!" She gasped as another pain came. She screamed as the black, merciless hands of pain dug at her insides once more.

"I'll help you myself," he told her gently. He bent her knees and pulled her tunic up to her waist.

"No!" she cried. "I can't . . . let you help! I don't want you . . . to look at me. Not . . . this way! Oh, God, Bryce, none of this . . . is like we planned!"

"You relax and quit worrying," he said, bending over her and wiping away her tears. "Now I helped deliver a baby not long ago. A white woman's family was killed by the—" He stopped and thought about how ironic this whole situation was. "By the Apaches," he went on. "They left her alive because she was with child, and she had the damned kid right then and there when we came across her. I think I know what to do, Shannon."

"No! I can't . . . let you!" she protested, grasping the post as another pain came.

"Shannon Fitzgerald, do you think after all these

months of searching for you, and knowing how much I love you, I'm going to just let you lie here and have this baby by yourself?" he said sternly. "This is no time to worry about being modest. And I'll be damned if I'll let any other man here help you." He bent over and kissed her again. "This is me, Shannon. Bryce. It's all right. After all we've been through, what does it matter? I love you."

She looked up into the beautiful gray eyes.

"And you're right. Things sure don't turn out like we plan them, do they?" he said softly, his own tears coming again. She knew he was wishing it was his child she was having.

"Oh, Bryce," she whispered. "I'm so . . . ashamed!"

"Ashamed of what? You tell me one thing you've done wrong, Shannon. One thing you have to be ashamed of."

She choked in a sob and closed her eyes.

"Bryce . . . I never . . . did anything wrong! How can I . . . make you understand . . . about Saguaro? Oh, God, Bryce, he loves me! And I love him. But I . . . thought you were dead . . . and I was so . . . scared . . . and lonely. And he was so . . . kind and good."

"Shannon, you haven't one thing to be ashamed of or that you have to explain. I'm not saying it's easy for me to swallow, but that isn't your fault. None of it is your fault. Now I want you to quit worrying about it and concentrate on getting this baby born so we can get you out of your pain, honey. Let's take one thing at a time."

The horrible agony came again, and she screamed in the worst pain she had had yet. "God, Bryce, it won't come! It won't come!" she sobbed.

"Yes, it will come if you just try to relax, Shannon," he told her. He kept his hands on her shoulders until the pain subsided a little, and then she seemed to slip into her own world of pain and labor. She lay limp and groaning, her eyes closed. Bryce wiped more tears from his eyes and went out for a moment, hesitating at the entrance.

Never had he been so confused. He hated and he loved Saguaro. He still loved Shannon—probably more than ever. But now she belonged to an Apache Indian—a renegade chief who raided and killed. It made him want to vomit. How many nights had he dreamed of holding her in his arms again, being one with her again? Now he would see her lovely body again, but in a bloody birth, the flat stomach he had dreamed about now swollen large with an Indian's child! Still, all that was important was her life at the moment. They would talk after the birth and see if they couldn't somehow piece their lives back together. He called Reynolds aside and the young man hurried over.

"Yes, sir?" the man asked anxiously.

Their eyes held. "I . . . need your total confidence and secrecy, Reynolds," Bryce told him in a strained voice.

Reynolds looked toward the wickiup entrance, then back to Bryce. "Sir?"

Bryce swallowed. "It's her . . . Miss Fitzgerald . . . inside the wickiup."

Reynolds's eyes widened. "The woman you've searched for?" he asked quietly.

Bryce closed his eyes momentarily and nodded. "She's . . . having a child. She needs my help,

Reynolds. There's no time to go into detail. I don't want the other men to know. You can understand."

"Yes, sir," the man replied, his heart aching for Bryce. "What can I do to help?"

"For one thing, let the others think it's just an Indian woman inside that I am helping. Tell them it's Saguaro's woman and because of that I want to protect her and let her give birth before we move on."

Reynolds saw the pain in Bryce's eyes. "Saguaro's woman?"

Bryce sighed. "Saguaro's." He rubbed at his eyes. "Heat some water and bring it to me along with a couple of clean blankets."

"Yes, sir, right away."

"Get Saguaro off to the side and tell him I'm taking care of the woman and will let him know when the child is delivered."

Reynolds knitted his eyebrows. "Don't you want Saguaro hung, sir?"

Bryce shook his head. "No," he replied wearily. "It isn't . . . what you think. Just do what I've told you, Reynolds. And keep this thing quiet, for her sake and for Saguaro's safety."

"Yes, sir." The young man left, glancing at the wickiup first once more. It was not his business to pry, only to obey this man who had saved his life once.

Bryce glanced over at Saguaro, who watched him pleadingly. *Damn you*! he thought. You've got me in one hell of a mess! How in hell can I deal with you the way I ought to when she . . . cares for you? Damn you!

He turned around and went back inside the wickiup. Shannon was tossing and groaning, sweating profusely. The blanket beneath her was soaked where her water had broken. For several more minutes Bryce worked with her, consoled her, until Reynolds called from the wickiup entrance. Bryce ordered him inside, and Reynolds entered hesitantly, averting his eyes from Shannon's bent knees.

"I . . . I'm no good at these things, sir," the young man said in a shaky voice, his back turned. He sat down the water and blankets.

"It's all right, Reynolds. Give me the blankets, and then I want you to keep her face bathed so the perspiration doesn't get in her eyes. You can do that much."

Reynolds did as he was told. By then Shannon's pains were almost continuous. "Hold her down," Bryce told Reynolds. "I think the baby is starting to come. I've got to keep her still and I'll need help."

Reynolds swallowed and moved closer to the tossing young woman. Bryce had a clean blanket beneath her now. Reynolds wet a rag and gently bathed her face. Her hair was matted with sweat and she groaned and whimpered, barely aware of either of their presence now, lost in the deep pains of childbirth. Her abdomen gripped her and bore down, trying to force out the life inside of her. She had no control now over what happened. She would give birth, and there was no way to fight it or stop it. The long, deep, searing pain tore through her, and she gritted her teeth and stopped breathing as she automatically pushed.

"That's good, love," Bryce told her gently. "It's coming now. It won't be long, Shannon."

"She—she's awful pretty, sir. Just like you said," Reynolds told him, studying the small face. "I can just see how pretty she must be, all dressed up in one of those fancy dresses the southern ladies wear, floating around a ballroom floor."

Bryce watched in appreciation as Reynolds washed her face again.

"I wish you could see her that way, Reynolds," he said quietly. He wanted to weep again. He gently ran his hands over her stomach. "She was the prettiest thing you ever saw." His voice began to break. "And she—uh—she was the sweetest, most innocent child . . . when I left her three years ago." He squeezed his eyes shut, wishing all of this were some kind of nightmare and he would wake up. But her next scream brought him back to reality, and the baby's head had begun to appear when he checked her.

"It's almost over, honey," he told her. "Just a couple of minutes."

"Bryce? Bryce?"

"I'm right here, Shannon."

"Oh, Bryce. You're alive! You're . . . alive!" She began sobbing uncontrollably. "My God! It's too late! Oh, Bryce! Bryce!"

He noticed the ring, which had fallen back on its chain and was lying by her neck. He reached down and gently fingered it for a moment.

"It's never too late for anything, Shannon," he commented. He bent down and lightly kissed her forehead. "It's never too late."

"Bryce, don't . . . go away!"

"I'm not going anywhere, Shannon."

"McGuire! Don't send me back there, Bryce. Don't send me back! Oh, God, Bryce!" she screamed as another pain ripped through her.

"Hang on to her, Reynolds," Bryce ordered as she

305

tried to get up now and lashed out in her pain. "Don't pay any attention to anything she says or does. Just hold her down."

"Yes, sir," Reynolds replied, already struggling with Shannon. He grasped her wrists and practically lay on top of her to keep her still.

"Let me go! Let me go!" she screamed. "Oh, God! God! Don't let him get me! Bryce! Bryce! Where are you!"

"I'm right here, honey. Your baby is halfway out."

"McGuire! Get him away! No! No! No! Bryce, help me! Help me!"

Bryce wished Loren McGuire were here now so that he could reap a proper vengeance on him. The Apache way. He realized now that it was not Saguaro who had taken this woman from him. It was Loren McGuire. If not for the man's attack, Shannon would not have fled Virginia so quickly. Bryce would have known her whereabouts and her trip would have been charted and guarded, and he would have met her in New Mexico with an entire escort to see that she got to Fort Bowie safely.

Reynolds hung on tightly, afraid he was hurting her as she struggled. Moments later he heard a smack and a squeak and then a baby's irritated screaming as it was rudely introduced into the real world. Reynolds turned to look and saw Bryce holding up a bloody and very tiny pink piece of life with shocking black hair that seemed too thick for its tiny head and body. Its arms flailed furiously and it screamed with amazing power.

"It's a boy!" Bryce said with tears in his eyes. How he had wanted a child like this! "Go tell Saguaro," he went on, "and get back in here and help me clean up the baby

306

and Shannon. Then we'll let Saguaro see the child and let Shannon rest."

"Yes, sir."

Reynolds ran out and Bryce looked at Shannon lying there weak and limp. He wrapped the baby in a towel and laid it on her chest.

"Shannon? Look, honey. You have a son."

She whimpered and opened her eyes, raising a weak hand to place it on the child's head. She studied the dark hair.

"Mine?" she said, sounding surprised. "I . . . really did it?"

"You sure did." Bryce replied. "It's a boy. That should make Saguaro happy." Shannon looked into his eyes.

"My poor Bryce!" she said, beginning to cry. "Oh, God, Bryce. You . . . wanted children . . . so badly." She choked in a deep sob and he took her hand.

"Now you stop that," he demanded. "You'll make yourself sick. It will all work out, Shannon. And a new mother shouldn't be crying. She should be happy. I'll clean up the baby and you, and then you will rest. You need it badly. You can just lie here and sleep and feed your son. I'll take care of everything else."

"Bryce," she wept, putting his hand to her lips. "I've never . . . stopped loving you, Bryce. Never! You . . . believe me . . . don't you?"

"Of course I believe you. And I've never stopped loving you, Shannon."

Shannon slipped into a deep sleep, while Bryce worked on the afterbirth, gently pushing downward on

307

the stomach that was now only slightly swollen, and wondering how on earth this tiny girl had just delivered a baby. She seemed so very small now, the way he had remembered her. Her legs were still slender and white, untouched by the sun because of her long tunics. Only her arms and face were tanned. She was still so small and lovely, but his heart was crushed when he looked at the baby, clean and quiet, lying beside her. How could she ever belong to Bryce Edwards again? Her loyalty would lie with the baby's father.

Bryce studied the child as it wiggled and made little gurgling noises. It had not yet opened its eyes to reveal their color—though eye color would probably change, anyway. But it was obvious his skin would be very dark, and his thick, straight, black hair was all Apache. Bryce found it almost incredible to think the tiny bit of life he was looking at had come out of Shannon's womb. He did not look as though he belonged to her at all.

But he did belong to her. And he was an Apache! An Apache! How ironic it all was, and how horribly real! Here was the woman he had mourned over all these months. He would never love another as he had loved her. He had finally found her—miracle of miracles. Only to learn she belonged to someone else; and to top it off, she belonged to a man Bryce was being paid to hunt down and place on a reservation. Would Shannon stay with Saguaro and submit herself to the filthy reservation life?

"Never!" he thought to himself. "I'll not let her. I'll keep her with me! She'll forget Saguaro and come back to the life she was made for."

He looked at the child again. Yes. He could love the

child, because it was Shannon's, and she would love it. The child would be no problem, and he would knock the teeth out of anyone who dared to insult her or the boy.

He turned and wet a rag in warm water and proceeded to wash her thoroughly, removing her tunic and taking his time—wanting to touch her and continue to drink in the reality that she was real and alive. Then he put one of his own shirts on her. She sighed and moaned slightly, not fully aware of what was happening.

His eyes rested for a moment on the full breasts he had so often dreamed about tasting and caressing again. He could not resist bending down and kissing one breast lightly before buttoning the shirt. So what if she was no longer his? He had been first to claim her, first to invade the small, sweet body. No other man could claim that, and he had that much to comfort him. Now he had to touch her sweet body again, kiss her again, or he'd go mad. He knew it was quite possible he would never get this opportunity again. He struggled against tears at the fearful premonition that, if forced to choose loyalties, this young woman would choose Saguaro. He was the father of her child. A woman's instinct and emotions could not lead her to do otherwise.

He reasoned with himself about the whole sitiuation, telling himself he must stay in control if he was confronted with the worst. To bring harm or death to Saguaro at this moment would destroy whatever love she still had for Bryce. He could not do that. Even if she remained with Saguaro, Bryce knew that she still loved Bryce Edwards. And as long as she loved him, there would be hope that somewhere, sometime, she would come to him and he would finally make her his own for all time. Yet how could he bear to lose her again, now that he had found her? How could he possibly let her ride away with Saguaro? And what would he *do* with Saguaro? Could he arrest the man and put him on a reservation or risk his being hung if Shannon chose to stay with him? There were some decisions to be made. Some very grave decisions. Shannon's well-being and happiness hung in the balance.

Bryce packed her bottom with the cattail down padding the Apache squaws had left behind, then covered her. The baby began to squeal tiny cries, which soon built into a hearty squalling. Bryce had planned to take the child out to show to Saguaro, but the crying made him nervous, and he decided a feeding first would be more important at the moment. He shook Shannon lightly.

"Shannon?" he said softly. She looked so very, very tired and pale. Her eyes were sunken and dark. The birth had been a long ordeal, and, combined with the shock of seeing Bryce alive and her fear for Saguaro, her body was relaxing into a badly needed sleep to regain its strength. He hated waking her. But there was obviously no other means of satisfying the irate infant who lay beside her screaming for some nourishment.

"Shannon," he repeated. "The baby has to eat."

"Saguaro?" she said in a half whisper. The name stabbed at Bryce's heart. The baby cried harder.

"Shannon, it's me. Bryce. You've got to feed the baby, honey."

"Hmmm?" She opened her eyes slowly and spoke as though drugged. "Bryce?" She came fully awake, and fear returned to her eyes. "You . . . hate me . . . don't you?"

"No, Shannon. I don't hate you."

"Yes . . . you do. I saw your . . . eyes! You don't understand at all!" she whimpered, beginning to cry.

"Shannon, you're in no condition to discuss any of it right now. Just roll on your side, honey. Can you do that? Roll on your side and I'll support the baby."

"Why are you . . . helping me?" she sobbed. "You shouldn't be." Bryce gently helped her roll onto her left side and propped some blankets behind her.

"I'm helping you because I love you, Shannon. Do you really think I'd blame you for anything that's happened? How shallow do you think my love is?"

She kept crying as he opened her shirt and pulled it down over her right shoulder. He scooted the baby under her and put a blanket beneath him to raise him up slightly so that he could reach her right nipple. He gently guided her breast into the infant's mouth, and the child's crying stopped immediately as it sucked away hungrily. Bryce could not help but admire the sight, even though the child was not his own. The sight of a child feeding at its mother's breast was very warming to a man, and what a beautiful mother this child had! If only it were his own son lying here now.

"Reynolds," Bryce called out as quietly as possible. The man was right outside the entrance waiting for more instructions.

"Sir?"

"Go get Saguaro. I don't think you need to worry about him escaping—not with Shannon and his new son here. Tell him he can come and see his son. I expect he has a right to."

311

Reynolds walked off into the quiet night, and moments later Saguaro appeared at the entrance and hesitated. Bryce looked up at him.

"She's pretty groggy right now, Saguaro. I don't think she even knows what's going on at the moment. You can come and see your son."

"Saguaro is grateful!" the man replied, his eyes shining with pride as he approached Shannon. He knelt down beside her, and Bryce was amazed at the softness in his eyes and his absolute worshipful attitude as he gently stroked her face. This was a savage Apache warrior, capable of murder and torture and heated revenge. The Indian leaned over to watch the child nursing. He touched the boy's head with the gentleness of a kitten and opened the blanket to check the hands and feet. The baby immediately gripped Saguaro's finger, and Saguaro had to pry the tiny fingers loose to get him to let go.

"He is strong!" the man said, grinning proudly.

Like his father, Bryce thought resignedly. He watched Saguaro cover the boy back up and then bend down to kiss Shannon's cheek. He said something softly to her in his own tongue, and to Bryce's surprise, Shannon replied sleepily in the same language. Had she become more Apache than he had thought?

Bryce fought a fierce jealousy, struggling not to let that jealousy override his love for Shannon and his respect for her feelings and wishes. It was childish to do so. She claimed Saguaro had never forced her, which meant only one thing. Again came the surging need to kill Saguaro at the thought of his taking what belonged to Bryce Edwards! The only saving grace was the Indian's obvious love for Shannon, and the knowledge

312

that Shannon would never have consented unless she had feelings for Saguaro, and certainly not if she knew Bryce was still alive. At least this Indian had apparently helped her forget the horror of Loren McGuire.

Bryce turned away, unable to watch any longer. He sat down on a crate on the other side of the fire from where Shannon lay and lit a cigarette. Saguaro remained behind Shannon, now stroking her face again. She still seemed to be more asleep than awake. Saguaro looked over at Bryce.

"You love her?"

Bryce turned back around and glared at the man. "I've always loved her. I've loved her since she was fourteen years old, Saguaro! That's seven years ago. Seven years!" He could not help the bitterness in his voice. "I left her three years ago and she was to come out here a year later and marry me. Then things got all botched up. Her brother was killed and her father got sick. She stayed with her father until his death."

Bryce paused and took a drag on his cigarette. "Then, unknown to me, she . . . was attacked . . . forced to kill her attacker . . . and she ran off without telling me. I guess she thought if she told me, the authorities would get word of the message and have her arrested. All I know is she must have been scared to death. I had no idea where she was. All I knew was she had killed the man and fled. I've searched for her for months and months. And now I've finally found her, and she's giving birth to an Apache child!" The last words were spit out, and Bryce stood up and turned away again.

"There is one thing you must believe, white soldier. If Saguaro knew you were the one, Saguaro would have

313

brought her to you," the Indian told him. "That is truth. Saguaro found her at stage station. The old station attendant dragged her out . . . stripped her . . . offered her to us in exchange for his life. I had him killed for his abuse of her. Her face was bruised and swollen. I ask her if she has people. She say no. She has no one. She say her man is dead. She cries. Saguaro put a blanket around her and take her back to Sierra Madres with him."

Bryce took another deep drag. "I don't understand, Saguaro. That's not what you normally do. Why in hell didn't you kill her or sell her . . . or rape her?"

"The Apache does not rape. I have now proven this by way I treat White Flower. Only white man cannot keep his manpart small. This woman was abused by white men, but never by an Apache."

Bryce almost wished she had been raped. It would give him a good excuse to have Saguaro hung. But this man had been kind to her, which only compounded Bryce's confusion.

"It is true that she was abused by her own kind," Bryce said calmly. "She's been cleared of any fault back East. I've had it all investigated, Saguaro. There's no worry about the authorities anymore. It was . . . quite obvious . . . what happened." He turned to face the Indian. "And we aren't all like the man who hurt her, Saguaro. Most of us have great respect for women, especially ladies like Shannon."

"I not say that you are that way. You are great and respected man. But Saguaro is tired of lies that are told about Apache men and white women. They not true."

Their eyes held. Bryce nodded. "I know they aren't, Saguaro. Especially now. You still haven't answered my question, though. Why did you treat Shannon differently? I've seen the dead bodies of women you've killed."

"This one was different. Her cries and struggles remind Saguaro of his own dead wife. She touch my heart. She not even full-grown woman yet. She was so small and lovely like a child, like Saguaro's first wife." He looked down lovingly at Shannon. "I looked into her eyes, and I could not harm her. She was like frightened deer. Soon I learned she had no one. She tell me she is very afraid to go home, where she will go to prison for killing man who hurt her. She weep much over what happen to her."

Saguaro bent down and kissed her again, and Bryce felt sick at the thought of the lecherous McGuire putting her through the horror of his vile attack.

"She tell Saguaro there was only one man she would have wanted after that, but that she had been told that man was dead. Man at station, he tell her her man was killed in Apache massacre. She lose so much, she believe him. She think all people she love are dead. She was homeless. So Saguaro gave her a home. Saguaro gave her love. She has friends among my people, who all love her. She was good squaw to Saguaro."

The Indian looked at Bryce, his eyes flashing now.

"But Saguaro never touch her until he sees the want in her own eyes! She was not forced." His voice softened again, and he looked back down at Shannon. "She grow to love Saguaro because she is alone and Saguaro care for her. I protect her with my life. Twice she was attacked by Mexicans, and Saguaro save her. Saguaro sat with her once for many days through a terrible sickness that almost took her from me. And

315

then she knew how much Saguaro love her. Day finally come when she look at Saguaro with want in her eyes. Now Saguaro has given her a son. She need this child. She had no one, just as Saguaro had no one. Now three of us have each other."

Bryce threw down his cigarette and stepped on it.

"Saguaro, you have nothing to offer her now. She can't stay with you. Your way of living will eventually kill her, and you know it."

Saguaro rose. "You say that because you want her for yourself!" he growled. His fear of losing Shannon began to build.

"No, Saguaro. I say it because I love her . . . very much. And I don't want her to suffer. If you love her, you won't want her to suffer either."

Saguaro's breathing quickened, and he blinked back tears. Bryce wished very much this man's love for Shannon was not so obvious. It would make things much easier. And he had always felt sorry for Saguaro for the horrible way the man had lost his first wife and two baby boys.

"Saguaro cannot live without White Flower and his new son!" the Indian said in a whisper. A tear slipped down his cheek. "Do not take them from me!" he said in a strained voice, struggling to remain in control. It was very unmanly to show tears in front of someone else. Yet the big Indian could not control them. His only consolation was that Bryce Edwards had been shedding some of his own. It had been very obvious when Saguaro entered the dwelling.

"You . . . have power . . . to take them from me!" Saguaro went on, his fists clenched. "But Saguaro is asking you not to do this. And do not put us on

316

reservation. There she would die. But if Saguaro can live free, he will take care of her. Saguaro protect her. Saguaro love her. She is mine now! I would take care of her. It is my promise!"

Bryce stepped closer. "It's true you made her your woman. But that was when she thought I was dead. I love her, too. I need her, too. I was her first man, and I've waited years to make her my wife! And as far as a reservation goes, I have no choice but to put you on one, Saguaro. That would be getting off easy, believe me. I could have you hung for some of the crimes you've committed. For Shannon's sake, I won't do it. But I'll be damned if I'll let her live on a reservation!"

Saguaro suddenly hardened, and his eyes now filled with hate.

"I see," he hissed. "So, it is fine for Indian to live in filth and humiliation. You would let our own women and children sit in their waste and lick hands of white man who hands them their food! But it not good enough for your own kind! You are like all the rest." Saguaro spat on the floor in disgust. "If this is what you are going to do with Saguaro, then keep my woman with you. But Saguaro will not stay on reservation! He get away and he take his woman back! And she will go with Saguaro, because child she nurses belongs to Saguaro!"

Bryce sighed and ran a hand through his hair. There was no stronger tie among the Apaches than family. He knew this man would do whatever it took to be reunited with Shannon and his son. He doubted any other race had a greater love and affection for its children than the Apaches.

"Look, Saguaro, I'm doing my best to make

317

reservation life better. I . . . I didn't mean that statement the way it sounded. I just—"

"It is no use, white soldier! White Father in Washington will never see it our way. It is all useless." The Indian turned and knelt back down beside Shannon. He took her hand and watched his son, still sucking away at his nourishment. "Please," the Indian said quietly. "Do not take White Flower from me. And do not take my new little son. Saguaro has lost much. I take good care of them both. I take them to village of Mangas Coloradas, where it is peaceful."

Bryce felt totally torn. He knew that this Indian loved Shannon as much as Bryce himself loved her.

"Saguaro, I have to take you to the reservation. Don't you understand? It's my duty!"

"If you truly love this woman, then your duty is to do what she wants," Saguaro replied, rising again. "I say you and Saguaro both want same thing. We both love her. So, we both want her happiness. It is for her to decide. If she say she will stay with you, then Saguaro will go to reservation. But Saguaro will escape! He will not harm or steal White Flower. If she stay with you by choice, then there is nothing Saguaro can do. He wants only her happiness. But if she say she wants Saguaro, then you must find a way to let Saguaro go free. For her sake. She cannot live on reservation. It would be impossible. Soldiers and guards there would mistreat her because she is a white squaw. They would insult her and my child."

Bryce studied the man silently for several seconds. The time he dreaded had come. He would be torn between love and duty. "All right," he finally said calmly. "We let Shannon decide. She's been through enough. I'll not do anything to destroy the little happiness she's found. Whatever she wants, that's the way it will be. If my career suffers for it, then so be it. I couldn't care less about that. I'll not force her into anything."

Saguaro stepped closer, and the two men eyed each other. Both were of equal height and stature—great leaders in each of their races. Saguaro put his hand out to Bryce and Bryce gripped it firmly.

"Always you and I are in battle," Saguaro commented. "Yet Saguaro has deep respect and kind feelings for you, white soldier. Now woman will keep us forever apart. We can never be good friends now. Perhaps no Indian can ever be good friends with white man."

"I like to think otherwise, Saguaro." They squeezed hands. "I can't say I haven't thought of killing you— several times—tonight," Bryce went on. "But my common sense tells me you've done nothing wrong in this. Her problems started with her attack and losses back in Virginia. You gave her shelter when she had none—friendship when she had no one. I probably owe the fact that she's even alive to you. I love her, Saguaro. I'll do whatever she decides. Tomorrow I'll talk with her, after she's rested."

They released hands.

"When I look at you," Saguaro told Bryce, "I see that her choice will not be an easy one."

"But it's your son who takes his nourishment from her breast," Bryce replied. "Do you really doubt what her decision will be?" Bryce's eyes teared again. Saguaro turned and looked at her and his son once more. He looked back at Bryce.

319

"Tell her I wish to name boy Chaco, for great canyon in north of Arizona. There are two sides to canyon—and they can never meet. It is fitting name."

The Indian turned and left. Bryce stared at Shannon, his heart aching. Then he moved to lie down carefully behind her. He wrapped an arm around her, and whispered her name—then wept with a bitter mixture of jealousy, anger, love, and desire.

Chapter Eighteen

Shannon awoke to the wonderful smell of bacon. How long had it been since she had had bacon? She could hear voices and some laughter outside. She lay still, moving only her eyes, to see Bryce with his back to her, bent over a small fire and cooking. Her eyes immediately teared and her heart felt crushed at the predicament she was now in. Bryce looked wonderful! And he was alive!

She watched him quietly. He wore no shirt, and his physique was more magnificent than she had remembered. She felt an old stirring and sweet, reawakened love as she studied the golden hair, which was thick and nearly to his shoulders now. His skin was tanned dark.

He suddenly turned to look at her with the beautiful, soft gray eyes she had almost forgotten.

"I thought I felt eyes on me," he said with a smile. "How are you feeling?"

"Since when did you become a midwife?" she asked him.

"You're forced to learn to do a lot of things out

here," he replied, turning the bacon again. "Doctors and other means of civilization are hard to come by. So, we make do sometimes."

"Yes. We do, don't we?"

Bryce turned his gaze back to her and saw that tears were slipping down the sides of her face.

"Hey, now, none of that," he told her, smiling sadly. He moved over and brushed the tears away. "You are going to eat a very big breakfast, Miss Fitzgerald. And then I'm going to bathe you."

"Bathe me?"

"In this weather and with all your bleeding, you need to be bathed often," he answered her as he checked the baby. "And I certainly don't mind doing it," he added with a wink.

Shannon blushed deeply and turned away.

"It's nice to see my little girl still blushes," he told her, bending over and kissing her cheek.

"Oh, Bryce, don't say that!" she whimpered, crying again. He sighed and took her hand.

"I didn't mean that the way it sounded, Shannon. You know that. I was just . . . you just reminded me of the little girl I left in Virginia three years ago, that's all. It's nice to see you look and act almost the same."

"Except that I've just given birth to an Apache warrior's child!" she choked out. "I can imagine the things that are going through your mind . . . and through the minds of all your men! Dirty . . . ugly things! It isn't that way at all!"

"Shannon, no one is thinking those things, least of all me. The men don't even know there is a white woman in this wickiup. I've explained it's Saguaro's squaw in here and because Saguaro is a valuable

322

prisoner I decided to help her through a dangerous birth. They all know Apache men won't go near their wives during a birth; it's against their religion. So my helping out makes sense. I've told them I intend to see Saguaro and his new family safely to the reservation to show the Apaches we care. It could help bring some peace. That's my excuse for being in here to help you and holding up here for a day. I don't know if the men would swallow my story for much longer than that."

"Where is Saguaro?" she asked anxiously. "Is he all right?"

He quelled renewed jealousy. "He's fine—under guard outside. I let him see the baby last night."

"Then you know," she sniffled. "You know he loves me and that I didn't just—"

"Shannon, it's all right. I understand. I truly do."

"You haven't harmed Saguaro?"

"Do you really think I would, knowing he helped you?"

"Oh, this is all so horrible and confusing!" she sobbed. "I'm so glad to find you alive, Bryce. We've found each other . . . yet we still can't have each other."

"Hush, Shannon. Please calm down. Here. Look here at your new son. You've hardly looked at him yet. By God, you did one hell of a job last night, woman. I never dreamed you had it in you." He held up the boy for her, and Shannon's tears subsided as she studied the fat, dark, wiggling infant.

"Oh, Bryce!" She began to smile. "He's beautiful! Perfect and healthy! Was . . . was Saguaro happy?"

"What do you think? You know how an Apache man feels about sons." He placed the boy in the crook of her arm. Shannon watched him.

"I also know you wanted sons of your own, Bryce," she said softly. "I'm so sorry for how all this has turned out."

"We'll talk about it later, I told you. Right now you're going to eat."

She noticed the scar across his chest and gasped.

"Bryce! What happened to you!"

He saw her staring at the scar. "Apaches," he said curtly.

"Oh, my God, Bryce!"

Their eyes held for a moment. "When I got this," he told her, "my entire unit was massacred. That's probably when the message was sent through that I'd been killed—the message the man at the station had heard. But I wasn't killed, although for a while there, I was wishing I was dead. I was a pretty sick man for about three weeks."

"You must . . . hate them all," she said in a near whisper, more tears coming. "And I . . . I have learned to love them, Bryce. The only reason they—"

"Shannon, you don't need to explain the Apaches to me. And I don't hate them all. I fully understand their predicament, and I'm very ashamed of some of the things our own people have done to them. Believe me, I'm not unsympathetic. I'm doing my best to keep the peace on both sides. Now let's eat and then we'll talk."

"What will you do with Saguaro?"

"I haven't decided yet just what I'll do with him. I don't even want to think about it. I just want to look at you for a few minutes and enjoy the sound of your voice. All this time I've thought you were surely dead, but something inside of me kept telling me you weren't."

324

The baby fussed and Shannon tried to sit up. Bryce was instantly at her side helping her. He propped her against a saddle he had brought in, placing blankets between the saddle and Shannon. He started to open her shirt so she could feed the baby, but she grabbed his hand and blushed deeply.

"Honey, I helped you feed him last night. You have nothing left to hide." He kissed her forehead. "Besides, I like to watch. It's a very pleasant experience for a man to watch a mother feeding her child. It's all right, Shannon. You feed Chaco, and I'll feed you at the same time."

"Chaco?"

"That's what Saguaro named him—for Chaco Canyon. He said the two sides of a canyon can never meet, and it was a fitting name." Their eyes held for a moment, then Bryce opened her shirt and she held Chaco to her breast. Unwanted tears came again, as she bent down to kiss the precious baby's head. Perhaps, in the end, this child would be all she had. She would die for him. Whatever happened, nothing would separate her from this child.

"And does Saguaro think that he and I can never truly be one?" she asked Bryce, as she gazed at the child. "Is that why he likened this child to a canyon?"

"Who knows?" Bryce replied, turning and stirring the bacon again. Shannon wondered to herself if that was the way it would turn out. Was it really possible for them to mix their two worlds together for a lifetime? She already felt her world drawing her away from Saguaro now, as she watched the man she once was to marry prepare her breakfast. She looked down at Chaco again.

325

No! she swore to herself. *I'll not take this precious child from his father.* Saguaro had lost too much. She looked back at Bryce. What about poor Bryce? He was so alone! So alone!

"This is all so crazy," she said aloud, covering the baby and her breast with a towel. "When you left me I knew little about men and wondered how I'd been able to let you look at me or touch me . . . and here you've—" She sighed and the tears came again. "How . . . humiliating!"

"I wouldn't call having a baby humiliating, Shannon. It's quite a miracle, and I'm very proud of how you came through it. And I happen to love you very much, so don't be ashamed. I'm just glad you're all right. I was a little worried there for a while." He turned and pushed on her nose. "And to me you're still the little lady I left behind in Virginia—a little sunburned, but otherwise, no different."

"But I am different, Bryce! Saguaro is my husband. This child seals that."

"Stop it!" he said quietly, looking away from her. He poured some coffee and turned to look at her. "When you married Saguaro, you didn't know I was alive. I was the man you promised to marry!" His jealousy was showing now. He breathed deeply. "Damn! I'm sorry, Shannon. I didn't intend to try and win you over by making you feel guilty."

She looked at him sadly. "I'm going to have to make a choice, aren't I?"

Bryce sighed. "Eat," was all he said. He sat down beside her and fed her bacon and biscuits and coffee, while she, in turn, fed Chaco. Little was said for a while. They finished eating and Bryce changed the

326

baby. Shannon swallowed her pride and allowed him to bathe her while the baby slept. Her love for Bryce tore at her heart as his gentle hands moved over her body. How good and beautiful things could have been between them!

Bryce seemed to read her thoughts as he washed dried milk from her breasts. He glanced at her, and in the next moment his lips were tasting hers in a kiss of passion and desperate need. She reached around his neck and he pulled her tight against him, pressing her breasts against his own bare skin and glorying in the feel of them touching him. His lips left hers and moved to her neck, and his hands gently rubbed over her back and moved to caress the breasts. He spoke in a shaking, whispery voice.

"God, I love you, Shannon! I want you so! Please come back to the fort with me. We'll get married. I'll help you raise Chaco. I'll love him like my own."

"Bryce, I have to think," she whispered. "Please let me talk with Saguaro—"

His lips were on hers again before she could finish, searching, pressing, wanting. He lay her back and moved on top of her, smothering her with his passion. His lips moved down toward her breasts.

"Bryce, please don't!" she whispered. "Please, Bryce! I'm married. Apache style or not—I'm married now. You must understand that. I'm married to Saguaro and I love him!"

Bryce stopped at the whites of her breasts. He looked up at her with tear-filled eyes.

"And tell me you don't love me!" he groaned.

She closed her eyes and touched the thick, sandy hair. "I can't!" she sniffled. "Is it possible . . . to be in

327

love with two men . . . at the same time?"

She opened her eyes and a tear was on his cheek. He sat up and wiped it away and put a clean tunic on her that he had found in her little bag of belongings.

"Bryce?"

"I'll bring Saguaro in again to see you," was his curt reply. He put on a shirt and tucked it into his pants so that he looked like a proper officer. Then he yelled out for Reynolds, who came running. "Go get Saguaro!" Bryce snapped.

"Yes, sir." Reynolds hurried away.

Shannon watched Bryce closely. "Thank you," she told him quietly. Their eyes held until Saguaro entered. Shannon smiled as her Indian husband came inside, and a moment later Saguaro was embracing her, kneeling beside her and Chaco.

"You look well today, my White Flower!" he told her, pulling back and studying her. "Saguaro was afraid for you. But last night I see my beautiful son, and I have never loved you so much! He is handsome and strong—a fine son for Saguaro! He helps me forget sons I have buried." He sat down beside her and pulled her to a sitting position, and Shannon rested her head against his shoulder. Bryce swallowed his jealousy and walked silently out of the wickiup.

"I tell white soldier who love you that you are free to make choice, White Flower," Saguaro told her after Bryce left. "Apache world is not your world, yet your son belong with his father. This white soldier loves you. Saguaro knows he would care for you as Saguaro has. I tell him if you choose to go with Saguaro, maybe he find way to set Saguaro free so we do not have to live on hated reservation."

328

"And if I choose Bryce?" she asked, looking up at him. His face fell.

"Then Saguaro will be taken to reservation. But he will find way to escape. Saguaro must be free! You know that. Yet he never be free of White Flower. Forever you will hold my heart in your hands. And to be apart from my son would be like having blood removed from my veins. But Saguaro will honor your choice, because Saguaro love you—want you to be happy."

If ever there was a time when a person could divide herself, now would have been a welcome moment. When she was in Bryce's arms, Shannon felt she could stay there forever. Yet here was a man who had been her friend and her lover, her protector and provider for many months now. This man loved her. He had already lost so much. And she did not doubt that he loved her as much as Bryce did.

"I love you, Saguaro," she told him. "But I need to talk more with Bryce."

"And your choice?"

She took his hand and kissed it. "You are my husband. In the white man's eyes, we are probably not considered married. But in my own mind and heart, and by your own ceremony, we are. The child I just delivered is your son . . . our son . . . conceived in love. A son must be with his rightful father. It is fitting. And a woman's heart clings most strongly to the father of her children."

Saguaro blinked back tears and touched her face. "It is great sacrifice you make. You trade safety for danger. You trade comfort of white man's world for hardship of Apache life. You trade good eating for

329

hunger—a fine home for simple wickiup. You are better squaw than any I have known. You will live in honor among my people!" He smiled through tears and kissed her cheek. "I only hope your white soldier friend will let us go free," he added. "He has power to keep us both. He has reason to hang Saguaro. He could do so and be done with the man who keeps his woman from him. Yet he does not do this. It is because he loves you and will not hurt you, even if it means losing you again. He is great man."

She broke down and put her arms around Saguaro's neck and wept on his shoulder. "Oh, God, Saguaro. I love him! Surely you know I still love him! My heart is so heavy!"

Saguaro held her and kissed her hair. "It is to be expected. Saguaro knows your heart is torn. Saguaro will love you and care for you, and our son will take away the hurt and bring you happiness."

"I feel like . . . I'm destroying him!" she sobbed miserably.

Saguaro pulled back and kissed her lips. "You must be sure, White Flower."

The baby stirred and they both looked at their son. Shannon turned back and met his eyes, dark pools of love—so very different he was! Yet, in many ways, so very much like Bryce.

"I'm sure," she said softly. "It's just . . . so hard. Bryce is a good man, Saguaro. And he . . . has no one. But I'll not take your son from you, and I'll not sit back and watch you be dragged off to a reservation. If I stay with you, he'll let you go. But even if he didn't, I would stay with you anyway. I love you. It's the right thing to do. Once we leave here, I'll not mention Bryce again. I

330

promise. It will be settled, and forgotten."

"Maybe you not speak of him. But he not be forgotten. Not in your heart. Forever there be ghost of Bryce Edwards between us. Today you prove your love for Saguaro and for our son—and prove you are strong and brave. You not be sorry for decision. Saguaro not let you be sorry."

"I know I won't, Saguaro," she whispered. He touched her face gently.

"Thank you for my son," he told her, a tear slipping down his cheek. "And for . . . not leaving me." He quickly rose and went out.

"I go back now," Saguaro told Bryce outside. Reynolds accompanied Saguaro back to where the prisoners were being held and retied Saguaro's wrists. Bryce went inside the wickiup, feeling a stabbing pain in his heart when he looked at her. He could already see by her eyes what her decision would be.

"I . . . have some things to tend to," he told her with a strained voice. "Have to get some gear packed . . . tend to the prisoners. I'll give you some more time to think." There was a boyish hope in his eyes that brought an aching pity to her heart. He turned away and Shannon lay down and wept. She was the only one who could decide the fate of two good men.

Chapter Nineteen

It was two hours before Bryce reentered the wickiup. Shannon looked up from where she sat near her new son. Their eyes held, and Bryce knew all hope was gone.

"You'll stay with Saguaro, won't you?" he asked dejectedly. She watched his eyes. How handsome he was! How lonely! How she loved him! Bryce! Her Bryce!

"Yes," she replied quietly.

"You'll die out there, Shannon," he said bluntly. "If he could keep you in one place, it wouldn't be so bad. But the Apaches are a hunted people. They have no place to call home anymore. It will get worse, Shannon. Much worse. It's no life for you."

"I can't help that," she replied, looking down at her lap. "I belong to Saguaro. I love him. I've just borne his son. The man has lost everything that mattered to him. I'll not take little Chaco from him. I simply won't do it. And I'm not afraid, Bryce. Saguaro takes good care of me. And I'll be loved. I'm just . . . sorry—" The tears

333

now began again. "I'm so sorry . . . you're so alone. It isn't fair. How could either of us know . . . it would turn out like this." She broke down and covered her face and wept. Bryce walked over and sat down beside her. He sighed and reached over and caressed the beautiful hair that he loved so much.

"Don't cry, Shannon. I'll survive. My only concern is for you. Come on now, stop crying." He pulled her over and she rested her head on his shoulder. "Tell me everything, Shannon. What the hell happened?"

"Oh, Bryce, it was awful! First Bobby, and then Daddy was so sick. Mr. Danner was so good to me and watched me so closely. Then I . . . got called into Barrett Carter's office." She sniffed and wiped at her eyes. "Mr. Carter told me all of Daddy's money was gone! Oh, Bryce, he stole it! I know he did. But what could I do with Daddy sick, and I didn't know anything about his dealings! I was so . . . scared. I just wished you were there. I had to let Marney go, and all the servants . . . everyone but Mr. Danner. We sent Marney and Parker North for their safety."

Bryce held her tightly. "None of it should have happened," he said dejectedly. "I feel like this whole thing is my fault. I thought I was doing the right thing, giving you another year to grow up—another year with your father and all. . . ." He put a hand to her face and sighed.

"Bryce, neither of us could foresee what would happen. I never dreamed Bobby would run off like that. When Daddy died, all I could think of was to just get out—get out of Virginia and get to you and never go back! Everything was gone! All the household belongings had been auctioned off. The house was almost

334

empty and already sold. I packed everything and sent Mr. Danner to the train station with my trunks and a telegram for you while I went to the funeral. I came back to the house. I just ... walked in ... thinking Mr. Danner would be back by then. But he wasn't there! Only ... only Loren McGuire was there!"

Her tears returned full force and she covered her face. Bryce held her tightly, trying to quell her trembling. He felt her hysteria building.

"Shannon, take it easy. You just had a baby. You'll make yourself sick."

"But he ... hurt me ... so bad!" she sobbed. "Oh, God, Bryce, I tried to get away! I tried! But he was ... so big and strong. He kept ... hitting me and hitting me!"

She drew up her knees and doubled over, and Bryce held her tightly, kissing her hair and fighting his own tears. If only he had killed McGuire in the first place! How wrong and twisted everything was! If only he'd killed McGuire. If only Bobby hadn't run off, bringing on her father's illness. If only he had brought her West with him three years earlier.

"He did such ... vile things!" she whimpered. "Said such ugly things! He hit me ... so hard!"

"Don't, Shannon. Don't think about it."

"But I have to! I ... killed him! He ... beat me ... tried to rape me! I ... I had a handgun near me ... in my handbag. Mr. Danner made me carry it, but I ... never used it before. I ... McGuire was ... on me ... trying to take what belonged to you! I had to stop him! I had to!"

"It's all right, honey. Of course you had to."

"But I thought ... no one would believe me ... and

335

even you might not. You'd think I was . . . raped and spoiled, and I had even killed someone! I was so afraid . . . you'd hate me!"

"My God, Shannon, how could you think that!"

"I don't know. I just . . . Oh, Bryce, it was all so horrid and ugly! I just . . . put the gun to his side . . . and pulled the trigger. And then he was cursing me . . . trying to choke me . . . so I . . . shot him again! Oh, God, Bryce!"

He rocked her gently, rubbing her back and kissing her hair while she wept.

"It's all over now, Shannon. It's all been cleared. You haven't been to blame for anything, honey. But I can imagine what went through your mind after that, knowing you were completely alone and your father had made so many enemies. And Loren McGuire had lots of money behind him. I can understand your fear."

"I thought they'd make me look like the guilty one. I couldn't bear the thought . . . of answering all their horrible, intimate questions, and being put on trial . . . and maybe go to prison. I've heard what happens to women in prison. I couldn't let them take me, Bryce! I just had to get out to you! You were all I had left, even if you wouldn't want me any more I . . . I knew you might at least help me. So I just . . . ran. I couldn't let you know, because I was afraid someone would trace me. And the more I . . . ran . . . I knew I'd just look more guilty. So I kept . . . running and running. I paid people to give me rides in wagons. I traveled . . . on the trains, sometimes under a different name. Men . . . looked at me . . . the way Loren McGuire looked at me. If I hadn't had . . . money—"

She wept again, and Bryce was amazed at this young

336

and inexperienced girl's uncanny ability to survive against such odds.

"You're one hell of a woman, Shannon Fitzgerald. I never dreamed you had it all in you. So—you got as far as the station east of Apache Pass?"

"I'm not sure where I was at all," she said, sitting up straighter and blowing her nose. "It was like the middle of nowhere . . . some canyon or something. I was the only passenger. I hadn't told the driver who I was. He told me to wait inside while he switched teams, and the old man inside kept . . . looking at me . . . like Loren McGuire did. And I thought, since I was so close, if I told him who I was to meet, it would scare him off. So I spouted off your name and he told me . . . you'd been killed . . . in a massacre. Oh, Bryce! I just . . . wanted to die!

"And then Saguaro and his Apaches came. I was so frightened! Flaming arrows came crashing through the windows, and in moments the whole place was on fire. I tried to get to my bag so I could get my gun . . . and kill myself before the Apaches could get me. But it was behind a wall of flames! And the next thing I knew, the old man was shoving me out the door . . . offering me to the Apaches like a side of beef!"

She trembled and wept, and Bryce kept stroking her hair, studying its beauty, thinking how she still had that childlike innocence about her, even after all she'd been through. How he loved her. How could he let her go away from him?

"I . . . waited for a lance to sting me . . . or to be thrown down and raped," she went on, blowing her nose again and shaking. "But Saguaro, he just talked so softly to me, and he put a blanket around me and told

337

me not to be afraid. He said he was taking me with him. And still I thought some horrible fate awaited me when we would get wherever we were going. But I had no choice. And where else did I have to go? Who else did I have?"

She calmed down somewhat and turned her face to his, studying the sad gray eyes.

"Saguaro treated me with nothing but respect and kindness, Bryce. It took me a while to realize that he truly meant me no harm. He slept with me for three months, Bryce, without touching me rudely one time. He was so lonely. He told me . . . all about his wife and sons. And there were many nights when he woke up weeping, and I would . . . hold him. That was all there was to it."

She closed her eyes against the hurt she could see in Bryce's eyes.

"How can I explain it, Bryce? Saguaro became my security. He protected me . . . provided for me . . . and he loved me, Bryce, to the point of all but worshiping me. He was so kind, and gentle, and good. We lived in the Sierra Madres. It was beautiful where we were. I made many friends with the other women. I learned to do things the Apache way. I can weave blankets and baskets. I know how to soften deer hides and make clothes and moccasins from them. I can even make a fire from sticks and rocks." She brightened a little and looked at him again. Bryce grinned a little, but the smile was full of sadness. He looked her up and down lovingly. "I guess I . . . don't look much like the girl you left back in Virginia," she said quietly, looking at her calloused hands.

Bryce gently rubbed her now soft and slightly

338

pouched stomach. "You aren't so awfully different," he told her. "And you don't need to tell me the rest. You fell in love with Saguaro—partly because of the man—partly because he was all you had."

She reddened and looked down at her lap.

"He saved me from that horrible old man. And later some other squaws and I were attacked by Mexicans, and Saguaro saved me again. And then I got terribly sick, Bryce. I almost died. But every time I regained consciousness, Saguaro was there . . . talking to me . . . holding my hand. When I got well, he held a big celebration, just because I had lived. The whole village joined in. They brought me gifts and flowers and treated me like a queen. And Saguaro's love for me, it just burst from him like rays of light from the sun. He'd been so good to me, Bryce.

"We . . . got married . . . by Apache custom. That was soon after I'd been sick. Saguaro was . . . he was . . . going away. I was afraid he might be killed. It was . . . so much like that day . . . that day you left." She looked into his eyes again, devastated at the hurt there. "Can you possibly understand what was going on inside of me, Bryce? I needed Saguaro. He had become my whole world. He was the only living being who cared about Shannon Fitzgerald. I thought I couldn't return to my own world."

Bryce reached up and pushed a piece of her hair behind her ear.

"The animal side of man in me wants to kill Saguaro and throw you down and show you who you really belong to, Shannon," he told her. She reddened and looked at her lap again. "But the side of me that loves you for more than your body would never let me do

339

that. I love your heart and your soul, and I know how you think. I respect your feelings. And I want you to believe me when I tell you I understand—all of it. I know exactly what fears and what sorrow were going through your mind. I can see how you thought Saguaro was all you had. I don't ever want you hanging your head like that, as though you have something to be ashamed of. It hurts me to see you do that."

She looked back at him with grateful eyes. "Oh, Bryce!" She embraced him tightly around the neck and he put his arms around her. "I love you so much, Bryce." she whispered.

"So why was Saguaro bringing you north, especially in your condition?"

"He didn't want to," she said with a sigh. "But we were attacked by the Mexicans. They found our camp. Oh, Bryce, it was terrible! So many Apaches were killed . . . even women and little children! Again, Saguaro risked his life to keep me from being hurt. They tried to take me away, and Saguaro was wounded fighting for my life. If Cochise and his men hadn't been there—"

"Cochise!" Bryce exclaimed. Shannon sat up straighter again.

"Yes."

"You traveled up here with Cochise? He's in the area?"

"Yes. But, Bryce, I don't want you to use what I've told you to go after them. I've learned to love these people. They aren't at all like everyone makes them out to be. They just want to be free, Bryce. Free to roam and hunt . . . to love and be loved. The settlers are taking away everything from them. They've been

340

cheated and lied to for so long. Wouldn't you fight back if some foreigner came and tried to steal everything that was yours? Your land? Your food? Your woman?" She suddenly blushed and looked away.

"Someone *has* stolen my woman," he said softly. She cried quietly, putting a hand to the side of her face.

"Please, Bryce." she said in a whisper. He stroked her hair gently.

"Shannon, to be honest with you, I'd have been surprised and maybe even a little disappointed if you had quickly decided you'd go with me. You've reacted the way any woman of quality and worth would react. You want to stay with the man who fathered your child. I just want to know one thing. Do you love Saguaro more than you love me?"

She remained turned away and shook her head. "No," she answered painfully. "God help me! I want so much to stay with you, Bryce. But . . . I can't. I love Saguaro, too. Not like I love you, but probably as much . . . just differently, that's all. I love him enough to be happy with him, Bryce. If I went with you now, it would be taking the easy way." She sighed. "Saguaro gave my life some meaning, Bryce." She turned to face him now. "After all I'd been through . . . I . . . I hated myself. I felt . . . dirty and humiliated. Saguaro took away the ugliness and made me feel . . . respectable again. I . . . I couldn't keep what little respect I have for myself if I just threw him aside now and went to you, not after all he's done for me, Bryce. And I can't take his new little son from him. It would be *impossible*. You know how the Apaches feel about their children! It would be like shoving a lance through his heart. I

341

have to stay with my son's father, even if it means . . . leaving you behind. God, I'm sorry, Bryce!"

She broke into new tears and buried her face in his neck. Bryce himself was too choked up to speak. They simply sat there for several minutes, enjoying what they knew would be their last moments together, possibly forever, this time.

"I love you, Bryce," she whispered. "You'll always remember me, won't you?"

"Jesus, Shannon, how could I ever forget you? I'll not marry, you know. Never. I'll wait. The day might come when you're lost and alone again and you'll need me. When that day comes, I'll be there."

"But, Bryce, you should marry. Don't throw your life away for me. Don't make me live with that."

He pushed her away gently and grasped her arms, gazing lovingly into the sea-green eyes.

"There's no other woman I want, Shannon. I've loved you for seven years. When I saw you last night, I knew for certain you were in my blood to stay. It's you—or no one. No matter what happens, I want you to remember me, Shannon. Don't ever be ashamed or afraid to come to me for help. Do you understand? I'll always be somewhere near you. I'm stationed at Fort Bowie right now."

"Oh, Bryce, you know I don't want to hurt you!"

"It's all right. At least . . . at least you're alive. And as long as you're alive, there's always a chance . . . a little thread of hope to cling to. I intend to wait around for that chance, even if it takes ten years."

She closed her eyes, wishing all of this were just a bad dream, wishing all the past three years had not happened. But they had, and it could not be changed.

"What will you do with Saguaro, Bryce? You have the last word, you know. I don't want him to suffer. Can you understand how it is for a man like him to have to live on a reservation? He'd die there. And I'd die with him. And I'll not have my baby grow up that way. I want him to be free and proud like his father!"

"I don't know what I'll do, Shannon. I guess I'll have to figure out a way to free him without losing my rank and reputation. It won't be easy, considering how badly the government wants his hide."

"You'd do that? You'd let him go?"

His eyes gave away the bitterness beneath his yearning love.

"Not for him, Shannon. For you. Saguaro and I both agreed we would do whatever you decided. You've chosen him, and rightfully so. You've just had the man's baby."

"Oh, Bryce!" she hugged him tightly.

"Don't go thinking I'm some kind of gallant knight, Shannon, because I'm not," he told her, closing his eyes and gritting his teeth. "It's taking all the strength I have not to put a bullet in Saguaro and take you away with me." He ran his fingers through the silken hair. "But if I did that, I'd lose your love for certain, wouldn't I? You'd never love me the way you love me now. I'd rather be apart from you and know you still love me, than to have you with me and hating me for killing Saguaro. If I did that, you could never truly be mine. Every time you looked at me, you'd think of Saguaro. But I'll tell you this much, Shannon."

He pushed her to arm's length again and grasped her arms tightly. Their eyes met, and his revealed the terrible jealousy again.

"The day will come when you're mine, Shannon Fitzgerald! Mine!" he said almost angrily. "I've thought of nothing but you at night all these years. Someday you'll be in my bed, and no other man will ever have you again!"

"Bryce, that can't happen. I'll probably never see—"

He did not let her finish. He was kissing her, and he forced her lips apart, groaning in his desire for her. He did not stop until he felt her responding and knew that she wanted him. It was what he had to know. She reached around his neck and kissed him hungrily, wondering at how lovely life might have been if not for the war, and her father's death . . . and Loren McGuire. Bryce left her lips and moved his lips over her neck, as his hands caressed her body. She could feel him trembling.

"No matter what happens," he said in a near whisper, "nothing can change our love, Shannon! Nothing! You'll run in my blood forever; and somehow, someday, you're going to belong to Bryce Edwards. I've loved you since that first day I helped a little fourteen-year-old girl pick herself up off the steps, and for the last three years I've dreamed of that beautiful afternoon we shared. I was your first man and nothing can change that—nothing!"

"Bryce, please don't! It hurts too much!

"Tell me again," he said passionately, as he kissed her neck and cheek. His gentle lips were reawakening things inside of her that were better left asleep. It was not right that she should want this man now. She was married to Saguaro. "Tell me you love me, Shannon."

"Oh, Bryce, you know I do."

He kissed her again, while he deftly unlaced her

344

tunic. He had to touch her again, taste her once more. It could be the last time. He pulled open the tunic and moved his lips from her mouth to her neck, her shoulders, her breasts, tasting, gently tasting. She grasped his hair and whimpered, glorying in the touch of those forbidden lips.

"Bryce, please," she whispered. "You said you respected my decision. Don't make it so hard on us both, Bryce!"

"I love you," he whispered. Over and over he repeated it, the gentle lips kissing and caressing, moving from her breasts to her neck and then her lips again, while he gently cupped a breast in his hand.

"Bryce, please!" she whimpered, grabbing his hand away. "We can't change the facts, Bryce."

He pulled her close and wept quietly, and Shannon Fitzgerald was wishing she were dead instead of in this terrible middle position. Two men. Two handsome, strong, brave men loved her with equal passion. Most women were lucky to find one good man. She had two. But there was only one Shannon Fitzgerald, and one of the men had fathered her son.

"Bryce," she whispered, stroking his hair again and drinking in the glory and security of his arms, "we must stop now. My decision has been painful enough. Please let me do what's right and keep my self-respect."

He squeezed her tightly and patted her back.

"Yeah," he said in a strained voice. "It's just . . . I searched for so long, Shannon. I'm so damned happy to find you. But letting you go again . . . it's worse than not finding you at all." He breathed deeply and pulled away from her, wiping at his eyes with his shirtsleeve. "At least you have a son . . . and Saguaro . . . to help

345

take away the loneliness," he said, with a tone of bitterness, as he laced up her tunic.

"Oh, God, Bryce, don't say such cruel things!" she implored him.

"I'm sorry. I just . . . I feel like someone has driven a sword through my heart. And I . . . I guess I'm feeling sorry for myself. At least you found some happiness and are safe, thank God. I was afraid something much worse had happened to you. You just remember what I said, Shannon, about my always being close by. I'll worry myself sick over you. You'll live a life of wandering and danger. What if Mexicans get hold of you?"

"I'll be all right," she replied, trying to sound sure of herself. "Saguaro is brave and strong—and he'd die for me, Bryce. I'll be protected and I'll be loved. But you'll always be deep in my heart and in my prayers. You know that. I loved you first, and I loved you the most. But life just doesn't seem . . . to go the way we want it, does it? It's as though someone . . . somewhere . . . wants to keep us apart." She put her hands on either side of his face. "And even though I'm not with you, you'll be loved, Bryce. Please remember that always. My heart will be with you, wherever you go."

She sniffled and her lip trembled, and they hugged again. Bryce kissed her cheek and stood up, walking toward the wickiup entrance.

"Now to figure out just how to keep Saguaro from going to the reservation . . . or to prison . . . or to the gallows," he commented.

"Bryce, will you be court-martialed?"

"Not if I'm clever enough to make it look like an escape." Their eyes held a moment.

346

"What you're doing," she said softly, "only tells me how much you do love me."

"Maybe I'm crazy," he commented. "Crazy in love, I guess. But I happen to owe Saguaro my life. It so happens his own men put this scar on my chest. Saguaro could have finished me off, but he spared me, because I had searched out and tried to prosecute the men who murdered his first wife and sons."

Her eyes teared again. "I . . . didn't know. It's all so strange . . . the way you've been thrown into involvement with Saguaro. I remember when you used to write me about him. It's almost frightening to realize how little control we have over our fate, isn't it?"

He sighed. "Yeah," he replied, a little sarcastically. It was then they heard the war whoops, and at the same time Reynolds was at the wickiup entrance.

"Indians, Colonel Edwards! A scout just rode into camp—about three hundred Apaches headed this way!"

Bryce grabbed his rifle.

"Oh, Bryce, it must be Cochise!" Shannon gasped. "The squaws who got away—they must have got word to him."

"Jesus Christ! He'll slaughter every one of us!" Bryce shouted as he checked his rifle. Shannon's heart pounded with fear and mixed emotions. Would she see the Apaches she had grown to love murder the white man she loved? What a horrible predicament!

"Stay here and lay low!" he ordered. "Lie over the baby!"

"Bryce, wait!" she screamed. But he had already gone out, and she could hear orders being shouted and a bugle blowing. Moments later there were gunshots.

347

"Oh, God! God!" she screamed, pulling little Chaco into her arms and weeping bitterly. More gunfire. She could hear horses circling—circling—Indians screeching and shouting war whoops—men crying out in death. Was Bryce one of them? Would Saguaro be one of them? Was Saguaro sitting tied and helpless? Reynolds had said there were three hundred Indians. But Bryce had only about a hundred or maybe a hundred and fifty men with him. He was far outnumbered. And Cochise considered all white men his bitter enemy.

The fighting went on for what seemed hours, but it was actually only a few minutes. The Indians suddenly rode off, and Bryce hurriedly shouted new orders to prepare for a second attack. But moments later Cochise approached alone, waving a white flag.

Bryce put down his gun and walked out to meet him. Shannon wondered at the strange quietness. She kissed Chaco and let go of the baby and struggled to the entrance to the wickiup, gasping when she saw Bryce and Cochise facing each other, standing apart from the rest of the men. From where she stood, she thought she saw blood on the side of Bryce's face.

"I call off my warriors when I see it is you," Cochise told Bryce. "I tell you once if we meet in battle, Cochise will spare you, if he can. Give me Saguaro and his braves, and you will go free, white soldier. There are many of us. We will kill all of you if you do not do as I ask. You know Cochise means his promises."

Bryce turned to look toward the wickiup and Cochise looked over also. The two men looked back at each other.

"You said you knew of no white woman," Bryce told

the Indian leader quietly. "That's the woman I've been looking for. The woman I love! The woman who was to marry me! And I find out she belongs to Saguaro."

Cochise's eyes saddened. "I did not know of woman until she was already wife of Saguaro," he told Bryce. "This is truth, white soldier. By then, I was at war, and I needed Saguaro to fight with me. She was already with child. Cochise decided it was better left alone. I did not want to be responsible for Saguaro losing woman he loved. It would have been no use to tell you after that."

Their eyes held and Bryce had never felt more defeated, both physically and emotionally. He had no recourse, either in this battle or with Shannon. He had lost on all counts.

"I want Saguaro and his warriors—and White Flower," Cochise repeated to Bryce. Bryce looked around at his men.

"If I hold out, it will only bring death to many of my men," he told Cochise. "You take Saguaro, Cochise. But we'll meet again."

Cochise grinned a little. "I am sure we will, white soldier."

Shannon watched him lovingly from the hidden position inside the wickiup. She knew Bryce was using this as the out he needed to let Saguaro get away. How she loved him! The pain rose in her heart as Bryce stood helplessly by while Cochise's Indians surrounded the soldiers. One of the warriors hurriedly cut the ropes that tied Saguaro and the other Apaches. Saguaro grabbed a rifle from one of his Apache friends and walked up to Bryce.

"Now there will be no reservation for Saguaro, ai?" he said. Bryce did not reply. He wiped blood from his face where a bullet had caused a piece of rock to fly up and cut him. But the wound just kept bleeding, and a second later, blood ran down his face again. He turned and walked with Saguaro over to the wickiup.

Cochise followed, still on his horse.

Shannon stepped out, a blanket hooded around her to hide her identity. She met Bryce's eyes, seeing the terrible pain. But the choice had been made. "Thank you," she said quietly. "For . . . everything." She stepped closer. "I will love you . . . always. Always."

"Prepare a travois!" Saguaro ordered some of the other warriors. "We must leave quickly!"

Men began moving about, and Saguaro stepped up to Bryce. "We have spared your life again today," he told him. "But Saguaro knows that even if Cochise had not come, you would have found a way to spare mine, for the woman's sake. You will always be an honored and respected man in Saguaro's eyes. But again we must be enemies, though neither of us wants to be."

"Just take her and get the hell out of here, Saguaro!" Bryce said dejectedly. Shannon reached out to him, but Saguaro grabbed her arm.

"It is best the parting is done quickly, White Flower," he told her. "Come."

Shannon kept looking back at Bryce as Saguaro led her to the travois. He gently laid her down on it and carefully secured her in place. She clung to Chaco and kept watching Bryce.

"We will be free now, White Flower." Saguaro was telling her. "Free! There will be no reservation. We will go to our new home now and enjoy our son."

Shannon looked up at him.

"I love you, Saguaro," she said softly.

Bryce felt his heart shattering, bit by bit. He would never forget the past few hours for the rest of his life. They could be the only time he would ever see this young woman again. In moments she would be gone. Should he shoot himself? No. Some day she would surely need him again. Shannon's few belongings were packed onto the travois.

"We go now," Saguaro said, looking from Shannon to Bryce. Shannon looked at Bryce again, and Saguaro did not object when Bryce walked closer.

"You're wounded," she said through tears.

"It's nothing. I'll be fine."

"Oh, God, Bryce, I love you!" she sobbed. "Good-bye!"

He wanted to hold her once more, but he dared not now. "Good-bye, Shannon Fitzgerald," he told her. He swallowed and fought tears and was unable to say anything more. Saguaro leaped up on his horse.

"You are man of men, my white soldier friend," he told Bryce. "I take good care of her."

Bryce glared at Saguaro. "You do that, Saguaro—or I'll find you and I'll hang you from the highest tree I can find!" he hissed bitterly. Shannon watched with an aching heart, hating herself for the pain she was bringing to Bryce Edwards.

The large contingent of Apaches turned and headed north behind Saguaro and Cochise. They took with them most of the soldiers' weapons and some of the horses. Shannon wanted to scream out, but she only pulled little Chaco closer. She watched Bryce until he disappeared into the heat waves of the Arizona desert. He stood immobile for as long as she could see him— watching her being dragged away from him. Bryce

351

Edwards had suddenly appeared in her life again, and just as suddenly left it. She wished she were dead, and knew he felt the same way.

"Bryce!" she whispered. "Dear God, help him!" She broke into deep sobbing. They had parted so quickly, with barely a good-bye. Saguaro looked back at her.

"Do not cry, White Flower. Saguaro love you. You have given Saguaro son. You are Apache now. You have chosen Saguaro, and for this you will always hold a place of honor among my people—and in Saguaro's heart."

But she was thinking of another man at the moment, and the look in his eyes when he had given her the lovely engagement ring she still wore around her neck, the ecstasy of one afternoon she had spent with her grand soldier, in another place, in another time.

Chapter Twenty

During the long months between August of 1861 and
the spring of 1862, Bryce Edwards suffered a loneliness
worse than what he had experienced thinking Shannon
was dead. Almost daily he would take out her letters,
those first, innocent, sweet letters she wrote when she
was only fourteen, so oblivious then to the real world,
to cruelty and hardship. Where was that Shannon
now? The thought of her riding off on a travois with a
half-breed baby in her arms and dressed like a dirt-
poor Indian squaw was painful torture for him.
Shannon! Once a belle of the South, educated, refined,
beautiful. Now the vision of her sun-browned skin and
her beautiful red hair worn in common braids haunted
him at night. In his dreams she floated with two faces:
one creamy white and lightly highlighted with rouge
and soft eye shadows, the red hair swept up into a
perfect coif; the other vision of a tanned face, plain and
sad, the red hair in braids, the green eyes wide with fear
instead of innocence.

The only thing that preserved his sanity was the

heightened action brought on by more Indian problems. He was kept busy patrolling the territory and safeguarding the settlers and miners against scattered Apache raids. Sometimes he met with success and saved settlers or miners who were being attacked. But more often he arrived too late. It was impossible to determine just where Cochise or Saguaro's men, always elusive, would strike next, and usually the damage was already done by the time Bryce arrived on the scene. It seemed neither Saguaro's nor Cochise's rage and revenge would ever be quite satisfied. Bryce knew that their whole purpose was to frighten out all whites and keep Arizona and New Mexico for themselves.

"They're doing a damned good job of it," Bryce mentioned once to Reynolds. "But it's a fruitless effort. In the end they'll die—and fail."

His biggest worry was Shannon. He was sure she was being moved from place to place, and he was right. She and Saguaro had moved from Mexico to the Dragoon Mountains—then to the White Mountains farther north. Mangas Coloradas, still attempting to remain at peace with the whites, moved on to the Pelongillo Mountains and bothered the settlers little.

Bryce's problems with the Apaches were now compounded by the fact that Confederate troops had appeared in the area to try and make a claim on the western territories, although their efforts met with little success. They were not only sought after and attacked by Union soldiers, often including Bryce and his men, but they were also plagued by Indian attacks. The "graycoats," as the Indians called them, had no forts like the "bluecoats" in which to fortify themselves.

They were forced to camp in the open and were laughingly ignorant of the land and its maze of mountains and canyons. Consequently, they were quite vulnerable to the wily Apaches, and were often attacked and killed for supplies and weapons, which were very useful to the Apaches in their own personal war against the whites.

Bryce found it surprising that the Confederates had come so far West, when they were having trouble holding the states they already had. Now he was faced with a two-front war—and he was almost grateful for the Apache attacks on the graycoats. He was sure the Indian harassment would drive out the Confederates, which was fine with Bryce, whose jail facilities were already filled with Confederate soldiers waiting to be transferred back East to Union prison camps. The additional activity resulting from the Civil War kept Bryce busy, and the young army doctor at Fort Bowie had his hands full, as well, patching up both Union and Confederate soldiers—and Apache Indians, who were brought in when captured and later accompanied to a reservation, from which they usually promptly escaped again. The ongoing circle of trouble helped keep Bryce's mind off Shannon, his days now filled with activity and decisions, his nights spent in sweet slumber brought on by mental and physical exhaustion.

For Shannon, life had become nomadic, but happy, in spite of the hardships; she was happy not only in Saguaro's love, but because of her little Chaco, who soon became her whole world and helped relieve her heartache over Bryce. She had given up Bryce, and a world of shelter and comfort, for her little son, so that the child could be with his rightful father.

Saguaro continued to be kind and loving. Shannon was resigned now to her Apache life. Her little Chaco would grow up to be a fine and handsome Apache warrior, like his father. During the first eight months after his birth, little Chaco grew into a fat and happy bundle of joy. It seemed he was always feeding at his mother's breast, never getting quite enough. But Shannon didn't mind. The sight of his little brown fist against her lily-white breast gave her great pleasure, and a little bit of happiness she might never have had, if not for Saguaro's love.

But Shannon worried about Saguaro's raiding, fearful that one day he would be caught and hung—or killed in battle. She wanted very much for Chaco to grow up to know his strong and brave father—to understand why Saguaro did the things he did—to be taught by Saguaro to be honest and brave. She taught herself to live from one day to the next, never daring to think about tomorrow, and she became content merely to wake up alive each morning and see Saguaro lying next to her, unharmed. But in those wee hours of the morning, she sometimes allowed herself to compare Saguaro and Bryce. She would watch Saguaro sleeping, and see that he was just a man, after all—not a savage. She thought about him sitting straight and tall on his horse, his long, black hair hanging over his shoulders, his wide-set, handsome face painted for battle, his nearly perfect physique set in rock-hard, fearsome rigidness, she saw a man who was all man. Yet so was Bryce, in every way. She wished she could find more fault with one or the other. But it was impossible. And even though Saguaro was not educated, it did not make him any less a man than Bryce. He was brave and beautiful—totally honest—a man of his word. He was intelligent and wise, just as good a leader of his own people as Bryce was of soldiers. Yet how different the two of them were—completely at odds in the outside world, yet both of them totally in love with the same woman.

It was on one such morning when she lay watching Saguaro that he suddenly opened his eyes, startling her at first. Their eyes held quietly for a moment.

"You think of him?" Saguaro asked.

She sighed and turned her back to him. "Sometimes. I'm sorry."

He gently rubbed her bare back. "Do not be sorry, White Flower. I know that you think of him, just as I sometimes think of my first wife." He leaned over and kissed her neck, then stroked her hair lovingly. "Tell me, White Flower. Why do whites think that because a man does not live as he lives, it makes the man worthless? I do not understand this thinking. They have their way. Apache has his way. And the white man does not trust Apache's word. Yet white man lies to us and cheats us. This is why Apache is angry and kills. But they turn around and say Apache not keep his word and cannot be trusted. Saguaro gets all mixed up when he listens to the forked tongue of the white man. And he has such great hunger for land and wealth." He sighed. "It is all foolish. Land is here for all of us."

She turned back to face him, and he drank in the beautiful green eyes and full white breasts. "I wish I could answer you, Saguaro. I truly do. I guess to my people land and wealth and education are all very

357

important. It makes them feel powerful—secure. Most of the whites in this country came from other lands, Saguaro. My own father came from a place clear across the Atlantic Ocean when he was very young. He and others came from places where they were abused, overtaxed, imprisoned for doing nothing more than to speak out against the government. I guess in a way, they were once like you are now—chased out, abused, hunted. Maybe it just goes on and on, Saguaro. Maybe it never stops. If it isn't our own war between my people, or the Indians against the Mexicans, or the whites against the Indians, man would find something else to fight about. It seems to be in his nature—the desire for power, a determination to protect what he considers belongs to him. It's all quite foolish when you think about it."

"Ai, White Flower. So, it will never end." He quietly pondered the irony of it all for a moment, then kissed her forehead as he gently ran a big hand over her milky skin. She had regained her figure again—small and trim and firm. He pulled her close. "I must tell you, White Flower," he said softly, his voice choking slightly. "We will not grow old together. I feel the Spirits talking to Saguaro and telling me this. Saguaro not live to be old man."

"Saguaro, don't say that!" She put her arms around his neck and he gently rubbed her bare hips.

"It is truth. You must promise Saguaro that you will raise our son to be proud and brave and honest."

"You know I will try."

"If something happen to Saguaro, my own people know they are to get you safely to white soldier who loves you. He is one of few white men Saguaro trusts.

358

He is also strong and brave. He would love Chaco because Chaco belong to woman he loves."

Shannon leaned back and studied his eyes. "Don't talk of these things, Saguaro. You bring me much happiness. I feel safe and loved in your arms. I'd die if anything happened to you!"

He shook his head sadly. "No. You would only go to the white man . . . where you belong. I know this. But we will not speak of it now, as you say. I only . . . I fear I may never make love to my White Flower again, if we do not break Apache custom of not touching until the child no longer nurses. Saguaro needs White Flower."

"I need you, too, Saguaro," she whispered. "I want to make love. I was afraid to tell you because of your customs."

In the next moment his lips were on hers, and in only seconds she was parting her legs and he was moving between them, and then she was crying out with the glory of having him inside of her. His kisses smothered her cries, and they clung to one another in an almost desperate fashion as she arched up to take in her Apache husband.

"My White Flower!" he whispered, as his life poured into her.

"I love you, Saguaro!" she replied, digging her fingers into the dark skin of his back.

That same spring the large village of Cochise and Saguaro was visited by a band of Mimbreno Apaches, who brought with them Mangas Coloradas, their aging chief. The chief was only semiconscious and was bleeding badly. Shannon stayed cautiously in the background as the village became mass confusion and Cochise's wife, Coloradas's daughter, began wailing and carrying on in her own tongue.

"What has happened here!" Cochise demanded of Coloradas's men, as others carried Mangas Coloradas to Cochise's tipi. A fierce-looking buck stepped forward, his eyes blazing.

"We go back to New Mexico to live peacefully, as Coloradas wanted us to do!" the man spat out. Shannon strained to understand. "White miners!" the man went on. "They not obey treaty. All land around Pinos Altos belong Coloradas and his people. They tell us it is ours in treaty. But gold has been found there. Whites come from all directions—swarm the hills like ants!" The man threw up his hands in wonder. "They come and they come and they come! Still, Coloradas say we must keep our word about no raiding and killing. But already they build their towns and tall poles with wires that talk! They see Indian, they shoot him— for nothing! Already they have stolen some of our young squaws and raped them! We cannot show our faces or they shoot us! So Coloradas think of way to make them leave. He say he will tell them where there is even more gold. He travel to different camps and carry white flag of peace. He tell each miner same story. He not like to lie, but he think he can get rid of them this way. He tell them that far in north there is more gold than in Pinos Altos. But one miner tell another—and they all get together and decide Coloradas is lying. They laugh at him. They spit at him. They beat him with large bullwhip. Over and over they beat him, until his skin is torn and bleeding and he cannot rise or speak! I witness this myself as they hold a gun on me!

360

He beg me to bring him here to Nahlekadeya, his daughter. I do what I can for him, but he is very sick and still can barely speak."

The people mumbled among themselves.

"This is an example of white man's ways!" Cochise roared. "Coloradas is old—and has tried to live peacefully with them. He is a great and noble and honest man. He abides by treaty, but they do not. And look how they treat a great Apache leader! They beat him nearly to death! Even yet, he could die!"

People's voices rose and warriors raised their fists.

"Coloradas whispers for us to bring him to you, Cochise!" the Mimbreno warrior continued. "Because he say you will help him. He wants you to come with him to Pinos Altos and help him kill white miners!"

The crowd quieted and Cochise paced. It was so still that the only thing Shannon could hear was the wind and the soft crying of Nahlekadeya in the tipi with Coloradas. She thought for a moment of the historic occasion she must be witnessing, and again she felt apart from the real world, as though she were reading a story and pretending she was one of the characters.

She suddenly felt a torn allegiance, wishing she could tell Bryce what was happening here. She was sure the miners would get to him first with their own version of the incident. Now there would be more Apache raids, and the whites would only be after Apache hides with even more vengeance; and the soldiers, including Bryce, would be right in the middle of it all. She could lose Saguaro *and* Bryce! Her heart pounded. She had never considered that possibility.

"This is my decision." Cochise finally spoke. "First we must heal my father-in-law—then sit in council. My

361

scouts tell me there are many bluecoat soldiers moving into Arizona from West. It is something to do with this war they fight far away where the sun rises. They are bluecoats—searching for graycoats along the Rio Grande in New Mexico. We can attack them as they come, and wipe them out. This would mean fewer soldiers to stop us from raiding in New Mexico. We will be able to get even more weapons and strengthen our hold on our territory. This could mean some great victories for Apache—against bluecoats, graycoats, and miners! First come soldiers and their weapons. Then we kill miners! Now that Coloradas is willing to fight, all whites in territory will be faced with a united Apache nation! Thousands of Apaches will make war as never before!"

All of the hundreds of warriors present cheered, including Saguaro. Drums began beating furiously, and squaws laughed and chanted, while the men began working themselves into a frenzied thirst for white blood.

Shannon only stood and watched sadly. She did not have to have Cochise's speech completely interpreted to know what he had said. Bryce would now be in great danger, as well as Saguaro—maybe even herself and little Chaco.

July of 1862 found Cochise and Saguaro riding with seven hundred warriors toward Apache Pass, where they intended to intercept about a hundred and fifty Union soldiers spotted several days earlier, headed in the same direction. Other soldiers had used the Pass many times, but Cochise had waited until Mangas

362

Coloradas was healed before he plotted the trap he had spoken about that spring.

Cochise knew that the approaching soldiers were very likely headed toward New Mexico and the graycoats were still holding some positions along the Rio Grande. The bluecoats would have to go through Apache Pass, as did most other soldiers who traveled through southeast Arizona. Cochise and the others would be ready! It would be a great victory for the Apaches! The scouts had told Cochise that the soldiers were being led by a very important bluecoat who had many stars on his uniform. Cochise dubbed the leader "Star Chief," and decided the man might even be more important than Colonel Bryce Edwards at Fort Bowie.

Cochise, Saguaro, and Coloradas all decided to show Star Chief the power and skill of the Apache Indians. Perhaps if they could impress the important bluecoat with their great number and force, the bluecoats would stop fighting against them. Maybe then they would tell the Great Father in Washington how mighty and undefeatable the Apache was, and the Great Father would return all of the land to the Apaches. Shannon had tried to explain to Saguaro just *how* great and powerful the president was, but Saguaro could not comprehend such might. He had never been outside his own world of deserts and mountains. He had never seen the great locomotive. He had no comprehension of just how many thousands upon thousands of whites there really were in the East, nor did he understand that more and more land would be needed to support them all. And so, when Cochise left that day to prepare for his battle with the bluecoats, Shannon only sat and wept, feeling a deep sorrow for the waste

363

of such fine, strong men who just simply did not understand the kind of odds that faced them.

The Apache leaders' plan was to stack rock piles along the cliffs of Apache Pass, behind which they would hide. Slits would be left between the rocks through which they could shoot, while enjoying the excellent cover.

"Saguaro!" Shannon had pleaded when he left that morning. "Watch for Bryce! He might be there."

Their eyes held. Then Saguaro picked up his rifle.

"He will not be there. These are soldiers coming from the West, not from Fort Bowie."

"But he might be there! And what about you? You—might not come back!" She tried to force back the tears, but they came anyway. Saguaro walked up and gave her a hug.

"If Saguaro sees the white soldier Edwards, he will not aim for him. And neither would Cochise. And do not worry about Saguaro. Saguaro can take care of himself. Always I come back to you, White Flower. Do not weep. What must be done, must be done. We have not asked for this. The greedy whites have forced us. It cannot be stopped. Saguaro is sorry you are caught between."

He quickly left her, and he rode away amid chilling howls and screams, the thundering horses soon vanishing in a cloud of dust.

As the Indians made ready their trap along the rocky wall of Apache Pass, Bryce and one hundred of his own men headed toward the same vicinity to meet the leader of the California Volunteers who were headed into

New Mexico to root out the Confederates. The "Star Chief" was General James Carleton, and he was accompanied by a Captain Thomas Roberts and a hundred and thirty men. Bryce feared the worst when Carleton and his men arrived in the area. He knew Carleton to be an Indian hater. Although the California Volunteers were coming to hunt Confederates, they were bound to run into Apaches. Bryce would have little say in stopping the higher-ranking Carleton from doing something foolish regarding the Indians, but he would at least try to advise the man as best he could.

On the morning of July 13, Bryce and his men joined Carleton and his Volunteers west of Apache Pass, near Fort Buchanan. The two factions of soldiers rode toward each other, and when they came close officers shouted down the lines and dust rolled as all the men came to a halt, long lines of bluecoats stretched out behind each leader. Horses whinnied and an eagle screeched overhead as Colonel Bryce Edwards and General James Carleton saluted one another. Each sat tall in his saddle and presented a commanding appearance.

"I've come to be of whatever assistance I can, sir," Bryce told Carleton.

"Appreciated, colonel. I'm told you're quite familiar with the Apaches."

"I am. You'll have more trouble with them than you will with Confederates, General Carleton."

"I'm not afraid of the Indians, Colonel Edwards. You shoot them—they're dead—and that's all there is to it. They're ignorant and unorganized fighters."

"Begging the general's pardon, but they're far from

365

ignorant when it comes to fighting, sir. They're very smart—very wily. And they're extremely organized—vicious, cunning, brave fighters who do not go down easily."

Carleton grinned. "Maybe so, Edwards, but I have something with me that will scare the Apaches right out of their war paint."

Carleton turned and pointed to two wagons being pulled along in the middle of his company's line.

"The guns on those wagons are called howitzers, Colonel Edwards. I'm sure, as an officer, you're familiar with such weapons."

Bryce felt his dislike for Carleton growing. He glared back at the man, whose smile was a sneering and sarcastic one.

"Of course I'm familiar with howitzers," Bryce replied. "But we don't see them out here much. They're being hoarded for the civil war back East."

"Well, these guns are mine to use as I wish, Colonel Edwards. And if the Apaches give me any trouble, they'll be showered with shrapnel from those weapons. The smoke and the fire and the noise those guns produce will make the Indians think twice about giving us any more trouble if they should attack us, I assure you."

Bryce eyed the guns again and suddenly thought of Saguaro. The Apaches would be little prepared for the thunderous howitzers. How easy would it be for Bryce to find Shannon if something happened to Saguaro? The fact that she lived with the Apaches now made his job and his decisions many times more difficult.

"Very impressive, General Carleton," Bryce said aloud. Both men were magnificent specimens of good

366

soldiers, both sure of themselves as they sat there in full dress uniform, the envy of the rest of the men and the epitome of prime officers. But one man lacked an important ingredient for dealing with the enemy—compassion. Bryce looked over at Reynolds, and they exchanged a look of apprehension. Bryce could see that Reynolds felt the same way about Carleton as Bryce himself felt.

"I am told you actually have a few friends among the Apaches," Carleton told Bryce. Bryce looked back at Carleton.

"I do," he said flatly.

"Too bad," Carleton replied. "I hope none of them gets involved in a battle with me, Edwards."

"Yes, sir," Bryce told him, glaring harshly at the man. "So do I."

Carleton cleared his throat. "We'll—uh—camp here near Fort Buchanan tonight, Colonel Edwards," he said in a strained voice. He cleared his throat again. "We'll head for Apache Pass in the morning. Thank you—for joining me and reinforcing my troops. How far do you intend to proceed with us?"

"I'm here to help in case of Apache attacks," Bryce replied coldly. "I'll see you through into New Mexico to the Rio Grande and help you root out some of the Confederates there. I know the territory well."

"Very good," Carleton said curtly. "Once we cover part of the Rio Grande, I'm sure I can take it from there and you can return to Fort Bowie." He cleared his throat again, feeling uneasy under Bryce's penetrating eyes. "After all," he continued, "while we're down there taking care of the Confederates, you'll be needed here to continue to deal with the Apaches, won't you?"

"Yes sir," Bryce replied, pushing back his hat a little. "I suggest you send scouts on ahead in the morning before we hit Apache Pass."

"And I'll not send scouts ahead," Carleton replied. "If the Indians want to attack, then let them. I'm eager to try out those guns."

"I'm sure you are," Bryce replied rather heatedly. He saluted Carleton, and both men turned to organize their men to make camp.

Chapter Twenty-one

The next morning found the soldiers moving east through prickly pear and hedgehog cactus toward Apache Pass. Peaceful little bluebells and lupines were quickly trampled beneath horses' hooves, the life that they clung to among the mesas and buttes of the Dragoon Mountains quickly snuffed out. The soldiers were all business, and they paid little attention to the beauty of the desert and mountains and the lovely colors of the bits of life that managed to bloom from the barren land.

By the second day of their joining troops, they reached Apache Pass, where they planned to get a fresh supply of the delicious spring water that could be found there. The Indians also used the water whenever there were no soldiers around. The stage station at the pass had not been in use since the battle there between Cochise and Lieutenant Bascom the year before. Since then, the Apaches had made it impossible for the coaches to continue to move, and the Butterfield stage line was temporarily closed in that area. The buildings

369

sat empty now, and the wind howled through the ghostly canyon.

The better than two hundred soldiers moved through the pass toward the springs, unaware that they were being watched silently by seven hundred Apaches. The bluecoats prepared to dismount, when suddenly the canyon came alive and roared with rifle fire from behind rocks that seemed to be doing the shooting all by themselves.

Men screamed out and fell from their horses, and all was confusion for the first several minutes, as soldier after soldier fell wounded or dead. Arrows sang through the air, penetrating men with their lethal sting. Horses reared, and the call of retreat was blown on the bugle. The bluecoats made a run for it, leaving behind the dead and wounded to be picked up later. At the moment, they had to flee for their very lives from the cliffs that spit out bullets and arrows. Some of the soldiers tried firing back, but there were no targets. The Apaches were too well hidden.

As the soldiers moved out of the canyon, Cochise and Saguaro and the others stood up and screamed out cries of victory. Their howls and yips were magnified by the acoustics of the canyon, and could easily be heard by the humiliated soldiers. General Carleton was furious.

"I'll teach those redskins a lesson they'll not soon forget!" Carleton roared, as he thundered around on his horse shouting orders to reorganize.

"Sir, we can circle from behind—" Bryce started to say.

"To hell with that!" The general whirled his horse and ordered the men to go back into the canyon and to

370

bring the guns. Minutes later, soldiers were again charging into Apache Pass, this time better prepared. The Apaches again rained down bullets and arrows on them. The canyon thundered with the roar of rifle fire, echoed with the cries of men gravely wounded, screamed with the whinney of horses, and sang with the victorious war whoops of the Apaches. More soldiers fell, and one of the wagons that carried a howitzer tipped on its side when the soldier driving it lost control of the horses in the confusion.

An arrow suddenly penetrated the neck of Bryce's horse. The animal whinnied and reared, then fell on its side. Bryce jumped off, barely in time to keep from being pinned beneath the animal. His foot caught in his stirrup, and the horse got partially to its feet and ran a short way, dragging Bryce with it, before it finally fell dead. Bryce, his uniform torn and his back and arms bleeding, managed to wiggle his foot free. He pulled his rifle from the saddle and aimed it up at the rocks, but again, there was nothing to aim at. Little puffs of smoke could be seen amid the maze of rock formations, but the Apaches were invisible.

From up above, Saguaro took careful aim, then hesitated. The man he was aiming at was crawling away from his dead mount—a prime target because he was hurt and was moving slowly. Saguaro could not be sure if it was Bryce Edwards, but the man wore an officer's uniform and had light hair, as his hat had fallen off and Saguaro could see his head. Saguaro picked another man to aim at. He pulled the trigger, and the soldier fell dead.

"Everybody take cover!" Carleton was ordering. "Get that wagon back on its wheels!" he shouted, riding

371

up to the men who were hiding behind the overturned wagon that carried the howitzer. "Point one gun to one side of the canyon, and the other to the other side! Blow the hell out of them!"

Bryce's back felt on fire. He saw one of his men bent over and bleeding, and he ignored his own pain and got up and ran to the man's side, grabbing him and pulling him behind a large boulder.

"Colonel Edwards!" the young private groaned. He rolled onto his back, and an arrow protruded from the boy's stomach. "Write—my mother—for me!" he whimpered.

"You'll write her yourself!" Bryce replied. But the young man did not reply. He was already dead. Bryce felt a depressing emptiness.

"Damn it all!" he whispered. He got up and ran over to the wagons with the guns and ducked down. Several other soldiers were running for the vacant buildings for cover, while the men on battery duty had righted the howitzer wagon amid arrows and bullets. Carleton was with them. He glanced at Bryce, as the men positioned the guns.

"Are you all right, Colonel Edwards?" he asked, truly looking concerned.

"My . . . horse dragged me," Bryce replied.

"Well, this will be over with shortly, and then we can tend to your wounds."

"I wish you wouldn't use those guns, General Carleton," Bryce told him. "I think if you let me go up there and talk to Cochise and Saguaro—and I'm sure that's who's up there—if I just tell them we're on our way to the Rio Grande and mean them no harm—"

"Nonsense! They started this, Colonel Edwards, and

372

I mean to finish it!"

Cochise and Saguaro were watching from above with curiosity, as the soldiers below struggled to maneuver the guns into position.

"Look at the strange weapons on the wagons," Saguaro commented.

"Ai," Cochise replied. "Do not worry. They are nothing more than the small cannons the Mexicans have used on us. They make noise, but do little harm."

Cochise had barely finished the sentence when a deafening roar was heard, and smoke and fire belched from the strange new guns. The Indians stopped shooting and listened, as a whirring sound filled the air, and, seconds later, great thunderous booms shook the rocks on both sides of the canyon.

The Apaches suddenly screamed and ducked, as bits of flying metal screamed through the air and showered them, penetrating their numbers and killing many of them with only one shot from the great guns. Rocks also came crashing down from the vibration of the howitzers. The guns belched again, and the deafening boom was heard again. More Apaches yelled out and collapsed. Some of the Indians spilled out of their strongholds and fell to their deaths in the canyon below.

Saguaro, Cochise, and Coloradas all watched in shock. These guns were many times more powerful than the small cannon of the Mexicans. The Indian leaders quickly ordered their men to retreat from the spring waters and let the soldiers have the water they wanted. Now the soldiers could kill many men with only one shot. This was something new—and terrifying for the Indians, who had no means of fighting such power. Saguaro was beginning to believe Shannon's stories of how powerful the white men could be. Perhaps the Apaches truly would lose everything! Bryce stood up and watched the canyon walls closely as things quieted. A few more Indians were shot in the back from below, as they scrambled up and out of the pass to reorganize and leave the area to the soldiers.

Those soldiers left standing on two feet cheered and hugged each other, and they were ordered by Carleton to move in and claim the water. Bryce struggled against his pain and walked back to study the dead Indians, searching for Saguaro's face. To his relief, he did not find him. Carleton was busy running around giving orders and basking in his quick victory. Reynolds was soon at Bryce's side.

"Sir, you're wounded!" he exclaimed. "Let me help you!"

Bryce did not reply right away. He just stared at all the bodies. "In a minute," he finally replied. "I have to be sure Saguaro isn't down here, Reynolds."

Bryce kept walking among the bodies as the soldiers set about the grisly task of burying the dead Indians in a common grave. The dead soldiers, after being identified, would each have their own grave. Bryce looked at each Apache's body before it was moved into the large hole. None of the bodies, torn and bleeding from the shrapnel, was that of Saguaro—or Cochise.

"I don't feel particularly proud of this victory," Bryce said quietly to Reynolds.

"I understand that, sir," the young man replied. "Please let me fix up your back, Colonel Edwards. You'll get an infection."

Bryce sighed. He headed for his tent and spent the

rest of the night in excruciating pain from the deep scrapes and cuts. He slept little, between the pain and his worries about Shannon. Was Saguaro all right? Where was his village? Would the Apaches come back? He drank whiskey to ease the pain.

The next morning Bryce forced himself to get into a new, clean uniform. It was torture to put on a shirt, but he intended to remain with Carleton until the man reached the Rio Grande, where it was less likely the Apaches would bother him as he moved east. If something was going to happen to Saguaro, Bryce wanted to be there and know about it so he could immediately go after Shannon. He walked over to Carleton's camp and suggested men be sent back to Fort Buchanan to warn any other soldiers who came through the fort headed east to beware of Apache Pass for the next few weeks. More Volunteers were due to come east from California. Carleton agreed to the warning.

"Give them an extra order," he told Bryce with a half-sneering smile. "Have them tell the commander at Fort Buchanan to wire the order to the other forts in the area. Tell them from now on there will be no leniency of any kind toward the Apaches. When they see one, they are to shoot him on sight."

Bryce felt his temper getting the better of him again. "Pardon me, sir, but—"

"That's an order, Colonel Edwards, and orders are to be obeyed!"

Bryce gritted his teeth. "Yes, sir!" he replied curtly. He left to round up some men to carry the messages back to Fort Buchanan. He decided as he walked that it was possible he would have to resign from the army

375

before he would obey the vicious and uncalled-for order from the general. He would flatly not obey it, and if the army and Washington didn't like it, they could all go to hell! He could kill an Apache as fast as the next man when in battle. But to shoot one down, young or old, for no particular reason other than being an Apache, was repulsive.

"Now what do we do?" Saguaro asked Cochise and Coloradas. "You have seen what their new weapons can do!" He felt desperate, realizing what a losing battle they were up against. It would never end now. Not until the Apaches were all but obliterated.

"Perhaps we can kill them off a few at a time," Coloradas suggested. "A scout has just told me about thirty bluecoats who have left the pass and are headed West toward Fort Buchanan. We could leave right now and cut them off! Perhaps they are going for help. We kill a few here. A few there. It is all same. It still plants fear in their hearts. Not all soldiers ride with same weapons they used on us yesterday!"

"Ai," Saguaro agreed. "Let us go and attack those who have left the others!" They quickly rounded up their warriors and thundered off to catch up with the men Bryce had sent back to Fort Buchanan. Before long, the bluecoats were spotted by the crafty Apaches. The painted Indians swooped down on the soldiers, seemingly rising out of nowhere, shouting and screaming the dreaded war whoops. The pursuit turned into an all-out horse race as the soldiers, outnumbered, began riding hard for cover. But the Indians' ponies were soon upon the soldiers, and in the fight that followed it appeared the Indians had the upper hand, until Coloradas fell unconscious from his horse, gravely wounded in the chest.

Cochise quickly ordered a retreat, and the soldiers, rather than pursue the issue, gladly took their chance and hurried on toward Fort Buchanan.

Cochise and Saguaro knelt beside Coloradas.

"Is it bad, my father-in-law?" Cochise asked the old man.

"Very . . . bad," Coloradas gasped. "I will . . . not be able . . . to help you now . . . Cochise." The old man passed out for a second time. Cochise and Saguaro looked at each other.

"I will not let him die!" Cochise spat out. "He agreed to help us. Now Cochise will help Coloradas. In the town of Janos, in Mexico, there lives a great surgeon. This wound cannot be healed by our own medicine man. I have heard of this doctor's skills. He is known to heal many things. I will take Coloradas to Janos and surround the town! I will order the doctor to make Coloradas well, or the whole town will die! This doctor will help my father-in-law, or he will die, also!"

"Coloradas is old, Cochise. Do you think the doctor can really heal him? It is a very bad wound."

"He will heal him—because his life will depend on it!" Cochise replied with a fearful look in his eyes. "Let us bandage him up and prepare a sling. I must go quickly! Right away! He could die before I get there. I would like you to remain here, Saguaro. Lead the rest of the warriors back to our hidden village. Stay there with them. Protect them. Lead them in battle if it becomes necessary. Cochise will return with Coloradas, and then we will be rested and ready to again do battle."

"Ai. I will do as you say. But we will lose much time, Cochise. Many soldiers get away now. More miners will come."

"Ai. This is so. Our end might be in sight, Saguaro. But if we die, we will die proudly—with dignity and honor! We will not waste away on their filthy reservations!"

The two men shook hands.

"Tell Nahlekadeya and my children not to be afraid," Cochise added. "Cochise will return, and he will bring Coloradas, alive! Tell Nahlekadeya that Cochise will take good care of her father. I do not want her to weep or be frightened."

"I will tell her this," Saguaro replied. Coloradas was prepared and Cochise soon left, heading south with a saddened heart. He took two hundred men with him. Saguaro took the remaining warriors and went back to his village. It would be good to return to White Flower. He wished to talk to her more about the strange powers of the white man. But when he reached his village, he learned that White Flower was not there. He searched for her among the women who came out to greet the returning warriors. Some of them looked at him strangely. Some of them turned away and wept. Then he spotted a young woman nursing Chaco. Saguaro felt his blood run cold. He jerked his horse to a halt and leaped down, and the crowd quieted. He stepped up to the young woman who held Chaco.

"Where is White Flower?" he asked, his eyes blazing.

"She . . . was stolen!" the young woman answered. She looked at her own husband with frightened eyes and ducked into her tipi. Saguaro looked at the woman's husband and spoke through gritted teeth.

"I have returned from a saddening defeat. Now I find my woman is not here to greet me. What has happened! Did the white soldiers take her?"

The brave looked at Saguaro with tears in his eyes.

"I wish that is who had taken her, Saguaro," the man replied. "But it was—the Utes."

Saguaro actually stumbled and another brave grasped his arm.

"She went to bathe with four other squaws," the third man told Saguaro. "It has been so peaceful here. Utes have not raided for many, many moons. We thought them involved with white settlers, just like we are. Nor did we worry about soldiers, because you and Cochise and Coloradas were keeping them busy south of here. So we sent only two braves to guard the women. Utes attacked with such quietness, we did not even know what was happening until it was too late. Both guards and other four squaws were murdered! We know it was those outlaw Utes from southern Nevada because of lances they leave behind. White Flower was missing. They—have taken her alive, Saguaro! It is lucky she not have Chaco with her, or they surely would have killed child. You still have your son, Saguaro!"

"Nooooo!" Saguaro roared, whirling and lashing out at the braves. He pullled a knife and rammed it into the belly of one before he could step back. "You were supposed to guard her! I promised her nothing would ever happen to her! And I promised the white soldier I would take care of her!"

The injured brave collapsed to the ground and his sister screamed and ran to his side and began wailing over his body. The others stood and stared, afraid to speak to Saguaro.

"I told the white woman that one day she would come between Saguaro and his own people," an old woman said to another squaw. She was the one who had talked to Shannon the day of celebration. "She has stolen his heart. He will never be same man now, if he not find her."

Saguaro circled, looking at all of them. He was rigid, the muscles of his back and arms bulging in fury. His breathing was labored and he blinked back angry tears.

"All of you know what will happen to her! She is white! *White!* They will sell her to the Mexicans! We must go and try to find her!"

"We want to help, Saguaro," one of the braves spoke up. "We go with you. We are sorry, but we not expect such a thing to happen. We were taking good care of her. That is truth, Saguaro!"

Saguaro threw a lance into the ground. "This is what happens when we are forced to fight the cursed whites! It takes us from where we belong! Will our persecution never end?"

Some of the women began weeping openly. Saguaro mounted up on his horse again.

"I want one hundred men. Fresh braves from the village. Those who returned with me are tired and some are wounded. Tend to their wounds. I am leaving you with many more men, so the village should be safe." He turned to look at a brave with whom he was good friends, and who had participated in the fighting at Apache Pass. "Redback! You will be in charge. Whatever decisions you make are what the People should do. I will go now and raid the Ute camps that

380

are close by. I will find out what I can. Then I will ride to Mexico and search for White Flower!"

"Saguaro!" another brave spoke up. "Perhaps the white soldier will help you search for her. The soldiers have power with the Mexicans."

Saguaro nodded. "The one called Bryce Edwards might help—for White Flower's sake." His eyes saddened. "But Saguaro is ashamed to tell him what has happened. Saguaro has broken his promise to white soldier!" His heart was heavy. He wanted to scream out his agony, to kill himself at the thought of what would happen to White Flower if he didn't find her soon. But he could not end his life yet. First he must find White Flower and help her.

"Bring me my son," he said in a strained voice. The young squaw who had nursed Chaco brought the boy back out and held him up to Saguaro. Saguaro took the boy, holding him out to study him. Chaco laughed and reached out for his father's nose.

"You will be reunited with your mother, my son!" he swore to the boy. "This is Saguaro's promise." He held the boy close for a moment, then handed him back.

"I ride to western ridge of our camp now. I wish to be alone," he told the others. "I want a hundred men to meet me there before the sun's bottom edge touches the ridge as it sets. There will be little sleep for any of them before White Flower is found!"

Chapter Twenty-two

It was the first of August, 1862, when Saguaro appeared at the gates of Fort Bowie carrying a flag of truce. Captain Hollander, the man in charge in Bryce's absence, ordered the gates opened, and he stepped out alone to face Saguaro, after first ordering that no soldier fire on the Apaches.

"But, sir, what about General Carleton's orders about shooting down the Apaches?" one of the men protested. "That's Saguaro out there! We could shoot him down right now!"

"Colonel Edwards left strict instructions not to shoot on sight. You know he objects to Carleton's command. We answer to Colonel Edwards, not General Carleton! I'll not be responsible for the death of an Apache leader like Saguaro. If you want to answer to Edwards for it, go ahead and shoot!"

The man scowled and backed off.

"There are better than a hundred Indians out there," Hollander went on. "You can be sure they'll come back with a lot more than that if we shoot their leader when he's sitting there with a truce flag in his hand. And we're shorthanded. Now open the gates. I intend to talk to the man and see what he wants."

The large wooden doors of the stone fort's gate creaked as the man opened them slightly to let Hollander step out. The soldier walked up close to Saguaro.

"What brings you here under truce, Saguaro?" the man asked. "Are you surrendering yourselves?" He was suddenly struck by the terrible look of desperation in Saguaro's eyes. The man's face was set like stone and painted in wild, bright war paint. His eyes glittered with hatred and looked almost maniacal. At the moment Saguaro was the most fearsome-looking Apache Hollander had ever seen.

"Saguaro needs to talk to white soldier Edwards—quickly!" the Indian replied.

"He's not here, Saguaro. He's somewhere east of here—riding with General Carleton to root out the graycoats and show the man the way through New Mexico to the Texas border. Can't I help you?"

Saguaro's face was shadowed with disappointment. "Saguaro needs Bryce Edwards's help! Saguaro is riding to Mexico. Wanted white soldier to come—bring men—help Saguaro!"

"Help you?" Hollander almost laughed. "Help you what? Raid Mexican ranches? That's the craziest thing I ever heard. Saguaro! You aren't making sense at all. Your war with the Mexicans isn't any of our affair. We're only concerned with what you're doing in Arizona against our own people."

"You do not understand!" Saguaro replied anxiously. "My woman. White Flower. She has been

384

stolen—by Utes. They will take her to Mexico and sell her as a slave. She will die there, if Saguaro cannot find her! Bluecoats have power to tell Mexicans to give her back. They will not listen to Apache."

Hollander frowned. "Why would Colonel Edwards be concerned enough about one Apache woman to go all the way to Mexico to try and find her? You're talking crazy, Saguaro!"

Saguaro realized then that this man and the others probably still did not know the true identity of White Flower. "Just tell your Colonel Edwards. He will understand. Maybe you can send men to Mexico?"

Hollander sighed and pushed his hat back. "I'm sorry, Saguaro, but that's impossible. We've been left here with very few men, and I have no authority to go releasing some of them to go on a wild goose chase to Mexico—with Apache Indians, no less! It's totally out of my jurisdiction, Saguaro. And we have no quarrel with the Mexicans at the moment. For me to send men down there would be like—well, our men represent our government, Saguaro. Do you understand? In our way of thinking, we have to consider the whole picture, not just one part of it. I'm damned sorry about White Flower. Maybe when Colonel Edwards gets back—"

"It will be too late!" Saguaro growled. "Time is important! Tell Edwards. Send him message on wires that speak. Tell him Saguaro go to Mexico to find White Flower. Tell him Saguaro need his help. He will come! Tell him! I go now!"

Without waiting for a reply, Saguaro whirled his horse, and the hundred or so warriors thundered south.

Hollander removed his hat and scratched his head, wondering why Colonel Edwards would care about

Saguaro's problems. He walked back inside and said to the telegrapher: "Get a message to Colonel Edwards if you can find him," he ordered. "I don't know why in hell it matters, but tell him Saguaro's wife, White Flower, has been stolen away by Utes and is probably in Mexico. I hate to bother the colonel with something like this, but for some reason Saguaro seems to think he would want to know."

Throughout August and into September, Saguaro raided every Mexican ranch in northern Mexico with a heated fury. The Mexican Army was quickly dispatched to try to find the renegade Saguaro, who swooped down on ranches, often killing everyone in sight, for no apparent reason. The Mexicans were confused by the sudden and unexplained raiding. Many of Saguaro's warriors were also killed in the raiding, and Saguaro himself was wounded. He took his remaining men into the Sierra Madres, hiding in the mountains for several days to tend to his wound and the wounds of his other men, before setting forth again on more raids in search of his white squaw.

During the weeks of his frantic search, Shannon Fitzgerald lay in a state of shock, unaware that anyone was searching for her. For six weeks her home was an old barn, on the property of a man named Santo Zia, a wealthy Mexican rancher who had bought her from the cruel Utes. Her wrists and ankles were becoming calloused from the leather straps that had held her throughout her traumatic ordeal. The vile things Zia had perpetrated against her, combined with his skill at painful torture when he was displeased, had driven

Shannon's already delicate mental state to the breaking point. She only lay and stared now, her mind automatically shutting itself off to all feeling and knowledge.

Occasionally, visions of a chubby, dark baby would float through her subconscious. She could hear his laughter and kiss his cheek and watch the baby's lovely green eyes dance. His little arms would hug her, and she would be at peace inside herself. It was only in those moments when she pretended she was safe and holding her little Chaco again that she could bear to think at all. Otherwise, she lived in a mental vacuum. She did not speak. She did not cry. She had no feelings—either mental or physical.

Her traumatic experiences over the past years, combined with the final horror of being taken by the Utes and then the evil Santo Zia, were too much to bear. For the first days of horror she had been carried on horseback by the Utes, bound and blindfolded, given barely enough food and water to keep her alive. Then came the worse horror of being sold to Zia. It took only a few days of lying tied and suffering his repeated rapes and torture for Shannon Fitzgerald to lose all sanity, all touch with reality. Surely all was hopeless now. She would never be found, either by Saguaro or Bryce Edwards, and she would never see her little Chaco again. She was doomed to a living hell. All was gone now—Virginia, family, the men she loved, her son. There was nothing left but to hope for death. Her mind went first, and her body was slowly but surely following.

*   *   *

Early in September, in a hotel room in northeast Mexico, Bryce Edwards adjusted his neatly cut, well-tailored, dark suit. The fancy threads were accented with a vest and a white, ruffled shirt. A gold chain watch hung from the pocket of his vest. He studied himself in a mirror, adjusting his expensive hat.

"Bryce, I've never seen you look so handsome!" Mona told him, walking up to stand beside him.

He turned and looked at the voluptuous prostitute whom he had befriended over his lonely years of service in the West. He did not doubt that Mona Jackson loved him, and at times he felt sorry for her. But there was only one woman in his heart, one woman he had truly loved enough to marry. Now that woman was surely in dire suffering, if she was even still alive. He had managed to get six weeks' leave, explaining to no one how he would be using it. He needed help in his plan to find Shannon. Mona provided that help, out of her own love and sympathy for Bryce Edwards.

He glanced down at her billowing white breasts. "And I like that red taffeta dress, my dear Mona," he replied. "You look every bit the part of a kept lady."

"Well, that's what I am, so it isn't difficult to play the part, darling," she replied with a grin. Bryce smiled sadly and bent down to kiss her cheek, then looked her over fondly.

"I appreciate what you're doing, Mona. And you look beautiful. We'll hit another tavern tonight and do the whole act again. Maybe we'll find her this time and I can get you out of these two-bit towns and get you home. I know you hate it down here, and so do I. Remember now, I'm Randall Corey, and I'm your pimp."

"I won't forget. We've been through this too many times now. You're looking for one of your girls who ran away. You intend to get her back. You're looking for a white girl with red hair and green eyes who may have ended up a mistress to one of the wealthy Mexican ranchers. Bryce, why don't you just get a bunch of your men and ride down here and search all the ranches? Just barge right in and raid them, like Saguaro has been doing."

"That won't work. Saguaro's raiding will get him nowhere, Mona. And neither would mine. Besides, as a representative of the U. S. Government, I can't do that. Anyway, when you raid the Mexicans, they just get stubborn and mad, and you never do get what you're after. This way—buying them drinks, talking friendly to them, I can get them to talk. And if I offer enough money, they just might lead me right to Shannon."

His face darkened and his eyes turned to ice.

"If and when I find out who's got her, Mona, that man will die very painfully and very slowly!" he hissed, his jaw flexing in anger. "If there's one thing I've learned from the Apaches, it's their technique for torture. I never thought it would come in handy for myself, but if Shannon's been used the way I think she has—"

Mona shuddered at the look on his face. "I hope I'm not around," she commented with raised eyebrows. "How long do we have left to search for her, Bryce? Don't you have to get back to duty soon?"

"I have another three weeks. Now that Saguaro is concentrating on the Mexicans in search of Shannon, there won't be much trouble with the Apaches for a while back home. They say Cochise is laying low

389

waiting for Coloradas to recover from a wound. My unit will do all right without me for a while."

"You and Saguaro—both out searching for the same woman. It's all so crazy. You fight each other, and now you're both fighting the Mexicans in your own ways."

"Yes, but Saguaro doesn't even know I'm here. I only know he's been down here raiding. I just hope one of us finds her, Mona."

"How will you know if Saguaro finds her?"

"I won't. But I have doubts he'll ever do it his way, anyway. And there's one thing for certain; whoever finds her, she's not going back to the Apaches this time, no matter what! She stays with me this time. I'll never let her out of my sight again!"

He turned and adjusted his hat again, blinking back tears. "God, I can't stand the thought of it!" he whispered.

She put an arm around his waist. "Bryce, don't. You've been over it and over it. You've blamed yourself, Saguaro, the Utes, the Mexicans, the Civil War—everything you could think of. But no one is to blame, Bryce. Our lives seem to be dictated by fate sometimes."

He turned and embraced her, and she could feel him trembling. "Thank you, Mona. I don't know what I'd have done if I had to come down here alone, especially at night, when it's so damned quiet I think I'll go mad with my thoughts—visions of her in the hands of some bastard Mexican!" His embrace tightened. "You shouldn't be here helping me. It might only mean losing me. You know that if I find her, I'll never be coming back to El Paso to visit you."

"All I want is for you to be happy, Bryce. I love you,

390

and I'll help any way I can." She leaned back and looked into his eyes. "Besides, the thought of that poor child in the hands of those men sickens me. I've been through that kind of awful hell and humiliation myself. Not exactly the same way, but I've been through it. I wouldn't wish that on anyone. It's too late for me now. Let's hope it isn't too late to salvage something of the old Shannon Fitzgerald."

Their eyes held, and he kissed her tenderly, then held her tightly again. "Thanks, Mona, for all of it . . . all the times you've helped me through the lonely nights, knowing I only came to use you to relieve my need for someone else. And thanks for coming here with me. You're a good woman. And if not for Shannon, I could love you."

He kissed her shoulder and she gently pulled away. "Oh, no, you couldn't, you handsome soldier, you. Army colonels don't love and marry prostitutes." She gave him a smile and a wink. "But I appreciate the gesture, love. You're okay. God knows you've given me a hell of a good time in bed and some very nice memories."

He saw the look of love and sorrow in her eyes and smiled sadly. He turned to adjust his hat once more, then looked her over, studying the perfect figure beneath the revealing red dress, the black, upswept hair and vivid blue eyes. "You're one of a kind, Mona." He kissed her forehead. "And don't worry about anything. I'll not let any of those Mexican bastards touch you, understand? That's why I have this gun along." He patted a small hidden holster that held a .45 caliber Colt derringer.

"What woman would be afraid with you by her side,

Colonel Edwards?" she replied with a smile. "I just wish it was me they had taken in the first place, Bryce. I could have stood it. After all, what's left for a man to do to me? I've already been through it all."

"Not the kind of treatment you'd get down here. And if it did happen to you, I'd come down here looking for you, just the same as I'm looking for Shannon."

Her smile faded. "Would you . . . really?"

Bryce flashed a handsome smile. "You bet I would!" He put his arms around her. "Shall we go, Miss Jackson?"

"I'm ready, Mr. Corey."

They left the room to continue their search.

How many times Bryce and Mona had searched through taverns and brothels in how many little Mexican villages, neither of them was sure anymore. So far, they had turned up nothing; but Bryce Edwards was sure that for a few gold coins, someone, somewhere, would know something, and would be willing to share the information.

They entered yet another Mexican saloon in still another small town, and Mexican eyes turned to stare at the beautiful, lily-white woman on the arm of the handsome, expensively dressed man. Bryce pulled out a chair for Mona, and a fat man wearing an apron came to the table.

"Just whiskey," Bryce said briskly. The man nodded, understanding the American word for the drink. His dark eyes lingered on Mona hungrily until Bryce gave him a warning look. The man turned to get the whiskey, eager to serve the wealthy American. Ten or so patrons continued to stare at Mona, while Bryce pulled out a thin cigar and lit it, then scooted back his chair and stood up, taking a gold coin from his vest pocket and holding it out.

"Gentlemen, do any of you understand English?" he asked, turning around the room and showing the coin. The men studied the gringo with the light hair and fancy clothes. They mumbled among themselves, glancing from each other back to Bryce. Finally one of them spoke up.

"*Si, señor*, I understand the English."

"Good. I'm going to tell you something, and I want you to tell the others in Spanish when I'm through." The man in the apron brought the drinks, and Bryce paused to take a swallow of whiskey. He looked back at the patrons and smiled, then began walking around the room, flashing the coin. They studied his fine clothes and expensive boots and hat. He looked every bit the part of a wealthy pimp.

"My name is Randall Corey, gentlemen. I am from New York, originally. But for the past several years I have been running a very fine—uh—brothel, in New Orleans." He nodded toward Mona, who sat giving seductive looks to the eager men. "That woman there is my—traveling companion, shall we say? A man should never go anywhere without a woman, should he? After all, we all need something to keep us warm at night, right?"

The English-speaking Mexican interpreted, and they all laughed and eyed Mona hungrily.

"They say what a good job you have!" the interpreter told Bryce. "Ah, señor, such beauty!" The man laughed again and put his hand out to Bryce. "I am Coca," he said with a broad grin. "What is it you want, gringo? Perhaps Coca can help you, and Coca will receive favors from the beautiful woman you have with you in return?"

Bryce eyed Mona sideways. "Perhaps," he replied. He held up the gold piece again. "This is a twenty-dollar gold piece!" he told them all. "You all know the value of gold—in any country."

Coca interpreted, and all the men grinned and nodded.

"I'm looking for someone," Bryce went on. He walked back to his table and took another sip of whiskey. "A woman," he went on. "A white woman. Pretty, like Mona here. But this woman was a little smaller—only about five feet, two inches tall. She had reddish hair and very green eyes—and she had an accent like people from the southern part of the United States have."

The men looked at each other. One heavy-set one; unkempt and wearing ragged clothes and a large sombrero, frowned and listened carefully as Coca interpreted. He watched the gold piece, thinking of how much whiskey and women he could buy with it.

"What do you want this woman for?" Coca asked. "Do you wish her harm?"

"For twenty dollars, why should you care?" Bryce replied. He pointed to Mona. "But if you're worried about it, just look at that one there. Does she look abused?"

They all eyed Mona again, and she felt totally naked beneath their stares.

"But—why is it you search for the one with the red hair, señor?" Coca asked. "Manuel—over there—" he pointed to the heavy-set peasant. "He wishes to know."

Bryce looked over at the man, struggling not to show his excitement. At last! A thin thread of hope! He looked at Mona, who scowled slightly and tried to tell him with her eyes to be cautious. Bryce walked closer to the fat Mexican and waved the gold piece under the man's nose.

"Tell this man that the woman worked for me. She was one of my best girls. But then she made off with some of my money. I've searched every whorehouse in New Mexico and Arizona for her. And I thought maybe she ended up down here—either by choice, or some Apache buck could have had a good time with her and then turned around and sold her to one of the wealthy Mexican ranchers down here. I'm aware some of your richer citizens buy white women for their own pleasure. She could be a slave down here somewhere."

Bryce turned back to Coca. "If this woman is some man's slave, then it serves her right for stealing from me. But either way, I want her back, Coca. She owes me! I intend to see that she pays me back through her services. I'll pay any man generously who can lead me to the little bitch, and I'll also pay the man who has her at the moment—or the pimp. A man has his pride, Coca. I do not like my little whores stealing from me. She was a very naughty girl. Tell Manuel if he thinks he knows where the girl is, I'll give him the gold piece now—and if it turns out to be her, I'll give him another twenty-dollar gold piece when I find her. I will also let him lay with her before I take her back with me. If it turns out not to be her, he can still keep this twenty-dollar gold piece."

Coca grinned and rubbed his hands together.

"What . . . what about Coca, señor? Does Coca get something for doing all of this talking for you? I . . . I would like the woman over there," he said, nodding to Mona. "Promise me her for the night, and Coca will give your message to Manuel."

Bryce frowned and glanced over at Mona. The man was putting him on the spot. Bryce desperately needed Manuel's information, but he was sure Mona was definitely not thrilled at the thought of going to bed with the smelly Mexican.

"My women come priced high," he told Coca. "They don't give out favors for nothing. You could all be lying. If I find the girl, then you can have your frolic with Mona there. She happens to be my favorite, and she doesn't give favors without a damned good fee or favor in return. Understand?"

Coca nodded disappointedly.

"*Si, Señor*, I . . . I will tell Manuel." He quickly interpreted the message about more money and favors from the redheaded woman if Manuel could lead Randall Corey to her. The man called Manuel grinned and removed his sombrero, fingering it nervously. Bryce put an arm out to the man and motioned for him to come and sit down at his table.

"You come, too, Coca," Bryce ordered. Coca sat down on the other side of Mona and eyed her hungrily, while Bryce ordered more whiskey for Coca and Manuel.

"Now, Coca, ask Manuel to tell you whatever it is he knows about a red-haired woman," he said to the Mexican, struggling to remain casual while the two Mexicans began talking rapidly in Spanish.

Bryce leaned back and lit another small cigar,

396

exchanging an anxious glance with Mona, who tried to tell him with her eyes to try to stay calm. Bryce sipped more whiskey, becoming impatient at the long conversation between Manuel and Coca. Were they merely cooking up something to get money out of Bryce? Coca finally turned to Bryce.

"Manuel, he works for a rancher east of here, señor," he told Bryce. "The man's name is Santo Zia. It is known to all of his men that Señor Zia—he likes the white women. He is married, but he hates his fat wife. He has been known to buy white women. When he tires of them, he sells them—or if they are not very pretty, he gives them to the *banditos*, to do as they wish with them. The *banditos*, they steal money and cattle for him in return."

"Sounds like my kind of man," Bryce forced himself to say, glancing at Mona again.

"Manuel, he say he is told by Señor Zia's bodyguards that Señor Zia buy a white woman about eight weeks ago. Manuel never see her himself, but the other men who tell him about it, they laugh about using the whip on the woman because she fight Señor Zia. She is taken to a place where she is used for his pleasure."

Bryce paled but managed to keep an unconcerned face as Coca babbled on.

"The men, they say she very pretty. Small—white. She have red hair and—uh—eyes green as the grass," Mona saw beads of sweat break out on Bryce's forehead.

"Go on," Bryce said in a calm, but strained voice.

"This is all Manuel knows. He say he hears the Utes bring this woman to Santo and that Santo paid much money for her because he thinks she likes the men and will be good in bed."

"Why would he think she likes men?" Bryce asked, his heart pounding.

"She was found living with the Apache Indians. Santo say any white woman who lays with an Apache buck is bad woman."

"He does, does he?" Bryce asked, eager now to meet and murder this Santo Zia.

"*Si, señor!* But the men who help him with her, they tell Manuel that she struggle and did not seem to like Santo so well. They laugh about it. Santo, he would have to hurt her to make her cooperate. Excuse me, sir, but you do not look well. Is the señor sick?"

Bryce downed the rest of his whiskey. "No. Just a little problem with your water down here," he replied. He breathed deeply and forced back tears of rage. "Is the woman still there?"

"This, Manuel is not sure of. He say Santo, he tires quickly of his women and usually gives them away or sells them, like I already tell you. It could be the redheaded one has already been sent away."

"Well, then, I guess we'd better move quickly, hadn't we?" Bryce replied, rising suddenly. "We'll go tonight!"

"Tonight! But why not wait until morning, señor?" Coca suggested.

"No!" Bryce snapped. "We go tonight. Right now."

Coca shrugged and told Manuel. Manuel also shrugged and said he would go and get his horse.

"Tell him to meet me out front in fifteen minutes, Coca," Bryce ordered. He rushed Mona out the door.

"My God, Mona!" Bryce whispered as they headed for their room to pack their bags. He was practically stumbling in his rage and horror.

398

"Hang on, honey. We'll get her out of there," she said softly. "You've got to keep yourself together or they'll catch on and you'll lose her again."

Bryce spoke little until they reached their room. Then he slammed the door. He grabbed the back of a chair and hunched over it and choked in a sob.

"Bryce? We've got to hurry, darling. We'll find her and we'll help her! We'll help her, Bryce!"

"Oh, God, Mona!" he choked out. He turned and embraced her, holding her so tightly she could barely breathe.

"We'll find her, Bryce," she repeated. "We'll find her."

Chapter Twenty-three

Bryce handed Mona his rifle, cocking it first. "You stay here and wait for me to get back," he told her. "I don't want you to see this, understand?"

"Bryce, you shouldn't go in there alone!"

"I'll manage. You stay behind these rocks, and if I don't come back, or if someone comes along and gives you trouble, let him have it and get the hell out of here! Manuel won't be giving you any trouble." He looked down at the unconscious and tied body of the man who had brought him to Zia's ranchero. "I tied him good and I don't think he'll be waking up for quite a while, anyway." He gave her a quick kiss. "Wish me luck, Mona. I hope to hell she's still there."

"Good luck. I'll be waiting, darling."

Bryce disappeared into the dark and Mona sat down to wait near the tied horses, the rifle in her hand. She shivered and pulled her shawl closer, trying to see through the darkness where Bryce had disappeared, but there was nothing to see, and the only sound was the singing of crickets.

Bryce crept through underbrush and climbed over a fence, making his way unseen to the door of Santo Zia's sprawling ranch house. A middle-aged Mexican woman answered the door and Bryce removed his hat.

"Good evening, ma'am. My name is Randall Corey. Is Señor Zia home?"

The woman eyed him warily. "How did you get here, señor? No one gets to this door without some of Señor Zia's men bringing him."

"I found my own way, ma'am, without being detected. Believe me, it's for good reason. I wish to see Señor Zia privately. I mean him no harm, I assure you."

The woman frowned and moved aside. "Come in. I will get him."

Bryce entered the marble hallway and the woman scurried off. Bryce studied the plush and expensive villa. It burned at his guts to think that the man who owned it bought women like so many cattle and used them in his own evil games. The house was neat and quiet, but there was no warmth. Everything was cool and dark. Rich red carpeting was laid farther down the hall where the marble of the entranceway ended. The walls were dark mahogany and the hall was lined with red candles, all lit. No voices could be heard as Bryce gazed around at expensive paintings and vases. Moments later, the slender Santo Zia walked to the entrance hall.

Never had Bryce Edwards had more difficulty staying in control. He forced himself to be patient. He must get all the information he could before he ended this man's life. Zia eyed Bryce warily. Bryce noticed everything about the man seemed cold and thin, including the hand Zia finally offered cautiously.

"How do you do, Señor Zia. My name is Randall Corey," Bryce said pleasantly.

Zia frowned. "And what brings you sneaking to my door in the night, Americano?" he replied. "I hope you realize I can summon any number of men to my aid at any moment."

"Of course. I am not a fool, sir. I am only cautious, for your own sake."

Zia's eyebrows went up in curiosity. "Oh? And what do you mean by that, señor?"

Bryce kept a kindly look in his eyes, all the while envisioning the horror of sweet Shannon at this man's mercy. "Could we perhaps go outside and speak alone?" he asked. "It concerns . . ." he bent closer to the man, "it concerns your interest in the white slave market."

Zia's eyes glittered. "Certainly, señor!" he said with a broad grin. "Come outside to the garden with me." He put a hand on Bryce's shoulder, sending a chill through Bryce's veins.

The two men went out and walked a slight distance from the house, where they sat down on a white wrought iron bench in the midst of a well-manicured garden. The hypocrisy of this wealthy man who put on such airs sickened Bryce. Insects of the night sang and there was no breeze in the garden that smelled of exotic flowers. There was a moon bright enough for the two men to be able to see each other.

"Now, Señor Corey, tell me what it is you are wanting," Zia said, lighting a thin cigar.

"Well, sir, I run a brothel in New Orleans. I also deal in the white slave market. You know—women bought

403

and sold for a man's pleasure, shall we say?"

Zia grinned. *"Si?"*

"Well, I've learned that the market is good here in Mexico. Now I happen to have two girls who get a little out of hand once in a while, and I'm trying to get rid of them. They steal from me and they run away and they do business without telling me. All in all, they're quite bad. But they are very pretty—and white—and I thought you might be interested in taking a look at them, or you might know of someone else who would like to see them. I asked around quite discreetly and found out that you do buy white women."

Zia eyed Bryce cautiously. "Who told you this?"

"Word gets around, Señor Zia. I would rather not say who told me. There are certain things I prefer to keep confidential. The fewer names mentioned, the safer for both of us. Right?"

"Hmmm. I suppose so," the man replied, still wary. "Why do you do this dealing yourself? You look like a wealthy man. Why did you not hire someone to bring these women—or why did you not sell them closer to home?"

"I brought them to Mexico because I figured I could get more money for them here. They're troublemakers, and the other pimps in my area aren't interested. And I brought them myself because—well, to tell you the truth, señor, I wanted to get out of Louisiana for a while—the war, you know. Things are very bad in the south right now. Very bad. And I felt like taking a little trip. Besides, I figure maybe I'll do more dealing in Mexico if this works out, so I wanted to come myself the first time and see just how things operate down here."

404

"We operate very discreetly, Señor Corey," Zia replied. "And you will find we pay well for white flesh."

"Well, like I said, these two are pretty—but a real handful. They need someone who will deal a firm hand with them," Bryce grinned. "I'm told you're very good at taming women. Perhaps you can show me a thing or two."

Zia laughed. "*Si, señor.* I have many ways to make a woman cry and beg. It can be very exciting! Maybe I will buy all of your little troublemakers, if you have more. And these two—Santo could have one for lunch, and one for supper every day, *si*?" The man laughed heartily. "Santo never tires of the women, señor. Oh, the games I play! I make them cry and whimper and beg for more—or sometimes they beg for me to stop!" He laughed again and slapped his knee.

Bryce swallowed and forced a smile. "Well, I can't have these troublemakers in my place, Señor Zia. I run a very smooth and sophisticated establishment. I often have to sort of weed out the bad ones, you know? But they're too pretty to just kick out. I figure I might as well get something out of them, right? Sort of like poor stock. You still expect to get paid for what little meat they have to offer."

Santo laughed. "Well, I do hope these little calves have much meat on them!" he said. "The one I have now—she is so skinny. And she will not eat for me."

Bryce's heart quickened. Shannon! "Well," he spoke up. "My women have lots of nice, white meat on them, nice full breasts, you know?"

"Ah, yes! This is good! Very good! And where are these women now?" The man could barely control his excitement, which gave Bryce the advantage.

"They're waiting in the barn, sir. I have a man watching them for me. I came in very quietly, after dark, because I didn't want to be noticed. I was sure you didn't want your family to know about this, and thought perhaps you wouldn't even want your men to know."

"Ah, no! I keep my women in a cellar beneath the barn. My wife has never known they are there. And down there, no one on the outside can hear their screams." The man chuckled from deep inside his evil heart. "And only three of my men know of my dealings with women. I am glad you were so cautious, but I am upset that you found it so easy to get through. I will have to do something about my security, or I will one night find Apaches lurking on my doorstep, no?" The man chuckled again.

Bryce nodded. "I can see your point." Both men rose. "Tell me, señor, do you have the skinny woman in the cellar now?" Bryce asked cautiously.

"Ah, *si*. The Utes, they bring her to me. They tell me she is whoring with some Apache buck. So I think maybe she likes the men, you know? But that one—she had no life. No matter how much Santo toy with her and make love to her or torture her, she does not cooperate and enjoy it. I finally give up on her. I was preparing to sell her to bandits."

Bryce averted his eyes to hide his fury. He lit a cigarette and remained casual.

"She is quite pretty—white, with red hair and green eyes. It is too bad I must get rid of her."

"I'm eager to see this place where you keep your women, Señor Zia," Bryce said in a strained voice. "And I'm sure you'd like to see the ones I've brought

406

you. Come to the barn with me and maybe we can make a deal. I told the men I have watching them that we would go inside and light a lantern, and that would be my signal to bring the women inside. I'd like to stay and see how you deal with them if you buy them, if you don't mind."

"Oh! *Si!* It is fine with me! I am quite anxious now to go and inspect them."

"Inspect them?"

"Ah, Santo Zia never buys a woman without stripping her and inspecting her—everywhere—if you know what I mean!" He laughed again as they headed for the barn. Bryce felt his mind exploding and his head ached with the tension of holding back his fury.

The walk to the barn seemed to take forever. When they reached it, Zia removed a lantern from near the door and lit it. He stepped inside and hung the lantern. Bryce closed the door after the man walked even farther in.

"Will your men come right away?" he asked, his back to Bryce. Bryce pulled out his revolver and pressed it into Zia's back.

Zia's blood ran cold. "What is this?" he asked cautiously.

"There are no other men, Zia!" Bryce hissed. "Just me! Me—and you! I want you to show me the girl you keep in the cellar—the redheaded one! Where is the door to the cellar?" Bryce's voice was cold and forboding. Zia began to tremble, realizing he had given this man too much information.

"What is this?" he asked again. "Who are you?"

"I'll ask the questions, Zia!" Bryce growled. He jabbed the pistol harder into the man's back. "Now tell me where the entrance is!"

Zia began breathing in short, frightened gasps. "Over there, señor, in the corner. What is wrong? Please, do not hurt me! Why do you do this?"

"This is the day you are going to die, Santo Zia!"

"Please, do not kill me, señor! I, Santo Zia, have done nothing against you. I have told you what you want to know. I have no quarrel with the gringo!"

"Well, this gringo has a quarrel with you!" Bryce replied. "I thought I'd seen and heard everything, Zia, but you are the most vile, putrid sort of human being I've ever been in contact with!"

Zia started to bolt away, but Bryce quickly kicked out, his foot landing in the middle of the man's back. Zia cried out at the jolt and went sprawling on his face. Bryce was on the man in a flash, planting a knee in his back. Zia grunted and Bryce hastily put away his gun. He grasped the squirming Zia's arms and bent them behind his back, hastily pulling out a piece of rope from his pocket and tying the man's wrists. Then he rolled Zia over. Bryce was half again bigger than Zia. He straddled the man and landed a big fist into Zia's jaw just as the Mexican started to cry out for help. He quickly pulled out cotton stuffing from another pocket and stuffed it into Zia's mouth and halfway down the man's throat.

"I'm going to thoroughly enjoy this!" he growled. He took a scarf from around his neck and tied it tightly around Zia's mouth and head, stretching the Mexican's thin lips as he did so.

Zia lay there groaning and squirming while Bryce looked around for a door to the cellar room Zia had mentioned.

A horse whinnied and snorted, and Bryce kept the lamp lit just bright enough to see what he was doing, but dim enough so as not to attract attention. He spotted a small wooden door at the back of the barn and hurried over to open it, revealing concrete steps leading downward. He hesitated, feeling nauseous, then descended.

Below he found a small room with a wood-burning heating stove in the corner. The only other piece of furniture was a bed. Chains hung from each post with leather cuffs that were adjustable for various size wrists and ankles, and now they held very small wrists and thin ankles.

Pain seared through Bryce's stomach at the sight. It was difficult to imagine that the tiny, battered, nude woman who lay there could truly be Shannon. He stepped closer, holding the lantern above her. Her eyes only stared into nothingness. Bryce heard an odd groan, and realized it had surged up from his own throat. Never had he known such horror as he felt at what he was seeing now. The smell in the room was putrid, and vomit rose in his throat. He swallowed and closed his eyes. Could this truly be the beautiful, innocent child he had left behind in Virginia? How could life be so cruel to one innocent human being who had never harmed anyone?

He set the lantern down and collapsed beside the bed in uncontrollable weeping. How much of this was his fault? How much was simple fate? None of it mattered now. This woman he cherished had suffered extreme mental and physical torture, and he should have been there to help her. None of it should have happened in the first place. If only he had brought her with him when he first returned from Virginia! He had made her his woman physically. He should have sealed it right then and there with marriage. How would he ever forgive himself for this?

He was an officer in the United States Army, fought Apache Indians, yet he had failed this tiny, helpless woman, the one person he loved beyond desire, the one person who had brought meaning to his empty life and given him hope of having a family and children and leading a life he had once thought he could never have. Now perhaps that hope was gone again. Even if she lived, her mind might never heal.

He moved to the edge of the bed, pulling out a knife and slitting the leather cuffs from her tiny wrists and ankles. He bent over and carefully pulled her into his arms, rocking her gently. She was like a rag doll, lifeless and limp. He pulled back and studied the face, the eyes still green but dull, with dark circles around them. He gently closed the lids and was glad when they stayed closed. He could not bear the vacant stare. He kissed each eyelid.

"Forgive me, dear Shannon," he groaned. He softly pushed the tangled hair back from her face. He wanted to help her, hold her, but there was no time. He realized he must hurry now. Some of Zia's men could show up at any time. He stood up and looked around the room for something to wrap her in. A whip hung on the wall, as well as a razor-sharp knife. A snake lay curled up in a cage on the floor. Did Zia throw snakes on his women to make them struggle and scream and to frighten them into cooperating? The room was a literal torture chamber. Never had he been so consumed with rage.

He picked up a blanket that lay in a corner and

410

shook it out. Then he carefully wrapped her in it and lifted her. She was easy to carry, more like a child than a grown woman. He carried her up the stairs and past Zia's struggling body and laid her near the door. He had a score to settle before carrying her to safety.

Without a word, he picked up Santo Zia's body and dragged it over to a large, square supporting post, where he shoved the man's backside against the pillar. He untied Zia's wrists and jerked his arms around behind the post and retied them. Zia started to whimper and slide down.

"You having trouble standing up, Zia?" Bryce said wickedly. "Here. Let me help you." He turned and grabbed a pitchfork, and Zia's eyes widened in horror as Bryce rammed the instrument through his middle and into the post. The horrified Zia tried to scream out in the awful pain and terror, but the gag prevented him from doing so. His face went white and his breathing was shallow, his forehead beaded with sweat.

"Now," Bryce said, standing back and watching the blood ooze out of Zia's middle. "That should hold you up."

Zia shook violently now from shock and pain. Tears streamed down the man's face at the knowledge that his life was swiftly being snuffed out.

"Well, look at that!" Bryce said, grinning. "The man is crying! How many of those women cried, Zia?" He lit a cigarette, watching Zia hang on the post, slowly bleeding to death. He savored the look of pain and ghastly horror on the man's face, and relished the man's pitiful moaning and crying as Bryce pushed hay around the man's feet.

"It was nice meeting you, Zia," Bryce told the man

with a grin. "And now I'm going to give you a taste of what it will be like where you'll go when you die!" He lit a match and threw it into the hay, and immediately the flames shot up in front of Zia, whose eyes widened so far it appeared they would pop out of his head. Bryce grabbed the lantern and smashed it into the flames, the kerosene causing the fire to flame up even more. "Good-bye, Señor Zia!" he said loudly. He quickly exited, picking up Shannon and kicking the door shut, hoping the fire would not be spotted until the barn was well on its way to a total loss, taking its evil owner with it. Even if it was spotted, it would be too late to save Zia from a horrible death, or, at the least, irreparable scars.

He crept through the darkness, Shannon little burden to him. He made his way as quickly as possible to the spot where he had left Mona, turning around only once to look back. Flames were already spitting out of the loft. It would not take long for the entire building to be engulfed. His heart leaped with joyous revenge at the sight.

"Mona?" he called out.

"Bryce! Bryce, are you all right?"

"Yes!" he replied. "Let's get the hell out of here and head north where no one will recognize us. They'll be scouting this territory for us now. Manuel and Coca both know I was here tonight. Once we get across the border, and I get back into uniform, no one will ever know who Randall Corey really was. They'll be looking in Louisiana for me."

"Oh, Bryce, I was so afraid! Did you find her?"

He walked closer and she saw the body in his arms. Her eyes widened. "Is she alive?"

"Barely. We've no time now to tend to her. I'll carry

412

her on my horse with me. Let's go! We'll do what we can for Shannon when we're in safer territory."

They mounted up and headed north.

"What do you think, doctor?" Bryce asked the physician who now examined Shannon. She lay still and small and white on satin sheets in Mona's elegant bedroom, looking out of place in the woman's large, rambling saloon/whorehouse.

"Well, physically, I'd say she'll make it," the doctor replied. "She needs to be fattened up, of course. She has one rib that's been broken and not healed right. There's nothing that can be done about that now without rebreaking the rib. The way it is, it will probably cause her some mild pain, but it will subside after a few months. She's badly bruised, inside and out. She's been tortured, that's certain. But she will heal. It's her mind that I can't do anything about. That's a matter of time, but it's possible she'll never come around."

The doctor shook his head and Bryce looked forlornly at Mona, who stood on the other side of the bed. The doctor pulled Shannon's soft flannel gown down over her and then covered her.

"Her heartbeat is good," he went on. "And I don't hear any congestion. She apparently was kept warm. I see no signs of pneumonia or disease." He frowned and sat down on the edge of the bed, pulling Shannon's eyelids open again and studying the pupils. "I'm not educated in mental problems I'm afraid. I guess only time and gentleness and love can heal that part of her. She should sleep quite a while, now that I've given her

413

the sedative."

He looked up at the devastated Bryce Edwards, who had developed new lines about his tired eyes, and whose face showed the strain of the last several weeks.

"I think you could also use a sedative, Colonel Edwards." He reached in his bag and took out a bottle of liquid. He stood up and poured some into a cup. "Here. Drink this."

"I don't want it," Bryce said in a near whisper, staring at Shannon.

"Drink it," the doctor commanded. "That girl is going to need you at your strongest when she comes around. So get some rest, Colonel Edwards, and take care of yourself so you can give her the help and strength she will need when the time comes."

Bryce sighed and took the liquid. The doctor put his other things away.

"Give it to both of them whenever you think they need it," he told Mona. "But no more than twice a day, and no more than a tablespoon at a time. Come and get me if you have problems with Miss Fitzgerald, such as vomiting or abnormal bleeding."

"I will, Arnold."

"She's bathed and sedated now," the doctor continued. "There's not much more I can do, I'm afraid. I think you had better get some rest yourself, Mona. You don't look good at all."

"I will, doctor. I'm going to go to bed soon and sleep for a week!" she said with a sigh. She led the doctor out into the hallway. "Thank you, doctor. That's a very nice girl lying in there. She's not one of mine, you know. She's a girl who came out here from Virginia to marry Colonel Edwards, but things didn't go quite

414

right, as you can see."

"Well, it's a damned shame!" the doctor replied. "Such a pretty, young woman. Practically a child yet. It's a damned shame," he repeated. "It's rough country out here, Mona. Only the really tough ones can get through it—like you, right?" He patted her hand.

"Let's just hope the girl lying in there is stronger than we think. Mr. Edwards loves her very much, doctor. I'm worried about him."

"And you're in love with him, right?"

She smiled sadly. "Come now, doc, you know women like me don't dare fall in love. He's just a good friend."

"Well, your 'good friend' will probably be fine after some much-needed rest. You just call me when you need me."

"Thank you. And—do me a favor. Don't ever tell anyone you saw us like this—where we've been and all. Will you promise me that? Bryce could get in considerable trouble if it was found out what he did down in Mexico."

The doctor grinned and kissed her cheek. "Mona, I've been coming to your place for a long time—either to treat your girls for some ailment or to do business with them. I've seen and heard a lot of things, and I've kept quiet about a lot of things. Doctors are pledged to keep their mouths shut. You know that."

Mona smiled. "Thanks, doc."

"Good-bye!" he replied, giving her a wink. He headed down the stairs. "Try to get some soup down her throat when she wakes up!" he called out. He disappeared around the bottom of the steps, and Mona reentered the bedroom where Shannon lay as still as death. She still had not reacted to anything or anyone since they had first found her.

Mona walked up to the foot of the large brass bed, where Bryce lay beside Shannon with his arms around her. He was already sound asleep. Mona sighed and went to his side, bending down and kissing his temple. "Good night, my darling Bryce," she whispered. "And good-bye. I've just lost you, haven't I?"

Chapter Twenty-four

For another week Shannon lay lifeless. Bryce and Mona managed to force soup down her throat, but not without considerable effort and a fear of her choking to death, for her body seemed to make no effort to function on its own, other than to breathe. She made no sound, not even to cry or utter a whimper.

Bryce was sure that in his whole life he had never wept so much. He was embarrassed and ashamed, yet he could not stop himself. To see this once beautiful and delicate girl in such a pitiful state was bad enough. But to realize it was his fault for not bringing her back with him four years earlier made her present condition almost unbearable for him. And then when he had had her back once more, he had let her leave with Saguaro! If only he hadn't let her go again! If only—if only!

"Bryce, you've got to stop blaming yourself!" Mona was telling him softly. She walked over and stroked his thick, sandy hair as he knelt beside the bed. "What's done is done. You made the right decisions at the time. How in God's name could you know what

417

would happen?"

Bryce grasped Shannon's hand and put his head down on the edge of the bed. "What should I do with her?" he asked brokenly. "I . . . don't know . . . what to do . . . what to say to her . . . how to help her."

Mona sighed. She sat down on the edge of the bed and continued to stroke his hair. "I don't know what to tell you, darling. I hate to say it, but maybe it would help to take her to Saguaro—try to find her baby. Maybe her little boy could help break this awful silence."

"I'll not take her back to him!" he seethed. "Never! She'll never leave my side again!"

"Bryce, sometimes there's a special something between a mother and her baby. If her baby is still alive, she should see him—hear his voice, touch him. It could help her, Bryce. He's the one sweet and innocent thing in her life now. The only connection she has left to a world of peace and love and innocence."

"Then Saguaro will have to bring Chaco to me! I'll not take her out there!"

"Well, it's for sure he won't come to El Paso. Maybe you could get word to him somehow. He doesn't even know you've found her yet. He has a right to know, Bryce. He loved her, too. And he's the father of her child. Why don't you take her to Fort Bowie and get a message to Saguaro? While you're waiting for him, you can work with her, talk to her, love her. Maybe between your love, and Saguaro's—and seeing her baby again—maybe she'll come out of it."

Bryce wiped his eyes and turned to look at Mona. "I owe you, Mona. I owe you a hell of a lot. Thank you for all you've done. Maybe you're right. But what if the kid isn't even alive! Maybe the Utes killed him. My God, Mona, if she comes around and finds out her baby's dead!"

"Bryce, Saguaro said nothing about his son being killed, did he? Surely he'd have mentioned that the night he went to the fort to get your help."

"I hope you're right. We have a few Apache scouts who could get word to Saguaro. I'll go to Fort Bowie and have them try to find Saguaro and tell him I've found Shannon. Do you have a girl about her size who could lend me some clothes for her?"

"I'll do better than that. Most of my girls wear dresses that wouldn't be something a little lady like Shannon should wear," she replied with a soft smile. "I'll go shopping myself and buy her some nice, simple dresses. And I know a woman in town, a widow woman, who would probably be glad to go to Fort Bowie with you for a while to help nurse Shannon. You'll need help, Bryce. You'll be too busy with your work to be sitting by her bedside constantly."

"I'd really appreciate that, Mona. I never even thought of that. Listen, get Shannon pretty things— pretty underwear and nightgowns. And get some nice things women like—you know, perfume and soap and such. And get her a brush, and—"

"Bryce, I *am* a woman! I think I know what women need and like."

Bryce smiled and looked her up and down. "Yeah, you're a woman, all right. Listen, I'll give you some money. How much do you think you need?"

"I don't want any. I want a different kind of payment. She sobered and her eyes teared. "You'll not come back once you leave here this time, Bryce

419

Edwards. I know it in my heart. I want you—for one more night. I know you're wrapped up in Shannon and her predicament, but I can't bear the thought of you leaving without—without making love to me once more."

Bryce glanced at Shannon, then back at Mona.

"She'll never know the difference," Mona told him softly. "And it could be a long, long time before she's ready to give herself to any man again."

"All right," Bryce said softly, taking Mona's hand. "Tonight I sleep with you."

Their eyes held and tears slipped down the beautiful prostitute's cheeks.

"I guess it's just not in the cards for a woman like me to end up with a man like you," she said sadly. "I love you very much, Bryce. And believe it or not, I hope she gets well and you can put your lives back together again. I want you to be happy."

Bryce put his head down on her lap and she stroked his hair. "It's a hell of a life, isn't it, Bryce?" she added.

He placed his hands on the sides of her hips and nestled his head in her lap. "Yeah," he whispered, the tears coming again.

Although a few rumors circulated and there were some remarks made in secret about Shannon Fitzgerald among the men, most of Bryce's troops at Fort Bowie could feel nothing but pity for Bryce, and for the woman he had brought back with him to the fort that November of 1862.

None of them knew the story behind her, only that she was the woman from Virginia that Colonel

420

Edwards was to have married, who had then disappeared. Where she had been, how and when he had found her, none knew. They could only guess because of her condition. Only Reynolds, who had been promoted to sergeant by then, knew the truth, but he was pledged not to divulge it.

The widow woman, Cora Nelson, had kindly accepted Bryce's request to come to the fort and nurse Shannon for him. Bryce had his men quickly erect a small one-room cabin next to his own quarters, where Mrs. Nelson stayed at night. And every night, unless he had to be away, Bryce himself slept with Shannon, embracing her tightly, trying to force his love through her strange, mental barrier, hoping that somewhere, deep in her mind, she was feeling that love.

On November 8, 1862, Reynolds banged on Bryce's door. Bryce was already asleep beside the still-speechless Shannon. He grunted and stretched as he heard the pounding again.

"Hang on!" he shouted out. He looked at Shannon. He always kept a lamp dimly lit in case she should wake up in the dark and be afraid. But she only lay in the same strange stupor. He sighed and quickly pulled on his pants and went out into the office and to the front door. He opened it to face Reynolds.

"What is it, Reynolds?"

"Scouts outside the gates, sir! They say they've found Saguaro. The man's afraid to come into the fort. He thinks it might be a trick to capture him"

"Does he have Chaco with him?"

"I don't really know, sir. The scouts said they can take you to him."

"I'll not take Shannon out there in her condition.

She's much safer here." Bryce ran a hand through his hair. "Listen, get Mrs. Nelson over here. Have her stay with Shannon. I'll go out to Saguaro myself and try to talk to him. I'll take a lock of Shannon's hair with me to prove to him I have Shannon. If Chaco isn't with him, I'll ride with him to get the boy if he wants. Surely if I offer myself as a hostage, he'll believe that I'm not up to something.

"Yes, sir." Reynolds left and Bryce quickly finished dressing. Then he took a pair of scissors and carefully cut a small hunk of hair from the bottom of Shannon's long, thick, auburn locks. He sat and watched her sleeping in the quiet of the night. She looked so innocent and lovely, lying there—as though none of the horrible tortures had ever happened to her. He bent down and kissed her lightly. By then Mrs. Nelson was there. Bryce put the lock of hair in his shirt pocket and went out to greet Shannon's nurse.

"I'll be back as soon as I can," he told her.

He put on his revolver and hat and grabbed a rifle. Reynolds had his horse ready and saddled. Mrs. Nelson thought Bryce a very brave man as the gates were opened and Bryce rode out into the darkness with the scouts to meet the hated and feared Saguaro.

The stars hung still and bright and a full moon cast a long shadow across the desert sands as Bryce rode almost silently with the scouts to Saguaro's camp. He was met by thirty more braves as soon as he was out of sight of the fort guards. The Indians led him to their leader. Bryce dismounted and walked up to Saguaro, who stood near a campfire. As soon as their eyes met,

Bryce could see that Saguaro had suffered greatly over the loss of Shannon. The man was thinner, and his eyes were filled with a terrible devastation.

"Where is my woman?" Saguaro asked in a strained voice.

"If you want to see her, Saguaro, you'll have to come to the fort. I'll not let her away from the safety of the fort again. She's in pretty bad shape, Saguaro."

"How can Saguaro be sure you even have her?" the Indian leader asked cautiously. "Perhaps you wish to capture Saguaro, because you hate him for breaking his promise to you to care for White Flower."

Bryce reached into his pocket and held out the lock of hair. "It's no trick, Saguaro. I have Shannon. Here's a piece of her hair. And I don't hate you, Saguaro. I understand you have a lot of enemies. You can't be everywhere at once."

Saguaro took the lock of hair and studied it. Its reddish tint glowed in the firelight. He squeezed it in his fist and blinked back tears. "I searched for her also," he said in a strained voice. "For two months I searched for her! I killed many Mexicans—raided many ranches! But I could not find her." He took a quick deep breath to keep from crying and looked at Bryce. "Tell me how you found her, white soldier."

"I disguised myself and talked my way through the Mexicans, Saguaro, pretending to be someone I wasn't. When I discovered where Shannon was being held, I went there myself, after dark. If it makes you feel better, I killed the man who had bought her. He had tortured her and treated her worse than an animal. He suffered, Saguaro. He suffered greatly and died slowly and painfully. And I thoroughly enjoyed every minute

423

of it."

Saguaro knew by Bryce's eyes that the man had died a horrible death, and it pleased him greatly.

"Saguaro thanks you for taking the proper vengeance!" the man said, his eyes blazing. "Maybe you have Apache blood in you, white soldier."

"After all my years out here, sometimes I think I do, Saguaro."

Saguaro actually grinned, but his eyes were still filled with a pitiful sadness.

"She's in a bad way, Saguaro," Bryce went on. "She's half mad. She doesn't speak or cry or groan or move. She does nothing but lie there."

Saguaro stepped closer, his face looking drawn and fierce in the firelight.

"This is true?"

"I've never lied to you yet, Saguaro. I simply couldn't bring myself to go dragging her out here in her condition. If you want to see her, you're welcome to come into the fort. I guarantee you'll not be taken prisoner. You have my word. I'm out here alone. You can hold me hostage if you like, while you go and see her. My men have orders not to touch you. But they also have strict orders not to bring Shannon out of the fort."

The big Indian blinked back tears. His lips pressed tightly together. When he finally opened his mouth to talk, his words came out haltingly, in a strained voice.

"When I captured White Flower she was . . . like a child. She cried so long . . . when she talked about man in Virginia. For a man to touch her wrong way . . . it was something she could not bear. And now this!" He closed his eyes and turned away. "There is no kindness left in this world. There is no peace. Only troubles. Always troubles and war and bad people." He shook his head and breathed out a sigh mingled with a groaning sound. "White Flower!" he whispered. He clenched his fists, then grabbed a lance and shoved it viciously into the ground. "I am glad for every Mexican I killed! Glad!"

Bryce gripped the lance himself, sharing Saguaro's feelings. He yanked it out of the ground and stepped closer to Saguaro.

"Saguaro, I had an idea that if Shannon could see Chaco, maybe it would help," he said cautiously. "A woman has a closeness to her children that can sometimes overcome such things. She needs her baby. Is your son still alive?"

"Ai," the Indian replied quietly. Their eyes held, and Saguaro nodded taking the lance from Bryce's hand. "I will have my son sent to you. I cannot return with you to the fort to see her. There is . . . too much hatred now. I do not trust your men to follow orders. I believe you that she is found and safe. I will . . . bring my son to you. I will pray to Usen that the child will help her."

"I'm sorry, Saguaro. I assure you you'd be safe. I know you want to see her."

Saguaro shook his head. "No," he said in a whisper. "It is over." He fought to stay in control. "Saguaro was unable to keep promise to white soldier to care for White Flower. Of this I am deeply ashamed, and my heart breaks with sorrow. Saguaro knows now that it is no good for her to stay with me. Once Apache was free and had much power. Still, we try to keep our land—to

425

chase out white men. Yet deep in our hearts, we know it is a losing battle. But our pride will not let us give up, white soldier. Apache has many enemies. Soldiers seek us, Utes and Mexicans attack us, whites shoot us down like rabbits. We have no home any longer, and little food. The sun is quickly setting on Apache nation. But White Flower is not truly an Apache. The sun should not set on her. She is too young, and my son needs his mother. Saguaro had her for a while. Saguaro will always have memories of happiness White Flower brought him, and fine son she bore him. It was good and beautiful between us. But deep in my heart, I knew it could not last. Our worlds are too different. Saguaro dissolves the marriage of his own free will and gives White Flower back to you. It is fitting. To come with me will only mean more danger for her, and an early death. I will give you no fight over keeping her. Saguaro loves her like his own life. He not be responsible for her death. But Saguaro must have some promises from white soldier."

"Of course, Saguaro."

"You will be gentle with her. You will wait until you see want in her eyes and you will marry her and be responsible for her—protecting her always and loving her as your own life."

"You know I will, Saguaro. I've never stopped loving her."

"The next promise is . . . is most important," Saguaro went on, his eyes tearing and his words coming in choked phrases.

"What is it, Saguaro?"

"My . . . son. He is . . . my life! My blood flows in

426

his veins! You must . . . love him . . . as you would love your own son."

Bryce knew the torture it would be for Saguaro to be separated from his little boy, especially after losing his first two sons to a horrible death. Apaches prized their children above all things.

"I will love him, Saguaro. You have my word. He's Shannon's child also. I know how much she loves him, and I'll love him because of that."

"It is most important. Give him . . . white man's education, so that he can live to be free and own land and not be an outcast. Do not let others make fun of him and call him half-breed. And most of all . . . teach him honesty and pride . . . courage. Teach him how to fight . . . and also how to be wise in his decisions."

"I'll do everything for him that I would do for my own son, Saguaro. And if I have sons of my own, they'll not be treated any more special than little Chaco."

"Saguaro's only comfort . . . is that he can trust word of white soldier Edwards." A tear slipped down Saguaro's cheek. "Saguaro will die soon . . . in battle. It is only way for an Apache warrior to die. Perhaps it will be different for Chaco . . . and for other Apache children. Do you think it will be?"

Bryce stepped up and grasped Saguaro's hand.

"I do, Saguaro. And I'll do what I can to see that it is. You're a man among men, Saguaro. Your sacrifice only shows me what kind of man you really are, and how much you love Shannon."

"It is best I go now and do not see her again. It would hurt too much to look upon her again. Soon others will come to fort with my son. It is best I do not see him

427

again after that. You will be his father. He will grow up knowing only you."

"No, he won't, Saguaro. He'll grow up being told about his real father . . . and knowing what a brave and strong man he was. He'll know the kind of pride that flows in his own veins."

Saguaro swallowed. "You would do this? You would tell him of his real father?"

"Of course, I will. And Shannon wouldn't have it any other way."

Saguaro put out his hand and Bryce took it, feeling the Indian trembling in an effort not to break down.

"My son . . . is bright and strong," Saguaro told Bryce, gripping the man's hand tightly and finding it difficult to let go. "I see honesty in your eyes. You are also brave and strong . . . like Saguaro. You make fine father. Good husband. Saguaro would want no other man to raise his son . . . but you."

"Thank you, Saguaro. I consider that a hell of a compliment."

"I will keep my son for two days first. I will walk with him and hold him, so that his . . . face and voice . . . will be burned into my memory."

"Keep him as long as you want, Saguaro."

"No. Only two days. When a man's heart is going to be torn from his body, it is best it is done quickly, so that the man does not have to dwell on thought of it. It is like knowing that soon you will be tortured, and you fear the pain. Then once it comes, you find the strength to endure it."

Bryce remembered the scars on the man's arms and chest and knew Saguaro had been through the terrible test of manhood that only the bravest of warriors would dare to endure.

"Saguaro, I—"

"It is done! Soon boy will be here. I will send a squaw to feed him and look after him until White Flower is able to do so herself. You have soldier's work to do. You cannot be running after small boy. We are much the same, white soldier. We both have work to do."

"I'm sorry we can't work together, Saguaro."

"Saguaro is sorry also. Perhaps my son will work together with your future sons, and sons of other whites and other Apaches will work together. Perhaps one day sun will rise to find Apache and white man living peacefully together. But it cannot be so for older ones who live now. There is only one way for today's Apache warrior to die!"

"It doesn't have to be that way, Saguaro."

"It does! There are many things about us you will never understand." Saguaro started to leave. "Tell White Flower . . . of my decision. Make her understand it is because I love her that I make this decision. It is best for her. She belongs in her own world. She will not think so at first. Make her understand. Tell her it is Saguaro's wish, and she is not to argue about it. She knows Saguaro's word is final."

"I'll tell her, Saguaro."

"Be sure she knows . . . that I searched for her . . . that I killed many Mexicans in my vengeance. Be sure she know how much I still love her."

"I'll tell her everything, Saguaro."

"Her name is Shannon now. White Flower is dead. You will not see Saguaro again, white soldier, unless it

429

is in battle. Good-bye, my friend."

The big Indian quickly disappeared into the darkness and his braves followed.

"Good-bye, Saguaro," Bryce said softly, a lump in his throat. "God be with you." He turned and remounted, riding out to meet the scouts who waited to accompany him back to the fort.

Chapter Twenty-five

Three days after Saguaro's visit, two scouts appeared at Fort Bowie, accompanying a young Apache woman who carried Chaco on her back in a cradleboard. Chaco was so chunky, and lively at fifteen months old that he seemed too big for the small woman who carried him, yet she didn't seem to mind the burden.

"Does she speak English?" Bryce asked the scouts.

"Some," one replied. "Her name Clay Woman."

"Assure her that as soon as Shannon is able to care for the boy herself, Clay Woman will be safely returned to her own village by Apache scouts."

One of the scouts spoke in his own tongue to Clay Woman. She replied softly, looking at the ground.

"She say it not matter. Her man is killed in battle with Mexicans. She is alone. Her children die of smallpox. She not mind caring for this child. Boy is weaned because her milk dried up. She ask if mother will mind."

"No, no! That's all right," Bryce replied. "It will

431

make it that much easier when his real mother can take over. She won't be able to nurse him now, anyway." Bryce peeked at the round, happy face and the large, green eyes that peeked out from the cradleboard. Chaco smiled instantly and Bryce chuckled. "He doesn't look the worse off for it. He's quite a chunk, isn't he?"

"Ai. He strong like his father."

Bryce sobered. "Is Saguaro all right?"

"Saguaro go off to be alone. Soon he leave Dragoon Mountains and move his people to another place. He not be easy to find, Colonel Edwards."

"Does he know about the orders for soldiers to shoot Apaches on sight?"

"Ai."

"Well, I don't always obey orders," Bryce told him. "And my men do what I tell them, not what some greenhorn from Washington tells them."

One scout grinned a little. "Saguaro say you only honest white man he ever meet."

"Well, tell him Chaco will be well cared for, as well as Shannon. What's the word on Cochise?"

"He is back—with Mangas Coloradas, who is healed from a grave wound. But Coloradas is weak now, and getting old. I think maybe he is thinking of giving up fighting."

"That's good news."

"Maybe. But only Coloradas speaks this way. Cochise and Saguaro never give up. They are younger. Do not expect raiding to cease, Colonel Edwards."

Bryce sighed and looked at Clay Woman. She was staring at the soldiers milling around the fort, her eyes wide and frightened.

"Clay Woman?" She turned her eyes to Bryce and looked at him from her mount. "You have nothing to fear here," he told her.

"White man look at Apache woman like hungry wolf," she said quietly, dropping her eyes again.

"She is afraid," one of the scouts spoke up. "She hear how some white men treat squaws."

It dawned on Bryce that this girl was as frightened around white men as white woman would be around Apaches.

"Clay Woman, I run this outfit, and what I say goes," Bryce assured her. "If one man lays a hand on you or looks at you crooked, you tell me and I'll promptly punish him. Understand?"

She nodded her head. "Saguaro say stay by you."

"Well, I have a nice little place for you to stay. And you have a very nice lady by the name of Mrs. Nelson to keep you company, so you won't be alone. I'd like you to live there and care for Chaco until Shannon is well enough to do it herself. Come with me now and we'll take the boy to Shannon."

He reached up for her and she let him lift her down from her mount. Bryce took her arm and she walked with him toward his quarters. Bryce explained Shannon's condition to the girl as they walked. They entered Bryce's outer office, and Clay Woman unloaded the cradleboard. Bryce removed Chaco and held him up high.

"This is one big kid!" he said, chuckling. Chaco giggled and kicked his chubby legs. "Say, Chaco, did you know I was the first person to ever lay eyes on you—even before your mother did?" Bryce said, swinging the baby up again. "I delivered you, you little warrior. Me—a soldier in the United States Army—delivering another Apache warrior into the world! How do you like that?"

He glanced at Clay Woman and she smiled.

"Does he walk?" Bryce asked her.

"Ai!" she replied. "But he never just walk. He only run!"

Bryce laughed. "I'll bet he does! Come on, Chaco. Let's go see your mama. You remember your mama, don't you? It's not been that long. All kids know their mama, no matter how young."

Bryce carried the boy into the bedroom, telling Clay Woman to follow but stand in the doorway. Shannon sat in a chair, fully dressed this day. Mrs. Nelson was brushing her hair.

"Mrs. Nelson, this is an Apache woman named Clay Woman," Bryce said as he entered the room. "She's going to live with you and watch Chaco until we get Shannon straightened out. That's all right with you, isn't it?"

"Oh, my, I don't mind!" the woman replied kindly. Her eyes lit up at the sight of Chaco. "And this is Miss Fitzgerald's son!" she exclaimed. She put down the brush and walked up to Chaco. "Oh, Colonel Edwards, he's the most handsome baby I've ever seen. Such lovely eyes!"

"He good boy," Clay Woman put in. "He easy to care for. But he run all time. I cannot catch him sometimes!" She smiled and Mrs. Nelson put her hand out to the girl.

"Welcome to Fort Bowie, Clay Woman," she told her. "Thank you for offering to care for Chaco. Colonel Edwards and I are hoping that seeing the baby

434

will help Miss Fitzgerald come around. It's such a sorry state she's in."

Clay Woman looked at the sober, staring Shannon, who seemed to be totally unaware of their presence. Bryce swallowed nervously as he kept hold of Chaco and approached Shannon. Clay Woman and Mrs. Nelson stood back to watch.

"Shannon?" Bryce said softly. "Look who I have. It's Chaco, honey. Your son is here. He's well and safe and healthy. Look, Shannon!"

He held the boy out and let Chaco touch her face with his little fist. Chaco's feet kicked against her thighs and he giggled.

"Say 'mama', Chaco. Tell your mama you're here."

Chaco just giggled and pulled at Shannon's hair. "Mama!" he finally said. He grabbed Shannon's nose. "Mama!"

Shannon gave no response, and after several minutes of effort, Bryce finally took the boy and carried him over to Clay Woman.

"We'll try again tomorrow," he told the girl. They left the room, and Shannon slowly reached up to touch her cheek where Chaco had touched it. No one saw the movement.

Every man in the fort gathered in the exercise yard, standing at attention before Colonel Bryce Edwards. Bryce stood before them, scanning them carefully. It must be cleared up for once and for all, to stop all rumors and to be sure little Chaco and his mother were treated fairly. There had been enough suffering.

He ordered them at ease. There was total silence as

the men waited for what they thought would be new orders, not expecting what was to come next.

"Gentlemen, most of you saw an Indian woman come into the fort this morning with a papoose, and you know she is staying with Mrs. Nelson, who is caring for Miss Fitzgerald. I will not go into details. I will only tell you that the boy's name is Chaco, and he is the son of Saguaro."

He could not read their faces, but a few glanced down and cleared their throats. "Saguaro has sent the boy here in hopes it will help Miss Fitzgerald recover from her . . . mental depression." He hesitated and took a deep breath. "Miss Fitzgerald is the boy's mother."

Reynolds glanced at Bryce in sympathy. Bryce held the eyes of his men steadily, showing no shame or apology. He could see that some of them were trying to control their shock.

"The details of what Shannon Fitzgerald has been through are not your business," he went on, not allowing his voice to waver. "Suffice it to say it has not been pleasant, and she has suffered months of hardship and horror, none of it her fault. She is a woman of quality and honor, of education and refinement. She is my betrothed, and as soon as she is well, we shall be married. Because Chaco is her son, she loves him as any mother loves her child. The boy will become mine. I expect both the mother and the child to be treated with respect. Any man who brings either of them insult or harm will answer to me! None of you has the right to judge Miss Fitzgerald as anything but a lady, an innocent child who has suffered because of the Civil War and other circumstances that determined a fate not of her choosing. Now she is safe and hopefully will recover fully. She is here because I am all she has left. She has lost her entire family. The boy is here at Saguaro's wish, so you need not fear an attack to take the boy. Saguaro wishes he remain here for safety and to be with his mother."

He removed his hat and stepped back slightly. "I share this with you because you knew Miss Fitzgerald was here and saw the Indian woman come in this morning. I felt an explanation of the boy's presence was necessary. None of this has any effect on our responsibility toward protecting the public and seeking out marauding Apaches."

He turned to his junior officers. "Proceed with your duties. That is all I have to say, except that the Indian woman, too, is to be treated with respect and honor, and any man who abuses her in any way will answer to me." His voice was strained, and the men watched him leave with mixed emotions, most of them feeling pity for him, and curiosity to see the mysterious Shannon Fitzgerald. She had been brought into the fort lying in the back of a wagon and had been quickly whisked inside Bryce's quarters, never to be seen since.

By the end of the third week after Chaco's arrival, Bryce's hope was dwindling. But again, he performed the daily ritual. His heart nearly stopped when he saw a flicker of life in Shannon's eyes this time, instead of the dull nothingness when Chaco reached out and touched her. But after several minutes of coaxing, she still did not move or make any sound, and her eyes suddenly dulled again. Bryce gave up, but he felt encouraged. He

437

set Chaco down, and the boy immediately ran toward the outer office. He tripped on the door sill and went flying, landing on his face and cutting his lip. Angry tears welled up in his eyes, and he started squalling. Bryce grinned and shook his head, picking the boy up. He set Chaco on his desk in the outer office and the baby continued to cry as Bryce pressed a hanky to his bleeding lower lip and tried to console the child.

In the bedroom, Chaco's wailing penetrated Shannon's dulled brain. "Chaco," she whispered. Her breathing became more rapid and her heart pounded. The baby! Was that Chaco crying? Were the horrible Ute Indians hurting him?

"Chaco!" she screamed out. "Chaco! Don't you hurt my baby! Chaco! Chaco!"

In the outer office Bryce's heart leaped and he sat momentarily frozen at the sound of her voice. Then he grabbed Chaco and headed for the bedroom. Shannon sat in the same chair as always, wanting to get up but shaking violently. She looked up at Bryce with wild, frightened eyes. He quickly walked to stand in front of her, still holding the now sniffling baby.

"Shannon!" he whispered. "Do you . . . do you know who I am?" She stared at him, breathing hard and looking scared to death. She suddenly leaped up and grabbed Chaco from his arms. She moved back into a corner, crouching down and clinging to Chaco.

"Don't you . . . touch me!" she screamed, clinging to Chaco. "And you keep your hands off my baby!"

"Shannon, it's all right. It's me—Bryce. You're safe now, Shannon.

"Go away! Get away from me!"

Bryce ran a hand through his hair and looked at Mrs.

438

Nelson, who stood in the doorway with Clay Woman. "At least she's doing something," he commented, almost in tears from the joy of seeing her come around. Mrs. Nelson walked up to him and patted his arm.

"Let me try," she said softly. He sighed and nodded. Mrs. Nelson walked close to Shannon and knelt down, smiling gently. "Hello, Shannon," she said softly. "I'm Cora Nelson. I've been taking care of you, honey. We've all been taking care of you. It's all right now, Shannon. Everything will be all right. See? We even brought you your son."

Shannon began to whimper now, tears pouring out of her eyes and spilling down her cheeks. She hugged Chaco tighter and buried her face in the baby's neck.

"Go away!" she sobbed. "Leave Chaco and go away! Don't look at me!"

Bryce motioned for the other two women to leave the room. He walked over to Shannon, kneeling down and reaching out to touch her arm. She immediately cringed as far into the corner as she could get and cried harder. The confused Chaco hugged her tightly around the neck, afraid of all the crying and his mother's firm hold on him. The boy's lip still hurt and bled slightly.

"Shannon," Bryce said softly. "None of it matters, honey. Do you hear me? You're here with me now, and you're safe. I've been taking care of you for almost two months now. I've been sleeping right beside you every night. I'll explain later how I managed to find you. Right now the important thing is that I did find you, and for the past two months you've just sat staring, Shannon—not speaking or reacting to anything. I was hoping Chaco would help bring you around, and he did. I'm so . . . damned happy, Shannon! I was so

439

afraid you'd never come out of it."

"Get out of here!" she begged through choking sobs. "I don't want to look at you! I don't want . . . to look at anyone ever again! Ever! Leave me alone with my baby!"

"I'll not leave this room until I can hold you, Shannon. Please, please let me hold you. I love you, Shannon. Nothing has changed that."

"You don't know! Oh, God, you don't know! You don't know!"

"Shannon, I know everything, honey. Everything."

"Go away! I'm . . . filth! Filth! Get away from me!"

Bryce felt his heart shattering at the words. "I don't want to hear you say that again, Shannon. Do you hear me? You're beautiful and good. You've not done one thing wrong to this day. Your heart is incapable of it. You were used, Shannon, against your will."

"Please, please go away!" she sobbed.

"No," Bryce replied firmly. "I'm staying right here. Now give me Chaco, Shannon. You're scaring him. I have a lady who will watch him for you while we talk."

"No! You . . . leave him here . . . and you go away!" she screamed.

Bryce grasped the child out of Shannon's arms, pulling at Chaco while Shannon screamed and grasped at him. He handed the now screaming Chaco through the bedroom door to Clay Woman, and she and Mrs. Nelson quickly left while Shannon screamed and scratched at Bryce to give the child back. She started through the door after the women, but Bryce held her, and she began fighting him and beating against his chest. Men outside turned to stare as they saw Clay Woman and Mrs. Nelson come running out of the office with Chaco. They could hear Shannon's screaming. They didn't know whether to be glad, or whether Shannon had gone completely insane.

For at least ten minutes, Bryce let Shannon flail wildly, kicking and scratching at him, screaming and sobbing and begging for him to let go of her and stop looking at her. She finally wearied and began to go limp, the strength in her small, too-thin body quickly draining. By that time, Bryce was himself crying at the sight of the broken woman who had once been so innocent and loving—so blissfully ignorant of men and life and the real world.

"I haven't waited all these years for you just to lose you now, Shannon," he told her sternly. "I'll not let what others did to you against your will come between us. I love you, Shannon Fitzgerald, and by God, nothing will ever separate us again! You're going to stay with me and you're going to let me love you, damn it! You're going to let me make it beautiful for you again. You're going to let me erase all of it, Shannon. All of it!"

She hung her head, now sobbing quietly, drained of all strength and resistance. Bryce pulled her against him and embraced her, kissing her hair. They stood there for several minutes, neither one speaking. Then he picked her up and carefully laid her on the bed. He lay down beside her and pulled her into his arms. She was limp and unresisting.

"We're going to start all over, Shannon," he said gently. He moved halfway on top of her and kissed her hair. "It might take a week—a month, a year. But you're staying with me now. And some day you'll look at me and see just Bryce—the man who loves you—the man who's loved you for eight years. And it will be the way it was before you left Virginia. You'll want me the way any woman wants the man she loves. Right now all you see is ugly, leering, strange faces. I know that. I understand that. But I'm going to change all of that for you. Someday it will be like that beautiful afternoon we spent together."

She merely continued to cry and did not answer him. He raised up slightly and kissed her eyes.

"I . . . can't . . . look at you," she whimpered. "I can't look at you!" She covered her face with her hands and he yanked them away, but she only turned her face into his shoulder.

"You'll have to look at me eventually, Shannon. Because I'm going to be with you almost constantly. Now there's a nice woman here who's been helping me take care of you. Her name is Mrs. Nelson. And there's an Apache squaw here named Clay Woman who will help watch Chaco until—"

"Saguaro!" she whispered. "Where's Saguaro!"

Bryce kissed her forehead. "He's asked that I keep you and Chaco and take care of you. It's too dangerous out there, Shannon. Saguaro knows that now. He loves you—very, very much. And the last thing he wanted to do was to part with Chaco. You know how close an Apache man is to his children. But it was his decision, Shannon. I didn't force him into making it. You'll not go back there. Saguaro knows things will only get worse for the Apaches. I'm sorry, honey. If he gave the okay and if you wanted to go back, I guess I'd have to take you. But I'm glad for his decision, because I'd already told myself I'd never let you out of my sight again. Never. I'll never forgive myself for not keeping

442

you with me four and a half years ago. Saguaro has dissolved the marriage, Shannon.

"Dissolved?"

"Yes. You're free . . . to marry me, hopefully. That's what he wants, and you know it's what I want. He asked me to be sure to tell you how hard he searched for you, and he did—very hard. He asked me to take Chaco and raise him to be strong and brave and free, with a white man's education and freedom to own land. I intend to raise that boy as my own."

"Oh, Saguaro!" she sobbed. "Poor, lonely Saguaro! He's . . . lost everything! Chaco was his whole world!"

"It was his decision, honey. He loves you too much to risk your life by taking you back. The Apaches are hunted from all sides now—by soldiers, by the Mexicans, by the Utes and the white settlers and miners. It's no good out there for you, Shannon. It's time for you to live the life you were meant for, as a colonel's wife."

"I can . . . never marry you . . . Bryce. Never!" she sobbed. "I can never . . . marry anyone now. I . . . can't even let Saguaro take me back. I'm not . . . worthy . . . of any decent man!"

Her sobbing heightened again.

"You're wrong, Shannon. You've made it through a hell worse than death, and you survived! I've never seen such strength in a person. And you have a handsome, bright son who would like to be with his real mother. It's time to look ahead, Shannon, not behind. Only ahead."

He kissed her hair again. But she kept her face buried in his chest.

"The last time . . . Saguaro and I were together . . .

443

we . . . we made love . . . because he said something would happen . . . and we would not be together much longer. How right he was!" She cried harder again. "Oh, God, Bryce, those horrible Indians who took me away! I . . . didn't know what was happening! And then . . . the horrible . . . whipping! Over and over!" She rolled away from him and curled up into a ball, gasping for breath, cringing and sobbing.

"Don't, Shannon," Bryce said, pulling her back to him again. "Don't allow your mind to dwell on it."

"But that . . . man! Santo! Santo Zia! The . . . horrible things he did! Oh, Bryce! I'm not the same! I'm filth!" Her hysteria was building and she tried to push away from him.

"That's enough, Shannon! I don't want you to dwell on it."

"But you don't know! You shouldn't love me . . . you shouldn't! Oh, God, I wish I was dead! Please just kill me, Bryce!"

"Don't talk stupid, Shannon. I love you. None of it matters. Not to me or Saguaro or God or anybody. And I don't believe you when you say you want to die. Not when little Chaco is next door waiting for his mama. Could you really take your life and leave Chaco?"

She seemed to calm down, and she let him hold her close again as she wept. "Please . . . help me, Bryce!" she whispered finally. "I want so much . . . to be . . . like the girl you left back in Virginia. She . . . seems so far away now."

"She isn't far away at all," he replied softly, his own tears coming. "She's right here. Right here in my arms."

444

He took out a hanky and wiped her eyes and held it to her nose. She reached up and took it from him and blew her nose.

"Shannon?" he said softly. He kissed her forehead. "You're still just my Shannon to me. Can't you believe that? You're just my little Shannon, and I love you so goddamned much!"

She raised her eyes slowly and finally met the soft gray ones. They held no malice—no hatred, no accusations. They held only love. Their eyes held for a moment until she finally closed hers.

"My God, Bryce! I'll never . . . be able to forget. Never!" she whispered. "I'll never . . . be a wife to you."

"Yes, you will, Shannon. I'm not the least bit worried about that. You will. And you also will forget. After today, we'll not talk about the last few weeks at all. We'll only look ahead, Shannon. Only ahead. You'll stay here with me and you'll enjoy Chaco and you'll let both of us love you and help you forget the ugliness and remember the beauty there is in life and love."

"What about . . . Saguaro?"

"You've never truly belonged to any man but me, Shannon. You've belonged to Bryce Edwards since that beautiful afternoon when you gave yourself to me so sweetly out of our precious love. You'll never belong to any other man from now on, either physically or in your heart. No man will ever touch you or own you again but Bryce Edwards. You're safe now. You're with me, and this is where you belong and where you'll stay."

"Oh, Bryce!" The tears came again, but at least this time she moved her arms to embrace him around the neck, and Bryce's heart swelled with joy. "Help me,

445

Bryce!" she whispered. "How can I ever . . . face anyone again!"

"Uh—begging your pardon, sir, but there's a wagon train just pulled in," Reynolds told Bryce after coming in and saluting first.

"So?"

"Well, sir, they're pretty damned happy to have made it this far through Apache country without being attacked. They're ready to celebrate. They said to ask you if you minded if they held a little dance tonight. They've got a couple of fiddle players and a guitar player and a man who calls square dances. They'd like to come inside the fort. The ladies will make food and coffee, and they won't chastise their daughters for dancing with some of the men, sir."

Reynolds blushed a little, and Bryce chuckled.

"And you wouldn't mind dancing with a few young ladies, right, Reynolds?" he put in.

"No, sir! But—that isn't the real reason I was hoping you'd allow it, sir."

"Oh?"

Reynolds glanced at the door to Bryce's private quarters, which was closed, as usual.

"I . . . I was thinking, sir. It might be good for Miss Fitzgerald, if you could get her to come. I mean, she's been here since the first of November, and here it is the end of February, and she's never come out of there. I'm in here all the time, and even I haven't seen her since she got here. The men . . . well, they'd like you to give her a message."

446

Bryce scowled a little and leaned back. "What's that?"

"They—uh—they'd all be real proud to meet the colonel's lady, sir. And they've grown real attached to the little boy, Chaco. They all feel like big brothers to the kid. They'd like to see Chaco and Miss Fitzgerald both at the dance tonight. There isn't one of them, sir, who thinks badly of her. She's become sort of a legend. They'd be right honored to meet her, and they're all hoping maybe there'll be a wedding soon."

Bryce lit a cigarette and glanced at the door himself. He sighed and took a deep drag on the cigarette.

"I don't know, Reynolds. I'll ask her. It took weeks to even get her to talk or cry. That was three months ago. In those three months, the only time she has smiled has been for Chaco. I've at least been able to send Clay Woman back, and Shannon takes care of herself and all . . . feeds the boy. She even cooks for me. But after that first couple of weeks, I gave up trying to carry on a reasonable conversation with her. She almost never looks me straight in the eye . . . won't let me hold her . . . help her." He sighed. He had held her just once, when she first came around. Since then he had slept on a cot every night and Shannon slept with Chaco. "She's removing herself from reality," Bryce continued, almost absently. "I'm worried if she doesn't come out of that shell soon, I'll lose her completely again. I'm not so sure things can ever be normal between us, Reynolds."

"I'm sorry, sir. I just thought . . . maybe if you could get her to come . . . maybe she'd enjoy it and would sort of get used to being around people again."

Bryce took another drag on the cigarette. "I'll talk to her. You tell those people they're welcome to come inside and have their little fling. And tell the men they'd better stay in line and treat the ladies with respect or they'll answer to me."

"Yes, sir. Thank you, sir. And you tell Miss Fitzgerald they'd all be honored to meet her."

"I'll do that, Reynolds. Thank you. Everything quiet out there today—the Apaches, I mean?"

"So far, sir. No messages from any towns or forts."

"Well, let's hope that doesn't mean they've cut the wires again."

"Oh, we've checked it, sir. We send messages back and forth just to be sure the lines are still open."

"Good. I'll talk to you later, Reynolds."

"Yes, sir." Reynolds left and Bryce turned to stare at the closed door. He could hear Chaco running and babbling behind it. He went to the door and opened it.

"Shannon?" he called to the little bedroom.

"Oh! Don't come in!" she yelled. "I . . . oh my!"

"What's wrong, Shannon?" he asked, alarmed. Chaco came running out with a tin cup and pounded it against the wall in play. Bryce hurried to the bedroom. Shannon stood before the dresser mirror, wearing a yellow taffeta dress just slightly low-cut that Mona had bought the day she had gone out to buy the girl supplies before Bryce took her to Fort Bowie. Shannon had never worn the dress. She considered it too fancy. Soiled women did not wear such lovely garments and parade around like ladies.

"I—" She fumbled with the buttons in front. She wanted to get out of the dress, but she didn't want to

448

undress in front of Bryce. She reddened and put her head down.

"Shannon, you look . . . beautiful!" he said softly.

"I don't! I . . . I don't know why I even put it on! I was just remembering . . . I guess. I thought you had left."

"Remembering? Remembering what? The night we danced on your seventeenth birthday and celebrated our engagement? I remember that very vividly, Shannon."

"Why?" she snapped, suddenly turning to face him with bitter eyes. "Because it was the last time you saw me young and innocent and untouched?" She breathed rapidly and fought tears as she struggled with the buttons. "Oh, damn! Please . . . get out of here so I can get this thing off!"

Bryce stepped closer to her.

"Shannon, don't you think you owe me something after all the years I've waited for you? I was your first man. I waited years for you to come and marry me. When you came up missing, I didn't give up. I searched and searched. And when I finally found you, I ended up delivering your baby, Shannon."

"Stop it!" she whispered, turning away.

"No. I've wanted you all this time, Shannon, and you can't get rid of me or run away from it. I let you go back with Saguaro because it was what you wanted, even though it was against my better judgment. And I didn't blame you. I understood how you felt about Saguaro and Chaco. But the worst happened, just as I had feared. And when you came up missing again, I risked my neck to get you back. And since then I've nursed you, wept over you, changed your messes, cleaned up after you, talked to you, worked with you, given you shelter, fed you. I've loved you almost eight years. I'd like you to do something for me . . . just one simple thing."

"What?" she asked brokenly. He stepped closer and put his hands on her shoulders and made her turn around.

"I want you to leave that dress on. Fix your hair and come with me tonight. There's going to be a little party outside. A wagon train arrived and they want to celebrate getting this far safely. I'd like to join them, with you on my arm."

"No! No, I can't . . . face . . . all those people . . . all those men who . . . know!"

"Shannon, Reynolds was just here. He said they'd all like to meet you. They'd be proud to meet you, he said. You're a legend, Shannon. Being around you gives people strength to go on. They know if you could do it, so can they. They're all lonely, and a lot of them are afraid. They're out here fighting Indians, and back where they come from, the nation is torn apart in war. It makes a man feel afraid and out of place . . . homeless . . . with no future. But you're living proof that there is always a future . . . always the ability to pick up and go on."

"I have no future!" she whispered, refusing to look at him.

"You're a fool, Shannon! You have me, and you have Chaco! You have a lot more than most. After all you've been through, are you going to give up now? You've won the battle, Shannon! Don't throw away the victory!"

He put his hands to either side of her face. "I love you. And I'm so very proud of you. I want to show you off. Please do this . . . for me . . . for Bryce. For one night you can be my Shannon again . . . the little girl I left behind in Virginia. Don't you understand that's all you've ever been to me?"

She finally raised her eyes to his, looking almost shocked.

"You really mean that, don't you?" she asked, sounding surprised.

"I've been saying it for weeks and weeks now. Of course I mean it. Shannon, when I look at you, that's all I see. Shannon Fitzgerald, gliding across the ballroom in her lovely gown, her eyes glittering with love . . . love for one man . . . me . . . Bryce Edwards. Do you know how much—" His voice choked and he swallowed. "How much . . . I'd like to see your eyes . . . look that way again?"

She closed her eyes. "I'm sorry, Bryce. I don't know if I'll . . . ever feel warm toward any man again. I'm sorry."

He kept hold of her face and bent down to kiss her lips tenderly. He felt a sudden hunger for her he had withheld for months. He loved her more than any man ever would. His kiss lingered, and he groaned lightly, kissing her harder and pulling her into his arms. She seemed to respond at first, but she suddenly pushed him away and whimpered. She wrested her lips from his and turned her face sideways.

"Let me go, please!" she said in a whisper. Bryce sighed and released her.

"Will you go with me tonight?"

"No! No, I can't!" she replied, beginning to cry

"I'm . . . sorry, Bryce. Truly I am!"

His eyes hardened slightly. "I'm leaving to check out a few things and meet the people from the train. I'll be here tonight and keep an eye on the men. But tomorrow I'll be leaving for a few days, Shannon."

"Leaving?" she asked, sounding alarmed. The thought frightened her. Bryce was all she had now.

"Where . . . where will you go?"

"I'm sending a patrol out to scan the area. It isn't necessary that I go, but I've got to get out of here for a while. I can't take the strain. I imagine I'll get to El Paso while I'm at it. I may be gone a week or two. You'll be watched well. And you have Mrs. Nelson to keep you company." He ran a hand through his hair. "On second thought, I think I'll take Mrs. Nelson with me and take her back home to El Paso. She's been here long enough and you can take care of yourself now."

"El Paso? That . . . that's where . . . that woman lives, isn't it? The woman who helped you find me? Mona?"

"Yeah, that's where she lives," he replied, almost sarcastically. "A man needs to feel wanted once in a while, Shannon. Mona wants me. She always wants me. I don't love her like I love you, but then there isn't much I can do about that, is there? We can't control our hearts. If I don't go and see her, I'll end up doing something that could destroy your mind for good. I can't do that to you. So I'll just get the hell out of here for a while. I'll—uh—see you later."

He turned and went through the door. "I'm taking Chaco!" he called out as he went into his office and on out the front door. Shannon sniffled and peeked through the window to see him walking toward the

452

gates with Chaco on his shoulders.

"Bryce . . . my Bryce!" she whispered. "I do love you! I do! I wish I could say it! But I'm . . . not worthy anymore. Oh, God, don't leave me now, Bryce! Don't leave me, I love you." She squeaked the words through tears and put her head down on the windowsill and wept.

arms with Chase on his shoulders.

"Boyce," Amy Boyce," she whispered. "I do love — yeah! do! wish I could say it! But I'm... not worthy anymore. Oh God, don't leave me now, Boyce! Don't leave me. I love you." She squeaked the word through tears and put her head down on the steering wheel and wept.

Chapter Twenty-six

Bryce watched the colorful skirts whirl as his men and the settlers danced to fiddle music. It was a warm, beautiful night, filled with laughter amidst the dancing, eating, and drinking. The entire fort was refreshingly alive, and those walking guard duty on top of the stone walls of the fort found it difficult to concentrate as they waited anxiously to be relieved of their watch so they could join the others.

A square dance ended, and several minutes later the fiddles began whining away, playing a waltz tune that sounded familiar to Bryce, but he could not remember why. Minutes later he heard whispers and saw people turning to look in one direction.

"Jesus, she's beautiful!" he heard one soldier comment behind his back. Bryce turned to see Shannon approaching the crowd and looking only at him. She wore the yellow dress.

"Shannon!" he whispered, his eyes lighting up.

She had applied ever so little makeup and her hair was swept away from the sides of her face and piled at the crown of her head, some of it gracing her slender back in long reddish waves of lustrous beauty. Bryce broke into a proud grin at the sight of her. Most of the soldiers gaped at the woman they had been wondering about all these weeks. In this desolate land, she was the most beautiful young woman any of them had set eyes on in months, but all knew that even among the prettiest women back East, this one would stand out. The settlers whispered among themselves as to who she might be, as Bryce stepped up to her and took her right hand, putting his left arm about her waist reassuringly. The fiddlers stopped playing.

"I'd like all of you to meet someone." Bryce announced. Shannon felt herself reddening slightly and refused to look at the other men. She moved closer to Bryce. "This young and very beautiful woman is Miss Shannon Fitzgerald—from Virginia. She's—" He stopped for a moment and looked down at her. He gave her another reassuring hug. "She's going to become my wife soon."

People broke into grins and some of the settlers came up to introduce themselves and congratulate them, many of them commenting on how brave she must be to agree to come to a post in the middle of Apache country to live. Bryce squeezed her hand, eyeing the rest of the men to make sure none of them looked inclined to insult her, with even a wrong look. To his relief he saw no sneers or looks of contempt, and now some of the soldiers were coming forward to introduce themselves and compliment Bryce on his beautiful bride-to-be. Bryce knew some of them were purposely trying to make him feel better, and he appreciated the gesture, and he also knew that Shannon's appearance was making them think twice. She was very obviously all of the lady he had told them she was.

"What would the little lady like us to play?" one fiddle player shouted out.

"Well?" Bryce asked her gently. "It's your choice, Shannon."

She raised her eyes to meet the lovely gray ones that were so filled with happiness at the moment. How she had loved him at fourteen! How much more she had loved him at seventeen, when he had taken her virginity.

"I . . . the waltz they were playing . . . when I walked out here. It . . . it's the one they played . . . that night we announced our engagement and everyone made us dance first alone."

She spoke so quietly he could hardly hear her.

"So that's where I've heard that song," he told her. "I thought it sounded familiar!" He looked over at the fiddle players. "Play the waltz you started a moment ago," he told them. "And I will dance with Miss Fitzgerald alone first. This one is all ours."

"Bryce, I can't—" she whispered as the fiddlers began playing.

"Yes, you can," he replied, putting one arm about her waist and forcing her out into the middle of the crowd. He whirled her around so skillfully it appeared they were floating instead of using their feet. It was obvious to all of them that Shannon Fitzgerald was a woman of class and breeding, as her small feet followed his step in perfect timing. She glided like an angel. Reynolds remembered her in braids and a single tunic, crying out in childbirth inside a wickiup. It was difficult to believe this was the same woman. He was very happy for Bryce, who he knew had suffered greatly over the past several years because of this woman he loved so much.

It was not long before everyone realized that Bryce Edwards and Shannon Fitzgerald were completely lost in only each other, as she raised her eyes to meet his. They were in another place and another time, totally unaware of their present surroundings. Their eyes held as they danced to the familiar tune, and they did not speak.

The ring was gone now, stolen by the Utes. But it didn't matter. It was only an object. The love that had placed it on Shannon's finger was still there. It had lived through civil war, the horror of murder and flight into a strange land. It had lived through an Apache raid and an Apache husband who had given her a half-breed son. It had lived through the worst horror of Mexican slavery and rape. It had lived through near insanity.

In the beginning there had been a fourteen-year-old girl who had dreamed about the handsome and brave soldier who fought Indians out West. And now here he was—still in love with her. He had never deserted her. He had waited—for so very long. So very long. Could a woman ask for more than a man who would still want her after what she had been through? And she had actually loved Saguaro. She still loved Saguaro, and could not and would not forget him. After all, he was the proud and handsome Apache father of her beautiful son. But never would her heart hold the special love for any other man that it held for Bryce Edwards.

Could she truly be a woman of honor again? Could

458

she find herself again through this handsome and virile man whose eyes glowed with love for her? Was it time for her to reenter the world she came from, after learning to live the life of an Apache squaw and then being a prostitute slave to the hated Santo Zia?

The dance ended, and they had little time to talk as both were surrounded by well-wishers and kind people who wanted to meet Shannon. Before they knew it, people were beginning to retire. The partying dwindled down, and Shannon had danced several more times, even with a few of the other soldiers. She had surprised even herself. It felt good to be dressed prettily again— to be looked at as a proper lady and touched gently and with respect. It was nice to have people talking to her and to talk back. The evening passed quickly, and then Bryce was guiding her back to his quarters. They went through the front door and then through the door to his private rooms.

"Let's not wake up Chaco," he told her. "I want to talk, Shannon."

"Chaco isn't here," she replied. "I took him over to Mrs. Nelson for the night."

"Why?" Bryce asked, surprised. She turned to face him, and her eyes told him the answer. She put her arms about his waist and rested her head against his chest.

"Help me, Bryce," she whispered. "Help me."

Bryce found the gesture unbelievable. He hesitantly touched her hair and removed the pins, letting it fall down over her shoulders. She looked up at him, and in the next moment their lips met. He felt her tensing up for a moment, and then she was responding, reaching up around his neck and kissing him back.

459

Bryce released her lips and their eyes held for a moment.

"It's time . . . you got your wish," she told him. "If you truly want me, Bryce . . . after all of this . . . then I'll not argue about it anymore. Few women could ask to be loved the way you must love me, after—"

"Don't say it, Shannon. I was . . . proud . . . when you came out there tonight. So proud. You look beautiful . . . just the way you used to look when I'd come to see you in Virginia. Shannon, I love you so much. So much!"

"And I love you, I've loved you such a long time!" They kissed again, hungrily this time. He picked her up and laid her on the bed, kissing her over and over, afraid to stop for fear he would lose this beautiful, thrilling moment. "This is Bryce," he whispered, moving his lips to her throat and bosom. "Just remember that. When I touch you, it's with love and respect and a need to have the woman I've waited for all these years."

He gently unhooked the buttons down the front of her dress, kissing her breasts, on fire at the sound of her quick breathing and soft whimpers. He groaned as he cupped a breast in his hand. He had seen and touched her many times during her illness out of necessity. But not in the act of making love; not in the beauty of having her give herself to him as a woman again.

Shannon felt the lovely bolt of desire shoot through her. She had felt this pleasure when Saguaro had taken her, and for a moment it brought back the sad, painful memory of her Apache man. But it was a love that could not truly be forever, and this was the man who had first taken her virginity. This was the man she had

460

loved first, and most.

Bryce! Her beautiful, golden Bryce! Here was the man she had loved and longed for since she was fourteen years old, the man who had taught her the beauty of giving her most precious possession to a man out of love and passion when she was only seventeen. How long ago that was! Could they recapture that moment? Could she ever be the old Shannon again? Perhaps. She only knew that if she was ever to be well and give this man the happiness he deserved, she must do this. She must try. She must let it happen.

They floated through the movements in blissful ecstasy. She felt her clothes coming off and did not fight it. His hands and lips moved expertly over her body, mingled with tender words of love and near-worship. What were these beautiful things he was doing to her? How could there be such a difference in men—men like Santo Zia—and men like Bryce and Saguaro?

There was no turning back now. Bryce was moving urgently, groaning, kissing, touching. His lips were on hers and she felt his gentle fingers probing her soft moistness and moments later she was crying out his name and clinging to his neck, both excited and afraid, proud and ashamed. Was this right? She had loved Saguaro, but out of respect and a sense of duty and because he had given her love and protection. He had been kind to her and helped her. Her life with Saguaro was more like another world—a world that could not last, because she was not born or bred for it. Yet it was a world and a part of her life that would live on forever in her heart, through her precious Chaco. She would never be ashamed that she had been the woman of

461

Saguaro! Never!

But now she was in the arms of the only man she had ever loved for no reason other than just to love him. In the beginning he had done nothing in particular to make her feel obligated to love him, as Saguaro had done. He had simply been her beautiful, gentle Bryce. And now he was moving on top of her. The one act both of them had waited to share again all these years would finally come to be. And it was every bit as gentle and beautiful as that first time. He whispered such lovely things to her. His hands were so gentle. But then there was the sudden penetration, and at first she cried out in remembered horror. The memory of being at the mercy of Santo Zia engulfed her and she started to panic and push at him. He embraced her tightly, kissing her warmly and moving his lips to her ear.

"Relax, Shannon," he whispered, sensing her sudden fear. "It's me. It's only Bryce. Think about that afternoon we shared back in Virginia."

"Oh, Bryce, help me forget McGuire, and Santo Zia, and—"

"Shhhh." He covered her lips with his own, and she calmed, beginning to move rhythmically with him. He surged deep inside of her, glorying in the ecstasy of finally bedding her again. It seemed only moments before his life surged into her, and she cried out, pressing her fingers into his back.

They lay there quietly for a moment, then he began kissing her tenderly, her hair, her eyes, her lips. "I was your first, first in your heart and first in your body, Shannon Fitzgerald," he told her softly. "You've always been mine."

He moved off of her and she curled up against him.

"Oh, Bryce, I love you so! Thank God you're alive and we're together this way again."

"We'll get married right away," he told her, kissing her hair. "I'll send for a priest. And he'd better hurry, or I'll have you pregnant before I can get another ring on your finger. I do not intend to abstain until he gets here. I've waited too many years to have you this way again."

He turned and kissed her hungrily again, and minutes later they were wrapped up in the lovely intercourse again. This night they would not be able to get enough of each other. They had too many wasted years to make up for.

On March 1, 1863 the final vows were said before the priest from Fort Buchanan, and as Mr. and Mrs. Bryce Edwards kissed, one hundred fifty soldiers cheered and guns were fired. Two cannons were set off, and Chaco had a field day riding atop shoulders the rest of the afternoon. Two soldiers who were reasonably good on the banjo and the fiddle strummed and twanged out some tunes, and the men danced with each other and with Shannon, who saw little of Bryce after saying her last "I do" and accepting her bridal kiss. But she did a lot of laughing, and Bryce relished watching her smile. She was his beautiful Shannon again. She had gained weight and her green eyes had life in them again. Today she wore a simple soft pink cotton dress, and flowers in her hair. It didn't matter that he had already bedded his new wife. He would enjoy doing it all over again. He would enjoy it for the rest of his life.

Five years, he thought. Almost five years since that afternoon of passion. And nine years since he had helped her up from the stairs the day she fell and was so embarrassed. How strange fate was. How strange life was. The same sweetness was still there in her, the innocent love, the desire to be a good wife and to please her man. She would be a wonderful wife and an even better mother.

Mrs. Nelson had stayed on for the wedding. She watched happily as Shannon danced and laughed. She had grown to care for the young woman very much and had stayed on willingly these past months since Shannon first recovered, because Bryce had feared Shannon would have a relapse. But it was now obvious that Shannon would be fine, especially with the support of the patient and faithful love of Bryce Edwards.

Mrs. Nelson would be escorted back to El Paso the next morning, after caring for little Chaco one more night so Bryce and Shannon could be alone. She would take with her a special letter from Bryce to Mona Jackson—a letter of love and good-byes, of deep gratitude and abiding friendship, and a promise to be there if she ever needed anything. Shannon knew about the letter and understood. Both of them had had someone else they could have loved and spent their lives with. But their first and only love could be for each other and no one else.

The newlyweds cut the cake Mrs. Nelson had baked for them, and their eyes held as they fed it to each other amid hoots and howls from the men. An extra room was being added to the little cabin where Mrs. Nelson had been staying. It would become Bryce and Shannon's home, and the spare room was for little Chaco.

"I do not intend to mix my pleasure with my work!" Bryce had told Shannon. "We will live in the cabin, separate from my office. There is no sense in your having to put up with men coming in and out all the time. Besides, my quarters are much too small for the three of us. And before you know it, it will be four—or more."

But for this night, they would stay in Bryce's quarters, where they could be alone, and it was not long before they were literally being pushed toward the office by all of the men, who insisted Bryce carry Shannon through the door, howling and whistling as the two of them went over the threshold and Bryce kicked the door shut. He set Shannon on her feet and looked down at her to see her blushing.

"Oh, how I love that blush," he told her. She smiled and looked down.

"Why do I suddenly feel so strange?" she said quietly. "Now you're really my husband, I feel . . . different."

"It's a good feeling, I hope."

She looked up at him with tears in her eyes. "It's a very good feeling. It's a wonderful, honorable feeling. I'm very proud to be Mrs. Bryce Edwards. Perhaps there's some . . . little bit . . . of honor left for me."

He kissed her forehead. "There's no woman in the world I respect more than the one standing before me this minute," he told her. He swooped her up in his arms again and carried her toward the bedroom. "Shall we officially consummate this marriage, Mrs. Edwards?"

"I'd be more than happy to grant you your husbandly rights, Colonel Edwards," she replied. Their eyes held and they kissed hungrily.

Bryce carried her through the door and laid her on the bed, hardly able to believe that from now on he would not just have to dream of lying beside this woman. She was here for real, and, finally, after nine years of loving her, she was his wife. When he made love to her, she was seventeen and innocent again. And he was her handsome, brave, but gentle soldier, come to claim his woman.

June of 1863 brought occasion for great happiness and great sadness for Shannon Edwards. She was pregnant, this time with Bryce's child. Bryce promised to get a good physician escorted to the fort as soon as possible. Shannon feared that her tortures at the hands of Santo Zia had damaged something that could cause problems with her pregnancy, and Bryce wanted to alleviate her distress. He did not intend to rely on the army doctor stationed at Fort Bowie—not for woman problems. He would have her examined by a physician who had experience in such matters, and he would have the man brought back to the fort when she was due.

"Bryce, you delivered Chaco, remember?" she reminded him.

"That was out of necessity. If I can manage to have a doctor here for you, all the better. I want no complications. You've had enough unhappiness, Shannon Edwards. I don't want you losing any babies on top of everything else. And you can bet I'll make sure I'm right there when it happens, honey. Apache wars or not, I don't intend to be away when you're due."

Their happiness over the pregnancy was overshadowed by the fact that lately more and more Apaches had been showing up at the fort to turn themselves in for reservation life. They were tired and beaten and diseased. They wanted a place to call home where they could stop running, even if it meant the hated reservation. It was a sorry thing to see such a proud and independent people coming in with heads hanging in shame and resignation.

Bryce could see the despair and pain in Shannon's eyes when she greeted the refugees. He wanted to stop her from running around trying to help and nurse all of them—feeding the children and clothing them, over-working herself for these Indians, but he knew she loved them and would only be more upset if he made her stop. And always she searched. For what? For Saguaro? Of course. He felt the old burning jealousy, unfounded now as it was. How could she not care? How could she not wonder about him? He and other men had heard her asking the small bands of Apaches who appeared at the fort about Saguaro. Where was he? How was he? Would he give himself up also? Had he married? No one stopped her from asking the questions, and no one blamed her.

And then on June 20, Reynolds came bursting into Bryce's office.

"Important message, sir!" he said, handing Bryce a note and glancing at Shannon. Shannon watched Bryce pale slightly as he read it.

"Is it . . . Saguaro? she asked anxiously.

"I'm not sure," he replied. "Mangas Coloradas is heading in the direction of Pinos Altos, supposedly to talk peace with the miners, according to the scouts. He's tired of fighting and raiding and wants to work

467

out some kind of deal."

"Is that so bad?"

Bryce looked up at her with concern. "Brevet General Joseph West is in that area. Need I tell you more?"

"Oh, Bryce, isn't he the one—"

"He's worse than Bascom and Carleton put together," Bryce interrupted, his face dark with distress. "If he gets his hands on Coloradas, then we've only seen the beginning of the Apache wars out here."

"What if Saguaro is with him?" Shannon asked, her eyes tearing. Bryce sighed and got up.

"Get my things ready, Reynolds. And hustle up about fifty good men. We're riding hard and fast for Pinos Altos. I doubt we'll get there in time, but we'll try."

"Yes, sir!" Reynolds left quickly and Shannon turned away from Bryce to stare out the window.

"Bryce, I'm sorry, but . . . I feel so sorry for them. I've learned to love them," she said softly. "If only . . . people knew how kind and good they can be. But no one cares. Their skin is brown, and the settlers and miners lust for Apache land that doesn't even belong to them. So they just . . . wipe them out like . . . like so many . . . flies!" She choked in a sob and covered her mouth with her hand. Bryce walked over and embraced her from behind.

"I'm sorry, too, honey. I guess there will always be certain people who are oppressed, falsely accused of things, taken advantage of."

"Oh, Bryce, this was *their* land! Their land! And we want to steal it from them and stick them on little reservations to live like animals. We want to take away

468

their dignity, their pride, their customs and language! Everything, Bryce, everything! Even to murdering as many of them as we can in the name of progress. My God, what are we doing! This is democracy? We preach about . . . about how wrong it is to move in and take over someone else's country. Yet that's exactly what we're doing now. We don't even keep our puny promises to them. We lie and cheat and murder—"

"Shannon, calm down. This isn't good for you in your condition. And you don't have to convince me of these things, honey."

"Then who do I need to convince?" she asked, resting her head against his chest. Sometimes I . . . I feel . . . ashamed . . . to be a part of the white race." She cried harder and Bryce held her tightly.

He sighed and held her. "I tend to agree with you. I'm finding it difficult to kill an Apache, Shannon. That's not good. It could get me in trouble, and it could get my men in trouble. I can't risk that. I'm thinking of resigning, Shannon."

"But . . . the army is your whole life."

He pulled back and met her eyes. "Not necessarily. It was when I was alone and single, but that's all changed now. I have a family now. We all should be living a more normal life. And after the way Saguaro treated you . . . took care of you . . . and now little Chaco being part Apache and loving him the way I do—" He kissed her forehead. "It's just a thought. You consider it yourself and we'll talk about it when I get back."

"Whatever you want, Bryce. I already know I'd rather not see you riding out to risk your life all the time. I've lost enough people that I love. I get so scared when you leave. So afraid you won't return."

He patted her head. "Well, this will be a peaceful mission."

"I hope you can help Coloradas. He's good, Bryce. And he's old now, and so very proud. And he's Cochise's father-in-law. If they harm him—"

"I'll see what I can do." He turned away to put on his weapons. "Maybe you and I together could do more for the Apaches some other way, Shannon. Maybe I could go back to Vrginia when the war is over and run for Congress or something. I could fight for the Indians' rights. Or we could be reservation agents and make sure they get a square deal that way. You could teach the children, and I could help the men learn trades. I don't know. I'm not even sure yet. I only know that when I ride out to defend settlers or miners, I sometimes feel like I'm helping robbers and killers."

"Bryce, be careful! If . . . if killing an Apache means saving your own life—"

He looked at her lovingly. "I have a new and pregnant wife waiting for me, not to speak of my little stepson. I'll be back Shannon Edwards. You can count on it."

He grabbed her close and kissed her hard. "I love you. You stay right here, no matter what, understand? You'll always be safe here." He turned and yelled for Chaco, who had been sitting in a corner stacking little blocks of wood. The boy grinned and jumped up and ran to Bryce, who picked him up and swung him around.

"You be good to your mama. Daddy's going away for a little while."

"Me go?" the boy asked, grinning broadly.

"Sorry, buddy." Bryce kissed the fat, dark cheek.

470

"You stay with mama." He set the boy down.

"Me go!" the boy said, now beginning to pout. Bryce looked at Shannon.

"Stubborn . . . just like his father. I wonder whose side he'd fight on?" Shannon smiled sadly and looked down at Chaco and patted the top of his head.

"I wonder," she said softly. Bryce kissed her once more, this time quickly on the cheek

"Take care. I have no idea how long I'll be gone," he told her.

"Me go, Father!" Chaco said, his lower lip beginning to protrude.

"No, Chaco. You be a good boy now." He winked at the child and went out. Shannon picked up Chaco and the boy wrapped his arms and legs around her.

"Me go," he whimpered through puckered lips. She patted his bottom.

"Not this time, honey," she replied. She watched Bryce mount up, looking as he always did, so very grand to her when he sat in full uniform on his mount. "Father has gone to . . . to help a great Apache leader, like your real father is. Let's pray he doesn't have to fight them; and let's pray that your own father isn't involved."

A tear slipped down her cheek and Chaco's little brown hand brushed it away when he happened to touch her face.

Chapter Twenty-seven

Mangas Coloradas neared Pinos Altos with his small party of warriors and made camp. He sat down wearily, his old wounds making him tire quickly now. He wondered to himself about just how he would approach the miners.

It was time to settle peacefully with the miners, if possible. Cochise and Saguaro had argued with him, warning him it was foolish to entertain such an idea. But Mangas was getting old. He wanted peace—for himself and for his Mimbreno followers. He could see that the masses of whites would continue to come, despite anything the Apaches did to stop the flow. It was like trying to stop a rainfall by setting a bucket in the middle of a field to catch some of the drops.

The night was quiet, and the fifteen men Mangas had brought with him all sat in a circle, looking sullen and dejected. Was this the way it would end for all brave and strong Apache warriors? Would they all rot away on a reservation, with nothing to do—no game to hunt, no place to really call home, no pride left?

Mangas sighed. He did not like being on the outs with his son-in-law, Cochise. But Cochise was young and still full of fire. And he was coaxed now by a rising young and angry warrior—a man who was fast becoming a leader of the Apache revolt, one who Mangas was sure would not give up the fight for many more years to come. His name was Geronimo.

As Mangas sat pondering his plans, a Mexican approached the Apache camp, waving a truce flag. Mangas rose, still a tall and commanding man in spite of his age. He walked up to greet the Mexican.

"Why are you here?" he asked the man cautiously.

"I come in peace, Señor Coloradas. There are soldiers nearby. They send me to tell you they wish to speak of peace and would be honored to have a word with you."

Mangas looked at some of his men.

"It is a trick!" one of them suggested. "Do not trust this man!"

"He carries a flag of truce," Mangas told them. He turned back to the Mexican. "Who is the leader of the soldiers?"

"Capitán Edmond Shirland, Señor Coloradas. He is a member of the California Volunteers."

"I prefer to meet with a star soldier," Mangas replied. "But if the capitán wishes to talk peace, maybe I should go."

"Si, señor!" The Mexican turned and hurried toward the soldier camp, and Mangas ordered his men to follow. They all grumbled among themselves about their leader's foolishness.

"Remember what happened to Cochise at Apache Pass!" they reminded the old man. "Remember how

474

the soldier leader named Bascom tricked Cochise! They put on smiles and shake your hand, then they stick a lance in your belly!"

Coloradas waved the man off. "I am old. They wish me no harm," he assured them. "And I come with few men. Surely they see I do not wish to make war. I only wish to talk."

The Mexican reached Captain Shirland before the Indians did, and by the time Mangas neared the soldier camp, he saw the white flag raised above the large tent where the captain obviously had his quarters.

"There. See?" Mangas said, smiling. "All of you go back to our own camp now and wait for me. I will go and talk with the capitán and come back soon."

The warriors scowled and obeyed their leader's wish. They all left, and Mangas headed toward the soldier tent. And then, as suddenly as a blink, several soldiers leaped out of the brush and surrounded him, cocking their rifles.

"Just keep walking, Apache!" one of them sneered. "Every soldier in the territory has been searching for you for months. And by God, now we've captured you. Just like that!" The man laughed and shoved the rifle barrel into Mangas's back and pushed him. "Get going!" he ordered.

Mangas's heart fell. So, his men had been right. Was there not even one white man who could be trusted? This would be his end, he was sure. He no longer had any thoughts of peace. He hoped the Apaches would rise up and kill every settler and every soldier in New Mexico and Arizona.

Mangas's hands were bound and he was kicked and shoved and half dragged through the night to a different camp so that the Apache warriors would be confused and unable to find their leader right away. The head of the second soldier camp was none other than General West himself. The general came out to greet Mangas by the firelight.

"Well, well, well," the man said, holding his head up in a cocky manner. "And so at last we have one of the great Apache leaders." West looked like a child beside the statuesque and overshadowing Mangas Coloradas, who stood straight and tall, in spite of his age and present cruel treatment. Coloradas glared at West, realizing even more what a great mistake he had made in trusting the paleface soldiers.

"What do you want us to do with him, sir?" one soldier asked eagerly.

"Do?" West chuckled. "Well, private, I'll tell you. I intend to set an example with this man. After tonight, the other Apache leaders will think twice about waging any more war against the settlers, miners, Mexicans, or the soldiers." He stepped up close to the guard who had asked the question. "By tomorrow morning, I want this man dead, private. You needn't tell me how you do it. I do not want my name involved, nor will I allow yours to be involved. But I want him dead. Do you understand? Dead! I'll take care of the report about his . . . attempted escape."

The private grinned, and Mangas Coloradas was dragged away. General West retired to his tent to have a good night's sleep.

The next morning found Bryce Edwards riding into General West's camp. Bryce dismounted and asked to

476

see the commanding officer and was led to the general's tent. General West came out to greet Bryce.

"Well, and who is this who has come to pay a visit?" the man asked with a broad grin. Bryce did not like the man's eyes. They did not smile along with his mouth.

"I'm Colonel Edwards, sir—Bryce Edwards."

"Edwards." West frowned a moment. "Oh, yes! Why I've heard of you, Edwards. You've worked with the Apaches out here for years, haven't you?"

"Yes, sir."

"In fact, I believe you just got married . . . to a woman who I'm told—uh—lived . . . with an Apache warrior for a while? I believe she . . . had a child by the man?"

Bryce glared at the general, who was thoroughly enjoying the suggestive tone he had insinuated into his voice. Some of the men from West's camp looked at Bryce curiously.

"The former Miss Fitzgerald's story is a long one, sir," Bryce said coldly. "But never did she dishonor herself. The details are not your business, nor do I need to stand here and defend her, to you or anyone else. I came here to see if you have seen or heard from the Mimbreno Apache leader, Mangas Coloradas. The man was headed this way to talk peace with the miners. I can handle any situation that might arise out of his efforts, sir, so that you won't be bothered with it. I'm acquainted with the man, and of course, with the Apaches in general."

"Well, Colonel Edwards, the—uh—situation . . . has already been handled. So you may go back to your own territory."

"What do you mean . . . handled?" Bryce asked, his

477

heart pounding.

"We captured Coloradas, last night."

"Captured?"

"Oh, well, not exactly. We lured him to our camp on the pretense of talking peace. But then you know the orders, Edwards. Wipe them out. The hell with peace, remember? I do hope you've been obeying that order. There is only one way to treat an Apache. Now actually, I think it's a rather unfair order myself. I personally wanted to treat the man fairly, since he did come in peace. I thought I might take him to the reservation and ask our men in Washington just what to do with him. But I'm afraid the men I left to guard him let him get away and the—uh—miners . . . had a field day with the old Indian. By the time my men found him . . . well . . . there was not much left they could do to help the poor soul. I suppose I should chastise them, for being so careless with their prisoner, but after all, they know the orders about Apaches. They would have killed the man themselves, more than likely. I'm afraid Mangas Coloradas is dead now, Colonel Edwards."

West tipped his hat to Bryce and nodded slightly. "Perhaps you would like to take the remains back to his people, if you're so inclined," the general went on. "The body is lying over there . . . in that ditch," the man sneered, pointing to a ditch where horse manure and human waste was dumped for sanitary purposes. "I'm afraid the man's head is missing. One of the miners must have decided to keep it for a trophy. The official report will say that he was killed while trying to escape."

Bryce glanced over at the ditch and felt his eyes

478

burning with hatred and tears. He turned back to look at West, who had already turned around to walk away. Bryce knew it was all planned and that more than likely it had been West's own soldiers who had killed Coloradas, but there would be no way to prove it. He quickly started to leave, not even wanting to see the body, wondering what kind of torture the poor old man had suffered at the hands of the soldiers before he died. He was suddenly ashamed of his blue uniform as he mounted up to head back to Fort Bowie. Then he turned back and forced himself over to the ditch, so that he could bear witness to the violent excesses of his own race.

Even as he rode for home, Mangas's warriors were already riding hard for their own holdout in the Dragoon Mountains to tell Cochise and Saguaro what had happened to Coloradas. And if the word Apache struck fear in the hearts of settlers and miners up to this moment, then there was no describing what it would mean to them before Cochise and Saguaro were through avenging the death of their great Mangas Coloradas! And the rising Chiricahua leader, Geronimo, was giving them new fire.

Saguaro and Cochise split up, each taking warriors and hitting settlers and wagon trains with mighty vengeance and determined hearts. What had been done to Mangas Coloradas was vile and unforgiveable! Every soldier, every settler, every miner must die! Never again would the white man's promises be

479

believed. Never again would the Apache even consider peace. The whites would long remember the Apache's power and fierce pride! And they would long regret what they had done to a good and honorable Apache leader!

The raiding started before Bryce and his men could even return to Fort Bowie. And as a result, Bryce was detained extensively, making rounds and helping victims of Apache raids.

In the third week of July Bryce and his men neared Fort Bowie. They were not more than a day's ride from home when they passed through a canyon and heard the dreaded war whoops. Apaches appeared along the ridge of both sides of the canyon. They had so cleverly hidden themselves, not even Bryce's scouts had detected them. Before Bryce could organize his men, the Indians came swooping down from both sides. Bryce's quick guess was that there were approximately half again as many Indians as soldiers.

"Dismount and fire at will!" Bryce shouted to the men. The bugler's horn squeaked in the middle of sounding for battle as an arrow pierced through the bugler's heart. Horses reared, and most of the soldiers yanked the reins of their mounts and forced the animals down to use them for cover. The firing of rifles in the canyon was deafening, mingled with the whinnies of frightened horses, the shouts of men and the ever-chilling war cries of the Apaches. The Indians circled the soldiers, screaming and shooting, but the soldiers had the advantage, being stationary and able to take better aim. Many of Bryce's men were killed before they were able to organize, but once they had taken positions, Indians began falling rapidly under the guns of Bryce's well-trained men. Bryce was kept too busy to notice Saguaro himself watching from farther up the canyon wall. Saguaro raised his arm and the warriors suddenly backed off, splitting up and riding off to each end of the canyon.

"Do you think they've given up, sir?" one man asked Bryce.

"Hell no! Get ready. They'll be back—stronger than ever! See what you can do about the wounded—quickly! I doubt we have much time."

"Yes, sir!"

Bryce's prediction had been correct. Within ten minutes the Apaches mounted a new attack, riding in from each end of the canyon, their fierce, painted faces set in determined revenge. This time, although those in front fell almost instantly from a volley of fire from the bluecoats, the others kept coming, riding right into the troops instead of circling, and, in moments, most of the men were engaged in hand-to-hand combat. Bryce swung his rifle and landed it in the middle of one Apache, and in the next second he was ducking a hatchet. He scrambled for his knife and raised up, lashing out at his attacker, whom he suddenly recognized. Both men froze.

"Saguaro!" Bryce said in a near whisper.

"So," Saguaro said through gritted teeth. "Here we are again, white soldier!"

The two men circled each other.

"Don't make me kill you, Saguaro. You know I don't want to!"

"Like you did not want to kill Mangas Coloradas?" the Indian roared.

"I had nothing to do with that! You know me better

481

than that. I rode to Pinos Altos to stop what might happen. I got there too late, Saguaro. But I intend to let Washington know what really happened!"

"And you think they care?" Saguaro laughed, his bronze and magnificent body circling Bryce's equally brawny one. He gripped his hatchet tightly. "We might all die, my white friend, but we will die proudly—in battle! We not die in shame, as Mangas did! The word Apache will long burn in hearts of white man! It will long live in his fancy books!" The big Indian swung at Bryce and Bryce jumped out of the way.

"Saguaro, don't do this!" Bryce growled.

Saguaro looked at him strangely. "Why not end it right here and now?" he said to Bryce. "Your men shoot well. I have lost many men. I have already told them if it was you who was leader, they should stop, and battle will be between only you and me. Look around you. Already my men are riding away again. Your soldiers have won. But our battle is not yet ended!"

Bryce kept his eyes on Saguaro, but he was aware that the man was right. The fighting had quieted. One soldier cocked a rifle and aimed it at Saguaro.

"Back off!" Bryce commanded. "This is between me and Saguaro!"

Bryce's men watched in near shock. They had simply to shoot Saguaro to save their leader. Why was he risking his neck this way? Saguaro smiled.

"Now you understand, don't you, white soldier? This is the way it has to be. For many weeks now Saguaro has lived without a heart. It is too painful. My woman belong to you now. My son belong to you. Soon all of my land will belong to your people. Saguaro has nothing now, nothing! Apache people have nothing.

Saguaro want to die proudly—in battle! And he has chosen the greatest man among white soldiers to do that battle with!" The Indian swung again, and Bryce came to the awful realization that Saguaro wanted Bryce to kill him. The thought of it tore at Bryce's guts. Shannon loved this man! He was the father of her child!

"You aren't being fair, Saguaro. I don't want to kill you!"

"Your men have won. If Saguaro is not killed, he will be taken prisoner and sent to reservation or maybe hung! Saguaro does not intend to be so dishonored!"

The Indian lunged at Bryce and they fell to the ground with Bryce grasping the hand that held the hatchet, while Saguaro held Bryce's wrist that supported the hand with the knife in it. They rolled and tumbled, and Bryce finally managed to get a foot in Saguaro's stomach and push up, sending the man flying over his head. Bryce rolled and got up quickly to meet a hatchet slashing out. It sliced across Bryce's shoulder, and Bryce cried out. He darted back, and it took him a moment to realize Saguaro could easily have made the hatchet go deeper. He could even have let go of it and let it fly and split into Bryce's chest. The man was deliberately losing this battle!

They circled again, and Bryce found himself ordering his men again not to shoot or grab Saguaro. If this was the way the man wanted it, then he should have his wish. Saguaro was literally begging to die with dignity.

"She's fine, Saguaro," Bryce said as they circled. "She came around. She's my wife now. She's even pregnant again. And Chaco is healthy and happy."

He noticed the Indian soften slightly, but then

Saguaro suddenly lashed out at him again and Bryce jumped back.

"She loves you very much, Saguaro. She wanted to see you once more, but I told her you didn't want that."

Saguaro lunged again, and Bryce's men watched anxiously as the two men struggled with hatchet and knife again and rolled on the ground. Dead and wounded soldiers and Indians lay strewn everywhere, and what was left of Saguaro's men who were able to get away watched from the top of the canyon walls.

Saguaro's hatchet came closer to Bryce's throat, and both men were straining and sweating as Saguaro seemed to truly be trying to kill Bryce. The arm Bryce used to grasp Saguaro's hand of death was shaking violently as the men pitted muscle against muscle in what would obviously be a struggle to the death.

Bryce would never know if he had found that little bit of extra strength, or if Saguaro had allowed it to happen, but he suddenly pushed hard and managed to roll Saguaro onto his back. He slammed Saguaro's arm against a rock as he did so, then pushed hard on the jagged piece of rock so that it cut into Saguaro's skin. Saguaro gritted his teeth and held on to the hatchet, at the same time struggling with the hand in which Bryce held the large knife.

Again, it was muscle against muscle, this time with Bryce on top. Bryce pushed harder on the hatchet hand, and it bled profusely now. Bryce bent the now-weakened wrist hard, and Saguaro grunted and let go of the hatchet. But the Indian immediately rolled Bryce over again and quickly got up and kicked Bryce in the stomach.

Bryce grunted and Saguaro lunged for the hatchet,

but Bryce moved fast and charged into Saguaro, shoving him away from it. Both men tumbled and struggled, and then Bryce was on top of Saguaro again, his knife against Saguaro's throat.

Saguaro lay very still, and their eyes held. It would only take a slight move for Bryce's very sharp knife to cut into Saguaro's flesh.

"My son—is happy?" Saguaro asked as he lay there panting.

"He's getting lots of love, Saguaro," Bryce replied, himself breathing hard and sweating. He pressed the knife closer. His own blood from the hatchet wound now saturated his uniform and dripped onto Saguaro's chest. "He'll be as proud and strong as his real father."

"Then . . . time has come," Saguaro panted. "To end it all. Saguaro . . . can no longer live . . . without a heart. Help me . . . to die . . . with dignity."

Bryce's eyes widened with horror. "No, Saguaro!" he whispered.

"Yes!" Saguaro roared. The hatchet was within his reach. Saguaro grasped it and raised it and swung. Bryce deflected the swing and lunged with his knife. Saguaro grunted as Bryce buried the blade deep in his chest. The two men watched each other and Saguaro actually smiled.

"Tell . . . my son . . . and White Flower . . . how much Saguaro loved them!"

The Indian's body jerked and his eyes widened, and then he stiffened and a very long sigh whispered through his lips.

"Saguaro?" Bryce said quietly. He was still on top of the man. "Saguaro?" he yelled louder. "Saguaro! Goddamn you!" Bryce was in tears now and his men

485

had to struggle to pull him off Saguaro's body. "Goddamn you!" Bryce kept screaming. They held on to Bryce for several minutes while he kept cursing Saguaro, and he finally quieted down, wiping angrily at his tears. His men released him and he stumbled over to his horse.

"Clean things up here," he said brokenly to Reynolds, as he clung to his horse's neck. "Make up . . . a travois. I'm taking Saguaro . . . to Fort Bowie . . . to Shannon."

"Yes, sir," the young man replied quietly. The remainder of Saguaro's warriors, who had watched it all, rode quietly away and disappeared into the hills.

Bryce wearily mounted his horse, refusing to let anyone treat his own wound, which at the moment he did not even feel. He sat rigid and struggling with tears as Saguaro's body was secured to the travois, and several minutes later they were ready to leave with the wounded. Fresh troops would be sent back to bury the dead.

Chapter Twenty-eight

Shannon heard the cry to open the gates and heard someone else shouting that Colonel Edwards was finally back.

"He's wounded! A bunch of them are wounded!" she heard another man yell. She grabbed Chaco and ran out of the cabin to greet the returning troops, many of whom were bandaged and bleeding. Bryce rode in front, his uniform covered with blood, his eyes bloodshot and filled with pain.

"Bryce!" Shannon screamed. "My God, what happened!"

Bryce halted his horse and looked down at her in sorrow, as other men scrambled to help the wounded, both white and Indian.

"I . . . killed Saguaro," he told her flatly. He studied the rapid changes in her face—from concern to shock to hate to sorrow to love and back to concern. She glanced at the travois.

"It's him," Bryce said brokenly. "He practically . . . begged me to do it, Shannon. He said he . . . couldn't

487

live any longer . . . without a heart. Chaco . . . was his heart, Shannon."

She could see he had been crying. She knew there was more to the story than the fact that Bryce Edwards had simply killed an Indian without compassion or feeling. He dismounted as she forced her legs to carry her to the travois, where she knelt down and uncovered Saguaro's face. His eyes were now closed in death. Shannon burst into sobbing and threw herself on Saguaro's body. Bryce's men forced themselves to turn away from the sight of a white woman, now married to a respected colonel, weeping over an Apache warrior, while her half-breed son stood nearby looking puzzled. Bryce stood behind her, saying nothing. She had the right to mourn over this man who had loved and protected her. She wept bitterly, with tears for more than only the loss of Saguaro.

Bryce knelt beside her, hesitantly putting a hand on her shoulder.

"They . . . killed Mangas," he said brokenly. "They burned him . . . and shot him and scalped him. They . . . even beheaded him . . . and just . . . threw his body into a ditch."

"Oh, my God!" Shannon wailed, clinging to Saguaro. "Oh, God, forgive us!"

"The Apaches will make war now as never before, Shannon. Saguaro attacked us. They . . . lost the battle . . . and Saguaro . . . he seemed to be . . . asking me to kill him. I didn't want to do it, Shannon. We got into a hand-to-hand combat, and . . . damn it, Shannon, he . . . he didn't want to be arrested and maybe die like Mangas died! He said he . . . wanted to die . . . with dignity. I knew what he meant. God in heaven forgive me, but . . . I knew what he meant!"

His voice choked and he closed his eyes and struggled with his emotions. Shannon raised up slightly and looked lovingly at Saguaro, gently stroking his face.

"You . . . did right then," she told Bryce. "This was the only way a man like Saguaro could die. He knew . . . that they were going to lose anyway," she sobbed. "Not just the small battle today. But they'll all . . . lose, Bryce, won't they?"

"I'm afraid they will, Shannon. My God, I'm sorry! I'm so damned sorry! I . . . didn't want to kill him. He forced my hand."

Shannon turned and pulled Chaco close to Saguaro.

"This is your real father, Chaco," she said softly. "I don't know how much a two-year-old can remember, and it's been eight months since you've seen him, darling, but this is Saguaro." Her words became difficult. "And he . . . loved you so much, Chaco . . . that he would rather die . . . than to live without you." She held the boy tightly and cried. Chaco reached out and touched Saguaro's face curiously.

"Sleep?" the boy asked.

"Yes, darling," Shannon said through her tears. "Your Apache father is asleep now. He will . . . join the Great Spirit . . . and he'll watch over you forever."

Shannon finally pulled the boy away and leaned down to kiss Saguaro's forehead. "I would have stayed with you," she whispered. "You knew that, didn't you, Saguaro? I would have stayed with you if you had asked. And I would have been happy. I'm so sorry, Saguaro!" She put her head down on his shoulder and wept again. Bryce touched her arm.

"We'll give him a respectable burial," he told her. She sat up and turned to him.

"Can't you . . . can't you have some scouts take him to his people?" she asked. "They should do it. He should be buried out there somewhere . . . where the land is wild and free . . . like he was."

Bryce nodded. "All right. Whatever you want, Shannon."

She studied him—the tired and desolate eyes—the bloody uniform.

"Thank you, Bryce." She reached out and touched his face. "I understand," she assured him. "So much has happened since that night we danced so gaily back in Virginia, hasn't it, Bryce?"

He took her hand and kissed it.

"Yet here we are," she continued. "Even this can't come between us, Bryce. We won't let it."

She stood up and Bryce got to his feet. He put an arm around her shoulders to support himself as they slowly made their way to his quarters where she could tend to his wounds. Shannon asked one of the men to take care of Chaco while she helped Bryce.

"I'll—uh—I'll be sure it goes into the records what a great leader he was," Bryce told her wearily.

"I know you will," she sniffled.

She helped him through the door and led him to his chair. He sat down wearily and she quickly opened his shirt and grimaced at the bloody wound. "Oh, Bryce! Saguaro did this?"

"I'll be all right. He could have planted the hatchet deeper, Shannon. I know he could have. The whole thing makes me sick. I'll never forget it for the rest of my life."

490

She pressed clean gauze to the cut. "It will get worse now, won't it, Bryce?" She used her free hand to help him get his shirt off.

"Definitely. We may be involved in a civil war right now, Shannon, but I'll tell you this much. That war will end in another couple of years—maybe three. But the wars with the Indians have just begun. They've just begun. Not just here, but everywhere as the West becomes more and more settled. They're already having considerable trouble up in Montana and the Dakotas with the Sioux. Our determination to do away with the Indian race is taking a foothold. It's sickening. What a waste of a beautiful people! And we haven't heard the last of Cochise. No, ma'am. I won't blame him one damned bit either for whatever he does, after seeing Mangas Coloradas the way I did. It was the most gruesome thing I've ever seen. Things are going to get bad—real bad. And there's a new leader in the wings, Shannon. He'll pick up with Cochise now and carry on. And from what the scouts tell me, this one will be feared more than Cochise or Coloradas or Saguaro ever thought of being feared. They call him Geronimo."

"Geronimo? I don't believe I ever met him when I was living with them."

"Mark my words, you'll hear his name for a long time to come. The Mexicans already talk about him as though he were some ghost who comes screaming out of the night to murder and plunder. They say he's clever and tricky. And when he goes into battle, he rides without an ounce of fear or hesitation." He sighed and shook his head. "Geronimo." He shook his head again. "Don't expect the Indian wars to end soon, Shannon.

I'd say we'll be fighting Indians until Chaco is well grown."

"Oh, Bryce!"

"That's my prediction, Shannon. We have a long, hard struggle ahead of us." He reached out and touched her face. "But then you and I know all about hardships and struggling, don't we?"

She sniffed and removed the bloody gauze, replacing it with new gauze. He touched her hair.

"The drums of war seem to be beating everywhere, don't they?" he told her. "This whole nation is at war for some reason or another. The Civil War is what helped drive us apart in the first place. But our own hearts . . . they beat just as loudly for each other as the war drums beat, Shannon. We've got each other now. That will see us through all of it."

"Oh, Bryce, when will it end?" she asked in despair.

"I don't know. We're a growing, learning country. We're stumbling and falling and making mistakes, just like a child does when he's growing up. We'll just have to keep . . . picking ourselves up . . . and starting over, like you've done with your personal life. This country is going through a kind of hell, and it's taken both of us along with it."

He stroked her hair as she lay her head in his lap and cried. He held the gauze to his wound himself with his free hand. "Shannon, I'm getting out. I can't hunt them down any longer, and I'm too sympathetic to be of use to the army. What do you think of farming or ranching? I may even look into being an Indian agent. Like I told you before, I could help them more that way, and you could teach them, and Chaco could grow up among his own kind where he wouldn't suffer the humiliation whites would throw at him if we moved back East or to a more civilized place."

She looked up at him. "Oh, Bryce, I would be very happy to work on a reservation. I don't think I could ever go back to Virginia now. The West and the Apaches are too embedded in my blood now. And I . . . I'm so glad you want to help them."

He sighed and held her eyes. "You sure? You married an army colonel, you know. How about just plain Bryce Edwards?"

She smiled. "That's all I ever really loved. The man, not the uniform; the beautiful man who wore it. It doesn't matter to me what you do, as long as we can be together, as long as nothing ever again separates us."

"That, my dear, I promise will never happen again."

She wiped at her tears and returned to dressing his wound, while outside, the scouts were leaving, dragging the travois with Saguaro's body on it, to be returned to his people for burial at an unknown site in the distant, rugged mountains that the man had loved. But not as much as he had loved the woman he had called White Flower, and not nearly as much as he had loved his son. But there was no room for love and happiness in the life of an Apache warrior.

Shannon glanced at the doorway when the scouts shouted for the gates to be opened. She looked back at Bryce, deep sorrow in her eyes.

"He will always live, Shannon, in the wind, and in Chaco. And he's happy now. It's time for you to be happy, too."

Author's Note

Please write me at 6013-A North Coloma Road, Coloma, MI 49038 and let me know if you enjoyed my story. I do hope you will look for my many other novels. I love hearing from my readers, and I answer all letters.